A Bold Rebellion

THE NETWORK SERIES
BOOK TEN

KATIE CROSS

www.katiecrossbooks.com

Chapter One

Leda sucked on her front teeth, lifted an eyebrow, and shook her head.

"The Sisterhood is doomed."

We stood inside a room tucked into a forgotten corner of Chatham Castle. An exquisite porcelain tea set petaled around a quaint table. The distant sound of scullery maids and an occasional slam sounded. Otherwise, this castoff room was nearly silent.

Steam luffed into the air from the spigot of an extraordinarily old tea pot, graced by a curved top that ended on a single, glazed leaf. Tea cakes, bowls of different tea types, and delicate spoons filled the silver tray beneath. As a piece of art, the arrangement was stunning, highlighted by a sprig of bright orange flowers.

As an offering from Leda, the arrangement made me very nervous.

Eyes rolling, I plopped onto a proffered chair. Mud flecked my bare ankles and feet. I pulled a twig from my hair, spelled it away, and prayed I didn't smell like sweat. The last-minute sprint brought me here just in time, and Leda's eyes held nothing but judgment.

"Don't be dramatic," I muttered, batting away a section of spider web. "The Sisterhood isn't doomed. We're . . . busy."

She stared.

I tried not to squirm.

"I brought you here to work on tea etiquette and salvage what little exists."

"The fate of the Sisterhood doesn't rest on tea etiquette, Leda. And if it did, I probably wouldn't have anything to do with it."

More demure, Leda lowered into a chair across from mine. She encapsulated the definition of decorum as she carefully reached for her silk napkin and spread it on her lap. A twist of her eyebrow implied I should do the same.

I refused.

This situation was entanglement.

Her forearm rested on the table top, fingers rubbing together as she sought patience.

"You see, Bianca, the fate of the Sisterhood *does* rest on tea etiquette. If you can't impress the Council Members for long enough to entertain them during tea, then we have no hope of receiving funding. Did you memorize my talking points?"

Her imperious lip pinch infuriated me. I slapped a hand over my eyes and groaned. "Yes! I memorized them."

"State them."

"Right now?"

"Yes."

Grumbling, I said, "The Sisterhood is a two-woman entity formed to protect the Central Network High Priestess."

"Aaaaand?"

"And?" I threw my hands in the air. "What else is there? You think we should only focus on Scarlett. I disagree. But you didn't list *that* as a talking point."

With a long suffering born from fury, she said, "Why are you speaking to Council Members in the first place? The answer is found in talking point number three."

I acquiesced, but only to end this torture. "Our goal in speaking with Council Members is to provide context and understanding so they can appreciate the strategic position of the Sisterhood relative to weakening aspects found in the Brotherhood."

The dry words stuck to my tongue. How I managed to wrench that political drivel out, I'd never understand.

Mollified, she folded her hands in her lap. "And you reviewed my key indicators of emotional distance in a negotiation? When to engage and when to retract?"

"You understand you're initiating a total takeover, right? We're *both* in the Sisterhood."

"This is survival, Bianca." Her pale eyelashes fluttered. "If you want to be a bonafide entity in the Central Network, you must receive funding and currency from the Council and the other leaders. Marten and Scarlett already approve. We lack only the Council. They will require intensive convincing. Now—talking points. Again."

"We don't need to review talking points again. They put me to sleep. Leda, these make sense for a *negotiation*. Meeting with Council Members isn't a negotiation."

"Aren't you convincing the Council that the Sisterhood has value? That is a negotiation. Actual currency isn't exchanged, but something far more valuable: time, trust, and belief."

Leda, prim and proper as ever, sat with her back straight and hair sliding over her thin shoulders. Her differently-colored eyes set on me with a determined stare. She wouldn't look away until I corrected whatever vainglorious mistake I made this time.

I had one last jab to land before I let her win.

"Why can't *you* hold these meetings?"

"If I felt that would work, I would have already conducted

them," she retorted icily. "For better or worse, you, and you alone, are viewed as the Sisterhood. It is through you that we must receive approval."

With a sigh, I dropped the sapphire cloth napkin on my lap. A veritable white flag, though I wouldn't go down easy.

She relaxed.

"Your first Council Member meeting approaches in a week. To attend your first meeting without preparing would be foolish. You may have survived the wilds of Carcere," she said quickly, before I could interrupt with that exact point, "but the world of politics is very different. I thought it would be wise for you to practice your verbal repartee before you meet with individual Council Members and share our new mission statement."

Mission statement.

The words felt like hot ash in my mouth. The more appropriate phrase would be *Leda's mission statement,* but I didn't have the energy to fight her. We needed something. Though imperfect, her slant was a starting point.

She eyed me as I reached for a cookie, waylaying my hand toward the tongs at the last possible second instead of grabbing it outright, as I intended. Gripping the tongs with an eye roll, I grabbed two cookies.

"You are going to practice a question-and-answer session today," she continued. "It may be wise to consider it an interrogation."

"With you?"

A maniacal gleam brightened her eyes.

"Not with me."

At that moment, the door slammed open with the *crack* of wood hitting the wall. I didn't have to ask who stood back there, because Aurora's presence announced itself. Like an attack of invisible knives, the new Central Network Ambassador raced into the room, borne by the smell of ink and dried rosemary.

Aurora Fontaine was a whip of a witch. Salt-and-pepper hair

piled in a neat afro atop her head, designed in a swirl like frosting on a cupcake. Judgment whetted her tight umber eyes, tucking deep into the fold and recesses of her intense stare. She wore ostentatious rings on skinny fingers, and held judgment in every twitch of her full lips.

Aurora nodded as she bustled past me, the table, and hooked around to stand next to Leda. The same conspiratorial gleam filled her eyes, and I bit back a hex by sheer willpower.

The good gods.

I'd die first.

"You won't take it seriously if I practice with you," Leda said with a smirk of pure gloating. "So I requested Aurora's time. She's very busy and has a lot going on." Leda sent Aurora a subdued, but sincere, smile. "So we'll only ask for thirty minutes."

Jikes.

Thirty minutes of *negotiation* with Aurora?

No one would survive.

Leda rose to her feet with the grace of a Priestess. "I know that I don't need to tell you, Bianca, that the betterment of the Sisterhood rests on your answers. And I certainly don't need to drive home the point that the Council Members don't see this as an investment in the Sisterhood as an entity, but in you as a witch."

Her points drove home with an unnecessary sting. "No," I ground out. "You certainly don't need to remind me."

Yes, we'd spoken about this ad nauseam for weeks, but it wasn't until I stared down Aurora Fontaine that I understood exactly what Leda signed me up for. Death by questioning and mission statements. The Sisterhood didn't sound as fun anymore.

Leda drummed her fingertips along a piece of parchment near her tea plate, where an empty cup awaited Aurora.

"Here are some suggested questions, Miss Fontaine. Of

course, feel free to ask your own questions. You already understand our goals with this practice, and with meeting Council Members." Leda cut a piercing stare to me. "Starting next week."

I ignored her.

Probably would forever, after this.

With a wide smile on her full lips, Aurora lowered into the chair. Her ample brilliant red and purple toned skirts settled around equally ample hips. The bodice, a mild-mannered orange, should have clashed with the wild colors. Somehow, it didn't. On any other witch, it would have appeared gaudy.

On Aurora, it made a statement of power.

Aurora waved her hand toward the tea pot. Water flowed into her cup, followed by a train of other items. Grains of sugar, a steeper of loose leaf tea, a dash of cream, and then a spoon. The orchestrations of tea time executed flawlessly, and without a single verbal command.

"Miss Monroe," Aurora said with a stuffy tone that suggested we'd never met before. "It's a pleasure to speak with you."

I lifted my shoulders. They wanted to play a game? So could I. I could put on a mask like the best of them, and dance to their desired tunes. No matter how boring or pointless it might be. Nevermind that I could be checking on Scarlett instead of this foolish mess.

Not that Scarlett required all that much protection when holed up in her office, protected by routine and stationary Guardians. Protecting her, and her alone, might be a rather boring endeavor.

Didn't see *that* talking point, either.

"Miss Fontaine," I countered blithely, "thank you for having me."

Aurora smiled like a cat. "I hear you have an idea to bring a Sisterhood into the Central Network?"

The words *I do* lifted from my throat, but talking point

seventeen had been explicitly against *inefficient statements such as* I get that *or* I do, *instead of the more concise and immediately communicative* I understand *or* yes.

"Yes," I said.

Aurora pressed her lips and hummed. I expected her to have a sip of tea, but she disregarded it. Ah, a power move. Leda mentioned this in talking point twenty four. Part of an *engagement or retreat* strategy. Depending on the witch, the conversation, the time spent with them, and the general energy of the air, I could take silence as an invitation or a stopping point.

Which one should I employ here?

I had no idea.

Following Aurora's lead, I bided my time by selecting a tea sachet out of a bowl with a pair of tongs and setting it in my cup. Using a spell, I tipped the hot water on top, though I didn't want tea. I preferred coffee. The only sound between us was the clink of porcelain.

Leda's tension elevated behind me, which meant I'd chosen wrong. Aurora's silence was an invitation, then?

Aurora cleared her throat. "Would you care to tell me *why* you want a Sisterhood?"

"I'd love to."

Setting aside my spoon, I summoned every word that Leda drilled into me for the past week, recalling them with easy memory.

"Recent events, dating back several years but including the past eight weeks, have proven that the Central Network requires a more targeted and precise protection detail for our High Priestess. The Brotherhood of Protectors are maintaining a steady, occasionally overpacked schedule, which negates their response. I believe it's time for us to do something new in protecting our High Priestess."

The boring and rote reply ended with my awkward, delayed, last-minute smile I almost forgot to tack on.

Had I said that right?

Mixed a few words up?

Probably, but the gist remained on point. In the reflection of a windowpane, I could see Leda relax ever-so-slightly. Reaching for my cup, I stirred the tea and picked up the handle to sip. Twenty-six more minutes of this?

I'd die.

Aurora scratched her cheeks, lips bunched. With painstaking care, she braced her elbow on the table, leaned toward me, and whispered, "Want to try that again?"

"Did I mess up?"

"Did you?"

Blinking, I said, "I don't know."

Aurora regarded me, then exhaled. "You're a demmed fool and a mindless puppet, to boot."

Choking on my own surprise, I nearly blasted her with hot tea. To Leda, she cried, "You brought me here to listen to a recitation of facts you cooked up for her?"

Leda gaped.

Irritated, Aurora returned her attention to me. She stared so hard into my eyes I thought she'd leave holes. "That is the most mindless and insulting drivel I've ever heard someone say, and you look dumber for saying it." Aurora's gaze slid to Leda. "Did you ask her to memorize that rubbish?"

Leda, who always composed herself more quickly than me, cleared her throat. Her reply of, "Yes," rang clear as a bell.

"It'll cost you the Sisterhood, you twits."

Rolling my lips together to keep from laughing, I could only stare as Aurora set her tea down, leaned back in her chair, and glowered. Did she just call Leda a twit? Me, too? Definitely both.

Delightful.

Aurora jabbed a finger at me. "I asked you about the Sisterhood, not the Brotherhood. Why would you end with them?"

My breath caught. "I . . . I don't know." The words, *because Leda told me to!* sounded even worse.

Leda stood stock still right next to the door, white rimming the edges of her wide eyes. Fists bunched, skin pale, she trembled on the spot. How long had it been since someone with Aurora's authority questioned her?

Aurora slammed a hand on the table. The delicate porcelain trembled under the hard *whack.* She leaned closer. "Who are you?"

"Bianca Monroe."

"I said," she demanded, "who *are* you?"

"I am Bianca Monroe, the Head of the Sisterhood."

Scowling, Aurora whispered, "That's right you are. The Head of the Sisterhood. You remember that. You go into this without apology. Don't mention the Brotherhood—they don't matter. Your lack of confidence and passion was the worst part of this entire interview. Negotiation over."

She pushed out of the chair, skirt swaying.

Certain that all of my self-respect would stride out the door with Aurora, I hurried to stand. My chair clattered to the floor in my haste to stop her.

"It's not that our Sisterhood would be helpful," I cried, "but we're necessary."

Aurora paused, back to me. She cast her eyes to the floor, but her attention returned to me. Drawing in a shaky breath, I forced myself to continue.

"There are things that others do well, but I do better. I am the Head of the Sisterhood because I'm strong where they are weak, but they don't know they're weak yet. That's why we're here. Because they *don't know* they're weak. But I do. I see it."

Aurora's jaw tightened.

She half-turned.

A small concession. Just enough. I had a feeling the only

thing that kept her in the room was my confidence, so I leaned into it.

"After Carcere, we know that Scarlett needs a more trained force to keep her safe. A force that could help the Brotherhood in equally unexpected ways."

"You said you only served Scarlett," Aurora countered.

"We serve Scarlett only," Leda confirmed.

I said, "I'm suited for both," and ignored her wrath.

Aurora spun to fully face me, disgust replaced by the mildest glimmer of curiosity. "Why should it be you?"

"Who else?"

She paused, head tipped. A rush of fear that she'd say someone else's name opened up inside of me, then closed. My question stood on its own.

Who else, indeed?

This time, I took Aurora's silence as an invitation.

Correctly.

"I was born for this, Ambassador. Not because of my father, my childhood in a dangerous forest, or the experiences I had with Mabel at a Network school. Not even because of the gods, but because of me." I pressed a hand to my chest. "There's something innate in me that was born for this. I'm ready before the Network is ready, because that's how it works."

Aurora lifted her chin, studying me with a daunting and open appraisal. She licked her lips. "I see you, Miss Monroe. I hear what you're saying. I look forward to hearing more."

With that, Aurora spun on her heel and slid out the door, vanishing in a swirl of enigmatic colors and dizzying emotional capacity. Her final harrumph, directed at Leda, punctuated her abrupt departure.

* * *

Leda avoided me for the rest of the day.

Grateful to think away from her brooding glare, I found myself on the trails where I truly belonged. My feet flew over a variegated carpet of fallen leaves, their burnt orange undersides mottled with brown and hints of yellow. Like moon slivers, they peeked around branches. Sun spurts in a dark forest.

I leaned into a sprint.

Pressing.

Pressing harder.

Racing.

Racing faster.

My heart thrummed like hummingbird wings against my ribs as I transported over a wide creek, moving so fast the magic was little more than a slip of blackness before my foot hit firm ground. With robust breaths in and out of my lungs, and the forest soundtrack clattering in my ears, I soared.

You belong to us.

We belong to you.

Leda's snappy indignation followed me through a close tunnel of branches arching overhead in a verdant dome. Her certainty that Scarlett was the right path haunted me. The trees sensed my agitation. *You belong to us,* they repeated in synchronicity that ballooned, filling me from bottom to top with overlapping voices.

Quick-fire and mercurial, my feet raced, raced, raced. I sprinted until it felt like my body came apart at the seams and my muscles stopped, though my determination continued. I leaped a gigantic root, landed on the other side, and collapsed in surrender. Tumbling side to side, I stopped rolling in a root well.

The canopy stared back.

Ribbons of sapphire spiraled out beneath me when I rolled onto my side, wincing. Jikes, but that would hurt for days. Had I bruised my rib again? My toes didn't bleed, which was a miracle. I stubbed them—sometimes broke them—far too much.

When I pressed my hand to a tree root, the burgeoning blue

light sought me. It pooled under my fingertips, swirled around my palm, and spread like a spiderweb into my fingers, my arm, my chest.

"Deasylva?"

The smell of honeysuckle drifted by. A certain and rare sign of the forest goddess. How curious to have her pop up today. Panting, I leaned against the tree roots.

"I have . . . a question."

Her purring response surprised me.

You may ask.

"You're really here?"

Always in my forest.

"But you don't *always* respond when I speak to you."

No.

Her simple statement remained. Understanding that she wouldn't explain, I gave up hoping. Deasylva did what she wanted. "There's a lot to say. Give me a second to figure it out. Didn't think you'd respond," I added in a mutter.

I know your heart, daughter of the forest. Share your concerns with me that way.

Not entirely understanding what *share your concerns with me that way* meant, but having a vague idea, I loosened my restrained thoughts. They gushed free like a broken dam, heavy with thrashing concerns about the Sisterhood, Aurora's biting disappointment, and Leda's certainty on how to stabilize the future around Scarlett alone.

Somewhere in the outpouring, I tossed in the Central Network Council.

Papa, too.

There is much.

"Tell me about it," I mumbled.

Finally calm, my hand drifted away from the tree. Sweat trickled down my forehead. Having rough bark under my touch was reassuring, but not required. Deasylva spoke to me everywhere. She interrupted deep thoughts while I ran along a dried stream bed or awoke me in the middle of the night.

Somehow, I did feel better.

Unburdened.

You seek control, daughter of the forest. This is not wisdom's path, nor yours.

Scoffing, I said, "That doesn't sound right."

No?

"I'm not trying to control anything. We're trying to convince the Council that we need them to give us currency and legitimacy. There's a vast difference."

As you say.

Her calm reply stirred my exhausted ire up again, but it settled quickly. Irritation required too much energy.

Be on your way, daughter of the forest. There are witches to help.

Chapter Two

Tomasso gurgled as Priscilla switched him from her left hip to her right, a pile of drool draining over his fingers and wrist. Unbothered, she popped the finger out of his mouth and gave him a damp cloth. He fussed, then began to chew it like it would save his life.

"Teething," she said primly, and pivoted.

The low murmur of a school purred in the background as I followed Priscilla out of the kitchen, down the hallway, and toward a set of spiral stairs that led to the attic.

"The school year is already busy." Priscilla's breath hitched from hauling Tomasso's thick form up the stairs. We passed the second and third floors without encountering students. I idly wondered where Ava, Baxter's niece and Priscilla's most challenging student, hid.

"Full class this year?"

"All three years," she replied. "Our first-year class is particularly rowdy."

Priscilla came to a dead stop at the top. I halted at the last second, nearly slamming into her back. Before I could ask why, my attention snapped to an attractive, middle-aged woman with black hair. Streaks of white silvered the strands, pulled into a coif at the back of her head.

Priscilla said, "Camila?"

My heart caught.

Camila.

Camila Aldana was the unofficial High Priestess of the Eastern Network. She wore a gown, not a dress, with a gaudy display of jeweled colors. Earrings sparkled from her lobes as she smiled at Tomasso, who reached for her with a gummy smile. She accepted Tomasso's lunging body with a quick peck on his cheek. Her gaze lingered on me.

"Camila," Priscilla said hastily. She patted back her mussed hair. "Uh . . . welcome. Have I forgotten—"

Camila cut Priscilla off with a wave of her hand. "No, no. Forgive me, Priscilla. I wouldn't fathom bothering you in the daytime while school is in session if it wasn't very important."

Priscilla nudged her chin higher. "What's wrong?"

"I came to ask a favor." Camila turned to me with the most solemn eyes I had ever seen. "Of Miss Monroe, the Head of the Sisterhood."

* * *

Through a magical and silent communication magic, I sent the only other Sisterhood member, Leda, a quick mental message. *Developments happening at Priscilla's.* The sentence would travel right into Leda's mind, placed there as gently as a thought spoken in my voice.

Her immediate and pert reply followed.

Oh?

Camila Aldana surprised Priscilla and me at the school. She wants to speak with the Head of the Sisterhood.

I pictured Leda's astonished blink, her long expression, and slow straightening away from her neat-but-cluttered desk at the High Priestess' office.

Stall. I'll be right there.

Camila regarded me with a hungry rapacity, as if I held her life in my hands. I avoided Priscilla's questioning gaze, though it bore into me from the side.

To Camila I asked, "Your Majesty?"

A hint of a smile appeared on Camila's face at my respectful, but improper, deference. She *wasn't* the Eastern Network High Priestess. Her son, Cristian, held the throne. Cristian had not taken a wife, so the title went to her as a ceremonial symbol, but no one here would argue semantics.

"Your reputation has reached the Eastern Network, Miss Monroe." Her tone and cadence had a soothing pitch. "Even before you began the Sisterhood of Protectors."

A month ago, Former Council Member Greyson, an inmate in Carcere, a magical prison located in the Eastern Network, threatened my life and Scarlett's. He sent letters, stalked, and eventually led me to the broken down island prison in a fight for my life. Despite his arrogant boasts around greater strength, I had prevailed.

Greyson would stand trial against the Central Network Council tomorrow. He would have been executed weeks ago had Cristian not asked for us to wait.

I cleared my throat. "Thank you for letting me know. I wasn't aware that news of the Sisterhood had reached your shores."

"Only through diplomatic channels." Camila gave a reassuring smile as she motioned to Priscilla, her *diplomatic channel*. Whatever Camila was or wasn't, she was a gentlewitch. Her love for Tomasso was more than apparent. He clutched her jewels with sticky hands, and didn't elicit a single sound of concern from her.

Priscilla said, "I mentioned—"

"It's fine, Cilla," I said easily, but didn't take my eyes off of Camila. Something restless and frightened lingered in her wise eyes, and my curiosity grew despite it.

You definitely want to be here, I sang to Leda.

I'm trying!

"Do you come to Priscilla's often, Camila?"

My attempt to stall wasn't dissuaded. "Weekly," Priscilla said with more affection than I expected.

Camila returned with a doting smile. "Tomasso reminds me of my Niko." She tickled him with adoration. "He has his father's spunk, and his mother's wisdom."

Camila spun to glance at the doorway into Priscilla's personal quarters, our original destination. Priscilla's office, bedroom, and living space occupied the entire attic, which used to house the former teacher Miss Mabel. With her nurturing care and a bright attitude, Priscilla had transformed this dastardly school into a place of learning and safety.

"We can go inside the living room," Priscilla said, and her lightness spoke to deepening curiosity. "It will be far easier to speak there than in a stairwell."

Tomasso, happy to see a pile of toys awaiting him on a circular rug, squirmed out of his grandmere's arms and crawled for them as fast as a beetle. Camila lowered to the ground next to him, her skirt belling around her. She was far more grandmere than pseudo High Priestess. No wonder Priscilla was fond of her.

With a *hem* to clear her throat, Camila said, "If the Sisterhood is indeed as formidable and powerful as rumors say," she cast a wry look at Priscilla, "then I was wondering if I might hire your help. I say *I* very intentionally. The request is my own."

My lips opened to ask a question when a pinch over my left shoulder stopped me. *We can find out a lot, so let her speak,* Leda said. *Though we won't accept it.*

Her hand brushed my shoulder, though I saw nothing. An

invisibility incantation, then. Wise. Camila would be less open and explicit if she knew the Central Network High Priestess' Assistant listened.

Camila continued on, blithely distracted by Tomasso. "The Eastern Network is facing many troubles, as I'm sure you know?"

"I'm aware, yes."

"You know what the *Chatterer* newsscroll reports?"

"Yes."

"Then you only know half of it. What you see is one fish in the school, so to speak. There is so much more that many witches don't know about. Not because of Cristian hiding it, either."

Priscilla sat in a chair with her hands in her lap, head slanted in a curious expression. The rhythmic *snip, snip, snip* of pruning shears rose from outside in a soothing rhythm.

"What isn't known?" Priscilla asked.

"The newsbooks are reporting criminal chaos. Riots, looting, mischievous acts, that sort of thing. What's really happening is chaos in our Council. There are Council Members that want to oust Cristian, and others are loyal. It grows . . ." Camila swallowed, "out of control. We are trying to prove that the opposing Council Members are directly related to the riots, but it has been difficult. Our East Guards ranks have been depleted since the Battle for Letum Wood. The insurrectionists know and are taking full advantage of the fact."

A pit sank through my stomach. Niko, Cristian's brother, and former High Priest of the Eastern Network, died over a year before in the Battle for Letum Wood. Under Niko's reign, the Eastern Council had been difficult to manage and fickle. Niko acted badly on poor information, which worsened a prior legacy of strict Aldana men.

"These Council Members seek not to overturn Cristian,

Miss Monroe, but the entire Aldana family. There is another person who wants the throne."

"Do you know who?" I asked.

"I can guess. We speak mostly from rumors and nothing confirmed. He is Council Member Giuseppi, and I can think of nothing he'd love more than to forge a new dynasty."

At the mention of his name, Priscilla's expression darkened.

"He has obliquely threatened to end the Aldana dynasty in the past," Camila continued, her throat working as she swallowed. Priscilla gasped, a hand to her heart. Her eyes went immediately to Tomasso. Camila held up a staying hand, but nodded sagely.

"Yes. As rightful heir to the throne, Tomasso will be in danger if we can't control the riots and the Council. That is why I came today." She hesitated. "When I met with you yesterday, Priscilla, you mentioned Bianca's scheduled visit today. It's why I invited myself. I can't tell Cristian what I'm doing. Yet."

Leda's hand tightened around my shoulder. I'd almost forgotten she'd slipped in. *Don't refuse yet,* she said.

I won't.

The pressure eased.

"What is it you want from me, Camila?" I asked.

A sense of relief overcame her as she whispered, "Please help me save my family by helping us find this insurrection leader. I need to know your answer within the next three days."

* * *

Only a minute later, I stared at the doorway where Camilla had retreated.

Leda's official pronouncement filled the silent room as she removed her spell. "I'd say she's mad, but I have too much respect for her." She stood a few paces away, arms folded across her chest, brow furrowed.

Priscilla jumped in her chair. "Leda! I didn't know you were here."

"Sorry, Cilla. Bianca told me that Camila asked for the Sisterhood and I thought it prudent not to make myself known."

"You thought right."

Priscilla cleared the hair out of her eyes with a shaking hand and sank onto the floor next to Tomasso. He rocked back and forth on his hands and knees, babbling fast. Without Camila, the room felt strangely empty. As if she'd taken the air with her.

"I don't know Camila well," I said in a poor attempt to gather my thoughts, "but it's safe to say that I've never seen her that distraught."

Priscilla agreed with a murmur.

Leda paused at the window, where she stared out. The first-year girls gathered on the lawn, flocking like scattered baby chicks. Scrolls followed several as they wandered toward the edge of the forest. The steady *snip, snip, snip* of shears had quieted. Jorge, the groundskeeper, gathered clippings on the far side of the field.

"The implications of you agreeing to help Camila are tremendous and foolish," Leda declared. "It's a definite no."

"Why?"

"For one, it's too large of a mission. Find an insurrectionist leader?" She blew a raspberry. "They'd need an entire Brotherhood for that task. For another, you would meddle in politics that aren't ours."

She sent an apologetic look to Priscilla. "Forgive me, Cilla, but this isn't our fight."

"I understand."

Leda pressed on, oblivious to Priscilla's growing distress. "This morning, I approved appointment slots for you to speak to individual Council Members and sell the idea of the Sisterhood under our new mission statement. Their meeting to vote on legitimizing the Sisterhood takes place in five months. To work for the Eastern Network in the meantime?"

She shook her head, incredulous that I didn't think of this myself.

"The Central Network Council doesn't have to know until it's over," I said.

Her glare would have set me on fire. "You want to play the odds that they don't find out and you lose all trust?"

"If we're successful," I continued as if she hadn't interrupted my train of thought, "it'll be another convincing mark in our favor."

"They'll see it as working for the enemy."

"The East isn't our enemy," I parried. "They're our neighbor. The mutual cooperation the war against the gods inspired has erased most of that rhetoric."

She shrugged, merciless. "Rhetoric and logic don't matter when it comes to governing bodies of imperfect witches, Bianca. Appearance is the Highest Witch. Sorry."

"I disagree."

Leda glowered from beneath pale lashes as she faced outside, illuminated by errant strands of sunshine.

"Let me think on it for a moment. Leave me alone."

Leaving Leda to her crabby self—I didn't envy Hiddleston, Leda's solid love interest and the other Assistant to Scarlett, dealing with her daily—I spun to face Priscilla. She stared at Tomasso, drawn into distant thoughts. Making escape plans, I'd wager. Camila's visit would put Priscilla into an agonizing anxiety spiral, and I didn't thank her for *that*.

I set a hand on Priscilla's shoulder.

"Cilla?"

She sucked in a sharp breath, shoulders expanding as she yanked herself out of it.

"What?"

I smiled. "Just me, everything is fine."

Her body slumped. "Sorry. I . . . I was just thinking."

"Whatever happens in the Eastern Network, I promise I won't let anything happen to Tomasso."

Priscilla pulled him into her lap and curled an arm around him. He bellowed, waving chubby arms in a futile attempt to reach a sock filled with dry beans and tied at the top. She wouldn't release him. Her eyes misted.

"I won't let them hurt him, Bianca. I'd die first."

"You'd have to get in line," I replied. "I promise I won't let it come to that. If we have to sacrifice the Sisterhood's position before the Council to save Tomasso, I'd do it without question. Do you hear me?"

Priscilla studied my eyes. Eventually, she nodded. Her emotions cleared, throat bobbed as she nodded and whispered a husky, "I believe you, B. Thank you. Let's hope that's not necessary."

Casting a sidelong glance to Leda, I said, "It isn't."

Leda spun, squared to us, and said, "My official suggestion is no. We're not touching the Eastern Network mess, not with a ten-pace branch. We don't have any responsibility to the Aldanas." She hesitated, glanced at Priscilla, and amended, "Not to Cristian."

Priscilla nodded, but her expression remained blank.

"Not to mention," Leda added, "that this is directly oppositional to our newfound purpose for the Sisterhood: we are a two-woman force that focuses directly on care for the Central Network High Priestess. This is in exact opposition to our mission statement."

The mission statement made my toes curl. Yes, I agreed with it. Scarlett as a central figure was the Sisterhood's most likely chance to receive the legitimacy we needed from the Council. But it was *so* restrictive.

I stood. "I'll take that into consideration, Leda. Thanks."

She eyed me, suspicion thick as frosting.

"That's it?"

"For now." I broadened my smile. "But I'm not making the decision yet."

"Remember that I have worked my fingertips off coordinating these meetings. Your interaction matters to the reputation and longevity of the Sisterhood, Bianca Monroe. More than anything. Do you hear me?"

"I hear you."

"There's no time to save the Eastern Network!"

I jabbed a thumb toward Tomasso. Freed from his mother's anxious arms, he rolled onto his back and gnawed on the end of a smooth wooden toy that looked like a flute. Drool rolled out of it.

"We wouldn't be working to save the East. We'd work to save Tomasso."

Chapter Three

Forest glades and lush grass and fresh pumpkin scents welcomed me home as I alighted on the branch outside my door. A fire crackled in the hearth of my treehouse. A spray of golden autumn foliage bloomed outside.

I closed my eyes.

Breathed deep.

Home.

The trees warbled their rambling whispers and quiet cacophony.

She returns.

You belong to us.

We belong to you.

Always, I silently said, and a wave of sighs rippled in response. Wherever in Alkarra I stood, the forest was always home. A touchstone and reminder of where I belonged. When I departed, the forest missed me with an ache I shared. Returning felt so good.

A thrill zipped from my neck to my toes when a rumbly voice, accented with the Northern burr, said, "Merry meet, little troublemaker."

My eyes flew open.

Merrick approached with a charged grin and bare feet. He picked me up, swept me into his arms, and kissed me in a way that electrified every nerve in my body. I pressed my hand to his face, giving as much as I took. When he finally set me down, tufts of my dress fisted in his hand, a smoky haze filtered through his eyes.

"Merry meet," I purred, laughing. "That is quite a greeting to come home to."

He smiled, fingertips running down the side of my face. "I've missed you." His arm hooked my waist, drawing me into the treehouse we shared. Amanthis, the gigantic, magically powerful tree in which I lived, gave a wordless sigh of relief.

"How was your day?" I asked as he led me to the table, where our staple, simple supper awaited. Fresh bread, a crock of butter, and a chopped salad of greens harvested from the forest floor. We didn't enjoy much meal variation on a day to day basis, but it didn't matter. Merrick was willing to prepare, so I would eat.

He pressed a hand to my shoulder, gently pushing me into a chair. Water magically filled a cup at my elbow.

"Today was good. Busy."

"Meetings?" I asked.

"Briefings."

After I chugged the water in the cup and watched it refill, I asked, "Briefings about the Eastern Network?"

He cut me a sidelong glance. "Maybe."

My smug smile led him to shaking his head.

"It's uncanny how you receive information before the Brotherhood. What do *you* know about the East?"

"Things."

Two plates floated in my direction as he lowered into the chair across from me. Kissing him was one thing. Sitting in front of him, the power of those verdant green eyes locked on me, was another entirely. My stomach flopped for a wholly different reason: the indisputable and slightly unbelievable truth that he was mine.

All mine.

"What things, B?" he asked, nudging the salad to me. I grabbed a handful of leaves and slung them on my plate while he sawed a chunk of bread.

"Things about the High Priest."

He lifted an eyebrow, his task forgotten.

"Oh?"

I motioned to the bread. "Eat your dinner. I'll explain everything. But first, thank you." I stood to press a hasty kiss to his cheek. "This dinner looks delicious, and I was starving."

A responding little smile lightened his lips. "You make it simple, and you're welcome." Sternness returned to his face. "The East?"

While he smeared fresh butter on his giant chunk of bread and I picked through the salad, I caught him up on Camila's request, Leda's insistence against it, and Priscilla's general shock at the threat on Tomasso's life.

Merrick clucked through his teeth. "Leda's response is interesting."

"Why?"

"Because she's normally more open to risk."

Snagging a slice of bread off the cutting board, I said, "Sometimes. Political risk, she's more likely to mitigate. We couldn't avoid fighting the gods, and going after Greyson was required to keep Scarlett and myself safe. To her, supporting Camila is unnecessary."

His gaze became distant as he thought that through, then shrugged. While he chewed through half the loaf heel, I added, "I have three days to figure it out."

No hint of judgment or opinion colored his next question.

"Why would you take it?"

"To protect Priscilla and Tomasso, naturally. Plus, experience."

Merrick mulled that over a beat. "Speaking of experience, Rognvald asked me if I thought you were ready to run the Sisterhood."

"Really?"

"Last night."

I balled a piece of bread in between two fingers, scrutinizing every twitch of his neutral expression. Rognvald asking Merrick anything about me was a loaded topic. The Head of Protectors knew of our relationship. Normally, he didn't bring me up unless I was around.

"What did you say?"

"That you're the magical equivalent of a dragon in a toddler's body."

He hooted when I tried to kick him under the table, but his nimble footwork dodged my attempts. When his teasing subsided, the gleam in his eyes remained.

"I told him I thought you had it in you, and I didn't know anyone better qualified. Like a younger version of Regina."

The compliment delighted me.

"And?"

Merrick shrugged. "He wanted to know."

"Has Rognvald shown signs of not trusting your opinion?"

"No. He trusts both of us. He was being thorough. When the Sisterhood has occasion to work with the Brotherhood, he said he'd assign me to work with you when circumstances permit."

I straightened.

"Really?"

A sparkle brightened his gaze. "He thinks you'll listen to me, and that I have the wisdom of ages to impart."

I rolled my eyes so hard my head tipped back.

Merrick laughed outright.

"I'm only partially kidding," he added more seriously. "He'll assign me to help any mission where you request Brotherhood support. I have a vested interest in keeping you safe."

"The other Brothers wouldn't?"

"I didn't insinuate that."

The touch of his hand under the table, grabbing my ankle and running his fingers along the inside of my foot, sent a shiver through me.

I smiled. "Thanks."

With my foot propped on his knee, weighted by his hand, he propped his other elbow on the table and leaned forward.

"Anything you want to talk about?"

I shrugged. "Not really."

"Good, because we need to discuss our handfasting date."

His easy tone held no guilt. Smirking, I asked, "Oh, you're not going to ask me to handfast you through some great surprise?"

He chortled and reached for my hand. I gave it, allowing his fingers to wrap around my wrist, testing the size. Witches in the Central Network and random parts of other Networks announced their intention to handfast through a cord of engagement. Men and women wore one until handfasting, after which the cords were tucked away as a keepsake.

Merrick chewed on his bottom lip.

"Do you want it to be a surprise?"

"You already live with me as it is. No one will be shocked when we make it official."

"It's not the asking that has me concerned," he admitted with a tempestuous stare. "Your father and I have already discussed it at length, and he's resigned to the reality that I'll be his son-in-law."

It was my turn to hoot in response.

He added, "It's my family."

"Your family?"

"Not that they have any problem with the handfasting. You know they adore you. Jacqueline definitely likes you more than me," he grumbled. "But . . . it's the Northern Network customs that have me concerned. Traditions are . . . intense . . . when it comes to handfasting. There are steps and rules and ceremonies and stuff."

Bridling my smile, I retracted my leg. My ankle dropped away from his, and he scowled. With a shove of my plates, I rose from my chair and joined him. When I settled on his lap, facing him, the scowl dissipated to growing heat in his ever-present appreciative stare.

Hands on his shoulders, I asked, "What kind of stuff and tradition does Northern custom require?"

"Dinners. A lot of food centered around the handfasting month."

"Month?"

"Mm hmm. Before the handfasting day there's the family dinner, the parents dinner, the couples dinner, and the siblings dinner. Not to mention the family announcement, and exchange of items of inheritance. On the day of, there's the pre-ceremony breakfast, then the ceremony. There's a passage of rites between families, and then another meal. Dancing that evening, a few more vague traditions. . . ."

He trailed away, and I was glad for it. The stacking events grew more daunting with each recitation.

"An elaborate meal, prepared by the bride, the morning after the handfasting," he tacked on with a knowing look.

I laughed outright.

"Everyone will either starve or die."

His knuckle grazed my skin as he drew it down my cheek. "There's a lot to handfasting in the North, B. I'm frightened it'll scare you away, because there are also memories and importance baked into each step. It's not something I can say *no* to without hurting feelings."

Matching his energy, I asked in a low voice, "Do we have to be part of it?"

"As the bride and groom?"

The shock in his question made me laugh. "No! Of course we have to be there, but do we have to do *all* of those?"

"I'd find a High Witch this moment and make it official, if we even need to do that. But this will be the first opportunity we have to gather them all together since my father died. The Hughes family will travel far and wide for a wedding. It's . . . a way he lives on."

He trailed away, gnawing on the inside of his cheek. Night fell, drawing shadows over the windows. The glowing fire reflected in the panes, and a cool breeze swept inside with the sweet scents of leaves and fresh rain.

I repositioned myself, closing what little distance remained, with my palms splayed on either side of his stubbled cheeks. My knees hugged his thighs. His heart beat a steady plod in his throat.

"What is important to you is important to me, Merrick. That includes your family traditions." I waved a hand around the treehouse. "It's part of merging our lives together in totality, not just name. Tell me what you want, and we'll do that. All right?"

He softened as his arms tightened around my waist.

"Thank you, B. Let me meet with my mother and my sister. This is important to them. The first handfasting in the family is a symbol of continuation. It's seen as the survival of our family and is celebrated in more ways than following handfastings, like Jacqui's. I want to honor those traditions, because they also honor my family."

Foreheads pressed together, I whispered, "Me too."

We dissolved into a hungry kiss, forgetting the turmoil of the Eastern Network, the delight of working in conjunction with the Brotherhood, and the reality that awaited innocent witches on the other side of Alkarra.

For this moment, I belonged to Merrick.

To the forest.

To myself.

* * *

A Northern Network shieldmaker peered at me with tight eyes and lowered lips and spoke in a raspy growl.

"You are rather specific about the details and requirements of your shield."

"Perhaps."

I know what I want in my shield, and I haven't found it yet, I silently added to her growing lour.

With an annoyed lip quirk, she withdrew the shield I inspected and set it on the floor below her. Her scowl could have lit water on fire as she rummaged for a different one under her counter.

Regina, elbows on top, stared outside with a low-level frown and lowered brows. Under my breath, I asked, "Are you all right?"

She bolted upright.

"W-what?"

"Are you all right?"

Her instant stress calmed. "Fine. Thanks."

She pursed her lips and shoved off the counter, wandering across the room to stare out a different window. A brilliant mountain vista sprawled on either side of the northern cottage. I'd never been to this quiet village hours away from known humanity, tucked in a valley with two steep behemoths on either side. Fall had already come and almost gone this far north, where snow kissed the blanketed heights.

A thump on the counter drew my attention to the shieldmaker.

"This one?"

She produced a shield wide enough to cover me from shoulder to shoulder, but not much else. If I turned, it would protect my torso thanks to a dip on the lower edge, and a peaked top. I stepped away, withdrew Viveet, and moved through a sword routine. Heat flared in my cheeks when I fumbled, knocking Viveet into the edges of the shield and nearly chipping her blade.

Embarrassing.

The shieldmaker scoffed before I replaced Viveet and returned the shield. "I'm sorry, but I think I prefer the round."

With an icy glare, the woman shoved the shield out of sight.

"Then we are done."

Regina snatched my arm and tugged me out of the shop, sending an equally icy stare over her shoulder. We headed down a winding path, toward the bottom of a low hill. The yellow grass, bent in half and dry from early winter snows, scuttled in a breeze. Cottages with thatched roofs peeked out of saplings. The sounds of chopping firewood rang through the idyllic valley.

I nodded to a stream snaking through the grass. "Let's head over there. I need a drink. Meanwhile, tell me what's on your mind."

She sent me a sidelong glance.

"What?"

"You're brooding."

Her lips parted to protest, but she stopped midway. With a humph, arms swinging wildly, she said, "I'm not brooding."

"Disagree."

Another uncertain glance.

"You want to know?"

"I wouldn't have asked if I didn't."

Regina mulled that over and sighed. "Fine, but it's about your father."

Wryly, I said, "Yes, I assumed."

"You really don't mind?"

Her disbelief fueled my exasperation. "Yes, I don't mind! I asked, didn't I?"

"You did," she murmured, puzzled. Another minute or two of thought passed. We stopped at the stream. I lowered, running my fingers through the silky water. Freezing cold. The level was low, with smooth pebbles paving the way. A leaf rippled on top as I cupped my hand and drank. Regina crouched, hugging her knees.

"I don't know how to talk about your father and our relationship." She barely breathed as she said it. "I certainly don't know how to discuss feelings with . . . with Derek's daughter. But I don't know any other women to talk to. They're all Masters."

Her nose wrinkled.

"That's probably weird?" I ventured.

"Weird." She tapped her teeth together before exclaiming, "He's gone! He's *still* gone and I have no idea where. It's my fault," she added bitterly, "because I said, *I understand,* and *take your time*, but now I'm frustrated. Worried, too, the blighter! He won't say where he goes. He writes, but I don't see him."

The rambling sentences barely formed into something I understood. Before I could clarify what *still gone* meant, she continued in another burst of frenetic energy.

"I don't know what to do, Bianca! Nor what to think. I . . ."

Regina blinked so hard, and with such absorption in the problem at hand, that I wondered if she prevented tears. If she hadn't looked so mystified, I might have laughed.

"I'm angry," she snapped, then softened. "Mostly, I'm worried. What if he's not well? What if he wanders forever? Will

I wait at home like a purposeless waif? I don't think he's with other women." A quick snap of her fingers broke the air. "The man isn't that daft. But still . . ."

She blinked harder. To conceal, not to reveal. She turned away, the elegant slenderness of her neck drew me to the bushel of curls around her ears. There was a fierce brilliance about her profile set against the rugged backdrop of the mountains. She shook her head, curls tossing.

"I'm sorry, Bianca. This isn't your problem to face, or to fix. I shouldn't have brought it up to you. It's between me and your father. We need to talk, that's all. But there's little chance of it lately."

Intermingling relief and sadness followed her heartfelt apology. I didn't want to be involved in this, now that she mentioned it. Yet, I felt for her. When she spun to meet my eyes, her equilibrium had restored. The disquieted parts faded.

"I'm retiring," she stated calmly.

"What?"

"I'm leaving the Masters next month. There's less than two weeks left of my service before I'm done and I'm in a panic. I'm not sure what to do next. Derek was part of my plan."

"Next month?" I squeaked.

Neck tight, she nodded.

"Does anyone know?"

She shook her head.

"Nadira?"

Regina hesitated, then nodded again. Nadira, High Priestess of the Northern Network, surely must know. Another Master, too. Whoever would take her place. To keep it a secret, though? I didn't dare ask her motivation to hide the decision.

I licked my lips. "Oh. That's . . . soon. And so . . . big."

To her credit, she didn't scoff at my pathetic attempt to provide support. "Most pertinent to this conversation, Derek doesn't know."

"Why not?"

"I wanted to tell him in person. My retirement might mean something for the two of us. It might . . . create pressure. I don't want that."

"If you're retired, you can share a life."

Regina drew a deep breath in through her nose. "Yes, exactly."

Pressure.

I understood.

The calm, cool calculation I revered in her had returned utterly, like a mask sliding into place. I missed her near-frenetic side. The transparency of her chaos seemed far more real in that state than this one.

"My retirement means that we could share a life. Not evenings after work, or whenever he finished a house project. His home is done. My career is closing in a beautiful sunset. We are as unstable and undecided as ever."

My heart cracked for her. What an awkward and impossible situation. The silence swelled, leaving space for me to think. Mama didn't drift up with the same power as she used to. When I spoke with Regina, I didn't see her in Mama's shadow anymore. The two could never interpose—they were too different. As awkward as it felt to comfort a woman who loved my father that wasn't Mama, my heart ached on Regina's behalf.

"I'm sorry this is happening, Regina. Honestly? I haven't heard from him much either."

She reared back. "Really?"

"Really."

"That's . . . odd."

"Very."

"I thought . . . well . . ."

"You thought he was avoiding you?"

"Yes."

Scoffing, I said, "He's avoiding all of us."

Eyebrow high, she asked, "Marten, too?" A confirmatory nod made her lips part, brows crash. "But that's . . ."

"Unexpected?"

Her focus tapered. "When was the last time you saw Derek?"

I shrugged. "Three weeks ago?"

"That long?"

"He's written a few letters, but not much else."

"Does he tell you where he's going?"

"No. He shows up whenever he wants, or if I ask. If I send a message and ask him for help, he comes. He doesn't explain where he goes or what he's doing. He's evasive and vague."

Questions filled her eyes. My hope to comfort her with facts missed a wide mark. Regina crouched next to the stream, trailing her fingertips along the top. Leaves shuddered over the top of flat rocks. She lifted her head, stared downstream at a hare with a twitchy nose and long ears scenting the air.

"Do you think he's building a different life?"

A laugh nearly bubbled out of me. I schooled it into submission to ask, "Where would he build another life?"

"I don't know," she said matter-of-factly, as if she'd realized the concept. "I'm worried he's avoiding me because I've done something wrong."

"He would tell you."

Regina rubbed a hand over her face. "This is bloody well why I didn't bother with this before!" she growled, standing. "Men are every bit as dramatic and difficult to understand at fifty-something than they were at twenty five. It's worse at this stage because I have a whole life behind me and a lot of routines I don't feel like changing."

I laughed, breaking the strange air.

With a budding smile, Regina said, "Thank you, Bianca. Next time, I won't burden you with my frustrations. I'm sorry."

"No apology required," I said quickly. "We all need a

friend." With a hand on her arm, I said, "He's worth it, Regina. I promise."

She cracked her first smile. "Thanks for reminding me." Regina nodded to the trail. "Let's head east. There's another shieldmaker at a village not far from this one. She makes shields if you ask really nicely, and bring her bags of barley. If you have a specific vision, she's the shieldmaker that you want."

Chapter Four

Late afternoon the next day, the Central Network Council converged in the Council Room at Chatham Castle to discuss Greyson's execution and the events leading to it. Those of us not on the Council—myself, Merrick, a handful of Coven Leaders, some journalists from the *Chatham Chatterer*, and maids ready to refresh drinks and snacks—collected in the hallway like old books waiting on a shelf.

Bright sapphire banners hung from the walls, flapping in a gentle wind that breezed in from open windows. Summer began her graceful glide into autumn, heralding chilly mornings and warm days. Stained glass sparkled, beams of sunshine raced in ribbons onto the floor. Two maids swished by, trays filled with water pitchers and dinner appetizers. The tranquil scene was pleasant and nerve wracking at the same time.

Considering the Council that awaited, my stomach twisted into knots and my palms turned clammy. I kept my hands balled in fists as I stared at a hideous painting of a wood nymph emerging from a scorched tree husk. My foot tapped a quick staccato on the rug. I cracked the knuckles of my right hand.

Merrick, tall, dapper, and golden, stood at my side.

"B," he drawled.

"I know, I know. I'm being . . . intense."

He cast me a sidelong glance, a hint of a smile interrupting the stubble along his jaw. He shaved his beard a few days ago, which made him an entirely different witch. I preferred the stubble.

"The interrogation isn't on you, B. Why are you so nervous?"

"Because Scarlett is recounting all the events that led up to Greyson's capture, and that heavily involves me." Squirming, I whispered, "There's something very unnerving about all ten leaders of the Network staring at me while Scarlett dissects every single decision I made."

Merrick sent a wayward smile to a passing Assistant. He kept one hand on his sword as he said, "True. It's not pleasant."

With a studious eye, I asked, "Why are *you* coming to the meeting?"

His tone had a mysterious evenness when he said, "Rognvald told me to show up." He turned the subject by saying, "Scarlett promised to keep the purpose of the meeting centered around Greyson and the mission, not the Sisterhood." His rich Northern burr sent a chill dancing down my spine. His presence soothed me, whether I'd admit it or not. "Scarlett promised she's not going to entertain questions about you unless it directly applies to his actions and incarceration. As you requested," he added in a dry tone.

A month ago, I asked Scarlett not to divulge the details over how the Sisterhood had prevented Greyson from killing our High Priestess and myself. Not that I had anything to hide, but the whole experience set me . . . off kilter.

My straightforward plan for the Sisterhood to mimic the Brotherhood lay on tenuous ground at the time. Grandfather had been right all along. The Sisterhood didn't need to mimic the Brotherhood.

We needed to be different.

At the time, I sought space to figure out what the Sisterhood was or would be before I had to defend myself against the Council.

Hence, Leda's mission statement.

Unfortunately, I wasn't sure I agreed with *this* version of the Sisterhood either.

My grace period ended today. The buffer had been enough time for Leda and I to slash our old Sisterhood strategy to smithereens. The biggest hurdle we faced was legitimizing the Sisterhood before the Council in order to make currency and create the career path. The rest would come later. In the face of pending questioning from the Council, I clung to the only certainties we had.

Two-woman force.

Served Scarlett.

I could get through this.

"This meeting is good," I said, parroting what Leda said that morning. "Recounting my decision-making process will stir up necessary questions regarding the Sisterhood that we can answer. The attention will help when I meet individual Council Members. Currency," I reminded myself. "Our next step is currency."

"Good." He nodded once. "Focus on your goal. Leave the rest behind. Everything will be all right."

Camila floated in the back of my mind. I had two days left to answer her heartfelt and plaintive query. Merrick's hand clasped mine, squeezing with gentle reassurance. "I'll be with you. Visible, even," he added with a chortle.

With the nature of our work, we rarely appeared in the same room together. I fought off my anxieties and smiled.

"Thanks. I appreciate you being here."

"Remind me to update you about our inevitable and future

handfasting," he added. "I spoke with my family last night. There's a problem, and her name is Jacqueline."

Before I could demand, *what did you say to her?* the double doors hiding the Council Room from view groaned. Merrick released my hand while they chugged open. A dozen eyes stared at me. Maids streamed by. Journalists tutted as they hurried past.

Scarlett stood in the middle on the other side of the room. She gave an amused and welcoming nod.

The Council awaited.

* * *

Scarlett caught my attention first.

Leda, second.

Greyson, third.

The former Western Covens Council Member had a gaunt appearance, unlike the healthy vigor of a few weeks ago. He stood in the corner, wrists and ankles locked by manacles. Protector-cast spells imprisoned him inside a glass-like barrier, nearly indestructible. Tysen, the newest Protector, stood slightly behind Greyson, and just to the side, able to see every movement.

Greyson met my curious stare.

He revealed nothing.

After defeating him in a match of cleverness and magic at the island prison of Carcere, he lost consciousness. I transported him to the Central Network and hadn't spoken with him since. Guessing how he felt about my victory wasn't hard. If he experienced disparagement or frustration, he didn't reveal it here.

Eventually, his eyes skated up, as if bored.

The giant doors chugged to a close as Merrick and I approached the table. Merrick slipped to the left, opposite Rognvald, who stood on the right. I remained at the end of the ginormous table that housed all ten Central Network Council Members and the High Priestess. Thirty paces long, if not more.

With a subtle nod, Scarlett yielded the floor to Rognvald.

"This is Brotherhood member Merrick Hughes, the leader of two Protectors assigned to the Eastern Network mission. He spent six months within all parts of the Eastern Network and sent daily reports on what he learned. If anyone understands the rising situation in the Eastern Network, it's Merrick."

By sheer willpower, I didn't look away from Scarlett as Merrick inclined his head to the Council. Rognvald stepped away from the table, opening Merrick to questions from the room. Unsurprisingly, there were none. He had nothing to do with Greyson and my encounter, and the purpose of the meeting wasn't to discuss rising issues in the East. Having him present, however, could mitigate argument points between Council Members later.

Scarlett kept her eye on me as she called to all present, "Thank you for attending, Merrick, Bianca, and others. We have just finished our brief on the timeline of events that brought Greyson to the castle, which leaves room for the Council to ask questions of Miss Monroe before we discuss the prisoner's sentence."

My eyes widened. *We have just finished our brief on the timeline of events.*

She what?

At my dazed expression, a slight smile elevated one side of her lips. I blinked, startled to realize Scarlett had done the scariest work already. She spared me the agony of grating Council Members who questioned every minuscule detail, then fought over what I *should* have done.

The realization was a heartfelt gift, and all my anxieties shattered.

Thank you, I mouthed.

She nodded.

Before any Council Members indicated a question, a voice rose from the corner. "High Priestess," Greyson called, "might I interject?"

Stunned silence cut short every noise. I couldn't even act surprised at the audacity. Greyson lived by a different set of life rules. Having been a respected member of this Council in the past, he knew exactly which threads to tug to unnerve everyone. A prisoner requesting an interjection before his finalized sentence was unheard of.

Scarlett lifted one eyebrow. "You have twenty seconds."

Leda's lips tightened in silent disapproval, but Leda drew hard lines for everything.

Greyson spoke with enough energy to summon a yawn, but little more. "Forgive me for interrupting, but I have something interesting to mention before you condemn me to death. I think you might find it worthy of sparing a few more minutes?"

Greyson paused a heartbeat, enough to absorb the span of silence. He plunged on.

"There is a rising insurrection in the Eastern Network. It does, in fact, have everything to do with my escape from Carcere."

A handful of Council Members cried out at his carefully-placed declaration. Based on Leda's irritated glare aimed my direction, I poorly suppressed an eye roll. No surprise overwhelmed me. Though no direct parallels had been drawn, it was easy to see the two chaotic circumstances merging.

Greyson spoke over the amplifying whispers. "The witch that began all the unrest for the Eastern Network was in Carcere with me. Carcere's destruction *was* an inside job, at least partially. Due to these circumstances, I know facts. Upcoming events." He turned to me and flicked the word, "Names," off supposedly impartial lips.

The cold chill of memories breathed down my shoulders.

"Soon," he stated to me, "there will be an attempted coup of

Magnolia Castle and the Aldana dynasty. It's the first in a series of growing rebellions. This takeover has been planned for over a year."

Blood whirled through my body in a fast circle. His specific mention of the *Aldana dynasty* wasn't a mistake. Camila had directly specified that danger existed. Their opponent wanted to wreck an entire genealogy, not the Eastern Network.

Horror settled on the room with a heavy weight. Only two Council Members appeared unimpressed by his declaration. Lovely-but-stone-faced Georgette over the Chatham Covens, and kind-but-militant Clare over the Western Covens.

Greyson blinked away from my held stare. Scarlett asked with a ringing voice, "And why should we trust what you say?"

"The Council doesn't have to trust what I say. Only Miss Monroe."

Outrage erupted. Voices sprouted in protest, hollering over each other, two of them shouting at Greyson, who yawned.

Keep it together, Leda snapped. *I can read every emotion on your face.*

I shifted from astonishment into a glare.

That's not any better.

Greyson called above the ruckus, commanding calm. "In exchange for information on the Eastern Network's insurrectionists, I ask something rather simple: a better imprisonment location while I await execution. I have accepted my inevitable death at your hands, but I don't desire to live in the darkness and shadows for my final days. I will help you, and the Eastern Network, fight the insurrectionists by telling you everything I know in exchange for a sentence of house imprisonment until my death."

Rognvald snapped, "Or I'll shove Veritas down your throat and you'll tell us everything you already know."

Greyson ignored him.

Scarlett quietly said to no one in particular, "It has already been attempted. He has inoculated himself against Veritas." Her declaration reminded me of Mabel. Only the really skilled villains managed to accomplish an inoculation against the powerful truth potion Veritas.

Council Member Georgette stood, commanding the room with her handsome features and an overstated style that was never gaudy. Her rock hard will clashed with mine often. Greyson had known Georgette as well, though I had no idea how deeply. Something bitter and unforgiving hardened her expression when she faced him.

All Council Members faced her. I couldn't help but join them. Georgette demanded attention.

"You're not worth the effort, Greyson. The Eastern Network's troubles are their own. The Central Network has had the most integrated, prosperous, and peaceful year of the last one hundred. I don't think we should make that worse by collecting problems that aren't ours."

A chorus of, "Hear, hear!" and thumping fists accompanied her to her chair. Scarlett, calm and mildly curious, scanned the room for other opinions.

Council Member Theodore rose to his feet. "If the East wants this information, they can get it themselves."

They're trying, I quipped to Leda.

She gave me a silent, long-suffering scolding.

Clare scoffed. "Because the Eastern Network did such a fantastic job taking care of Greyson last time?" She met Georgette's gaze from down the table, and added with a coldly amused smile, "I can't believe I'm saying it, but I agree with Georgette. We don't involve ourselves in matters that don't concern us."

Georgette gave a returning smile, however slight. Her slitted eyes returned to Greyson immediately after.

Greyson ignored her, too.

He stared at me, and I couldn't look away. A challenge lived in there, and the slight curl around the edge of his lips made me certain I didn't imagine it. Somehow he knew—or guessed at—Camila's request of me. Why single me out or point out that he knew names? What did he expect me to do with that information?

Don't be swayed by Camila's pretty request yesterday, Leda said, confirming my impression that she watched me like a hawk. *Georgette and Clare are correct. The problems in the East are their own and we must leave it that way.*

I know, I said to get her out of my head.

The Sisterhood serves Scarlett.

Her reassertion spoke worlds about her anxiety. My curiosity churned, influenced by tugs from Camila, Priscilla, Niko's legacy, even Cristian. While the Council and Scarlett debated the merits and risks of giving into Greyson, I met Leda's gaze. She glowered, already understanding exactly where my impressions ran.

What if he's right? I asked. *What if there is a coup against Magnolia? What if he knows who released the prisoners from Carcere and instigated this growing unrest? We can keep Tomasso safer by ending it.*

Greyson's an expert manipulator that's gone through extensive means to make himself immune to Veritas, she snapped. *There is no way to prove he isn't lying without embroiling us into a mess that isn't ours. Bianca, there are other ways to keep Tomasso safe.*

We can be master manipulators, too.

With a sigh in her voice, she said, *You are many things, Bianca Monroe, but a master manipulator is not one of them.*

Listen, we aren't going to give him what he wants. I agree. But what if finding this witch is easier than that? Think of the lives we could save!

There is no we.

There could be, though. That's what Leda didn't see. Her

position as Scarlett's Assistant kept her too busy and focused to view the possibilities that *I* saw.

A building pressure wrapped my chest. My breath came a little too fast as I stared at Greyson, the world tunneling into a dark halo. Prickling needles swept my skin at his half smile in response.

He knew.

He knew *everything*.

I jerked out of the trance. Leda wasn't wrong. He was manipulating the situation, but so could I.

He doesn't fool me, I reassured Leda before she burned me with her incoming anxiety. *But I don't think shutting him out is wise. There are assets here. You saw Camila. She's desperate. This rebel can't get rid of the Aldana's without massive loss of innocent life and a destabilization of their political structure.*

Don't you dare say a word, Bianca Monroe.

Do you trust me?

The question silenced her. I heard myself speaking before I knew what I was doing. "Why?" I shouted to Greyson. "Why do you want to make a deal?"

The question landed during a temporary lull in the escalating discussion. Half the Council swiveled my direction. For a flash, I thought I saw something real in his gaze. Something . . . pained.

"I miss the sun," he said.

"You'll never convince me that you're trying to see the sun," I countered, "but I do believe you know something. Many things, probably. Yet, you've failed to make anyone in this room care enough to commute your sentence. If you truly want to see the sun again, you must give the Council a reason to care more about the Eastern Network than they care about executing you."

The room held its breath as Greyson studied me with an appraising look that I'd seen in an umbrous room, over a table full of cards and an hourglass that drained the remaining seconds of my life.

"Stall your decision over my life for one week," he said. "Time will prove the attack on Magnolia Castle. That will show you what I know."

"Not good enough," I countered. "Tell us how to stop the attack."

"No."

I lifted a hand in a farewell salute. "Then good luck on the other side. I hear Hatha burns hot as hellfire."

Heart in my throat, I stepped back from the table.

Once.

Twice.

Greyson's brow lowered. My heart slammed in my chest with a painful *whomp* in time with my third pace. He called out, "You're not as good at this as you think."

"Same."

A flicker of a haunted smile appeared. "What sort of information do you want, Miss Monroe?"

"Something worthy of action. The cost of extending your miserable life has to make sense. Thus far, it does not."

His top lip curled ever-so-slightly as he considered. Quiet stretched into thin, fragile, spun sugar. The Council, riveted between us, didn't say a word.

He shoved an agreement out. "Fine. In Necce, there is a small curiosity shop. You'll know it by the lantern that hangs outside and burns a purple hue. If you're there in . . ." his eyes flickered to a grandfather clock against the wall, ". . . sixteen minutes, you'll hear their planning meeting. I suggest you start there."

Merrick shoved away from the wall, responding to Rognvald's immediate and sharp nod. He pried open one of the double doors and slid outside. I edged to follow.

"I would suggest," Greyson called in a lofty voice, "that you take no prisoners just yet. Listen to their plans. I assume your talent is strong enough that you can circumvent and catch them from there."

Merrick vanished.

I paused to say, "Your fate is your own, Greyson." To my greatest shock, a frisson of insecurity appeared in his gaze. To Scarlett, I said, "I'll return after the meeting, Your Highness, and give you a full report with Merrick."

She released me with a nod.

"Thank you, Sisterhood." The three words resounded. "You may go."

Leda offered no admonition. As I departed, the Council roared back to life and Georgette glared me out.

Chapter Five

D ark had already fallen on the Eastern Network, perfusing a twilight glow through the sky. Stars sprinkled out of the velvet like old friends. Leda spoke shortly after my transportation spell completed.

I presume you'll want access to Merrick through the communication magic? she queried with her usual prim politeness, dashed with an edge of displeasure.

Yes, please.

Rognvald has already granted it.

The ability to speak to Merrick without words eliminated many difficulties, particularly on a mission. Leda, Priestess of the Lokkan communication magic, had access to all conversations. She closed the individual threads, lest they annoy her all day. Rognvald, as Head of Protectors, heard any thread with a Protector in it. The lack of guaranteed privacy made it unlikely Merrick and I would use it outside of missions.

With a spell, I sent the Volare and Viveet to my treehouse. I had a feeling I wouldn't need them just yet.

Greyson's vague instructions led me to a specific coven in Necce: the Mayfair Coven. Known for eccentric shops and even more eccentric witches, it was the ideal place to gather if witches wanted to meet without drawing attention.

For one, it was far from Magnolia Castle. For another, Guardians didn't patrol here. Other Covens made far more noise and stirred up greater problems. Strange and calm. That was Mayfair.

Halfway into the Mayfair Coven, I sensed Merrick's magic turn around the corner of a building with a lighted lamp. The faintest purple hue emanated from the flame. The side alley smelled like rotten fish, which decorated the ground with cast-off bones. A rat scrambled out of a broken wooden box lying on its side. Levitating over the mess and the noisy cobblestones, I followed Merrick to the back porch and landed on my feet, invisible.

Merrick's whisper rumbled from nothing. "I thought you'd join me."

"Is that why you were so obvious?"

"Just in case."

"I'm flattered. Shall we switch to the communication magic?"

This better?

Much.

We faced a back door teeming with unseen magic. Obvious invisibility incantations and anti-jinx spells coated it, preventing witches from entering or trying to hex it. Their protection was overdone and garish, or simply intended to distract from more intricate incantations.

We wait, I suggested. *We're within the sixteen minute time-frame that Greyson suggested, so someone is bound to come along.*

Agreed.

Do you think it's a trap?

Merrick's blasé reply didn't surprise me. *It could be.*

While waiting for time to tick or witches to appear, I swapped for a lesser-known invisibility spell and strained to hear every sound. The scuffles of rodents, occasional rustle of distant life, was all I could hear.

Mere minutes after we arrived, approaching footsteps pounded close to the alley. A man and a woman left the main roadway, veering into the shaded side street. They strolled up to the back door and pressed inside without a knock. As it closed behind them, bright green light zipped around the edges.

I know that spell, Merrick said. *Only allows known witches, who've given blood to it, inside.*

What happens if you haven't given blood?

Burns. Really, really bad ones.

Any other way in? Rognvald asked.

Not easily.

Eyes on the ground, I said, *Yes. Sort of.*

Merrick's silent question was palpable. I crept closer to the building. The indomitable magic protecting the interior strengthened with each step. Greyson made infiltration sound easy, but of course it wasn't.

I knelt to the side of the door. Holes riddled the wall, chewed by mice and rats. Light peeked out from within, little dots set against time-warped wood. Unlikely that the witches would have thought to magically shield against rodents.

If I transform, I can get inside. As a mouse, I added, for Rognvald's benefit.

Better to be a rat, Merrick responded. *They have faster minds.*

Would it be worth it as a mouse? A rat wouldn't fit through the tiny holes. Or . . . I could transform from mouse to rat.

Thanks to years of practice, transforming from witch to rodent wasn't a problem. I'd transformed into a cheetah while captured by Mabel. My abilities weren't as strong then. Yet, changing while transformed required precise maintenance of magic and exquisite control.

Worth a shot.

I'm going in, I said.

Merrick replied, *Understood. I'm going up. There's an attic I want to assess.*

I recast the invisibility spell, which bought me eight minutes before I had to renew it. The simple magic drew little from my magical reserves. The morphing from witch to mouse, however, was . . . weird.

I initiated the spell with a held breath.

Slipping to the ground, losing altitude and physical body presence, and attempting to cram all the personality and soul that I possessed into a hundredth of my size wasn't painful. Neither could one call it comfortable.

When I fully shrank, my mousey nose twitched. Whiskers fluttered from side to side. My legs gave an involuntary leap when something swung behind me.

Oh.

Right.

I had a tail.

All good? Merrick asked.

It required effort to reply, *Fine,* and figure out the use of my tiny appendages. Four legs gave a distinct advantage, but required a moment of practice to coordinate. The giant ears, intense hearing, and increased sense of smell made for a jolting experience.

Finally ready, I said, *Transformation complete. I'm going in.*

No magic prevented me from slipping through the chewed holes. Immediately, a dank smell drew my attention. Curiosity sent me scurrying to the right for three seconds before I stopped myself.

Refocus, I thought. *Eavesdropping, not food.*

First lesson: beware the mouse urges.

Second lesson: simple thoughts worked better.

Scuttling again, I pressed on.

The vantage from the ground was wildly disproportionate. I hurried along the seam of the wooden wall, underneath a table, onto a wooden board. No wonder there had been mouse holes. This curiosity shop reeked of food. Based on the chairs ringing several similar tables, this was some sort of eatery *and* curiosity shop. Curios cluttered bookshelves like forgotten denizens.

Weird place, Mayfair Covens.

Across fathoms of space stood a group of witches. They towered overhead, inscrutable and unpredictable. Every movement made my pointed face quiver, then my legs, then my tail. The ripple effect irritated me to the end of my mouse toes.

Breath held, I waited for someone to out me. No witch thundered over to attack me with a broom. They didn't register my magical signature, which spoke to distraction, desperation, or concentrated magical use.

A good sign.

Torches and candles blazed, casting shadows on the unused furniture. The attendees shoved unused tables and chairs into the periphery, leaving an open space for witches to mingle. I scampered along the wall, following a strange scent that had vaguely familiar notes. Nothing I'd smelled as a witch, but it excited my mouse instincts. Fighting off the stirring urges and acclimating to four legs occupied my mind for too long.

A telltale stirring swirled through my tiny feet. The spell was fading. Forcing all my concentration and will power into magical use, I re-issued the transformation spell with a new intent.

Time to be a rat.

A boldly intelligent one, with a brain accomplished enough to take in scenery, though I wasn't *that* confident with transformation. Priscilla could manage it in a blink.

Magic bled away from my reservoir as I doubled, then tripled, in size. As I took on greater proportion, the squeezed-brain feeling dissipated. My thoughts opened. They automatically cataloged my surroundings, but with breathing room. I could think more easily around simplistic concepts. A long, whiplike tail, broader face, longer nose resulted.

After ten seconds, the magic held.

Well? Merrick asked.

Far more easily, I said, *I'm a rat.*

Yes, you are.

Ha, ha.

Anything?

Ducking under a table, I peered out. The sense that a hushed audience waited for my report lingered in my quiet mind. *Nothing important. There are eight witches. I need a hiding place.*

No one else replied, thank Alkarra. I'd explode if I tried to comprehend feedback from many Protectors, maintain the magic, and creep forward. To spare myself the agony of figuring out how to navigate a rat's body, I leaned into the instincts and let the bitty appendages take over.

Silent, I scuttled around the wall, past the tables, and away from flickering candlelight. A sinewy tail slipped around. That would *never* feel normal.

A cupboard of fine porcelain plates pressed against the wall, allowing room for me to slip behind. I wedged between the wall and the cupboard, my nose sticking out the side.

"Patience," insisted a reverberant female voice in Ilese. Chatter followed I couldn't understand. When a chair scraped across the floor, my legs jolted. I barely stopped myself from fleeing from the hiding spot.

Bianca? Leda asked.

Yes?

Do you need help with translating?

Not sure. I'll repeat what I hear. Someone else can figure it out.

Rognvald said, *Brody is fluent.*

Listening, Brody replied.

I'm in the attic, Merrick said. *Nothing up here. I can hear for the most part. I'll augment what B says.*

Best as I could, I relayed the words, the sounds. No other

Brothers communicated, freeing my mental space. In the cacophony, I recognized only a few Ilesan words.

Fight and *leader* and the Ilesan word *tortorra*, which could have been *beginning* or *fast endings*. None of those created any clarity. Some witches spoke quickly, with thick accents almost impossible to decipher. Names surfaced. *Frederico* and *Ricardo* and *palude*, which might have been the name of a marshland, or a derogatory slur.

One male agreed to the previous sentence, I said. *Another is protesting.*

As I warmed up more to the flow, it suddenly stopped.

A rap came on the back door.

My heart nearly seized. *Merrick? Where are you?*

On the roof.

Someone is at the back door.

The held-breath feeling continued as the door creaked open. A heavy pair of footfalls entered the room, and the hush deepened. "My friends," boomed a voice in perfect but mild Ilese, "Good evening."

Murmurs followed, each quieted in near reverence.

He's no one I've seen before, Merrick said. *He's protected by transformation magic. I saw a thick head of black hair and a normal physique before the door closed.*

New scents swarmed my rat nose. Fresh air. Salinity. A musky scent I couldn't identify. *He's familiar,* I said, *but I don't know how. I've heard his voice.*

The male figure chattered about *new rules* and *ever forward,* and *patience, patience, patience.* When all the witches started to speak at once, I lost my ability to decipher words. When the melee calmed, the new voice replied.

"Magnolia Castle will not die easily."

Did he mean Magnolia Castle as a structure, or the Aldana family? Ilesan phrases referred heavily on metaphor. My rapid transferral of his sentences was hasty and imperfect, but the general gist made his violent intent clear.

A modest smattering of applause accompanied his vainglory. With another repetition of the transformation magic—the invisibility spell had ceased, and I let it for now—a tug of weariness pulled on me.

Best I could tell, the conversation flowed into trivialities. The complicated threads of different witches speaking at the same time about various topics was impossible to distinguish. I felt strange all the way through.

Could rats experience headaches?

I certainly did.

I'm retreating, I said. *This is done. We've confirmed that Greyson was telling the truth.*

* * *

Scarlett and Grandfather met Merrick and me in the Gatehouse.

More often than not, Scarlett pulled everyone into her office for recaps. It had more space, and allowed Leda to take copious notes. Papa had done the same. Mildred, too, and all leaders before her. Tonight, Scarlett spoke to us at the Gatehouse.

Scarlett, with her pinched expression and slightly pale face, sought to change many practices. Or perhaps she was tired of the same scenery. She'd started far outside the political world as a teacher. Did her humble origins create a sense of imprisonment at the castle?

Her progress through teacher to Head of Education to High Priestess to Highest Witch testified to the stepping stones that prepare us.

Greatness lay ahead, not behind.

The Gatehouse had three main areas. It stretched in a large rectangle, with the Head of Guardian's office on the right, an open reception area in the middle—that had nothing but stone floors and a varied amalgamation of weapons with varying levels of importance—and the Head of Protectors office on the left. The Head of Guardian's office was three times the size of the Head of Protectors, allowing for a massive wooden table, around which many Captains congregated for weekly, sometimes daily, meetings.

Somewhere in the middle, I spied a room for the Sisterhood.

With a flick of his wrist, Head of Guardians, Talmund, spelled said giant table from his office and into the middle area, which allowed for more organization. Leda sprawled her paperwork on top, as did a Captain of the Guards assigned to Talmund. Clearly, Talmund had done this before.

Rognvald sealed the doors and windows, locking them, before he motioned toward the High Priestess. Scarlett stood behind the desk as she took command of the room. I felt a pang. Without Papa here, this would always feel a little empty.

To my deepest irritation, Georgette stood at Scarlett's side. The Council had voted Georgette into the respected position of Voice of the Council, a new job that the Council had organized the last several months without input from Scarlett. She brooked no opposition, which had riled Leda.

There's courting the Council and then there's giving in! she'd cried, nearly exploding with the pressure of holding it in after the announcement was released. *She can't lose power or control over the Council. You give a little, they take a lot. There has to be balance.*

She had fumed for days. While I didn't love Georgette, I saw no issue with the position thus far.

Merrick, Rognvald, and Brody stood near the Head of Protectors office, while Talmund and his Captain of Guardians, Sosha, who oversaw contingent placement and Captain assignments, stood near Talmund's side. Leda and I stood directly across from Scarlett, which gave me ample room to regard Georgette, who stood with her hands folded in front of her and ignored me.

"Thank you to our Sisterhood and our Brotherhood for providing the intelligence that we required," Scarlett said. She nodded first to me, then to the Brothers.

Thanking us first was intentional, Leda said.

"Starting with Bianca, please relate to Georgette, Talmund, and Sosha what you heard and observed. I ask you to relay it first so that Merrick's view, since he will report after you, can layer in extra detail. Finally, Brody will give his official opinion on the translations."

Half an hour passed by the time all three of us finished our recounting, answered questions, and established a bigger picture. Georgette, who said nothing the entire time, and looked at me when the strange power dynamic between us required it, kept a studious eye on the table, lost in thought.

"Thank you," Scarlett concluded as Brody finished. His scroll where he'd written notes replicated itself several times, distributing to each witch in the room. "Now that we have a tenuous confirmation of Greyson's information, I would like to assign our next steps to the individuals that will bear them."

Leda, with her brows drawn, appeared as confounded by the words *the individuals that will bear them* as I felt. Scarlett turned to Leda first. "Please write immediately to Cristian and request a meeting before the end of the hour. We will be informing him of the threat."

Georgette sucked in a breath.

Scarlett squared to me and ignored her. "Bianca, you will accompany me to the meeting, and your individual assignment will be given afterward, depending on what Cristian says."

I nodded.

To Rognvald, Scarlett said, "Please have the Brotherhood prepare a plan for imminent and secretive support to the Eastern Network. It's not likely that Cristian will ask for it, but I'd like to be prepared. This is to be kept silent, to only those in this room. The *Chatterer* or other such news sources should not know."

Rognvald nodded. "Yes, Your Highness."

"Also assign a Brother to invisibly accompany Bianca and myself to the meeting with Cristian. Preferably Brody or Merrick, due to their extensive dealings with the Eastern Network over the last six months."

Rognvald nodded to Merrick, who accepted with a nod.

Georgette's lips parted, eyes glazed. I couldn't help but share her surprise. Was Scarlett pressing forward with supporting the East despite the uproar just hours ago? The ability to act without Council support lay entirely in her purview, but she exercised it so rarely. I couldn't help but appreciate her moxie.

Scarlett whirled on the spot, her bell-like skirt swinging around her legs as she turned to Georgette, who had not yet asked the lingering question.

"Georgette, after we meet with the Eastern Network, I will update you on my plan. You may tell the Council before or after I have finalized all of our next steps to alert the Eastern Network, whatever feels best to you. In case the Council has questions, I plan to inform Cristian of the threat, offer secretive Protector support if he desires, but no Guardians."

Georgette straightened as if to speak, but Scarlett cut her off. Her voice was firm, but not unkind.

"To be clear, I am not asking permission from the Council, and will not be entertaining opinions on my actions until the situation has stabilized. Thank you for understanding."

Scarlett's voice rang through the room with tones of the strict teacher I met a whole different lifetime ago.

Well, that's something, Leda muttered.

"Thank you everyone for your help." Scarlett swept the room in a glance. "I'll keep you apprised."

The security magic unfolded from the door and window as she reached for the handle and tugged it open. Starlight spilled into the room with the brisk autumn wind. Grandfather sent me a wink as Leda and I followed at Scarlet's heels.

I love it when she commands, Leda said.

I couldn't help but agree.

* * *

Scarlett strode for ten steps before she stated, "There is great scrutiny on the Sisterhood right now, Bianca."

"I've noticed."

"With the Brotherhood actively involving you in a matter of great interest and security that does not originate with me, the Council will be doubly watching. I brought you into my meeting with Cristian to reaffirm the mission statement you and Leda have decided upon."

My hope sank like a stone. If Scarlett reiterated the two-woman Central Network team focused solely on the High Priestess, that meant my mission to the curiosity shop might be the last.

"Thank you, Your Highness."

She cast me a look that said my flat tone didn't fool her.

We passed a crowd of witches that hushed with reverence and parted around the High Priestess, whispering amongst themselves. It appeared to be a Network school on a tour. How did they look so young?

Scarlett gave them a subdued but sincere smile. The teacher, a woman I didn't recognize but who smiled with familiarity at Leda, waved. Scarlett nodded to her, murmured a warm, "Good to see you, Felicia," and kept walking.

"Can't we just cut the Council out and proceed?" I asked.

The foolish, grumbling hope was a wasted effort. "Funding," Leda interjected, and I loathed the word. "We want Georgette to see the Sisterhood aiding Scarlett *in regards to Scarlett only.*"

Scarlett sighed. "Unless you plan to work your tail off for a

Network that doesn't reimburse you a single sacran or pentacle? No."

"The Eastern Network needs our help, High Priestess."

"And we will grant it."

But not with the Sisterhood, came the silent continuation.

I bit my lip. Could I fault Scarlett? Not at all. She reiterated our boundaries. Problem was . . . I didn't like our boundaries.

While we passed into Chatham Castle, a letter fluttered in front of Leda, appearing mid air with a *pop* of sound. Without breaking a stride, she plucked it out of the way and daintily unfolded it. The bright emerald wax seal indicated Cristian's Assistant had already replied. I hadn't even seen Leda send one.

"Cristian will arrive on the hour, High Priestess."

Scarlett paused. "He's coming here?"

Leda nodded.

"Interesting. Thank you. I assumed we would go to him." Flustered by this unexpected change, she shook it off and added, "Please notify Rognvald and Merrick."

Leda's lips pressed. After five seconds of narrow-eyed concentration, she said, "Done."

Ah, magic.

What a convenient messenger.

After a moment of consideration, Scarlett added, "Of course, this means you'll need to contact Aurora immediately, Bianca."

The name *Aurora* sent a curl through my gut. Before I could protest or request that she never say the words, *you'll need to contact Aurora immediately, Bianca,* Scarlett continued.

"Of course our new Ambassador shall be present for the meeting with Cristian, and *you* will need Aurora's cooperation to earn the Council's trust. Like it or not. Leda and I will be busy preparing while you bring Aurora up to date with recent developments." She cut me a sharp look that reminded me of

Miss Scarlett, third-year teacher. "You *will* get along with Aurora."

"Yes, High Priestess."

Eyeing me, she added, "If you're lucky."

I barely suppressed a deep groan as we passed standing Guardians and headed toward the main, wide staircase. If there was one witch I didn't want to speak with—aside from Greyson — Aurora Fontaine was that witch.

At the top of the stairs we had been ascending, Scarlett and Leda bore to the left. I split to the right, headed for the Ambassador's turret.

Chapter Six

I only have to tell Aurora to come to the meeting, I reminded myself, fingers balled tight into fists. *I only have to tell her to come to the meeting.*

Summoning the Volare and Viveet made me feel marginally more prepared, though I'd never actually fight Aurora. Metaphorical readiness held some power.

Aurora's low, swift voice carried from her office as I stepped up the final turret stair and peered through a crack in the mostly closed door. She couldn't maintain an Assistant, which meant Grandfather's former turret was a chaotic disaster of roving messages, paperwork piles, and trinkets from every part of the Central Network. The coziness Grandfather once maintained was lost amid disorder and unregulated madness.

That was Aurora.

She muttered to herself as I watched, silent on the landing to her office. Half bent over her desk, her veiny hands propped around what appeared to be an unfurled scroll. She spoke to herself as if she expected an answer.

"Well, what did you expect?" she snapped to a letter. "A bloody god is providing magic for your witches. Excuse me, *former magical persons*, and you're frustrated that the culture of your Network has irreparably altered? I don't have time for your emotional pandering."

The letter turned to fire. Must have been from the Southern Network Ambassador, who had a habit of complaining. He couldn't have chosen a less-suited witch to vent to. I'd never seen Aurora care about any problems except those within reach of her thin, pointed glasses.

I rapped on the door.

"Come in, Bianca," Aurora called distractedly. "No sense in eavesdropping."

With the tips of my fingers, I pressed her door open. The dishabille spread to the doorway, barely allowing it to swing open. A trail led from my feet to her desk, then parted. To the left, a chair, to the right, another chair, both covered with paperwork, discarded shawls, or feather nubs.

"How are you, Aurora?"

"What do you want?"

"Scarlett sent me."

Aurora paused. Her gelid gaze slipped to mine, assessed, and returned to her desktop. Without question, she said, "I missed the Council meeting."

"Yes."

A string of curse words followed.

"Among other things," I added, thinking of the Eastern Network. "Scarlett wanted you to know that we're going to have a meeting with Cristian at the top of the hour. She has requested your presence."

"Of course she requested me," Aurora snapped. "I'm the bloody Ambassador!"

She snatched a flying letter from the air, opened it with equally hard fervor, and stabbed a letter opener into the header to pin it to the desk. I hid a wince. Grandfather had once taken great pains to care for this place, and many such pockmarks now littered the top of the desk. She didn't repair them with magic.

"And why," Aurora asked smoothly, "has the High Priestess sent you instead of her minion?"

Delighted and indignant at hearing Leda referred to as a *minion*, I forced the emotions to settle. I'd learned long ago not to reveal an emotional response to Aurora's words.

"Leda is busy helping Scarlett prepare for Cristian."

"Scarlett, hmm?"

Ignoring her vague reprimand for my familiarity, I continued. "There have been developments, and I'm here to brief you on them."

Aurora gave no immediate reply, but I knew better than to speak again. Unless I wanted a four-minute rant on the merits of patience, I'd hold my tongue and let her tirade run its course. No wise witch interrupted Aurora in the middle of a thought.

Finishing the letter, she straightened, yanked the opener from the desk, and flung it to the side. It clattered across the desk, dropped off, and shivered on the ground. The letter curled up and zipped into the air. A list of unmoving letters crowded around it. Read missives, presumably.

Aurora waved a hand.

"Proceed."

Grateful to get the recounting over with, I repeated the events to the detail I felt she cared about—which meant not to great detail. Yet. When Aurora adopted a furor for anything, she demanded headache-inducing clarity.

During the reciting, she kept her vibrant stare on the desk. I'd never seen a witch with such tight, coiled hair. The white streaks against her dark skin was a shocking contrast that worked well to her personality.

Aurora was a study of sharpness.

Her jaw clenched after I finished. She continued to stand perfectly still as other letters poured into her room. One day, she'd have to learn how to trust another witch with her missives. Until that time, she stayed up until all hours to stay abreast of her workload and only let vetted witches near her office.

The only reason I could enter was Scarlett's insistence.

Aurora received the Ambassadorship because she was the only candidate that the Council put forward to whom Scarlett agreed was a good fit. For my part, her lack of trust and unfiltered mouth required further vetting. Things hadn't gone well with the Northern Network Ambassador last I heard, but smoothed over eventually.

A crisis with the Eastern Network was hardly the proving grounds I would have desired for Aurora.

Yet, here we stood.

At the end of my review, Aurora asked, "What's your opinion?"

"About which part?"

"Greyson."

Surprised that she asked, I replied with halting honesty. "I think we'd be foolish to ignore him as a potential source of information, just as we'd be equally foolish to trust him."

The gleam in her eyes when I said *foolish to trust him* abated ever-so-slightly. Aurora's penchant for deep distrust and criticism of lackadaisical security measures couldn't be overstated. She was wasted as an Ambassador.

"What damage can he do from a prison cell?" she asked, with neither sarcasm nor innocence.

"Plenty."

"Agreed."

Aurora rose to her full height, a pace taller than mine. She selected another missive from the air. "I'll be there four minutes before the meeting. Go well."

* * *

When Camila stepped into Scarlett's office at Cristian's side, I felt neither surprise nor relief. Only a stewing sense of curiosity.

How interesting.

Tomorrow was my deadline for answering Camila. Fate, it seemed, had a plan.

In the weeks since I'd last seen Cristian, time had not been kind. Wrinkles ravaged the corners of his eyes, which sagged. His skin had a sallow tint, as if he hadn't seen the sun, or slept, in many days. Despite a bright smile, which lacked something, he appeared functional.

Two East Guards trailed behind the two Aldanas in the Eastern Network equivalent of half-armor. Less leather, more thin metal, shaped to fit shoulders and pectorals, but not their upper arms. Neither touched their swords—they wouldn't dare in Scarlett's presence—but their quick hands weren't far. A magical signature tailed them.

Do you sense it? I asked Merrick.

It's an East Guard. They always have one that's unseen.

My brow wrinkled. I didn't like that. Not one bit. Anyone could stroll into the room behind them. To Leda, I said, *Before we start, I want to see the invisible East Guard.*

Leda's forehead wrinkled.

There's an invisible one?

Yes.

I can't sense them.

I do.

Flustered at a magical capability we didn't share, Leda merely nodded and jotted a note on her paper.

I'll handle it.

Scarlett, busy with welcoming Cristian and Camila, didn't notice.

Aurora slid into the room a second before Hiddleston closed the door, remaining outside to prevent interlopers. She joined Scarlett, Camila, and Cristian in the middle of the floor with a friendly enough smile. Chameleon, that one. Aurora could be anyone she needed to be.

While waiting for it to start, I scanned the office from where I stood near Scarlett. Merrick, invisible in the far corner, gave off a low magical signature. The East Guard that entered remained a surreptitious presence directly behind Camila and Cristian.

As Scarlett returned to her desk, motioning Camila and Cristian into the plush chairs that awaited, Leda held out her note. Scarlett accepted it as she slipped past. The familiar smell of cumin wafted past my nose with her movement. Not missing a beat, she read it, set it down, and turned to Camila and Cristian.

"Before we proceed, I would like to make a request. Please have your invisible Guardian reveal themselves. We want to see their face."

Cristian's cheek gave a little twitch.

Ah.

What a telling silence.

They were hiding it, I said to Leda.

She murmured a stiff and furious, *I agree. This will be followed up with later.*

Camila had the presence to appear slightly alarmed, though serene. She kept her gaze on the ground as Cristian gathered his startled hesitation. "Of course, Your Highness. Ronaldo, you may reveal yourself."

A middle-aged Guardian sprang to life. Hints of silver gray lined his short-cropped hair, pillowing back. I met his cool stare for a full three seconds. "Thank you," I said. "I'm satisfied."

With a wave from Cristian, Ronaldo vanished. Scarlett pressed on, mitigating the tension. As she relayed the new events, Merrick said, *Nicely done.*

Thanks.

A recap of Greysons approach to the Council, his revelation of information, and the meeting Merrick and I had spied on required a handful of questions from Cristian's side. Scarlett blithely avoided informing Cristian that Merrick and one other Brother had been in the Eastern Network for over six months, chronicling the gradual decline of events against the Aldana dynasty. The violence reached a fever pitch when the magical prison, Carcere, had been breached and prisoners released.

Scarlett brought the accounting of events to its inevitable conclusion. "I requested your presence today to inform you about what Bianca and Merrick discovered on their mission to the curiosity shop in the Mayfair Covens," Scarlett concluded. "I hope this is of some assistance to you."

Cristian inclined his head. "Thank you, Your Highness. We are grateful for your openness and transparency."

"We are also willing to help you manage this rising problem if you require help from our Protector force. Particularly considering Greyson is under our custody, and that will not change."

She left Cristian the space to refuse, should he feel to save pride and not ask for help, but without straining relationships. The neutral approach created no real pressure. Elegantly managed, despite the tension it would certainly create in the Council.

"The offer is generous," Cristian murmured.

"If you do require our assistance, be assured we'll do what we can to assist you, short of providing Guardian support, as the need arises. We require utmost secrecy, however. It should not be known that our Protectors are involved."

"I understand. The situation is . . . fragile. There is not much that I can say to explain it more fully, except that to involve another Network—even quietly—could crumble what little standing I have amongst Council Members."

His liquid brown eyes met hers with a grateful, but weary, smile. "Your offer is noticed and I will keep it for a time when I need it. Let us all hope that time doesn't come."

Scarlett inclined her head.

"I understand. The offer remains."

Cristian braced his hands on the arm rests and stood. The slow unfolding of his lean body left me holding my breath, waiting for something unknown to erupt. Nothing in the room had shifted. Not magic, not witch.

I couldn't help my shock.

He *couldn't* use them?

Camila tensed, her fingers twitching. We had studiously avoided each other for the duration of this meeting.

"Thank you again for the information, Your Highness," Cristian concluded. "I will strive to deal with this information immediately."

* * *

That evening, the trees soothed me.

They sang quiet melodies as I sat on a branch and stared out. Legs crossed beneath me, hands on my knees, I distracted myself with their wordless songs. My rising ire settled. I more easily searched through my concerns and fears.

Cristian's quick departure shouldn't have ruffled me this much. Refusing the Protectors meant the Sisterhood wouldn't miss out on any action, yet I couldn't help my regret at his choice. He departed with all the flexibility and gratitude of a wooden board. Camila, her smile subdued but present, appeared reluctant to leave. Her eyes lingered on Scarlett, shadowed by all she couldn't say.

Politics.

What a disaster.

Approaching feet, and then a firm body, lowered behind me. Merrick's legs snaked around my sides, swamping me in his warmth. He pulled me close, and I gratefully leaned into him. His bent knees framed my body as I melted, spine pressed to chest, and fully relaxed. I trailed the tips of my fingers along his forearm, enjoying the crinkle of his hair.

His thoughts weighed so heavy I could have extracted them from his brain.

"Frustrating," he stated with his usual burr. "This whole thing with the Eastern Network is *frustrating*."

"Cristian's scared."

"If this rebellion truly rises, it will mean the downfall of the Aldana dynasty."

"Is it that bad?"

"It's heading that way. It all started with Niko," Merrick added with an unusually acerbic bite.

I spun to study his wrinkled expression, startled by the depth of aggravation. "You're very upset."

"I am."

"Why?"

"Because I spent the last six months touring the Eastern Network. The poverty and deprivation and death outside the cities, particularly in the marshlands, is appalling. Their own leadership doesn't appear to see it. In all my time, not a single Council Member was visible in the bereft marshes. Nor spoken of," he added.

"You saw quite a bit of ugly stuff over there, it sounds like."

"Stupid things," he immediately retorted, shoving a hand through his long hair. The loose braid disintegrated, spilling strands onto his shoulders in a heart melting way. "There's more destruction and suffering in the Eastern Network than the *Chatterer* or newsbooks report. Especially in the small towns. The distant places, away from Magnolia and Necce. The marsh witches have been left to starve and fight illnesses they don't have potions or Apothecaries for, and worse."

"Is it their Council Members, or Cristian?"

"Who can tell?"

His observations swirled into thoughts of Camila, Cristian,

and Greyson. I faced him fully, legs folded beneath me. "Council Members, it sounds like. Why are they ignoring marsh witches, do you think?"

"I don't know." He shook his head. "They're too poor to bother with, perhaps? Rural, too. There aren't many resources that go in and out of the marsh. Or they're trying to convince the marsh witches that the Aldana's are the problem, when *they* are the problem."

Ugly arithmetic.

"Do you think the Eastern Network can stop the uprising?"

"No."

"Really?"

Distress wrinkled his brow. "I don't think they can, B. It's big, and growing bigger."

"He refused our help for the moment," I drawled, "but that doesn't mean we can't help if we aren't detected."

He snorted. "Rognvald would birth a cow if I helped without his assignment."

I have no such obligation to Rognvald's authority, I thought, thinking of Camila and her plea. Framing Camila's request in light of Cristian's refusal for help brought a new angle of consideration into my decision. How important would it be for the Sisterhood to maintain that flexibility?

Our current mission statement negated it.

Which I loathed.

Flexibility is everything, I thought with raw understanding.

But would flexibility negate legitimacy with the Council?

Merrick broke into my thoughts with a heated statement. "I didn't agree with Leda's opinion about helping Camila before, but after Cristian's response, I understand. We're better to give the East a wide berth and let them fall as they may."

The removal of his support cost me courage. Merrick tried to remain sublimely neutral toward any Sisterhood decision I made, allowing me to proceed without fear of judgment. But this?

Frightening.

"Will the Protectors try to interfere anyway?" I asked, hoping to turn the focus away from me.

Merrick's lack of reply was all that I needed to know. In his hesitating eyes, I saw the answer. I pressed our foreheads together.

"I love you."

He wrapped a hand around the back of my neck. His whisper of, "I love you, too, B," expressed profound relief and weariness. I pulled him into my arms and held him.

Night descended and stars winked from high in the forest canopy.

Chapter Seven

A bouncy giggle drew me into a familiar Northern Network cottage, set against the backdrop of jagged teeth and saw-like mountain tips. Hints of pumpkin pie wafted from the stove. A bundle of hair, skirts, and firm arms flew into my chest. Jacqueline was little more than a flash before she slammed into me.

"Congratulations!"

I wrapped my arms around her and stepped backward, catching her before both of us toppled.

"Congratulations?" I set her down. "For what?"

Her mouth hung half open, eyes wide as saucers. "You're going to handfast my *brother*!"

Merrick, standing behind me, grunted. As he hurried deeper into the house where his stepfather, Drogo, stood, Merrick rolled his eyes.

"Jacqui, you've known that we're going to handfast for months, if not years! This isn't new."

"But it's *official*." Her eyes dropped to my bare wrist. She frowned. "Or almost official, anyway. I thought it was official!"

She whipped around, a hand on her hip to shout at Merrick. "When *are* you going to ask her?"

Merrick glanced over his shoulder. "Hey, B. You wanna get handfasted?"

"Sure."

"Set a date later?"

"Sounds good."

He returned his focus to Drogo.

Jacqueline steamed like a furious teakettle. I grabbed her hand, twirled her around, and pulled her away before an explosion tore the house in half. Jacqui followed me to the table, but not before sending Merrick a withering glare.

"Merrick says that handfasting is really important in the Northern Network," I said in a not-so-subtle effort to return Jacqui's focus to what she adored the most: celebration management. "What is it you want to do?"

Kalli, Merrick's mother, sat at a wooden table near wide, sunshine-bright windows. Whimsical reminiscence lightened her expression as she glanced up, a half smile on her face. Seeing me, her expression illuminated.

"Merry meet!"

While I embraced her—she smelled like mountain sage and sunshine—Jacqui braced her hands on the table and swept her arm over a scattered sundry of items. "These," she declared with recovered gusto, "are the items of inheritance."

"The what?"

Kalli said, "In the North, the first handfasting in a family conveys the items of inheritance, which are what you see on the table, to the first child who handfasts. That will be you and Merrick."

Jacqui, clapping prettily, cried, "It passes on who we are as a family!"

Knowing those implications, I comprehended the cache with a different regard. The items of inheritance occupied almost the entire table, tripling across several dozen things. Most appeared nothing more than trinkets, passed down through generations from former grandparents. As I studied the layout, it became clear that the hoard was split into two sections, one on either side of the table.

Jacqueline pointed to the top left corner. An arrowhead chiseled from stone, tied to a snowy owl feather.

"This belonged to our father. He called it his lucky arrowhead."

"Did he make it?"

"He did." Her fingers danced to the next item. A clay pot with a tiny lid canted open, revealing a gray, powdery substance. "These are the ashes of my grandfather." She tapped on a doll, sewn together with thick thread and gathered canvas. Four appendages and a horrific smile stuck from its ragged body. "This is my great-grandfather's. The doll was his favorite toy as a child."

I swallowed my rising panic.

The good gods.

What were we supposed to do with all of these macabre things? Kalli watched me closely, so I strove to keep an interested, delighted expression.

After Jacqui introduced me to a stained pillowcase that her great-great-great grandmother used to wipe the blood off her dying husband's head, I managed to choke out a, "What lovely heirlooms," and not sink to the floor in horror.

Kalli's careful scrutiny didn't waver as Jacqui finished the tour of items, gifted from both families, that dated back six generations. Most came from direct descendents—grandparents and great-great-great's—but others accompanied the main bloodline. Aunts and uncles, distant cousins, old family friends.

Anyone that passed on something of significance remained in the . . . cache. Including a pile of old rags at the far end of the table. By Jacqueline's account, they oiled the wooden stump of her seventh great grandmother and carefully preserved all these items by preventing jostling.

A full twenty minutes passed before Jacqueline made it through each piece. Halfway through, Merrick stood behind me, a hand on my shoulder. He gave me something to lean on, choked by disbelief.

"And there you have it!" Jacqui concluded with a wide smile. "Our family and our items of inheritance."

"That is quite the treasure trove," I said.

Merrick gently squeezed my shoulder. "There's a wooden box that holds them." He nodded toward the windowed wall. A rectangular wooden box stood open, the contents disgorged onto the table. "Every couple receives their own wooden box on their handfasting day, in which they put all the treasures inside."

"During the extended family dinner!" Jacqui cried.

Extended family dinner? I didn't recall him mentioning that particular meal when he brought it up days ago, but there had been so many it would have been impossible. Merrick blithely avoided eye contact by spinning to ask Drogo a question.

Drogo.

Merrick's favorite local escape hatch.

Delicate ceramic and wooden carvings littered the collection. Letters from Merrick's father lay betwixt other items with deep emotional significance. Amongst them, I recognized a whittled M, J, and A. Merrick, Jacqueline, and Ana, his younger sister that died while still a child.

"It's beautiful," I said.

Kalli stared at the box with a thoughtful expression. In measured tones she said, "For some of our family members or friends, these small offerings were all they had to give us. They constitute a great gift, and mean a lot."

Horrifying, but heartfelt.

"I can see why," I said.

Drogo joined Kalli at her side, a hand on her waist. She put an arm around his back. "As the first handfasted," she lifted her focus to Merrick, "these items will go to you. At least, part of them. I will keep my half, so that the spirits of my forebears bless this house until I pass. After which, you'll take them. Of course," she added with a clap, "we still have the box party."

"Box party?" I whispered.

Merrick's grip tightened. "The family puts our box together, bequeathing the items."

"As part of the dinner?"

"Separate."

"So it's another dinner?"

"Yes."

"I thought—"

"The extended family dinner is where we unpack it and talk about it," Jacqui quickly said. "We'll still have to box it. You see?"

The strain in Merrick's voice meant he sought to lighten the blow when he said, "We put it together during the box party, which is the next day. The items of inheritance will remain on display for the extended family dinner."

I needed a flowchart.

Jacqui twirled on the spot, delighted for a new reason to celebrate. "During the box party, we have a big dinner and invite all our friends with the extended family. We wrap and place the items together, in order of when they were received. Then we tell them the story of each item—with greater detail than I just gave of *course*—and the family takes the box to stain the wood and finalize it for the final handfasting dinner." She paused, then added, "But first, the extended family dinner where we unpack it. Right, Mother?"

Kalli nodded.

Jacqui beamed.

My chest tightened like a vise. Handfasting dinner? Is that the one *I* was supposed to fix? No, no. This sounded altogether separate. Kalli, beaming at Drogo with such delight, motivated me to wipe the anxieties away.

Later. I couldn't reveal my horror at this particular moment. Whatever value Merrick and his family placed on these traditions, I would share with him. Surely, it couldn't be *that* bad. Assembling the box, hearing the stories, would provide greater insight into the Northern Network life.

Not to mention the family I would join.

This was fine.

Fine.

As Kalli and Jacqui joined together, squealing with steady excitement around handfasting plans and dinner menus—something I couldn't bring myself to care about if it granted the Sisterhood every dream we had—I reached up, put my hand on top of Merrick's, and gave him a reassuring squeeze.

I thought I heard him sigh.

* * *

Council Member Henry is low hanging fruit, Leda said the next morning. *As long as you listen to him, act kind, and say a few words about what you need from him, he'll be immediately supportive of the Sisterhood. An easy win. If he starts talking to other Council Members about his conversation with you in a positive slant, which he's sure to do, it can only help.*

When is my meeting with Georgette? I responded.

Wryly, she said, *Dead last. When you know it's poison, you don't drink it. Also,* she added imperiously, *let this remind you of your real goals.*

Leda hadn't forgotten that today was my day to answer Camila, though I'd hoped for a lapse in her memory. Ironic, because the Brotherhood planned to launch another sleuthing mission into the Eastern Network. The rogue group at the curiosity shop had drawn Rognvald's interest when this morning's *Chatterer* headline declared an emergent state of unrest near Portafina, a known marshlands hub. Witches pillaged the local Coven offices.

Cristian didn't require our help yet, but Rognvald wanted intel.

Council Member Henry issued a squeal of delight, drawing me back into the moment. His aged fingers danced above square cucumber sandwiches perched on the edge of his plate. Cut into symmetrical squares and topped with delicate olives, he studied his for several seconds before he peered at me.

"Well, those are *quite* lovely!"

My smile grew pained.

We sat in the gardens, surrounded by a beautiful autumn day. Two maids spelled silver trays to their palms and set them on the round table where I sat, the persuasive sunshine on my face. Flowers perfumed the air, brought by the lightest breeze. It fluffed the forest leaves, stirring them.

Henry lifted his head with an exaggerated motion and blinked. "Well?" he asked, adjusting wide spectacles broken across the nose bridge several times. "How are you, Miss Black?"

"Monroe, actually."

"Oh, you're married?"

"Not yet. I took my mother's name instead of my father's."

"Not yet, eh? Will you be soon?"

Bemused by the odd slant of the conversation, I said, "Yes. Plans are in motion."

"What will your name be then?"

The question surprised me. Would I take Merrick's last name? Would he take mine? It went both ways. Some witches didn't change their name at all. I mentally hung it on the *talk to Merrick about it later* peg.

"You know? I'm not sure."

With a noise from deep in his throat, he drew taller, which wasn't very tall. Tufts of his perfectly white hair sprawled wide.

"Well, that's *quite* interesting. All this time, I presumed . . ."

His discourse trailed into compounding surprise when a maid lowered a tray with glasses brimming in red slush. Fina, who ran the castle kitchen, had a particular berry concoction she adored. These lazy fall days were perfect for it. If I had to get through this egregious small talk disaster, the slush would be worth it.

While he interrogated the maid on whether or not cardamom had been used in the recipe—for he was *quite* allergic —another voice pulled my attention away.

Mission into the Eastern Network has begun, Rognvald announced.

Thank you for letting me know, lingered on the tip of my tongue, but I couldn't bring myself to say it. If I thanked Rognvald for including me, it would acknowledge that I ate cucumber sandwiches with a Council Member instead of attending a high-profile and secretive assessment of the Eastern Network.

Embarrassing.

Not to mention peeving, chafing, and every other form of irritation I could imagine. Leda hadn't blocked me from updates, which was an oversight of pure luck. Rognvald wouldn't have included me if he'd known I met with Council Member Henry, which was another stretch of luck. I might run out, at this rate.

We're starting in Portafina, ending at Magnolia Castle. His voice echoed slightly, meaning he spoke to many witches.

Thank you, came Scarlett's voice. I almost froze. No wonder Rognvald was providing updates. Despite a general dislike of the communication magic, Scarlett also listened in. A new form of efficiency.

Probably Leda's idea.

"And that," Henry declared, "is that!"

He gestured with two fingers to his plate, mouth agape in a delighted smile. Petaled apple slices decorated the edges, highlighted by a strategically placed blueberry here and there. At the top, a spoon lay in a thick bowl of a creamy dessert, meant to be placed directly on the sliced fruit. Instead, Henry dropped a dollop in the middle of his food flower.

The maids hurried away, hiding their chortles.

"Council Member Henry," I said through a determined smile, "that is a lovely display you've made. How are the Tate Covens?"

"Fine. Just fine."

"Anything new?"

"Not really." He picked up a fruit slice with the edge of his fingernails, sucked the white mixture off, and waggled the piece. "You see that depth and cut line precision of the apple core? Incredible what chefs can do with knives."

Knives? I wanted to counter. *Leda brought me here to discuss fruit arrangements?*

I discovered a group of rebels hidden in a marsh, Brody stated. *There's a discussion about splinter groups, which are apparently forming off the main rebellion.*

Anything about a leader? Rognvald asked.

No.

Council Member Henry set his napkin on his thighs, leaned his forearms on the edge of the table, and declared, "Well! This is *quite* cozy, isn't it? Eating out in the wild, and all that."

A bird twittered overhead, swooping past the table. One of the maids returned, empty handed, and stood several steps away in case we needed her. She shifted painfully from one foot to the other. Conjuring a chair on her behalf, I set it in the grass at her side with magic. She beamed.

"Thank you, Miss Monroe!"

Henry, clucking, reached for a berry smeared with extra compote and cream. "Well, well," he sang, "*quite* a lovely thing to do for the maid. Sorry, miss!" He shouted, far louder than necessary. "I should have done so myself. Glad you're here. Have you seen these berries?"

The maid smiled wider.

"So, Council Member Henry," I called, attempting to divert his attention again. "Have you heard of the Sisterhood and the work that we're trying to do with the High Priestess?"

"Yes, yes. I have! *Quite* interesting stuff."

"Do you have any questions?"

"None at all."

With my fork tines, I speared half of a strawberry and lifted it to my lips. Distracted by a bee on the tip of his finger, Henry hummed, strawberry abandoned to his plate. No wonder Leda called him *low hanging fruit*. He'd probably support the Sisterhood simply because he enjoyed nature in my presence.

"You seem very fond of the outdoors, Council Member."

Brightening, he exclaimed, "Oh, yes." His voice lowered into a nervous stammer as he glanced at Letum Wood over my shoulder. "Too bad it's so unpredictable." A hesitating smile died on his lips. "You know . . . so dangerous. But beautiful," he tacked on, as if he waged a great war between danger and beauty.

Confirmed splinter group, Brody said.

How many witches in it? Rognvald asked.

Thirty present, but they're insinuating others. That's all I know.

I had to bury the urge to jump to my feet and demand, "Let me help!" Staying in one spot and participating in food art was unconscionable. Instead, I rose demurely to my feet and stuck out a bent elbow.

"It just so happens, Council Member, that I live in the forest. I don't find it all that dangerous most of the time. Not around the castle edges, anyway. Wouldn't a walk through the woods be delightful?"

He perked up. "Yes it would! Are you sure it's safe?"

"I have a good feel for the trees."

"What about dragons?" he whispered. "They're known to patrol the grounds."

"Not as often now that Almorran magic is gone. They've dispersed more widely across the forest these days."

His eyebrows waggled as he considered that statement.

"True."

"Would you care to walk with me? I can guarantee your safety and a good time. We'll spell the rest of the food to your office to eat at the end of our visit, if you like."

Henry balled up his napkin, shot to spry feet, and accepted my arm. "That is *quite* the invitation. Yes, yes. Let's have an adventure, shall we?"

* * *

Like a child, Council Member Henry was best entertained by movement. We strode into the forest, where the flora and fauna captured his interest. He oohed and ahhed over indomitable tree heights, roots sticking from the forest floor that loomed over his head, and flower chains forming delicate knots.

When a particularly bright cluster of mushrooms with white circles and purple tops appeared on the ground, Henry couldn't throw himself to the forest floor fast enough. On hands and knees, he exclaimed over each tiny toadstool.

Meanwhile, Merrick provided another update that made my heart flutter. *No sign of a splinter group in Portafina, but there are signs of meetings out in the marshes. A well known trail leads to an old house. Tysen and I are watching it, but not seeing much.*

Potential gathering place? Rognvald asked.

We believe so.

I squinted at the sun, nearly invisible with Letum Wood blocking it. We hadn't advanced far into the forest. Hints of Chatham Castle's gigantic gray bulwark peeked in between tree branches, but I couldn't ascertain how much time had passed.

Half an hour, perhaps? Our appointment was a strict forty-five minutes.

My thoughts fell into spirals around splinter groups, the Brotherhood, my position as the head of the Sisterhood, and Camila when Council Member Henry caught my ear.

"Have you ever, Miss Monroe?"

"Forgive me, Council Member. I was lost in thought. Have I ever what?"

"Seen such extraordinary creations?"

"Never. Letum Wood is rather special."

"*Quite* true."

He straightened, tugging at his pant legs to clear the fabric, and continued jovially down the path. Mud and dirt stained charming circles around his knobby knees. Chuckling under my breath, I followed. When I trailed my fingers along a tree root, blue light swelled to life and swirled to the ground.

You belong to us.

We belong to you.

Always, I crooned in return.

"Must say, Miss Monroe, that this is *quite* surprising. Never have I been invited on a walk in the woods by the castle. Enlightening. The forest is different in different places. Isn't that fascinating?"

"Letum Wood covers much of the Tate Coven, doesn't it?"

"Much, but not all." He lifted a finger to punctuate his point. "Not all. I hail from the unforested portion of it, and generally avoid going in alone. Bad experiences as a child, you know." He shuddered. "Dragons."

"I'm sorry to hear that."

"After this *quite* delightful stroll, so am I."

"We need to find you more adventurous friends, Council Member."

He pressed a hand to his face and laughed. Shaking his head

and dabbing at his eyes, he said, "We should turn back, Miss Monroe. Meetings, meetings. You know how it is. *Quite* busy."

Rognvald's final update issued as Council Member Henry and I crossed the lawn.

Continue the investigation, Brody and Merrick, where you are. Let's try to draw more details on the potential splinter groups. Return at dark ready to report to the High Priestess.

Interesting observations that definitely impacted Camila. Did the Eastern Network have a secretive force doing the same ground work? Unlikely, which is why Camila approached me. The denouement of my involvement in the situation was no surprise. Inevitable, no matter what angle I studied it. Frustrating, too.

I wanted to be part of it *all*.

Long after Council Member Henry gave his exalted and continuous thanks, and the maids swept away the table and food, I stared at the forest, lost in thought. One witch could help me with these conundrums.

Grandfather.

Chapter Eight

An hour later, Grandfather's wise eyes tilted on the edge of a laugh. His brow, wrinkled and high, seemed to ask, *Well? What are you going to do?*

I had no idea.

We stood in the lower bailey. Grandfather, despite his advancing age, insisted on a spar with swords before I caught him up on the news. Using a wooden training sword instead of Viveet, I happily accepted his offer. Somehow, after several minutes of back-and-forth, he'd pinned me into a corner with a wooden sword edge at my neck and I had no way of getting out.

He must have been faking his initial frailty.

For being his age, against a witch of twenty-three, it seemed impossible that he wasn't a little more winded, sweating, or at least struggling. His impeccable footwork and twinkling eyes didn't show a hint of upset.

"Well done, Grandfather." I panted in between words. "I concede the match to your superior skill. You . . . win."

He studied me, then dropped the sword. With a growing smile, he said, "I may be an old man, but I haven't lost my edge."

Laughing, I agreed. "You definitely haven't."

"It's not as much about superior skill as knowing your opponent." He held up a finger. "I have spent years watching you fight. You have tells, my dear. We all do. Of course, someone would have to watch and work with you for years to read you as I do. You're special, Bianca, but not *that* special."

I lowered my shoulders. "Thanks. I think?"

He spun on his heels, breathing a little heavier now that the fight was won. So, he *had* been posturing.

Wily witch.

I strode to catch up with him, wearing pants instead of my simple, long-sleeved dress. Other Guardians trained in pockets around the lower bailey, oblivious to our presence. The dull *thunk* of wooden swords clashed beautifully with the higher-pitched *clanks* of metal. The dulcet symphony reminded me of the handful of years when I trained the new recruits in swords. Those were steady, lonely days, mourning Mildred, Camille, and all those lost in the war against Mabel.

After more than five years since Mama died, and many others lost, I'd long learned that grieving amounted to the same thing: acknowledgment and letting go. Over and over and over again.

As we departed the bailey, I left those ghosts behind.

Again.

Grandfather guided me into the low, dark hallway that led into Chatham Castle, passing high stone walls and a small portcullis that blocked witches from entering the castle through the lower Bailey if enemies breached the walls. No one joined us, for which I was grateful. Grandfather's distant thoughts meant he had something on his mind. He wouldn't impart it with an audience.

"How are you feeling, Grandfather?"

"Fine."

"You're quiet today."

"I'm feeling . . . thoughtful."

"Want to talk about it?"

We petaled to the left, peeling away from the juncture that would take us deeper into the heart of Chatham Castle. There was a back way, winding through turrets and lesser-known hallways that required more walking, but had less people. Grandfather took it routinely.

"Perhaps," he said, hands folded behind his back. He cast me a sidelong glance. "But you also have something to discuss, and I'm far more interested in you than the thoughts of an old man. Mine are not as pressing as I think yours might be."

With a wry smile, I conceded. "An offer has come forward for the Sisterhood, and I need to reply before this evening. I haven't decided fully whether I accept it, as it goes against what Leda and I previously agreed about the mission of the Sisterhood. Well . . . *Leda* felt it would be our most appropriate focus. I . . . would appreciate your thoughts."

Solemnly, he asked, "Shall we discuss this in my office?"

I nodded.

With a lift of his arm, he invited me with him. "It's an honor to be with you anywhere."

* * *

The High Priest's office, smaller in size than Scarlett's, invited all witches with a cozy interior. Leather-bound tomes lined the wall, illuminated by candlesticks. Trinkets collected from a lifetime of service to the Central Network and subdued still-life paintings graced the rest. The familiar, cozily cluttered decor greeted me as we strolled inside.

As always, padded upholstery and a steaming tea set awaited. Grandfather motioned me into a chair with a tilt of his head. "Have a seat, my dear. Scarlett and I have other meetings that will begin in an hour. If I clean up before I speak with you, we'll lose our opportunity. I'd rather make the

Coven Leaders wait while I tidy up after a spar, instead of you."

He winked.

I smiled as I lowered into a chair across from him. "I can make this quick."

"No need. My time is plentiful for you."

He didn't sit behind the desk, but on the seat nearest mine. The tea poured itself. A sachet dunked into the hot water, and cream poured in billowy plumes, while I told him about Camila. Grandfather listened attentively, sipped, and hummed at all the right times.

Finishing with, "I *want* to help Camila. By extension, Priscilla and Tomasso. While I understand Leda and Merrick's concerns about having anything to do with the Eastern Network, I don't think it's fair to punish Camila. She's asking for help. The Eastern Network needs help. I can give it. I can't figure out a better definition for the Sisterhood than that."

"True."

"But," I continued down the same line of reasoning, "Leda will disagree. We decided to focus on Scarlett because we felt that would sway the Council in our favor."

He lifted an eyebrow. "It is a narrow focus."

"I'm noticing."

"Hmmm."

"What do you think?" I asked, hopeful.

For a long time, Grandfather bunched his lips and stared at his tea, frowned at a painting of Mildred, his former life-long partner and my grandmother. Setting aside his empty cup, he asked, "I think a lot of things, but none of them matter as much as your opinion. What do you believe is the best course of action?"

"Helping Camila," I said immediately. "She came to me; it would assist Priscilla, and help the situation in the East. The ability to do *something* is welcome. Scarlett doesn't have all that much danger in her daily life," I added in a mumble, considering the sheer number of hours Leda spent in Scarlett's office with her.

"What about your plan to position before the Council? I agree that assisting Camila will impact their approval. For good or ill," he added blithely.

"Well, that's something else I wanted to ask you." I hedged a smile. "What if I didn't tell anyone?"

I allowed the insinuations to trail out. For the first time, Grandfather smiled. "Certainly, it would be a bold rebellion, my dear. If you are to help the Eastern Network against the advice of your peers and, perhaps, your superiors, should you ask their advice, it wouldn't look good."

Leaning forward, I said, "I managed to help without being detected . . ."

"Then beneficial things might stem from that decision."

"Tomasso," I whispered. "I'm most worried about Tomasso and Priscilla. She's so happy at the school. He's so happy in the forest. If the Eastern Network stabilizes and this . . . Giuseppi witch . . . doesn't overthrow the Aldanas, Priscilla won't have as much reason to fear."

Grandfather's eyebrows came together in a wrinkled concern that made my gut clench. He saw hope and goodness everywhere. When Grandfather revealed distress, there was a reason to pay attention.

"I share your concern about Priscilla and her son. As Leda indicated, there are many ways to protect them, but perhaps nothing simple or easy. Priscilla would have to go into hiding. Not even Letum Wood would frighten the Eastern Network witches away enough to stop them from harming the child."

Historically, witches in the Eastern Network had a particular hatred for Letum Wood. They feared the high branches, the gigantic trees, thicker than several houses together. Something in the magic kept them far away. But not vicious, bloodthirsty assassins intent on hurting a child.

"The forest could help protect her," I said, "but only if they left the school. And Priscilla is happy there. She's independent. If she had to move . . ."

"Then she would," Grandfather finished softly. "She would make it work and find happiness again. But, perhaps, there are other avenues for you to explore before it comes to that."

"Do you think Cristian can fix this?"

"Not with his current Council. It is no small matter to rearrange an entire Council in the midst of a bloody rebellion."

His steady expression revealed nothing. If Grandfather approved of *my* rebellion, then it would make the decision for me. Except, he didn't reveal an opinion beyond a very expected and logical concern.

With a hint of humor, I said, "You aren't going to make this easy on me."

Grandfather leaned forward, clasped my hand in his. With a simple, "No," he made me laugh. He relaxed into his chair again. "You know what you want, Bianca. As the Head of the Sisterhood, you are expected to make your own decisions."

"And bear the consequences."

"Yes."

"Good or ill."

"Good or ill," he replied quietly. "And *that* is true leadership, my dear. Whatever you decide, you shall have my full support."

I already knew what I wanted to do.

What I *needed* to do.

Squeezing his hand, I said, "Thank you. I'll let you know if I require help."

"I am always on your side."

Chapter Nine

M agnolia Castle had never been a bastion of security, but considering the state of their Network, I couldn't blame them. The Battle for Letum Wood decimated their Guardian reserves, and recruits hadn't been plentiful. With riots scattering the Network, few remained. Those who protected the castle had their hands full.

After nicking a maid's outfit from a pile of laundry to avoid drawing attention with magic, I navigated off the first floor and into higher levels. No one questioned me—though I dodged a wily butler with a too-knowing stare—as I worked my way to the High Priestess' chamber.

Witches in the Eastern Network would likely recognize Bianca Monroe after the Battle for Letum Wood, but thus far, my popularity proved no obstacle.

Not far from Camila's personal quarters, commotion down a hallway drew my attention. Cristian stood outside of a room with double doors. Several witches flanked him. One of them stood out from the rest, with his tall figure, broad shoulders, tightly coiled curls and light green eyes.

Baxter.

How perfect.

The Ilesan words for *violence* and *responsibility* and *leadership* floated down the hall, whisking in one ear and out the other. Was it possible that the rising insurrection had finally named a leader?

I hoped so.

An enemy with a face was far easier to find. If that wasn't the conversation, their dour, drawn expressions didn't say anything good. Baxter could tell me about it later. I averted my eyes and kept going, stride never faltering.

The High Priestess' chamber was an opulent but simple room, with wide windows usually thrown open to fresh sea air. Crashing waves and sandy beaches sprawled below. I first met Isobel, a former High Priestess of the Eastern Network, in this room. Isobel, secretly the Almorran Master Angelina, had used me to free her daughter.

After her death, I received the Volare. The magical rug was strapped across my back, invisible thanks to an enchanted case. Like Viveet, which I tied to my thigh—made smaller by another innate spell in the sword—the Volare accompanied me everywhere.

Outside the High Priestess' chamber, I stopped. Camila had sufficiently changed it since Isobel died so that little remained except the original structure of the room. A faint blush of pink pillows decorated ivory divans, and greenery grew around the windows and doors, reminiscent of the inside of a magnolia flower.

Camila, hands planted on the back of a chair, gazed out, unseeing, onto splashing waves. A breeze gusted through dancing drapes. She leaned into the violent force, as if she bore a great weight and sought a reprieve.

After confirming that we were alone in the room, and no one approached from down the hall, I rearranged the linens in my arms. With a soft *tap-tap-tap* of a knuckle, I rapped on the door. She regarded me over her shoulder with some confusion.

"I'm sorry, I didn't request any linens."

I smiled and said, "I know," in the common language.

Her expression illuminated. Camila spun, a long skirt shimmering in a whirl around her legs. "Miss Monroe?"

"Can I close the door?

Eagerly, she waved. "Please."

The doors shut before I could reach for them. She must have sent a spell. They locked, sealing us inside. To be certain, I sent an incantation to block witches listening from the hallway.

"I came to respond to your request at Priscilla's."

Camila gripped her hands together, color blanching out of the knuckles. She waited, curved brows high in a studious question.

I set aside the linens. "It's a fraught situation."

She inclined her head.

"Indeed, it is."

"Regardless, I'd be happy to help you, and by extension, the East. If there's something I can do to assist you and innocent witches, I will."

Relief suffused her features. She smiled, eyes watery. "I understand. Thank you, Miss Monroe."

"Call me Bianca."

With a bent knuckle, she dabbed at her eyes. "Bianca, yes. Forgive me." She rooted through her pocket, seeking a handkerchief. "Please, forgive my emotions. I . . . I didn't think you would accept. I understand, particularly after the meeting with your High Priestess, how risky this venture is for you. I appreciate your willingness to do it."

"I can't guarantee that I'll be available every minute of every day."

"Of course not."

"This can only be known between you and myself."

Camila paused. "Not Scarlett?"

"Not yet."

"Surely, you will—"

"Eventually. Right now, she has other things to think about. Until I know what helping you will look like, I'll wait to tell her."

Camila blinked. "This will not come between you?"

"No."

"I would never wish such a result."

"It would take more than a quiet assignment for Scarlett and I to lose trust. I will tell her, but not until there's more to say. She's aware that you asked the Sisterhood for help."

Satisfied, Camila nodded. "Thank you, Mi—Bianca. Thank you. This is most appreciated."

"Where should I start?"

Voices rose in the hallway. Camila's gaze darted to the door and back to me. Her whispered reply lowered in tenor. "Now is not the best time to discuss it. I will be brief until a better time presents itself. The High Priest's of the Eastern Network have a habit of keeping the High Priestess *protected*, which really means *ignorant.*"

Unfortunately true.

With new energy, Camila said, "With that in mind, I need help knowing. Knowing anything."

"Anything?"

"About my Network, my witches, the violence. Anything."

The request haunted me. Because of the ornamental position the High Priestess held in Eastern politics, *knowing* was a bargaining chip. A position of power. Not so long ago, Isobel made the same request, and I snuck in a *Chatham Chatterer.* The entire operation had been a manipulation.

What prevented this from being different?

Everything.

And yet . . . nothing.

The reality that Camila could be manipulating me as readily as Isobel followed me here. Yet, *I* was different. My instincts honed. I wasn't a grieving teenager, lost in her own world. I trusted myself.

"My motivation is for my witches, Bianca. If this violence continues, I fear for the East. There are so many who suffer, particularly in the marshes. I need to know where, so I can send aid. I need to know who is doing it, so we can stop them."

Camila folded her thin arms around her middle as she sashayed to the window, staring out. Her haunted eyes highlighted a fragile elegance. I didn't doubt her motivation to protect her family, nor her witches. Her sincerity rang in loud tones.

But did she have the ability to change anything?

I had serious doubts.

Merrick likely knew more about the state of her Network. Greyson, too. He, the veritable trove of information that I sought to exploit.

"There is an upcoming ball here at Magnolia Castle." She tapped her finger on a folded piece of thick parchment. Elegant scroll designs decorated the edges, swirling like wind gusts. "Please, attend. Listen, observe. Council Member Giuseppi will be there. You can tell me what you hear about or from him. There may be clues . . ."

"You think Giuseppi is running the rebellion?"

"Yes."

Glancing at the date on the parchment, I nodded. Three days from today. "I'm not busy that night."

"You cannot approach me in public," she said quickly. "We shall have to meet in secret to discuss what you hear. We'll start our work together then, unless something arises that you think I should know."

"I'll inform you. Do you have witches keeping you safe in the meantime?"

"Yes." She waved a hand. "Ronaldo and . . . others. I will be physically fine. It's my witches I'm concerned for. Thank you, Bianca. You may rest assured in my secrecy."

* * *

Magnolia Castle never looked more appealing than three days later. Against spangled starlight and dark seas, the beloved Eastern Network symbol glowed. No moonlight smudged the dome, nor the horizon. The tripling expanse opened wide, unfurling far, with the light gleam of ever-blooming magnolia trees circling the lovely structure.

Raw, ornamental appeal.

I crouched behind a marble sculpture of a sand crab, scuttling up a piece of driftwood to fight a sea wyrm. The gigantic, ugly thing left plenty of space for me to hide. One of Grandfather's rare invisibility spells concealed me.

While I readjusted both Viveet on my hip and the Volare on my back, two female witches bustled by. Skirts spilled over their hips. Shoes clacked as they giggled, eyes darting with mischievous perusal. A shout from a nearby male, an orchid in his tailored suitcoat, drew their attention. They clattered to the open doors, hurrying inside while their male counterparts chased.

The purpose of this assignment, Rognvald drawled with an incandescence that issued whenever we spoke across the groups, *is to gather information. Mutual cooperation between the Sisterhood and the Brotherhood will ensure a wider net, so to speak. Report from your agreed-upon areas as you observe, and don't get involved.*

With punctuated precision, he reasserted, *This is an information gathering mission.*

Understood, Brody, Merrick, and Chi said. Once their unanimous assertion faded, I said, *Got it.*

I could have sworn I heard Rognvald harrumph. Involving the Sisterhood had been a strategic move for Rognvald. Not only had I given him the idea to include me, but it meant he had to provide only three Protectors instead of four.

And *I* could spy for Camila without inciting Leda's suspicion.

Win, win, *win*.

Minutes passed with little more than youthful laughs and rustling skirts. Very few faces were familiar here—I couldn't pick a Council Member out from the crowd. Nor did I know what Giuseppi looked like. Once the revelry began, I'd slip inside and eavesdrop to hear better.

A flicker along the far southern wall caught my attention. Turning that way, I leaned forward to see better. Was that a crack in the white stone wall?

No.

Impossible.

I rubbed the heel of my hand in my eyes to clear them. Before I could investigate further, a voice distracted me.

In position at the ocean, Merrick said. He patrolled on the other side of the castle, an eye on the ocean, in case rebels attacked from that side. Brody and Chi canvassed two other corners. I watched from the front, sensing whether invisible interlopers came from Necce. Cristian may not have asked for our help, but we gave it. Aside from the Battle for Letum Wood, this would be the Sisterhood's first official shared mission with the Brotherhood.

Any signs? Rognvald asked.

No magical approach from the front porch, I said.

Clear, Chi reported.

Clear, said Brody.

East Guards patrolled the hallways, mingling in pairs. Gratified to see them, I relaxed a little. They were the third pair in the last fifteen minutes, at least. Their thin faces and harried stares spoke to difficult times. Life in the East wasn't easy.

Ten minutes later, with only the shifting of a sea breeze twining through the leaves of the magnolia trees, a shuffling occurred. I spun, facing Necce. Several magical signatures approached.

Three witches advancing from Necce, I said.

Same on the east side, Merrick said. *Emerging from a small dinghy that just appeared on the waves, clearly transported.*

Confirmed on the north, chimed Brody.

Chi followed up with, *And the south.*

Violin strains arose from within, followed by a gleeful chorus of happy shouts. With the dancing to commemorate the official start of the festivities, all witches cleared the porch. Only three stragglers hurried up the final stairs, rushing inside.

Reminder, Rognvald drawled with a bored tone, *that I forbid any heroics. Unless, of course, you can save lives. In that case, don't be spotted, and don't be stupid.*

As he spoke, twelve invisible witches converged around the three I first saw. They stood in the middle of the courtyard. When I cast an amplification spell, noise swelled from within Magnolia Castle, too. Impossible to overhear what they said.

I advanced down the stairs.

Fifteen in the courtyard, I said.

All fifteen vanished.

They appeared in the next moment, scattered across the castle exterior. Ten concentrated on the north wing, an extension of the flowing white rock. Five others littered various points. My stomach clenched.

Not good.

The witches I see on the south have not moved, Chi said.

Same for the east, Merrick said.

Ten at the north, came Brody's harried reply. *I think—*

Heat flared.

A flash of white blinded me.

Seconds later, a percussive wave ripped across the grounds. Magnolia trees bent. The brilliant, stunning light exploded and sent me flying. I soared backward, skidding across my spine, rolling shoulder over shoulder. Grass and gravel ground into my back as I drifted to a stop.

Stunned, I lay flat on my back and stared at winking stars. The world rotated around a single point.

Utterly silent.

White petals floated overhead, cascading in a lazy dance. Falling rubble crashed with ash and fire. Smoke billowed near the corner of my eyes, rising black out of the otherwise sparkling castle.

Bianca? Chi asked. *Are you there?*

Fine, I said. My body ached as I elevated to my elbows, grimacing. Jikes, that spiral through the air hurt.

Brody?

Fine, he reported. *It was an explosion. They ripped a hole in the northwest edge of the castle. The witches disappeared a second before it blew apart.*

The screams began.

Still dazed, I shoved to my feet. The explosion knocked me almost senseless, but the invisibility spell hadn't failed. Hand to my head, I blinked several times. My ears rang with low, pulsing tones. The dull thud of my heart, and the wild, tinny sound that colored the background, ebbed.

Merrick's fervent voice pulled me from the tunnel.

B?

I shook my head, coming back into myself. *I'm fine,* I quickly said. *Fine. Just . . . knocked senseless. Are you all right?*

Fine.

Chaos reigned near the castle. A chunk of the white stone had been torn asunder, blowing rooms apart. East Guards poured out of various doors and windows, but no matter how I searched, I located none of the magic from before. Near the north end, a maid shrieked. I heard it through a fuzzy tunnel and the high-pitched ringing in my ears.

The magical signatures from before have disappeared, I said.

They're at the back, Merrick said, *infiltrating. They created the diversion in that wing and are moving from here, probably toward the High Priest's personal quarters.*

On my way in, Brody said.

Let's hope Cristian isn't stupid enough to be home, Rognvald muttered.

My mind instantly snapped to Camila. This Sisterhood mission had shifted from information gathering to safety creation. Camila said she had Ronaldo to protect her, but I wanted to be certain.

I'll approach from the main entrance, I said.

More clear-headed with each step, I drew in as many details as I could manage. No other magical signatures. Chaos on the north wing. Infiltration in the south wing. I could enter through the main entrance on the west and interrupt interlopers from the south while searching for Camila.

The wide-open doors welcomed me into the marbled elegance of Magnolia Castle. Distant shouts rippled through the corridors. I ignored the areas to the north and headed south along the main hallway.

In the main hall, I said. *No one here.*

I've already cleared it, Merrick replied.

I paused. *Then I'll go to the back cor—*

Cleared it, Brody said.

The good gods. I knew they moved quickly, but this was something else.

What about the south entrance?

Clear, said Chi, a frisson of frustration leaked into his tone. *I have eyes on it. Dealing with incompetent East Guards right now.*

Don't be stupid, Rognvald said, but I wasn't sure whether he meant Chi or myself. I didn't want to know. No matter how accepting the Brotherhood might be, the Sisterhood was still an outside entity. They had the benefit of years of training together and knew these seamless integrations, but I wouldn't relinquish my spot inside this mission, even if they didn't need my eyes.

I'd simply put my eyes elsewhere.

I headed into a side chamber Baxter once revealed to me during one of my visits. He'd pulled me into a hidden staircase in an effort to avoid spying Council Members. I paused short of pulling the correct handle, my fingers hovering above.

A sound stopped me.

What was it?

Oh. Fast breathing.

I shot backward as the hidden door burst open, nearly slamming into my nose. By sheer luck, I managed to dodge away just in time.

A man spilled out, brandishing a sword. A murderous expression heightened the promise of violence in his eyes. I sent a tripping hex in his direction and he toppled, sword splaying wide, which bought me time to cast a more complicated sleeping spell. As he struggled to stand, the spell swept him. His eyes closed. He sighed, slumped. Ropes appeared, securing his hands.

I flipped his sword off the floor with the tip of my foot, caught the handle, and inspected it.

Not bad, but no matching shield. Not a proper one. I tossed the sword aside. With a hovering spell, I sent the witch into the hallway. Ropes secured his wrists as he floated over to the wall, then slumped. Another spell scrawled the word *rebel* across his chest. Let the East Guards deal with him.

I returned to my original intent.

Hidden passages.

Clearing the hidden passages, I said. *I left one rebel in the hallway.*

A pause, then, *There are hidden passages?* from Rognvald.

I didn't bother hiding my smirk, nor did I reply. Although I didn't know the labyrinthine passages at all, I made my way toward the southern edge of Magnolia Castle by sheer luck and a floating ball of light.

Markings along the outside of each door revealed, in a different language, each location as I stumbled past them. Every few steps, a crack in the plaster, a broken board, or holes in the wall became obvious.

Magnolia Castle had a beautiful glory outside, but a skeleton structure within. The aging process was not so glamorous when inspecting the bone.

A stirring noise, and a familiar voice, stopped me at a door marked *Sangreata*. Might be the language of the ancients or a version of Ilese. I didn't know what it meant. The voice within drew my attention.

"*Ridicola!*" Camila cried, though I could barely make out the exclamation. Pinpricks of light created a sloppy design near the outside of the hidden entrance. A murmuring reply might have been an attempt to put her at ease, but it didn't work. She shouted, "Let me out!" in Ilese.

A door closed.

She thumped on it once.

Twice.

A string of profanity followed. My eyebrow lifted. I liked Camila more every day.

Someone had locked her into her room. Or *was* it her room? I had only a vague awareness of where I stood, and I didn't think I was far enough into the castle to be in the High Priestess' chambers. Nor high enough. This was the wrong floor . . .

Time for risk.

With my knuckles, I rapped softly on the wall. Her irate muttering ceased, apparently not far away, because I heard her low tones with clarity. While groping for the little handle that should be along the side of the door to open it, I rapped again. The invisibility incantation bled away when I closed the spell.

"Allo?" she called.

The door clicked open. I held my breath, and before emerging, whispered, "Camila, it's Bianca Monroe. I'm alone. I can prove it."

A pause, then the slow creak of the secret passage door opening. Camila stared at me, her face white. She clutched a giant candelabra in her veiny hands. She glanced at me, then at the door, and then at me again. In the common language, she exclaimed, "But what are you doing in the secret passage?"

"Information gathering. Want to join me?"

She nodded, irritation mounting. "Yes. They locked me in here like a child."

I made room. "We'll go somewhere else together."

Hesitation paused her for only a heartbeat before she followed me into the webbing walls. I reached for her hand, holding it tightly.

"Where should we go?"

Peering into the narrow, waiting darkness, she whispered, "To find Cristian and hear what's happening. That'll be to the right."

We crept along like two mice in the walls, instinctively following the ruckus heading to the south end of Magnolia Castle. Camila stayed close, her hand gripping mine. I paused at a junction with narrow, steep stairs heading to the left, and a flat turn to the right. I made a mental note to congratulate Baxter on his aplomb with subterranean machinations.

Son of a god.

"This should take us to Cristian's chambers."

"Is Cristian in his room?"

"Unlikely, but I want to check."

"Where would he go?"

"I don't know for certain. Ronaldo will try to move Cristian in unexpected ways in order to avoid pursuit. Former East Guards have joined the rebellion."

We stopped at a dead end near the southern edge of Magnolia. The complicated tapestry of these hidden passages rivaled Carcere, in some regard. Chatham Castle had her own hidden ingresses, but nothing like this. Commotion stirred outside our thin confines.

Merrick, what's happening?

Ambushes. The East Guards have Cristian in a room on the south side of the castle and the rebels are trying to get inside.

If this had been Scarlett, she would already be in the Northern Network, under guard with myself and the Masters. Like Chatham, the residential area of Magnolia Castle prevented transportation within, but not away. Staying here wasn't enough protection.

I'm securing a room with several Council Members and their wives, he added.

Are they aware you're there?

No.

Brody? Rognvald asked.

I'm still outside, Brody replied, *preventing three rebels from entering the windows into Cristian's hidden spot. All are unaware of my presence.*

Chi remained silent.

"Ambushes," I told Camila. "Not yet successful."

Her expression tightened. "I will sit with my son. I won't hide in walls."

Though I disagreed, it wasn't my job to tell her what to do. Extinguishing the light, I reached for a skinny lever along the edge of a narrow doorway and whispered over my shoulder, "I'll be ahead of you with a shield spell and will remain hidden."

"I'll keep it that way."

"Identify yourself as soon as the door opens, or they'll think we're attacking."

"I will."

With a shield charm ahead of me, I pulled the lever. The resistance gave way overhead when I pulled, swinging the portion of wall forward. As I stepped through the widening crack, Camilla called out.

"It's me! Camila. I came through the hidden passageways. Cristian's fourth middle name is Alessandro, and yesterday for an evening snack, the kitchen baked eel cakes with cream sauce."

A chiding, "Mere! What are you thinking?" could be heard in reply.

I flowed ahead of her into the room. A menagerie of East Guards surrounded a central figure pacing the floor. Quiet chaos resounded as a result. Occasional spurts of noise followed, then eased.

Cristian paused his frenetic back-and-forth. "Why did you take the hidden passageways?"

"He locked me in a room!" she hissed. The rest of her tirade was a blur of words I couldn't decipher. I turned my attention to cataloging the number of witches in the room and the situation itself.

I'm with Cristian, Camila, and several others.

Rognvald asked, *Details?*

Five East Guards. Closed windows, protected by magic.

The room was stifling hot and humid. Cristian, his dress shirt undone all the way to his navel, sweated through the fabric. A thin man with a thick mustache and beady black eyes stood closest to the door. Based on the regalia of his uniform alone, he was a high-ranking officer.

Cristian is fine. No other pertinent updates that I can see. I believe the Head of Guardians is here.

Understood.

Camila, finished with her tirade, stopped. Fists stacked on her hips, she glowered at her son. Cristian opened his arms, muttered something that sounded like comfort and a command wrapped together, and Camila melted into his embrace.

"Mere," he said with a sweet and soothing reassurance. "I didn't know they took you. I'm sorry. This is . . . frightening. We'll pull through it together."

Duly comforted, Camila said, "Thank you, Cristian. I only want to know."

"I hear you. Stay here, and we'll discuss our next steps."

Camila spun on her heel and headed toward a bookshelf. While Cristian's attention shifted to the Head of Guardians, I tailed close to her, whispering, "Don't stand here. Too many windows. Go to the far end."

With impressive smoothness, she continued walking, perusing the titles, and obeyed.

Incoming! Brody shouted.

Glass shattered in a spray. I lunged for Camila, slammed into her side, wrapped an arm around her waist, and whirled her away from the showering glass. A heavy metal ball dropped onto the spot where Camila just stood.

The floor buckled beneath the weight, boards splintering. She tucked into a ball on the ground. Glass shards skittered off my shield spell, but no one seemed to notice. Eyes wide, Camila stared at the spot in silent horror. In case rebels advanced, I cast an invisibility spell over both of us and held her tight.

East Guards activated with shouts.

The attacker outside is taken care of, Brody grunted. *They transported to the spot and hurled the projectile inside without warning.*

Why wasn't it protected with spells? Merrick thundered.

I had as many questions.

Sounds from without faded. *There are spells. Very old ones, if my senses are correct. They're weak,* Chi reported. *The rebels are retreating. I'm following.*

I'll join in case they split, Brody said.

While chaos reigned around the Guardians, aided by the Head of Guardians snapping orders left and right, Cristian vanished out of sight.

Finally.

The door sprang open as East Guards charged inside, nearly skewering a fellow Guardian, and incurring greater wrath from the Head of Guardians. They swilled around, confused. An occasional recognizable word slid through their conversation. *Perimeter* and *empty* and *prisoner.*

"What is happening outside?" Camila whispered.

"Not much more. I'll explain in your room."

Confirm retreat, Chi said. *They're meeting in a shop in Necce, on the very top floor. Several are injured. Five are missing.*

The hubbub eased off, leading to mass confusion as the East Guards stared at the heavy ball and broken glass. Wild gesticulations likely indicated they argued over the lack of spells on the glass panes.

"Can we go now?" she asked.

"If your East Guards don't kill us on the way out."

I released her and retracted the invisibility spell from just Camila. Straightening, she faced the chaos as a familiar male witch strode inside, East Guards tailing him.

"Ronaldo?" she asked.

A familiar Captain—the invisible one in Scarlett's office—let out a breath of relief. He shoved aside quarreling East Guards to join her. She held out a hand, which he accepted.

"High Priestess!" he cried. "I have been searching for you. Please, let us get you somewhere safe. How did you get here? When I heard they locked you in that room, I sought you."

Camila gripped his hand with both of hers. "I'm sorry, Ronaldo. Please, let's go somewhere safer."

Ronaldo barked at the three Guardians that flanked them. They regarded the disaster of a room in disgust, upper lips curled back. They clutched their swords, swept the room, and formed a protective bubble around Camila. Viveet would have added to the confusion, but my fingers itched to hold her.

Grasping Camila by the arm, Ronaldo led the way out of the room. Two Guardians surrounded her from behind. Trailing them, I strengthened my invisibility spell.

I'm with the High Priestess, I said to the Brotherhood. *I'll report when I return to the Gatehouse.*

I didn't tell them why.

Because the Sisterhood didn't have to.

Chapter Ten

Ronaldo swept the High Priestess to a hidden room with comfortable chairs and no windows.

Two Guardians stationed themselves outside of it: one visible, one not. While Ronaldo summoned hot tea, a change of clothes, and quietly commanded his Guardians, Camila puttered around, changing out of her glass-strewn clothes, brushing out her hair. Based on mutual warmth and camaraderie, they had worked together for years.

When Camila finally sat, Ronaldo explained the cascade of events. Her lips tightened with horror and sorrow. Her despair as he recounted the shattering of Magnolia's north walls cut deep.

Hearing the East Guard's perspective unwound the disaster one morsel at a time. If I translated correctly, the Head of Guardians was incompetent and lazy to his duty, resulting in a sub-par response from East Guards.

I thought of Giuseppi and rumors of rebelling Council Members and wondered.

While Ronaldo finished, I stood at the window, staring out. No other magical signatures appeared. All lay quiet except for

Magnolia Castle's quiet hum of life. Hopefully, Cristian retreated to somewhere safe for the night.

"Who put you in that room, High Priestess?" Ronaldo demanded.

"Council Member Giuseppi."

That information changed things.

Rage flushed Ronaldo's cheeks crimson. "Giuseppi, that rat! I will inform His Majesty immediately! This is an outrage. He has no authority to—"

"In time, Ronaldo," she said in soothing tones. "I couldn't tell Cristian about Giuseppi because the Head of Guardians stood in the room with us. We will, Ronaldo. We will."

Ah.

So the Head of Guardians *was* suspect also.

Poor Cristian. Who did he trust in his entire leadership force?

More sedately, Ronaldo asked, "How did you escape the room? It's a good thing you did. Rebels swept through that hall minutes later. You could have been harmed, taken, or killed."

Probably Giuseppi's intent, I silently added.

Camila lifted her head. "Although I know it is against our agreement, please reveal yourself, Bianca. I trust Ronaldo implicitly. He deserves to know."

Wary, I complied.

Seeing me, Ronaldo's eyes blew wide open.

"Bianca Monroe?" he breathed. "But—"

"Later, Ronaldo." Camila turned to me. "I owe you, Bianca. You saved my life, pushing me out of the way. Thank you."

Abashed, I only nodded. She waved me to sit down. I lowered onto the chair across from her. Ronaldo eyed me with mingled resignation and gratitude.

"Before you came to my assistance," she inquired with a politeness that belied the intense air, "did you observe anything of note that we should be aware of?"

Thankfully, her previous request asking for my help covered my tracks. I had no reason to mention the Brotherhood's presence, or assistance. I explained the rebels assembling and attack in the courtyard. Ronaldo posed the first question.

"The secret passages—how did you know?"

I held his gaze, saying nothing.

He glowered.

A hint of amused exasperation lightened Camila's voice. "Bianca has her secrets. We shall allow her to keep them, considering the great favor she has granted." Her thick eyelashes fluttered to Ronaldo. "If you will be patient, I shall explain everything in full after she has gone. We must respect her given time. Bianca, do you have final observations to impart?"

"Not at this time. If you desire, I'll continue to watch and listen until you summon me again."

Her eyes twinkled with a mixture of relief and mystery. "That sounds wonderful, thank you. As for payment—"

Standing, I cut her off.

"Later," I insisted.

"As you request," she said lightly. "Thank you again."

I paused before issuing the transportation spell. "High Priestess, have you noticed cracks in Magnolia's exterior?"

Lines formed on her brow.

"Cracks?"

"Outside."

Ronaldo spoke quickly. "The structure is as sound as ever, Miss Monroe. Occasionally, cracks appear in the foundation, but these are addressed with magic. We are short staffed at Magnolia Castle lately. They will be fixed."

Camila poorly hid her flash of surprise. Ronaldo's hurried response heightened my suspicion.

"Of course. It must have been a trick of the low light. Thank you. Merry part, High Priestess. I await your next summons."

* * *

Merrick drank me in with a hungry stare.

I returned it.

Oh, how I loved seeing him unharmed after a mission. Barely ruffled, truth be told. After scurrying through hidden passages, I gathered dust like a library gremlin.

A tense band simmered in Scarlett's office when I entered alone, neutral expression firmly in place. Merrick haunted my every step. Knowing Leda and Rognvald could hear every word we said through the communication magic stopped me from speaking directly to him.

The temptation was oh-so-difficult.

Grandfather sat in a chair near the fire, shooting me a welcoming smile. The advancing midnight hour made it difficult for him to remain awake. Leda fluttered near Scarlett's desk, organizing incoming missives, batting others away, sending a very specific stare to Hiddleston, who stood at the door, a pile of papers in his hand.

An *oddly* knowing stare.

Had she brought him into the communication magic as well?

How interesting.

Noting it to discuss with her later, I turned my attention to Scarlett, who surveyed me with pinched lips and ready consternation. Despite the late hour, she retained her energy. Over a month ago, the same couldn't have been said. Greyson had been poisoning her with a new tea. Her return to full health occurred within a week.

"You are the last to return, Bianca," she observed crisply.

"Forgive me, Your Highness. I ran into a High Priestess in distress and decided to lend my assistance."

Her rising brow revealed deep curiosity.

"Oh?"

Through the magic, I promised, *Full details later.* Scarlett, Leda, and I had direct connections while—however this complicated magic worked—neither Rognvald nor the Brotherhood would hear the promise.

Leda pinched her lips in response.

Scarlett's scrutiny traveled to my cheek, which started to sting. "Do you require an Apothecary?"

You're bleeding, Leda added.

Reaching up, I touched a tacky spot of skin near the worst of the throbbing. A bloody souvenir from the blast.

"Oh. Uh . . . no, Your Highness."

Merrick shifted, hands folded in front of him. I sent him a reassuring glance that brought a slight nod. Stress lined his features, but it wasn't untoward. Leaving the dishabille of the Eastern Network would set anyone on edge, particularly with Rognvald, Leda, Hiddleston, Scarlett, and Grandfather expecting a promising report.

We had none to give.

Rognvald sent me an annoyed eye roll that was more ribbing than serious.

I winked.

To the room at large, Scarlett said, "Now that the Sisterhood has returned and does not require an Apothecary, the debriefing may begin."

Rognvald launched the restatement of events by saying, "Chi remains with the rebels while Brody watches the castle. I'll fill them in later, Your Highness. As the initial attack has de-escalated, Cristian and Camila secured, and the Head of Guardians calling orders at Magnolia Castle, we felt it prudent to withdraw Merrick."

"Agreed."

While Rognvald continued a play-by-play of the events, Grandfather sent me a knowing and expectant look. A tea tray elevated from the back of the room and settled in front of me.

Ice clinked against the sides of a sweating glass of water. I accepted it, quietly gulping it down, while a cup of coffee arranged itself on the tray in front of me. When it finished, Grandfather gave me an encouraging head tilt.

I smiled with gratitude.

The ice water cooled my flushed veins, and the coffee bolstered my whirling thoughts as Merrick contributed his observations. The retelling happened around me as I set my half-full coffee cup down.

By the end, all eyes turned to me.

"The Protectors had the castle in hand," I said. "Because I knew an entrance to the secret passageways, I went inside and slipped around to hear and discover what I could. That's how I found Camila."

The truth of my words covered my responsibility to Scarlett, the Protectors, *and* Camila. Ideal that I could scout and listen for all three interests, so I felt no qualms leaving out Camila's requested angle. Based on the daggers Leda shot my way, my secret may not last long.

Explaining Camila, Cristian, and Ronaldo's interactions came easily enough. I stalled at the end, finishing with a hasty, "I think something else is happening in Magnolia Castle, but I can't say exactly what."

Scarlett's chin elevated. "What else is happening besides a rebellious war?"

"The Head of Guardians might be a rebel. Council Member Giuseppi put the High Priestess in a room swept by rebels minutes later. If that's not an assassination attempt, I don't know what is."

Rognvald scoffed. "The East has been like that for months."

Shaking my head, I said, "But there's something *more* to it. To the building itself, I mean. Magnolia Castle is . . . different. Weaker?" Blowing a frustrated raspberry, I said, "I'll figure it out and let you know."

Through the communication magic, Leda said in a tone that suggested she buried frustration very deep, *Shall we discuss your decision to* figure it out *more in-depth later?*

Sure.

Leda scribbled something on one of her eternal lists and returned her focus to Scarlett, who picked up the conversation.

"Thank you, Sisterhood. We look forward to your refined thoughts when you have them. In the meantime, Rognvald. What do you advise?"

"Continued monitoring." He gestured to Merrick and set a hand on his hips. "Merrick and Brody will have a rotating observation schedule. Brody will work at night, Merrick will work during the day."

"Agreed." Scarlett punctuated it with a nod. "Eyes on Magnolia Castle is wise." To Merrick, she said, "I wouldn't say no to a little inside observation as well. I'd like to keep a hand on this situation. If the Aldana regime falls, it could prove trouble for border disputes and inter Network affairs on a wide scale." She paused, then added, "There's a question of safety for one of my former students, as well."

"Understood, Your Highness."

Scarlett swung to face me. "Would you mind briefing the Protectors on how to find the hidden passageways, should they need it?"

"I wouldn't mind, Your Highness."

"Good. Thank you all for your hard work tonight. Rognvald, Merrick, you are dismissed. Leda, please remain for a few more minutes. Bianca, you may go, but I require your presence in the morning. The Council is meeting with Greyson again, and I'd like you to be there."

* * *

Merrick and I sat side-by-side, shoulders pressed, feet soaking in a lake blanketed by midnight shadows. Northern Network mountains cut jagged, dark behemoths into the starry view.

He handed me the heel of a loaf of bread, which I accepted. When I bit into it, creamy butter flooded my tongue. My ravenous stomach welcomed the midnight snack with a loud growl. He leaned back on one hand. His other pressed to my back, heavy against my spine.

"You did good, B."

I scoffed. "You, too. It's interesting to see the Brotherhood work together so seamlessly."

"Is it frustrating?"

"What?"

"That you're not integrated in. Yet," he added. "We acted without you."

Thinking it over, I shrugged. "At first, but I didn't take it personal."

"And then?"

"It forced me to do something different," I said loftily, "which may have been the best part of the night."

"You reported to Camila, didn't you?"

"Yes."

"You agreed to work with her?"

Unwilling to keep a secret from him, I said, "Yes. Several days ago."

He grunted.

Leda and I were at odds over what the Sisterhood would do in terms of scope, but versatility and ease of movement would be pivotal. While the Brotherhood had the leadership and rules for a bigger fighting force, Leda and I had the benefit of moving where the demand took us. We didn't await permission.

That was worth fighting for.

"Brody, Chi, and Rognvald said nothing about your performance," he added.

"A good thing?"

"Very. We only talk about the ones we're frustrated with. If you pull your weight and do your job, there's nothing to say."

"Thanks."

He rubbed his palm along my shoulders. The moonlight cast watery shadows on the lake top. I leaned into him, grateful when his arm came around me. His unique forest smell filled my nose when I breathed deep. Like the glades of Letum Wood, he held such power. In the pristine silence, I wanted nothing more than this exact moment.

"B?"

"Hmmm?"

"Do you want a cord of engagement?"

"No."

He chuckled. "Your response was faster than I expected."

"I don't need to think about it. Do you want one?"

"No. But . . . can I get you something else?"

"Like what?"

"It's a surprise."

Shrugging, I said, "Sure."

"Can I kiss you?"

Smiling coyly, I said, "Do you have to ask?"

He grasped the back of my neck and hauled me into a heated kiss. I collapsed into his arms, eager to forget the night, the questions, the frustrations. Scratchy stubble rubbed along my palm as we breathed together.

The handfasting routines, plans, and celebrations seemed silly and inconsequential against the starry night sky. Against life and death. A piece of parchment with an official Network seal didn't change what we had, but it did make it firm.

We lay on the lake shore, tucked tight. Creeping trees snuck closer, providing a screen that blocked us from the world.

Alkarra lay far beyond the circle of our two eternal souls.

Chapter Eleven

While raindrops plinked against the window panes, I descended a hidden passage starting in Grandfather's office. It meandered behind the walls, filled with scuttling rats, but allowed me to slip into the dungeons through a lesser-trafficked route.

With a spell, I commanded a torch to life, slipped it from the holder, and headed toward Greyson's cell.

A startled Guardian greeted me as I approached.

"Merry meet."

Awareness brightened his familiar gaze. Jack, a recruit I trained in sword work years ago. He broke into a wide smile.

"Miss Monroe!"

"Merry meet, Jack! It's good to see you again."

He nodded eagerly, but his excitement calmed into a question. "Why are you here?"

"Can I speak with Greyson?" I stopped myself short of saying, *and let's both act like I wasn't here.* The temptation to cover my tracks was subversive to the goal of trust in the Sisterhood, but I couldn't help the concern.

Jack stepped aside without hesitation. "Of course. Do you need any help?"

"No, thank you."

Close air wrapped me in a chilly embrace when I entered. Jack left the door open enough to spill a ray of light. Bars spanned the distance from ceiling to floor. Powerful incantations saturated the rocks and metal bars, preventing magical use within the cell.

Greyson stepped out of the shadows, eyes glittering as he emerged from his tomb-like cell. He'd lost weight and pallor. The gaunt way his eyes sunk into his head made my stomach sick. No wonder he bargained for better conditions.

He offered no platitudes, nor a smile. That glimmering stare, fathomless in its evil depths studied me.

His departure from the darkness swept me to another time, years ago, when Mabel had done the same. Unlike Mabel, who had been mere shades of her earlier self, Greyson looked exactly the way I expected.

"Miss Monroe," he murmured.

The same crystalline cleverness radiated from his eyes. The depths of his intensity had increased, no doubt due to lack of magic access, and a return to the prison environment he so loathed.

Facing him after the game of logic and magic stirred up a maelstrom of emotion. At the end was a pulsing, quiet light, armed with a hint of compassion. Sadness, too. Greyson rolled the dice and lost everything.

Twice.

He'd brought himself to the terrible circumstances that he loathed. How deep was his regret? Did he spend his waking hours attempting to figure out his next move? Did he live ahead for the next desperate swing of fate?

"Congratulations," he said. "You won the game, fair."

"Was it fair?"

Head tilted, he paused to consider. "I thought so."

"You stacked it against me."

"By definition, all games of logic and magic *are* stacked against you. It creates the opportunity to exercise your abilities and win. It wasn't meant to be easy, Miss Monroe, nor equivalent. How would that showcase your talents?"

"You're trying to convince me that you sought to help me?"

"You'll believe whatever you want." His dismissive tone couldn't have cared less.

He surveyed me. In his quietude, I remembered flashes of Carcere's suffocating hallways. The cradle of dark magic, hollowed out. The splash of midnight that never ceased. Thinking about him living in Carcere for months on end, I couldn't help a tightness in my chest.

"The Council is meeting again in a few hours," I said.

"I'm aware."

"Your death hangs in the balance."

He scoffed. "I never expected the reprieve of death so easily."

"I think you banked on it," I replied. "I think there's another plan and this is an offshoot. You didn't manage to win our game, but I don't think witches like you only have one game."

He chuckled. For a moment, I recognized the light of real amusement in his eyes. Arms spread, he asked, "What can I do from here?"

"That's not the right question."

He smiled.

I pressed my advantage. "The Council doesn't care about you, Greyson. They'll agree to any measure that eliminates you immediately. They won't want to get involved in the Eastern Network."

"If you think that is my goal."

"I didn't say that."

He spoke with the tone of a witch predicting the obvious.

"Georgette won't want to be involved in the Eastern Network's issues, and the sheep follow their shepherd."

His insinuation that all Council Members were sheep was blatantly false, but not Georgette's position as a leader.

After a long suffering scrutiny, he asked, "Camila requested your help, didn't she?"

When combined with the stunning arrogance of his wrinkled upper lip, his certainty caused little surprise. Unnerving, the way he predicted it. Almost as if he had insight, though that was impossible.

With a tilted head, he continued. "The guards have been speaking all night about a tussle in the Eastern Network. Almost as if someone had told you to expect attacks and you didn't listen."

"If you think that is our goal," I added lightly.

He smiled, and the tension in it unnerved me. "As expected. Let me wager a guess? The famed Bianca Monroe was there for the attack."

I returned his smile.

"Allow me to venture another guess? Sweet Camilla is locked inside the castle, desperate for help with Cristian at the helm, fighting Giuseppi. He's no Niko, you realize. Certainly, no Diego. That entire family lost all hope when Diego died. All of them are incompetent."

The stony words, spoken without inflection, felt like splinters driving beneath my fingernails. Although he inspired so many questions—how did he know Camila would ask for my help? What game did he seek?—I bit them back.

When I said nothing, another flicker of a violent smile appeared.

Vanished.

Chin elevated, he asked, "Why are you here in the wee hours before my next appointment with the esteemed Council?"

"To ask you a question."

"Answers come at a price."

Reaching into my pocket, I extracted a shiny red apple. He eyed it, unable to disguise a gleam of hunger. He was of no use to anyone dead, so Greyson received rations, but they didn't load his plate. Greyson swallowed hard. The gesture revealed a world of vulnerability.

"One answer, one apple."

He clutched the prison bars with emaciated fingers. "Depends on the apple," he retorted. "That might be a deception spell."

I tapped it.

"Poisoned?"

With a crunch, I took a bite and chewed. His eyes lingered on the juice on my lips. He hissed, teeth bared. I extended the apple. "Want it?"

"What's your question?"

Swallowing the delicious, crisp fruit, I met his gaze. The flicker of torchlight brightened his pale features.

"Tell me what you know about Magnolia Castle's structural foundation."

Greyson smiled a wicked smile.

"Oh, Miss Monroe. How lovely is thy wisdom. For an apple, I might have a little information you'd be very interested in. But if you advocate for me with the Council, I might have a *lot* of information." He plucked the proffered apple from my palm. "Shall we begin?"

* * *

Harried desperation filled the Council Room later that morning. I stood near Scarlett, my early appointment with the prisoner unknown. Greyson's observations about Magnolia Castle buzzed in the back of my mind. He'd been vague, yet oddly specific at the same time.

There is more falling apart at that castle than just the Aldanas.

Structural integrity is in question. Has been for years.

The rebellion plans to wipe out more than just the leadership. They believe it's time for a new start. The leader knows where the true heart of the East lies.

My heart thudded at those words. *The leader knows where the true heart of the East lies.* That could mean any number of things, but I hazarded a guess he meant Magnolia Castle, the jeweled symbol of the Eastern Network.

Leda bustled from Assistant to Assistant, using spells to distribute agendas, murmuring answers, and settling a pot of tea for Scarlett. Steam wafted free, diffusing into the air with the general hubbub of gathering witches.

Rognvald and Talmund slipped inside just before the double doors slid closed on the hour. Behind them strode three Guardians. One ahead of Greyson, one at Greyson's side, and the third bringing up the rear. Greyson occupied the corner, protected by the same barrier as before, with a placid boredom.

Once discussions of Greyson ceased, I could leave. Scarlett didn't require the Sisterhood protecting her in the Council Room, nor did I need to listen to the drivel of everyday problems in the Network. Not when I could gather more information about the Eastern Network issues with Baxter, who awaited my word.

Georgette stood. "Let us begin."

The room quieted. Leda finished passing out agendas while Georgette buzzed through boring generalities, announcements, and a review of those present. Ten minutes later, she met Scarlett's studious gaze.

"First order of business, Your Highness, is the sentencing of former Council Member Greyson. We deferred his decision to today out of respect for the Eastern Network, and by request of His Majesty Cristian Aldana."

Scarlett nodded. "Thank you, Georgette."

Greyson met my gaze over the top of the table. Curiosity burned bright. I could practically hear his unspoken question.

What will you do, Miss Monroe?

The idea that Magnolia Castle's physical infrastructure had anything to do with this rebellion was a wild one. A strange track to chase, mostly because what could it mean? While the leadership degenerated, did it matter what the castle walls did?

Yes.

Because *everything* mattered, and no one else was asking. I had a feeling Greyson knew it.

With my heart thudding in my ears, I leaned into Scarlett's side. As hoped, the entire Council focused on me when I whispered in her ear.

"Your Highness, do you trust me?"

Mimicking my low tone, she asked, "Why?"

"We haven't had time to talk about the Eastern Network and my hunch yet, so I can't explain right now. But I'm asking you to trust me."

Disregarding the entire Council staring at us, Scarlett met my eyes.

"I trust you."

"Push for time. Don't give him a house, but stall the execution."

"Stall?"

"Two months."

Scarlett thought about it, then said, "I hear you. Let me work."

She turned to the room at large. "I move that Greyson's death sentence be scheduled for several months from now instead of immediately. The unfolding situation in the East may require greater information, if the prisoner has it."

A general murmur arose from the Council. Assistants scrambled to take notes as Leda settled at Scarlett's side, managing a flow of paperwork as well as the proceedings. We hadn't spoken since the debriefing last night, which was for the best.

What are you doing? she asked.

The right thing.

Scarlett continued. "The prisoner has requested to be removed from the prison and sentenced to life in a house that he cannot leave. I do not support this."

Scarlett paused, allowing time for the Council to absorb her statement. If they truly wanted to punish Greyson for what he'd done, then torturing him with life in the dungeons was far worse than death.

"I move that Greyson remain in the dungeons, with an execution date set two months from now."

Georgette stood, her pretty face twisted into a glower. "Two months?"

To my deepest shock, Aurora stood.

"As Ambassador, I support a two month timeline. The Eastern Network is under great strain. We can maintain strategic and open alliances, without imparting precious resources, by simply keeping Greyson alive in case he is required."

Her eyes latched onto me. I couldn't read their fathomless depths, but had a distinct feeling that *I* was the reason she spoke. Scarlett wisely let the silence roll. Leda's assessing stare appraised each Council Member, undoubtedly locking down deeper notes on their expressions, emotions, responses.

Georgette's argument floundered in face of Aurora's unexpected support. Seeing no hands in the air, ready for comments, Scarlett called, "Those in favor?"

Eight hands rose, Aurora's amongst them. Her vote didn't count, considering this wasn't deemed *official* Ambassadorial work, but Aurora never withheld her power of opinion. Three hands did not elevate, including Georgette.

Greyson revealed no physical response.

With little change in expression, Georgette said, "Let the

record be shown that the Council supports the High Priestess' decision to delay former Council Member Greyson's execution for two months hence." She slid her cold gaze to mine. "I feel this is the most advantageous time to reiterate that the Council does not support meddling with Eastern Network affairs."

I hid a smile.

"We also," she said slowly and with obvious emphasis on me, "do not approve of subterranean work with the Eastern Network. Not even from witches outside of approved Network bounds that we cannot speak our approval into."

I held back the urge to say, *Not that* you *have any real control, anyway, Georgette.* Scarlett allowed the Council to speak their opinions into her work, but opinions were not final.

This, Leda said promptly, *is what it feels like to swim upstream. Do you see why your presentation is so pivotal to the Council? They already don't trust you.*

Don't you mean Georgette?

Leda silently huffed.

Georgette tapped a tiny hammer on a wooden circle.

"The prisoner may be removed. Next order of business."

Greyson tipped me a subtle, assenting nod. After Scarlett dismissed me, I'd sneak into the prison and see what further information on Magnolia Castle he offered. I sincerely hoped that whatever he said would be worth the risk.

And Scarlett's instant trust.

Chapter Twelve

In the last month, Carcere's interior had been emptied and swept clean. The giant turret was little more than stone and space. Loneliness perfused the abandoned island.

A stormy sky blew through the beaches and surly waves. Pewter clouds simmered above the sea, scooping close to the horizon. Splashes of foam littered the side of the turret, skittering sand across the ground. The thrum of rain raced closer, borne on wild winds.

Leda's exasperation added a punch to the moment.

Are you sure about this?

Not at all, I admitted. *Are you sure you want to help me?*

A fragile interlude forced me to wait.

I'm not a dictator, Bianca, she said with surprising softness. *We are allowed to disagree. Scarlett appeared proactive toward your idea the other night, so for now, I'll support it. However, you have another Council Member appointment coming up soon.*

Relieved for momentary peace, I said, *Thank you.*

Back to the task at hand: in exchange for an apple and encouraging Scarlett to keep Greyson alive, he told you to go back to Carcere? That's it?

Wind breezed past my face, drawing hair in front of my eyes. *Sort of. There were more instructions than that.*

Specifically, Greyson said, "Return to Carcere, and you'll find something interesting." Directions on navigating the interior had followed, but nothing else. The awareness that he might be leading me on a wild chase prevented me from telling Leda everything.

Curiosity could be a real witch.

Returning into Carcere was as lackluster as I expected. I stood in the archway, waiting for tightness in my chest, or visions of terror to streak through me. Nothing paralyzed me, because I had won. Greyson should be afraid, not me.

Are you at La Torra island? Leda asked.

Just about to enter Carcere.

Be careful.

I'll keep you updated.

I ventured within at a clipped pace, immediately registering the lack of weighty air. Spiderweb cracks along the stone led me farther down the corridor and into the interior. Under my breath, I muttered Greyson's directions, "Go through the same main corridor," as I passed into the Carcere abyss, a summoned torch in hand.

Still here, I said a few minutes later.

I hear you, Leda replied.

Her voice was as resonant as before. No ancient, livid magic caught up with me. Less oppression, more physical stonework. Whatever power had occupied this place leached away. Carcere was an abandoned, creepy building more than a magical monstrosity.

At the third branch on the right, I turned into an open doorway. Dirt and grime stained them less intensely than the rest. A long hallway awaited with nothing but stone walls. I slipped the torch from side to side, counting doorways.

Greyson's directions, thus far, hadn't been false.

A ripple of muffled sound resulted when I kicked a pebble. A flash of sunlight or hint of fresh air would be a welcome sign of life. Diving into a deep and unfathomable underground didn't rank high on my enjoyable list.

When the first left turn appeared, I pushed the torch into it first. A longer hallway headed into gloom. Doorways split left and right, narrowing to an alcove ringed by five or six cramped cells. Whoever structured this awful place meant for it to house hundreds of witches in sub-human environments. Victims, criminals, the deranged, aged. I couldn't fathom who passed through these stone walls.

Shuddering, I pressed toward the final cell block. *At the end,* Greyson had said, *in the fourth cell. You'll find my old home there.*

I approached the fourth cell on the back and slipped inside. Picturing Greyson in this miniscule area without enough room to lay down, nor enough room to stand, painted a brutal picture. Water and time wore unevenly on the walls, gliding in trickling waterfalls that degraded the stone.

The torch wavered as I held it aloft, seeking . . . something. What sort of clue could possibly exist amongst old straw and an overturned bucket that smelled foul? My stomach flipped at the accosting scents and I fought not to retch. When I swung the torch to the right, carefully avoiding the brittle hay, a glint of light flickered.

The corner seam emitted a flash of silver. Ducking, I touched the spot with my fingertips. A round medallion slid free, landing on the ground. The heady scent of torch oil filled my nostrils as I lowered the flames closer.

A rose gold coin, as thick as several sacrans stacked together, lay on the ground. Less coin, more carved medallion. Darkness made it almost impossible to see clearly, but when I scraped the top of my thumb across it, engravings indicated designs.

I tucked it into my pocket.

Can you still hear me? I asked.

Leda's voice returned, clear as a bell. *Yes.*

With relief, I issued a different spell. A ball of light floated in between bars and slid around. The successful use of magic meant Carcere's degradation had continued. I could transport home from this spot. Invisibly, I scoured every cell for clues. Finding nothing, I transported outside.

The rain-kissed sea awaited.

Gulping fresh, humid air, I pressed my back to the dank exterior and centered myself. Despite the terrible claustrophobia, I had one thing left to do. Peeling myself away, I padded around the exterior and to the wide hole in the wall. Wind scoured the air. Sand shifted beneath my feet as I studied the horrific entry point.

Massive building, somehow torn asunder.

Just like Magnolia.

A levitation spell elevated me to the explosion point, where a gridwork of cells marched to the left and right of the gaping hole. Whoever blew it apart did so from within. Light and fresh air poured onto the cells a floor below and into an entryway above. Only half the floor remained, revealing a cell blown wide open. Due to the suppressive magic, the witch must have sacrificed themselves, perhaps others, to complete it.

Did Carcere prevent magic in *everyone*?

Or most witches?

My eyes snagged on something in the far corner. A book lay canted open, the pages ruffling in the wind, as if tossed aside. I summoned it to me with a spell. Rain and fresh air and wind had destroyed the interior. Ink blurred. Smoke dulled the pages, several of which had been blown apart. Enough remained that I recognized a chart along the charred edges of a ledger.

I tucked it under my arm, confirmed nothing else remained. *I'm returning. I found several things.*

Meet me in my room. I'm eating lunch.

See you soon.

* * *

Leda, lips pursed to the side, studied the medallion first.

Remnants of lunch littered her table, set in the organized dishabille of her apartment. An open window fluffed the air with an autumn breeze that had a chilly edge. I never expected Chatham Castle's constant bustle to be welcoming until I spent time in Carcere. The quiet signs of life and sunshine were most welcome.

"It's a medallion," she declared.

"We agree."

Finally, I silently added.

"What's the difference between a medallion and a coin?" I asked.

Her long suffering tone reassured me that our usual repartee remained in place. "A coin is currency, Bianca. This is a medallion."

As if that cleared anything up.

I stood at her side, gently perusing the half-destroyed book. Not much remained, which explained why it was abandoned. Words along the spine or upper parts, not charred to a crisp, displayed recognizable Ilesan scripts. Shorthand, perhaps. The bigger boxes on the left side contained scattered syllables. Names. Two pages crumbled when I turned their delicate bulk, puffing into ash.

Leda tapped the medallion on the table, drawing my attention. "It's solid metal." She sat it down on the flat edge and frowned. "I'm not sure what the markings on the front and back mean. The best I can come up with is some sort of family crest. Wheat branches, do you think?"

"Or grass."

"It's a guess."

She looked at me for the first time since I entered, then held open her palms and closed her fingers in a grabbing motion.

"The book, please."

Grateful to hand it over, I slid it across the table. Instead of reaching for the medallion, I chose her abandoned lunch and snatched up half of a sandwich. The pillowy bread smelled like yeast and deliciousness.

"Clearly, this is a ledger."

"Clearly," I said around a mouthful of ham. She ignored me with the power of a thousand suns.

"Under what arrangement this ledger runs, I can't tell. There appears to be some purpose. If this column is prisoner names," she skimmed a dainty finger down a column near the spine of the book, "then that is most interesting. See this far right edge? Almost looks like checkmarks."

Her idle murmurs continued as she grazed through and over each morsel. I was grateful for the food and her thoughts. Punting the conundrum her way guaranteed I didn't miss a detail, and her quick mind consumed them readily. We were an important pair.

I needed to remember.

"I'm not sure how it's significant, but it must be," she concluded. "You didn't find this in Greyson's cell?"

"No, by the hole blown into the building. I can't say for certain that the medallion was Greyson's cell either. Simply that it was a cell he led me to and stated was his *home*."

"Good point. Did he tell you to look in the explosion area?"

"No."

She frowned. "Confounding. The medallion must be . . .."

Her eyes skittered to me with deep hesitation.

"Must be . . .?" I drawled.

"Important?"

"Why is that a question?"

"Because I hesitate to assign any good deed to Greyson! If he left the medallion in that cell and then sent *you* there, that assigns some level of planning or awareness. Did he have this planned? If so, there are motivations we aren't aware of."

"Assuming he left it behind on purpose," I countered, popping the last bite of crust into my mouth. The remnants of food appeased my rampant hunger for now. "He may not have meant to leave it behind."

"I can't imagine prisoners shuffled often."

"That's an assumption."

Irritated, she huffed, "True," and fell into thought. After a minute, she perked up. "You said the coin was hidden in the rock?"

"Wedged in, sort of. Not quite hidden. Stuck out enough to make it visible."

"Hmm."

Leda pondered it in her thoughtful way. After I finished her apple slices, she asked, "What do you want to do next?"

"Find the origin of that coin."

"How?"

"Not sure. I'm thinking that over."

"Not through Greyson, surely."

"We'll see."

Relief stained her lowering brow pucker. "Good. What about Camila?"

"No noise from her."

She arched a brow. "Really?"

"I agreed to help her," I said, grateful to air it. "It's the right thing to do, Leda."

Discomfort tightened her frown, but she didn't speak her opinion at first. A series of emotions passed through her eyes like smoke while she considered my statement. She peered at the window, lost in thought, while I continued.

"I'm emotionally involved in the Camila situation because of Tomasso. And I do like Camila," I added.

She scowled. "Whether you like someone or not shouldn't

be a reason to help them, jeopardizing your own safety and the success of the Sisterhood."

"Disagree."

"Bianca!"

"What?"

"The Brotherhood would never—"

"Doesn't matter." I cut her off with a slice of my hand through the air. "We aren't them, remember?"

Her mouth snapped shut, and she loured so abruptly I fought a laugh. Leda would burrow her heels into this hill and die on it, unless I could speak her language. This was the moment to *appeal to her logical side*, as talking point eleven had testified.

"Consider this new angle of our currency request to the Council?"

She perked up.

"Scarlett doesn't have a lot of requirements for me on a day-to-day basis, right? Guardians stand in the hallway as part of their rotation, and she conducts most of her life from Chatham Castle."

Grumbling, she assented with a nod.

"So something we need to consider is Georgette saying that I'm getting paid to do nothing. If they do give us currency, it will have to be based hourly. That's a start for legitimacy, but not really what we're hoping for."

Leda's lips slacked. Her brow elevated. "Oh. I hadn't thought of that." Frowning, she tucked her chin in and demanded, "*Why* hadn't I thought of that?"

"So," I continued, suppressing my glee at the win, however slight, "I can work secretly with Camila." I slowed my cadence a touch to get her attention. "If it goes well, and the Council is showing signs of coming to our side as I meet with them one-on-one, we can bring it up later. After it's settled."

Leda opened her mouth, closed it. Again . . . shut it. With a stymied shake and dazed expression she said, "Point taken. I . . . still don't agree that it's the correct angle, but I see that a compromise can be reached . . . for now."

No accord resulted, but I felt lighter. If anything, Leda and I remained firmly entrenched in our previous sides, but progress happened. I'd take the win.

She looked so lost I couldn't help asking, "Is something else wrong, Leda?"

Her neck stiffened.

"No."

"Really? Because—"

"I'm fine," she snapped.

Sensing my time for retreat had arrived, I held up both hands in surrender.

"Understood, as the Brotherhood says. I'll back off. I've already sent Priscilla a message about the ledger and medallion. I'm going to see if she has any thoughts. She replied already and invited both of us for dinner."

Leda sent me a look that suggested she wanted to be frustrated, but couldn't summon the energy. "I can make space for that in my busy schedule," she said imperiously.

I let her have the upper hand.

Gathering the empty plate and spelling it away, I asked, "Can we pull Priscilla into the magic?"

"She's not part of the Sisterhood."

"Neither is Hiddleston."

Leda stiffened so thoroughly she resembled a board, confirming my earlier hunch that she let him into the magic.

"Fortunately," I said crisply, "I am an excellent secret keeper."

Her cheeks flared. To spare her the agony of admitting she brought Hiddleston into the magic, I continued. "It'd be fun to have immediate access to Priscilla as a friend, and I want her to have immediate access to me. Just in case."

With a tone so neutral that she must be testing me, she said, "The Brotherhood also wouldn't allow someone into their communication magic on the basis of friendship. You know this in a personal way."

I cracked a smile.

"Good thing we aren't the Brotherhood, isn't it?"

* * *

That evening, Tomasso snoozed in the attic while Priscilla, Leda, Michelle, and I crowded around the dining room table, empty plates stacked to the side. Celia snoozed in a nearby chair, her mending abandoned to her lap. A fire crackled in the hearth, banishing a tentative cold that settled with the evening air.

Outside, the groundskeeper Jorge strode back and forth, pushing a wooden wheelbarrow. He didn't glance inside often, but when he did, his gaze slipped to Priscilla in a flash so quick I would have missed it if I hadn't watched. She kept her gaze off of his handsome profile.

"Let me get this straight." Priscilla leaned her forearms onto the table, staring hard at me. After more than a year as Head Witch of a Network school, she'd already adopted a pristine school mam severity. "You're helping Camila?"

"Yes."

Her hand pressed to her breastbone. "Because you want to help us?"

"That's her main reason," Leda said.

Michelle, nursing a tepid cup of tea, asked Priscilla, "Are there other reasons to go against the Central Network Council and help the High Priestess of a Network that once tried to kill you?"

Michelle's tone had all the inflection of a rock. I sent her an amused smile, recognizing the tell for what it was: concern.

"It's the right thing to do," I countered softly.

Priscilla set her elbows on the table and her head in her hands. Tears sparkled from her closed eyes.

"This is a disaster, Bianca. I'm sorry you—"

"Stop," I commanded. "Right now. You will never apologize again for letting me keep you both safe, and you're not the only reason. Just the most important one. Besides, I'm in a fight to be a better aunt than Leda."

Leda snorted. "Fat chance."

At our bickering, Priscilla gave a little sob. Michelle reached over, patting Priscilla's shoulder. "It's all right, Cilla," she whispered. "Everything's going to be all right."

"It's just so kind!" Priscilla wiped the tears from her eyes. "I . . . I'm so grateful."

"As ugly as it seems now, it will only get worse," I muttered, earning a glare from Leda. "As the rebellion in the Eastern Network progresses, so will Tomasso's insecurity. The best we can do is help Camila find out who is instigating the rebellion. I believe Greyson. I think the culprit is connected to Carcere's downfall."

"Until Cristian has a better idea who has instigated this rebellion, the Eastern Network will continue to flounder," Leda agreed with an air of surrender. As if she gave into the obvious because she must, but not because she wanted to agree. Her steady, authoritative voice seemed to stir Priscilla out of deeper anxieties.

Priscilla reached for the ledger, gently pulling it close. We fell quiet while she perused what remained. It wouldn't survive much more handling. Michelle sipped her tea, answering Leda's queries about her young daughters, Sanna and Isadora, and her latest pregnancy. Nicholas hoped for a boy. Michelle didn't care either way.

"It's a ledger," Priscilla said slowly, nose wrinkled as she swiped at a smudge with her thumb. "I can't make out many details. The final edge, on the left, with the check mark? That says *lealta*, which is Ilesan for loyalty."

Leda and I shared a sidelong glance. What reason *but* insurrection would any witch in a prison have to track loyalty? Priscilla brought the pages closer to her face.

"These *aren't* checks, actually. They're . . . letters. *Y, M,* and *I*. Just those three. Different loyalty assignments? Sort of like an *us, them,* and *indeci,* which would mean undecided."

"What better place to foment a rebellion than a bunch of angry, trapped prisoners with absolutely nothing to lose?" I asked.

Michelle, pale-faced, whispered, "Nowhere."

We waited in silence while Priscilla perused other pages, her teeth buried in her bottom lip.

"There are other columns," she finally said, "but they don't make sense. Might be locations?"

A *thump* in front of Leda drew my gaze to the side. She had created a more robust copy of the ledger and already had a quill perched in her hand. A glimmering bottle of ink appeared next to her.

Eyes on the page, she said, "Will you tell me the direct translations again? I'd like to have a copy of them, starting at the beginning."

While my thoughts swirled, Priscilla and Leda scoured the few available words. They finished in less than three minutes, as most of the columns were repetitive. Leda sat back. Fatigue tugged at the corners of her eyes, and I felt a stab of guilt. She'd likely had a long day with Scarlett, and still stepped into this at the end.

Such whole-hearted commitment, despite not agreeing on my direction. I couldn't help my respect for her dedication.

Priscilla gently closed the original ledger and pushed it across the table. "Thank you for letting me help. I agree with your assessment, Bianca. I believe it's a ledger not related to the prisoner, but the resistance. And thank you for doing this."

"You're worth it," I whispered.

A weary smile flashed across her face before she yawned, patting her lips with her hand. Her eyes flickered to the window. Darkness had long since fallen. Rain speckled the window panes with gentle taps. A hint of disappointment showed when she glanced at the empty outside, then stopped as quickly as it came.

Perhaps I'd imagined her attention on Jorge.

But I didn't think so.

Chapter Thirteen

Sweat trickled between my shoulder blades the next day as I swung Viveet overhead, twirled with her momentum, and readied to slam her into the bark of a nearby tree. Her brilliant sapphire flames bounced with a sparkling swirl.

Weight burdened my left arm, tugging muscles not often used until recently. I'd strapped a shield that I'd borrowed from the armory to my arm. After half an hour of sword routines, my shoulder grew tired. Good. I needed the challenge and skill that came with it. How embarrassing would it be to find the perfect shield, then not be able to use it?

My concentration, half on Camila, half on an idea to spy on Council Member Giuseppi, wavered just enough that I didn't see the body standing a few paces away until it was almost too late. A moment sooner than I expected, Viveet's edge bit into something that wasn't a tree.

Metal clashed with metal.

Papa's crooked grin flashed between Viveet's flames as our swords collided, blazing with sparks. His plumed a brilliant crimson, a rare flash of color he didn't often conjure when he fought.

He lowered his sword, bringing Viveet to the ground a second before I advanced.

I slackened my fighting stance.

"Papa!" I panted, delighted. "What are you doing here?"

He laughed as I collided with him, hooking my free arm around his waist. When I pulled away, a tired smile wrinkled his cheeks. He appeared a little leaner, but no worse for wear. I stepped out of his arms and sheathed Viveet.

"Where have you been?"

Leaving a hand on my shoulder, he said, "Out," and steered me the other way. "C'mon, B. Let's have lunch."

* * *

With a spell, I sent the shield back to the armory. The Volare, which I strapped to my back whenever I trained so that I was used to fighting with it, remained in place while I followed Papa's transportation spell elsewhere.

To the edge of a desert.

Heat undulated over baking lines of sand. We stood above a deep red canyon that dropped three hundred paces toward a gurgling river. The foamy white caps and dark depths hinted at chasmal depths. The stillness held notes of isolation.

"Where are we?" I asked.

"In the West."

"Obviously."

With a twitch of his hand, he beckoned me to follow. A footpath cut into the canyon wall, winding higher at a gentle grade. It tracked back and forth, fading into a suggestion of a path. He levitated along the edge, and I realized that Papa had found a hiding place.

This was where he'd been.

He led me to a cutout in the sandy red rock wall. A cave rolled into the ravine edge, tripling to darkness. Thanks to jutting ledges on either side, it was all but invisible from most vantage points. I released the levitation spell to cross the dusty floor. A bedroll, remnants of a fire, and bones scattered the interior. The delicate angles suggested a bird, and the arrowhead nearby suggested Papa shot it down.

"This is where I've been hiding," he declared, hands on his hips. "Well, one of the places."

Ah.

He admitted hiding. How . . . unexpected. Eyebrow high, I asked, "Where are the others?"

"Everywhere."

I made a noise and meandered around, eyeing the utter lack of possessions and the barren landscape.

"Why?"

"Because," he said softly, "I never have before."

My lips quirked to the side. "It would take a good amount of work to convince me that, in all your years in the Protectors, you've never hidden in a cave."

His cheeky glare was more humorous than serious.

"To clarify," I continued to spin in a circle, seeking details that might answer the burning questions his nomadic, strange life inspired, "you built a beautiful house in Letum Wood, taking painstaking care to complete every step and detail. Once finished, you promptly abandoned it, and Cat, to shoot birds with arrows?"

"No. To be free."

The quietly spoken words struck my heart. Before I could scrutinize his expression, he slipped around to stand at the edge of the cave. I joined him, peering down. My heart slowed from the exertion, but picked up again at the dizzying height.

"Jikes."

"Long drop." He nodded. "Good place to practice transporting mid fall."

"Have you been?"

"Nah. Don't need it."

We sat, legs dangling over the edge. Despite the burdened silence, it was a relief to be at his side. To see the wind tousling his too-long hair. A sense of wildness had returned to Papa, amidst advancing age lines. He certainly didn't seem *old*, but he'd lost the sense of indomitability that he carried as readily as Protector arrogance. This shift in Papa hinted at fallibility, and I didn't like that.

I leaned onto my palms, enjoying the distant view. A rockfall bloomed down the opposite canyon wall, triggered by a white-haired goat that sprang from crevice to crevice. Watching its progress was a calming fascination.

He shook his head, words thready and light, like a string of snowflakes sewn together. "I went on so many missions, B. So many places that I kept up here." He tapped his temple. "I promised myself that I'd see them with Marie. For years, she stayed at home so I could roam with my job. She dreamed of the day we'd travel together. So . . . that's what I'm doing. I've been traveling to all of them for Marie. Putting myself in front of each promise and then talking to her."

My heart twisted.

Oh, sweet Papa.

He motioned to the gorge. "This was one of my favorites."

With a hint of irony, I whispered, "Mama would have hated it."

He laughed, soft curls bouncing. "I know. It's too dry, too high, too lonely, too windy."

"She hated heights."

"All the better to get her to cling to me, I suppose," he added lightly. "It was a game we played. Trying to get her as close to me as possible."

"I remember." I smiled, inundated by memories of Papa chasing Mama around the yard, in the house, down the road. Gesturing around us, I said, "This is sweet, Papa. Really sweet.

At what point do you run out of places to go to with Mama at your side?"

He swallowed hard. "This one," he murmured. "This is the last one. And now . . . I don't know what to do with myself."

Turmoil brewed in his gaze. It reminded me of the conversation I had with Regina in the Northern Network. Her raw insecurity, and the sense that she shouldn't have given so much of the truth to her lover's daughter, but couldn't help it.

"What about Regina?" I asked, forcing levity in the query.

He eyed me.

"Why do you ask?"

"When was the last time you saw her?"

"A few weeks ago."

"Wrote to her?"

"Yesterday." His eyes sharpened further, like a whetted piece of flint ready to strike fire. "Why?"

"Did she write back?"

He motioned behind us. "Do you see any letters?"

Although I already knew what didn't wait back there, I made a show of looking.

"Nope."

His elbow to my shoulder almost knocked me over. "Out with it, B."

"It's not mine to share." His agonized expression dropped into something nearly unreadable. So I added with a blasé, "She knows something is wrong. If I were Regina, I might think your absence had something to do with me."

A look of contrition, mingled with horror, crossed his face. "That's . . . that's not it!"

"How would she know that?"

Papa's throat bobbed as he swallowed. "Thanks," he rasped. "I didn't know. I just asked her for space, and she gave it. And . . ."

He trailed away.

"For being so smart, Papa, sometimes you're really dumb. What else is she supposed to think?"

"I don't know!"

"What is really going on? Your tour of Alkarra is admirable and sounds very healing, but it reeks of hiding. I think it's sweet you fulfilled your promise to Mama and reached for the edge of freedom, but I'm calling you out. This is fear."

My genuine inquiry finally found its mark. Perhaps Papa had softened himself up enough to face it, or maybe I'd taken him by surprise.

"You're right," he whispered, gaunt.

Channeling his arrogance, I said, "I know."

"Leaving the Protectors was . . . challenging." He closed his eyes, shoulders slumping. "Not that I didn't genuinely look forward to the freedom. But . . . after I finished the house . . . I had nothing to focus on."

His palms opened. He stared at them, as if trying to figure out how something had been taken away. The fingers trembled. His thousand-pace stare grew yet more distant. "I just . . . I realized how much I've given to other witches. In the end, I was supposed to receive something back: time with Marie. The fulfillment of my dream. Instead . . . it was just wasted."

"What was wasted?"

"Years," he breathed. "Years of my life given to witches who hate me. Years of my life to a cause that died with Mildred. Whom," he added with a note of steel that rang with bitterness, "also happened to be my birth mother. Time with you. Time with Marie. I . . ."

The words he didn't say echoed through the gorge.

Gave up everything.

Papa's fingers curled into fists. He growled. "I had to leave. I needed to be somewhere I could think, escape the rage of it. So one day I returned to a place on the northern edge of the Eastern Network, not far from the mountains. There's an idyllic and tranquil lake there. I'd always promised myself I'd return one day, and of course I hadn't."

He stopped, eyes locked on something below, near the river. Several heartbeats passed before he shook out of it by running a hand through his hair.

"While there, it was like I could breathe again. Almost . . . I could have sworn . . . your mother. Anyway, I stayed the night. And then the next day came and went. And the next. Breathing was easier. Sleeping. Existing. Marie . . ."

Her name died on his lips.

Connections slid into place. He sought escape from himself. From feelings and emotions that had no screens behind which to hide.

"Where did you go after that?" I asked.

"To the West." His face was rote and stiff, locked in memories. "And it forced me to focus on finding food and shelter. Survival gave me something else to think about and it all seemed . . . easier."

"So you stayed."

"I stayed," he breathed.

"And you've been bouncing around Alkarra."

"Yes. I've never had the luxury of running away before. Now, I finally understand those poor souls whom I used to judge."

Relief over his emotional recognition was a real force. Papa understood his aversion at least, but that didn't soften the reality of his choices.

"And you haven't explained this to Regina?"

A momentary gauntness swept over him. Eyes wide with fresh comprehension, he muttered, "I'm an idiot."

Unable to help it, I laughed. "Why haven't you told her?"

"If I tell her, she'd understand."

"Exactly!"

When he didn't continue, I jabbed him in the side with an elbow.

"She'd understand what a mess I really am." He tapped his teeth together. "She'd never want anything to do with me, and I would truly mourn the opportunity to be with her more. She isn't Marie, but she is Regina. And I . . . I care for Regina. Deeply."

"Your penchant for being moody and unpredictable is not news to anyone, Papa," I retorted. He rolled his eyes with good-natured amusement, but didn't lose his solemnity.

"What if I'm too broken for Regina, B?" He motioned a hand over his body. "What if I'm not worth it? I'm advancing in age. I have no career. No part of the Brotherhood. I'm effectively forgotten by all of them," he said in a near hiss, "and can't pull myself together. She deserves better."

"So you're ignoring her?"

"I'm not *ignoring* her," he retorted with heat. "I'm . . . giving her space. Giving her a chance to decide if she really wants me in her life."

I slapped a hand on my cheek and groaned. "Papa! You're so bad at this."

He spread both arms wide.

"What?"

"She's already decided that she wants you in her life! Why do you have to go and muck it up by making assumptions?"

"She wanted *that* Derek!" he cried. "The Derek that once had purpose."

"Purpose is created!"

"Well . . . this Derek has none. She hasn't met this side yet and I don't want her to."

His snappy conclusion had pure terror in it, though he tried to play it off as irritation. He sounded entirely too much like me to hide it.

"You're going to lose her."

"Then maybe it's better for her."

"Don't give me that," I snapped right back, flaring with frustration. "You're making the decision for her. Don't you have any respect? Regina, of any witch in Alkarra, knows your situation better than anyone else. Not that you'd know why," I added with a particularly strong burst of vexation. "Because you haven't spoken to her."

His emotions matched my own in a rare display of ire. "What's that supposed to mean?"

I shot to my feet, stepping away from the ledge.

"Talk to Regina and you'll find out."

Unsure of what to say next, I strode toward the edge of the cave, near the trail, but stopped halfway there. He didn't call out to stop me, and I had a feeling he wouldn't. In this state, Papa wouldn't beg anyone to stay.

Yet, I couldn't leave.

Not like this.

Papa sought out help. He opened up. Imperfectly, but so had I. Our equal tempers matched, and I didn't want to leave like this.

Sighing, I spun around. He cut a morose figure against the canyon backdrop, with his broad shoulders low, his expression tortured. Even the way he kicked his heels against the ravine made me sad.

"Have you convinced yourself that survival feels better than the stability of a home and family who loves you?"

"No," he grumbled.

Hearing his defeated tone sent a curl of fear through me. Papa stood to face me. A slightly more repentant expression lingered there, but it had too much agony for regret. How could he stand against the greatest dangers that the Central Network had ever faced, but be afraid of himself?

Of the quiet?

Was this Merrick's fate, or even mine? Did loyalty and work for other witches lead to the same inevitable end? These questions led to uncomfortable roads that I'd think about later. I kept my attention focused on my unraveling parent, marveling that he should appear as lost as me.

"Grandfather seems to think this time to yourself is the best thing that's ever happened to you," I said to impart what little hope I could offer.

His lips lifted on one side with a dark chuckle.

"Sounds like him."

What more could I say?

No one but Papa could answer his own questions. No one but Papa could rid himself of the memories. Unable to fix his problem, I strode over and held out a hand. He pressed his palm to mine, turned them over, and threaded our fingers together. No matter how much I'd advanced into adulthood, his calloused hand still swamped mine. His tight grip reassured me that all was not lost.

"I'm here for you, Papa. So is Mama. You've taken her everywhere, now it's time to let her go. Create your own purpose."

He nodded, reaching a bent knuckle to his cheek to swipe away a tear. I stepped into the protective circle of his arms. His shoulders gave a little tremor.

"Do you think I'm too late?" he whispered.

Thinking of the defeat and anger in Regina's face didn't bring me much hope. Surely, she had some compassion to extend, but how much tolerance for male stupidity did a witch like Regina, who had deliberately avoided this type of drama her whole life, have?

Not much, I'd wager.

"I don't know, Papa."

"I'll talk to Regina," he whispered. "I promise."

We stayed there for a long time.

Chapter Fourteen

The next day, I sent a message to Camila without a signature.

I have questions and an update. I'll be bringing a friend.

She replied within twenty minutes.

I am available at noon in my quarters. Approach as before.

I burned it in the fire.

* * *

"I'll have you know," Baxter muttered with a mildly irate expression a few hours later, "that I had to hand write this list."

He set two curled up scrolls into my hands with a perturbed stare. I grinned, silently thanking him. When my fingers splayed the first scroll open, I chewed on the inside of my cheek. A list of names awaited.

"These are the witches that Ronaldo feels is a direct threat to Cristian, or has ties to the rebellion?" I asked.

"Yes."

Council Member Giuseppi topped the list.

I lowered onto a wooden chair that sat in direct sunlight, appreciating the wafting breeze off the Eastern Network shore. Gulls cawed, cutting swift shadows across the sand as they soared overhead.

Of course, I recognized none of the names. Not that I expected to. I had no insight into Eastern Network culture. With a spell, I transported the first scroll to Priscilla, who expected it. She'd reply with notes on each name.

"How did you do it?" I asked.

"Not god magic, if that's what you're asking."

"It wasn't."

He set his hands on the small of his back and leaned backward, his spine popping as he yawned. "I have used my time in the Eastern Network wisely."

"You made friends with Ronaldo?"

"And others. To your benefit."

"I appreciate your research on my behalf. It's far less suspicious when you poke around. Camila and I have reasons to keep my interference a secret."

"You're welcome," he said with a vague hum. He added less mysteriously, "This was the easier part. Your second request has proven more difficult. You know, it's really not that hard to find out information about Carcere. The hard part is trying to act like I don't need it."

He scowled when I laughed.

The second scroll was another set of names, these very different. "And those," he said, anticipating my question, "are the active Guardians who worked on or near Carcere at the time of the explosion, as well as others that I added on the end who have generally acted suspicious, per Ronaldo's experience. Mine, too," he added.

"Do you interact with East Guards much?"

"You'd be surprised."

These names were only words, but I would not send them to Priscilla. I set it in my pocket for a different witch to peruse. "Is their force truly diminished?" I asked.

"By more than half, I'd wager."

My jaw dropped. "More than half?"

He winced. "It's hard to peg an exact number down. Neither Cristian nor the Head of Guardians are upfront about it. I'm not sure Cristian can trust the numbers that the Head of Guardian reports, anyway."

"Jikes," I muttered, utterly unable to imagine half of our Guardian force gone. Cristian's life resembled swimming in bloody waters near ravenous sharks.

"Do you think the Head of Guardians is part of the rebellion?"

"Definitely. Do I have proof? No. It's weird, though."

"What?"

"The records for Carcere are minimal, and they have been for years and years. If it wasn't a prison island that the Highest Witch still used, though with less frequency since Niko's reign, then the whole place might have been forgotten."

His observation didn't surprise me. Little else existed on the spit of land, out of sight of the Eastern Network shore.

Baxter's shadow darkened the scroll as he lowered onto the chair next to me, wind tousling his hair. "Did you find what you needed about Carcere?"

"Not sure."

"What *are* you looking for on that gods-forsaken island? Literally gods-forsaken," he added with a quick, charming grin.

Baxter listened with contemplative interest while I explained my promise to Camila and the latest discussion with Greyson. If she could rope in Ronaldo without my permission, I could do the same with Baxter. He didn't appear surprised. I extracted the medallion, extended it in my palm.

"This is the medallion I found in Carcere. What is it? Leda thinks it could be a family crest."

He studied the engravings. "It *is* a crest."

"Oh?"

He brought it closer to his face. "Yes . . . I think I've seen it before. The families here all have crests. Pompous you know. Bloodlines."

A cross of bitterness slipped through his eyes, vanishing as quickly as it came. Considering the abusive and tempestuous relationship with his father, god of fire Ventis, the suppressed choler made sense.

"Too many crests to memorize them," he said, "but something about the bundle of grass in the middle is familiar."

"You think it's grass?"

"What else?"

"Could be wheat."

His lips screwed to the side. "No, I don't think so. Grass makes more sense for the East, particularly with all the marshes. Exquisite detail. You can see the individual strands . . ."

Lost in my own thoughts, I let his rambling observations on the medallion filter into the air. I'd studied the coin until my eyes wanted to peel out of my head. The Volare sprang out of the case on my back and caught me as I dropped in exhaustion and irritation, blowing a raspberry.

"When is your meeting with Camila?" he asked.

"In twenty minutes."

Baxter straightened, fingers wrapped around the medallion. "I'll come with you."

Slyly, I said, "I thought you might say that."

"You told her to expect me?"

"I said I would bring a friend."

He laughed, rubbing out his curls with a hand. They tossed with delightful bounces, wavy in the fresh breeze.

"How's Tipa?" I asked.

He snorted. "She's fine."

"Have you seen her lately?"

"Yes."

Nothing more followed. Though I longed to ask about details, I held back. Baxter always respected my desire to withhold information, I'd do the same. No matter how tempting it could be to pry into his slow-as-molasses love life and friendship with the female demigod, Tipa.

Demigods moved slow on everything.

"Ava hasn't stirred up trouble in a few weeks," he said with a frown.

"That's a good thing."

"It's suspicious."

"Definitely that, too."

Baxter shoved his hands in his pockets and glanced at the clock. "Let's go. It'll take a few minutes to walk through the castle, and you probably have some transformative disguise or invisibility spell to execute."

High Priestess Camila sat behind a desk, a quill in her hand, when we arrived at her office. Bedecked in my former maid regalia, with Baxter invisible thanks to a quick and rare use of god magic, I rapped on the door.

"Come in," she called without looking up.

The door closed behind us as I entered, then sealed with an incantation to block eavesdroppers. Her wide-open sea doors were shut, something I couldn't remember seeing in the past. Two East Guards stood on her balcony, eyes roving the beach below, which likely explained why she'd closed the doors.

The added security since their attack reassured me.

Beyond the East Guards, leaden skies approached, covering the sun with their ballast. Autumn had such cranky weather, no matter where I stood in Alkarra.

Camila's glance alighted on me with a welcoming smile.

"Miss Bianca, merry meet."

Smiling, I advanced. For cautious purposes, I kept the maids regalia and left the sound of a question in my greeting.

"My friend has come with me."

"Yes. Of course."

With a spell, she closed heavy drapes near the East Guards, preventing them from seeing inside. Light zipped around the periphery of the double doors, sealing it with an incantation to prevent eavesdropping.

Baxter appeared, and a wider smile graced her expression. "Baxter!" she cried, laughing. "You are always welcome. I knew you had a friendship, but I didn't know you were *this* trusted."

"Like you trust Ronaldo, I trust Baxter. I hope you will, too."

She merely nodded, gesturing to a cluster of divans near a low fire. The day was humid, but not chilly. The snappy flames lent more comfort than necessity. Baxter sat near me as we settled across from Camila. Curiosity and hope filled her expression as I updated her on my discussion with Greyson, the medallion and ledger, and Baxter's secret sleuthing trip.

When I finished, I pulled the scroll from my pocket and extended it to her. She accepted, running a finger down the middle to keep it open.

"These are the Guardians that worked on Carcere. Baxter spoke with Ronaldo on my behalf to obtain the information, which made it easier."

She blinked in rapid succession. "This is . . . most organized and thorough. Thank you, Bianca."

"Do you recognize any of those names?" Baxter asked.

She shook her head, lips bunched.

"Not really."

"We didn't expect association," I added. "We just wanted to make sure none of them stood out."

She handed it back with a grimace. "I apologize, but no names stir recognition or awareness."

"What about this?"

Brandishing the medallion, I passed it to her. She studied it, me, then it again. With astonishment, she said, "This is the Gallo family crest."

"Gallo? Who is that?"

"They are an old family, and very quiet. A lesser family. Culture splits full-blooded Eastern families into lesser and greater. Mostly a wealth and status thing, very frivolous." She grimaced, as if it pained her. "I haven't heard much of the Gallo family in the last several years, since Diego died."

Baxter's lack of knowledge mollified my disquiet that I hadn't heard of them. He tilted his head to the side.

"When you say *very quiet*, what does that mean?"

She shrugged. "They don't stir up problems. They come to required Network meetings and social events, but not many others. They don't host their own *revelees*."

Revelees, a term Priscilla taught me, was a music-inspired gathering less extravagant than a ball, and far more intimate. Witches of similar social castes gathered in a family-hosted *revelee* to dance, eat, and gossip, but rarely in large groups.

Pure torture, to my thinking.

"Were any of the Gallo family imprisoned in Carcere?" I asked, chewing on the inside of my cheek. "To explain why the medallion was there in the first place."

She recoiled at the suggestion. "Oh, no. That would jeopardize their standing in our social hierarchy. At least," she amended, "not that I'm aware."

"Any reason for the Gallos to hate you?"

"Aside from the usual tripe? Not really."

Noting that to think over later, I set aside populating plans to search for Gallo family history to withdraw a copy of the burned notebook. The original, so badly marred I didn't dare move it unless forced, remained with Leda.

"This is the ledger I mentioned. It's a replica of the original, which isn't in good enough shape to travel."

With delicate fingers, she carefully fanned open the pages, studying each one with intent perusal.

"I haven't seen this before," she murmured. "But I can confirm that it's not an official document on Network stationery." For a few sentences, she rattled in Ilese, which I translated only partially.

Under his breath, Baxter said, "The gridlines are made by a spell she recognized. A papermaker out of a city called Livorno. The papermaker specializes in stationery."

Livorno, a creative capital of the East, was a busy town bedecked with authors, sculptures, artists, and poets. The lodestone of the Livorno economy centered on wealthy witches who enjoyed the finer architecture and weather. In return, they paid ample artists to generate creative works for the entire kingdom.

"Then it wouldn't have been a ledger associated with Carcere?" I asked.

"Not officially, no. I cannot see all the written words." She brought it closer to inspect with a squint. "Only this one. *Lealta.*"

"Which means loyalty?"

"When strictly translated. But to the Guardians, it's colloquial. Ah . . . shorthand? They say it to mean *promised* or *agreed*. It's a step above being loyal. *Lealta* is sworn to a task, master, or premise."

"Does this indicate what that loyalty is attached to?"

"Not that I can tell."

"But the rebellion makes sense?"

Reluctantly, she nodded. "Yes, but I wish so much of it had not burned."

While Camila continued her perusal, Baxter leaned close. "Is it proof enough that Carcere *is* related to the rebellion?" The dark tilt of his voice sent a shudder down my spine.

"I don't know."

By the time Camila finished her perusal, the storm descended. Rain swept the glass doors in racing lines, coating the veranda with a shimmering puddle. Thunder drowned out the racing drops. I didn't envy the East Guards positioned outside.

Camila tapped a finger to her chin. "You know, I just thought of something."

"What?"

"Ricardo."

"Who is Ricardo?"

"Ricardo Gallo. He's a funny old man." Camila straightened, elbows propped on her knees as she rotated the medallion in her fingers. "He is the head of the Gallo family."

"How do you know him?"

"He was the caretaker of Carcere, I suppose you could say. Amongst . . . other things. The Gallo family are well known in the Portafina area. Marshes, grasslands, swamps." She tapped on the medallion. "That's why the grasses are their symbol."

Interest elevated the hair on the back of my neck.

"Oh?"

Baxter scrambled to read the Guardian list.

"No, no," she said softly. "Ricardo is not on that list. For years and years he cared for Carcere. There are ancient family ties to it. Now that I think of it, I'm not sure what happened to him after Carcere's breaking."

Instinct stirred up memories I had forgotten until this moment. Before I first ventured into Carcere, an old man met me at the turret. Wily and sharp, he caught my interest for more than one reason.

Ricardo had been his name.

"As the caretaker of Carcere," Camila continued, "he was one of the first witches that fell into suspicion after the prison was broken. Cristian questioned him personally."

"And discovered nothing?"

"No. The Gallo family have been loyal and, as I said, calm."

Or not, I thought, recalling the rampant destruction at Magnolia Castle not long ago. Thankfully, a name for the family crest and more information on the vague wording in the ledger was something to start with.

Camila floated the medallion to me with a spell. "Perhaps Greyson would tell you more, now that you have this? He clearly meant you to find the medallion, and you have discovered more than that." Her eyes sparkled. "You often do more than expected?"

I chuckled. "I try. Greyson doesn't know I found the ledger."

"The ledger could be leverage," Baxter said.

I shook my head. "I don't think so. Freedom is the only leverage I have against Greyson, and that will never happen."

Baxter clapped a hand on my shoulder. "Good luck finding a way to get him to cooperate. Glad I'm not in your shoes." To Camila, he offered a far more professional smile. "Thank you, Your Majesty, for entertaining my presence. Please, let me know if I can help you."

Camila beamed in her quiet way as Baxter bowed and vanished into another use of god magic. The door didn't open and close, but I sensed he departed. God magic and goddess magic could not detect each other, but the absence of his personality spoke loud enough.

"What is your plan, Miss Bianca?"

"I want to speak to Greyson first. Do you think it would be beneficial for me to spy on Council Member Giuseppi?"

Her eyes darkened. "No."

"But—"

"We know he is rotten. No need to prove it. It would be too dangerous for you, and we may not learn anything we don't know. If Greyson knows more about the rebellion and is pointing fingers at Carcere and the Gallo family—of all witches! —then it's worth it for you to chase." More sagely, she said, "No one else will."

Convinced, I nodded once.

"Then I will speak to Greyson and let you know."

"Thank you, Bianca. I cannot tell you what this means. Whatever I can do as you research more, let me know."

Chapter Fifteen

Scarlett swept through the halls of Ashleigh House, a former residence of some distant High Priest that time already forgot, with me at her side. Leda would highly disapprove that I didn't care enough about history to strive to remember.

The High Priestess commanded this space with her usual grace and dignity. Her swirling skirts arched around her in a lovely way. She wore her usual bun, tight at the back of her neck, her dark locks gleaming. Streaks of gray littered the top.

In a chamber on the other side of the property, a dozen or so High Witches awaited her presence in a leadership meeting. Leda, who prepared Scarlett's speech and worked with the Assistants of said High Witches, would meet us there.

As Scarlett strode with her billowing skirts, I spilled updates about Carcere, my official agreement to help Camila, and Baxter's involvement. Relief unburdened the weight on my chest as I opened up.

I studied her sidelong to gauge her reaction. This would be the first mission outside of her that I'd taken without her direct approval or involvement.

"And so," I said, drawing to a conclusion the summary of events, "it's possible Greyson is leading us on a merry chase about the rebellion instigator, but considering Camila's corroboration and Baxter's observations, I don't think that's entirely true. Camila would like me to continue looking into the Gallo family, if I'm willing. I am. To do that, my next step would be to speak with Greyson again. I wanted your permission."

Scarlett showed no outward reaction at first. We twirled around a corner, decorated by a stained glass mural, a painting of nude water sprites frolicking on a forest lake, and other frames with a similar penchant.

She took my revelations in stride.

"I agree with your decision to assist Camila."

"You do?"

"Yes."

With a breath of relief, I said, "Good. Leda hasn't been convinced it's wise."

"From her purview, that makes sense. From my side, I feel the risk is worth the reward."

"In light of the Sisterhood's latest mission statement?"

Scarlett's sidelong glance communicated amusement. "Leda is the closest approximation to a perfect Assistant as I've ever seen, but that does not make her perfect. Patience and proof is what you require to deal with her."

"I agree, Your Highness."

"You let me deal with ramifications around the Council, to which I believe Leda is most concerned. The insight you glean will be valuable, and I'm appreciative of your initiative. But please, in the future, don't feel as if you're protecting me by withholding information. This is a *Sisterhood*, which means we're in it together. You are not too much for me, Bianca. Nor are your aspirations."

Until she called out my fears for what they were, I hadn't

recognized them. Indeed, I had all those concerns. A nudge of humility resulted from her gentle chiding.

"Thank you, High Priestess."

She nodded at a passing witch, bestowing a warm, if not tired, smile. Scarlett could have transported directly to the spot, but had a habit of walking in between meetings. Not only to change her surroundings, but movement helped her thoughts settle. It provided the additional bonus of visibility to workers, which she highly valued.

"What are your plans regarding Ricardo Gallo?" she asked as we took another corner with her smooth gait.

"Hard to say."

"Finding him sounds like your main priority?"

"Yes."

"Do you hope speaking to Greyson could be helpful?"

"Could be anything," I countered. "But he's going to ask for more than an apple, this time."

Scarlett pressed her lips. "We cannot let him out of the dungeon, but I have no qualms with you speaking to him again."

"If he refuses to speak, can I upgrade him to a different cell?"

She contemplated for a long moment. "If we must, then yes. But don't take that action until you must, and do so with whatever discretion the Guardians can manage. I would suggest informing Talmund and Rognvald first."

"Naturally, Your Highness."

"Before you approach him again, please speak with Aurora. Inform her of your plan."

The request—more like a command—immediately irritated me.

"Why?"

She sent me a reproachful stare. "Aurora has more talent and presence than you think, Bianca. Her contributions to the ambassadorial process should not be understated, even with a prisoner of Greyson's . . . acclaim."

"Of presence, she has plenty."

"Take my request as a command, if you must. Just make sure you include Aurora. If you want to maintain diplomacy with her, I suggest she not find out I had to command it. Her diplomatic process is worthwhile."

"Not necessary," I grumbled. "I'll do it. There's also this other concern I have about Magnolia Castle itself."

"The structure of it, you mean?"

"Yes. It seems to be in disrepair. I'm wondering if the rebellion might attempt to bring down Magnolia Castle."

She frowned. Her rapid steps slowed, and the rustle and murmur of voices came from just ahead. Leda's white hair flashed in and out of sight as she moved around the interior of a room not far away, clearly preparing it.

As if she sensed our approach, Leda said, *Where are you? Right outside.*

Her head popped out of the room with a relieved nod and a brief smile for Scarlett, who had a quizzical expression on her face as she stopped to regard me. She didn't seem to truly see me.

"Why would the rebellion physically remove Magnolia?"

"It's a symbol," I countered. "A powerful and beloved one."

"It *is* beloved," she murmured. "The rebellion, should they truly want to overthrow and not tear down, would want to maintain the symbol and make a point of taking over. The requirement to decimate such a building would be . . ."

"Enormous?"

"Beyond that." She blinked, studying me with deeper intent. "What makes you think it's a potential problem?"

Saying *cracks in the wall* and *weaknesses in hidden passages* sounded utterly stupid when I considered them. They'd be worse to state.

"I'm trying to keep my insight open," I managed to say.

"Hmmm." Her quizzical stare didn't fool me. "Well, thank you for the update. I'll consider that line of questioning, but I have no ideas for you. Please, keep me apprised of your plans with Greyson, and good luck with Aurora."

You told her? Leda asked.

Yes.

A sigh lightened her voice. *That will make my life significantly easier.*

Scarlett shuffled to the other room, where noise levels lowered. "Let me know how I can help, Bianca," she tossed over her shoulder. "I trust the Sisterhood has this firmly in hand."

With that, she spun around and entered the room with her usual heartfelt and personal greetings.

Leda peered at me, peeved. *Council Member Clare had to cancel your lunch with her tomorrow. You can take that off your schedule until I find another time with her.*

She closed the door.

I sighed.

Chapter Sixteen

When I returned to the treehouse, Merrick stood at the table, hands pressed into the top. Ever since Rognvald assigned him to stalk the Eastern Network during the day, we hadn't seen much of each other. Twilight descended, so I wrapped my arms around him from behind and squeezed tight.

"Merry meet," I whispered against the strong planes of his back. He grabbed my arms and pulled me around to see my face. I kept my head tilted, hair dropping along my spine, and met his emerald gaze.

"How are you, B?"

"Let's never grow up."

Laughing, he said, "You must have seen your father."

"How did you know?"

"There's a tone."

I recoiled. "There's not a *tone*."

He sent me a smirk, and I glowered. Well, maybe there *was* a tone. His arms came around me in a hold as reassuring as Papa's. I pressed the shell of my ear to his chest and listened to the thud-thump of his heart until I couldn't bear the contemplative silence.

When I pulled away, he roused from deeper ruminations.

"Something you want to say?" I asked.

He returned to his previously surly expression. Dragging a hand over his face, he gestured to the table. "A letter came from my sister. Bloody nuisance, if you ask me. She's only going to get more difficult from here on out."

"About the handfasting?"

"And life!"

Merrick and Jacqueline had a habit of constantly irritating each other, so I failed to feel concern. Extracting myself from the circle of his arms, I lifted one of two pieces of folded paper off the table. At the top was a scrawled note from Jacqueline.

Please regard the list below as emergent and respond with immediate replies. We have dinners to plan and things to put into place, so your cooperation would be appreciated.

Above all, she added in a line that sounded far more like an exasperated Jacqueline, *pick a day already!*

My eyes widened over the next line. *Things We Require to Plan the Handfasting* scratched across the top. A list covered the front and back of the page and one side of another.

"There must be fifty requirements," I whispered.

"Sixty two."

Merrick paced in front of the fire. His shirt, half unbuttoned, was rolled up at the wrists, ending near his elbow. The taut muscles of his forearms rolled as he strode back and forth, twisting his wrists, as if they were sore.

"They want to honor every tradition," he continued, speaking as much to himself as to me. "*Every* tradition. Why are sisters so annoying? What does it matter? We don't need to fulfill every single tradition! My parents didn't even fulfill all of them."

"Which ones matter most?"

He threw his hands in the air with engrossing exasperation. "According to Jacqueline, all of them!"

I skimmed down her detailed list. The details were dauntingly specific.

Measurements required for Bianca's handfasting dress.

- Wrist
- Sleeve length
- Waist circumference
- Length from top of hips to floor
- Neck
- Elbow to wrist
- Elbow to shoulder
- Elbow to neckline
- Neckline to wrist

The thought of measuring for a handfasting dress wasn't as terrifying as a dress pieced together by Jacqueline. Knowing her, it would be elaborate, complicated, and require me to be sewn inside.

I ran my finger down the list. "Your sister certainly has a skill for details, doesn't she?"

He grunted, but resumed pacing. He folded his hands behind his back and stretched his shoulders with a grimace, all indicators that he'd spent time sparring with other Protectors. His mission aside, he still set aside an hour of physical work.

A niggling instinct pushed me to ask, "Are you hungry?"

"Starving."

Ah. Perhaps the issue of his surly glare would be easier to solve than I expected.

While I continued to peruse the list, which involved the line items, *Send a list of your favorite colors* and *also send your least favorite colors by the third day of next week,* amongst sundry other strange requests, I sent a spell to summon food from the pantry.

Whipped butter, leftover savory scones, a leftover crock of leto nut paste, and several handfuls of fresh-cut greens carried across the room. They settled on the table nearby. Nothing extravagant, but our daily meals had little flair. Merrick stopped pacing to regard the gathering supplies. I kept my gaze averted to avoid more explosive conversation.

He snatched a scone, the butter dish, tipped a corner inside, and scraped the edges free. Within seconds, he'd popped half of it in his mouth and chewed. The final page of the second parchment was a detailed list of the expected schedule for the weeks leading up to the handfasting. For two weeks, we'd have absolutely no space in our lives.

"Jikes," I muttered.

Merrick abandoned the butter to tear into the other half of his scone with a growl. I sent the letters to the bedroom, out of sight, while he calmed. He'd already devoured the first scone when I reached for the leto nut paste and a spoon, which sailed through the air from a distant pile.

"She's mad." He sat forcefully across from me. "That's what! I'm still on assignment. I might be on assignment then. We can't *plan* these dinners around our schedule."

"True."

"She's forgetting this isn't her handfasting."

"She's excited."

"She's a nutter."

"They're just . . . involved."

"It's embarrassing," he grumbled.

Unable to help myself, I laughed. "Why?"

"We could elope to the South and be done with it in ten minutes, if we do it at all."

The thought thrilled me, but the dream was implausible.

The celebration meant a lot to Jacqueline and his mother, and they meant a lot to me. I reached over the table and set my hand on top of his. His fingers twitched under my touch.

"Merrick, you know how much this means to them. It might be a little uncomfortable to spend this much time on a celebration that neither you nor I care about as much as them, but this *is* the only time either of us will be doing it. Don't you want it to be special?"

He softened, but only slightly. He grabbed my arm above the elbow, stood up, and hauled me into a kiss that left my toes tingling. He smelled like the basil and greens hidden in the scone dough.

He tore away with a soft grunt.

"I'm interested in a handfasting that represents *us*, not them," he said. "This is our day, Bianca. Our celebration. Other witches shouldn't control it."

"I love your mother," I countered. "She means a lot to both of us."

"I agree."

"I don't want this to come between us later. If they want to plan it and all we have to do is make decisions, that's easy, right?"

He plopped into his chair again with a martyric sigh. "Not easy," he countered, clearly unwilling to give up the fight, "but doable."

Taking the calm concession as a deferment to decide later—which we did more often than not—I set aside the lists to consider in the morning, when we weren't so tired. While Merrick scooped a spoonful of the savory leto nut paste swirled with clumps of garlic, I plucked a scone off the top of the bowl and tore a corner free. Specks of basil crumbled to the table. I swept them free with a wave of my hand, then used a spell to send them outside.

"It'll be easier if Jacqueline comes here to take my measurements anyway," I replied, "because I have no idea what they are. We can just answer her questions then. It'll be easy."

Merrick's returning scowl suggested he didn't agree.

"Besides," I added with a breezy wave, "she's right. We need to decide what day it's going to happen. Then you can see if Rognvald will let a different Protector cover that day—just *one* day," I hastily added when Merrick's displeasure deepened.

With greater resolution, I nodded once.

"A date is the first logical step. We'll discuss it in the morning."

* * *

Aurora glared at me from over the top of her ostentatious glasses without any glass. Sparkles along the arms reminded me of Camille. The decoration-only impact of her outfit left her looking disheveled and overdone, dripping with earrings, necklaces, bracelets, and rings. I stood inside her office, one foot poised out of the door, and tried to act like I wasn't hiding from her.

"Merry meet, Aurora."

Aurora's whetted stare sharpened, if possible. If looks could stab, I'd be bleeding. "What do you want?"

"An hour of your time."

"For what?"

"A prisoner interrogation."

Aurora folded her arms over her chest and leaned into her desk like a vengeful owl about to swoop. Unlike other leadership, she kept her chairs over cluttered to prevent witches from sitting. An intentional move meant to discourage people from staying too long in her office, something that few would ever desire.

She drummed her thin fingers along her elbow.

"Why?"

Leashing the full truth about Scarlett's command to invite Aurora, I said, "Your diplomatic process is respectable, and it seemed a good idea to ask for your insight."

"Sounds like something Scarlett would say."

"It is."

Aurora's glasses tilted down her narrow nose. She glared at me over the top. "Don't get sassy with me, Bianca Monroe. You may be the leader of an organization that no one except the High Priest and High Priestess recognize as a functional entity, but that doesn't give you unequivocal access to the castle and the ability to do anything you want."

You're right, I almost countered, *I have access without the Sisterhood,* but couldn't imagine a way of saying it that didn't sound like a challenge, so I kept my mouth shut.

Aurora waited, fingers drumming.

"As Head of the Sisterhood," I said carefully, "I don't have to justify my speaking with prisoners. Regardless, in this case, I have permission. Scarlett invited me to have you join, as she believes in your *diplomatic process.*"

Despite my attempt to remain even-keel, the challenge filled my response with a thrumming question. Would Aurora dive deeper? I had single-handedly brought Greyson to justice on my own. She knew I didn't truly require her, but her prickly personality lent few witches to give her work. If she wanted to stay in office and employed, she had to prove herself.

Scarlett was giving her a chance.

I didn't like being the vehicle for it.

Aurora made a noise in her throat and turned to look outside. Her profile silhouetted against crisp fall air that poured through windows and into her turret, mixing with heat from the fireplace on the far side. Seeing any witch in this office that wasn't Grandfather created disbelief every time.

Unfortunately—or, perhaps through some purviews, fortunately—Aurora knew her precarious personality had become a problem. Regardless of her positioning or not, she still rolled her eyes.

"Spare me the pain of false compliments," she muttered. "Just because you put someone in the dungeons doesn't mean you have any say in their inevitable fate. Why do you want to visit with the accused?"

"He's not accused. He's proven guilty."

"Whatever."

"I want to speak with him."

"About?"

"The Eastern Network. More information has come to light. Scarlett has given me parameters under which I can bargain with Greyson for more."

"What questions?"

"About something I found. At his behest," I added.

Her slotted gaze apprised me, thin lips making a sucking motion like a fish. Her fingers drummed higher onto her shoulder, where they rolled in perpetual motion for what felt like an absurd amount of time.

"How close to the Carcere explosion was Greyson in that turret?" she asked.

Surprised that her line of questioning didn't become more accusatory, I said, "That's what I wanted to find out."

"And?"

"And," I drawled, "I went back to Carcere."

Aurora's eyes gleamed. "Now *that* is the first interesting thing you've said today, Bianca." She rolled her hand in an impatient circle. "You discovered?"

Irritated, I tilted my head and served up my own version of glaring dagger. As usual, she ignored my wrath as child's play.

"If his cell is where he sent me, then he wasn't all that close. Different floors, from what I can tell." With a frown, I added, "At least, that's the best I can assume. Carcere is strange with the way it lays out. Assuming Greyson *was* in Carcere when this happened, which is the most likely scenario that we haven't proved differently, then someone must have let him out of his cell."

"Could it have been a result of the magic? Perhaps many witches found their freedom simply because the magic failed."

"I don't know," I admitted, recalling the dank hallways and splayed cells. None of them had the appearance of being broken or forced apart. "It would be impossible to know without deeper interrogations of involved Guardians, based on surface-level observations."

"Any similarities between the Carcere explosion and Magnolia?"

"I haven't looked into it specifically, but I'd wager there are."

Aurora snapped two fingers and several quills sprang to life from her desk, elevating above scrolls that rose out of a drawer nearby. She strode around her desk, tossing something on top. It bounced off, soared to a bookcase, and settled at the top with a flash of green light.

"Presence in Carcere at the time of the magical dissolution doesn't make Greyson guilty of insurrection," she stated.

"No one is charging him as such."

"Unfortunate, because it might help."

"Help what?"

She lifted a hand, as if I hadn't spoken. "Although," she sang under her breath, "there is something to be said for the value of observation, visual or auditory. He must have heard *something*." Aurora ticked a hand back and forth. "And what happened between his escape and the threats against Scarlett's life?"

"I don't—"

"I know." She flapped an impatient hand my way. "I know you don't know. I'm *asking* because you don't know."

Which made no sense, but the possibility of her coming around to my side made me not want to break the eggshells.

She spun around, muttering, "But being present at the time

of the dissolution does make him *valuable.* The question is: how to convince the Council to agree that he's important enough to justify leverage."

"You agree with me?" I asked.

"I didn't say that."

"You said—"

"I know what I said," she snapped, "but it wasn't in agreement with your observations. What are you offering Greyson in exchange for him answering your questions?"

"I'm . . . not sure."

"He won't accept just anything."

"Last time, I gave him an apple."

"I know."

"You do?"

"You'll need something more valuable. If we can offer something with high enough value, can you get him to recount what happened when the wall broke?"

Recalling my previous experience with him, I shrugged. "Maybe."

With expiring patience, she asked, "What ideas do you have? This is not my job to figure out, thank you very much."

"What about a full, hot meal? In case that's not enough, a book or two. He'll offer up information in exchange for comforts. I think," I tacked on. Knowing Aurora, she'd hold me accountable to every comment that crossed my lips. As Head of the Sisterhood, that seemed fair enough.

"Don't take any book." Returning to her bookshelf, she tapped her fingernails along the book edges, stopped, and pulled one free. "Take this."

The tome floated to my side. *Impossible Logic Puzzles and Their Games.* A sheepish sense of gratitude swept me. Yes, this was a better idea than a novel. Greyson thrilled to game-like challenges.

"See what you find out," she said.

Stymied by this sudden and unexpected turn into allyship, I ventured a tentative, "You don't want to come with me?"

"Not this time."

"Why not?"

"Because," she hissed, "I'm busy. Do what I suggested and it'll be enough. For now. Greyson will eventually want more in exchange for bigger information, which I will assist with should you require assistance."

"May I ask why you care about—"

"No."

"I just—"

"No!"

Sensing I wouldn't get anything else, I muttered, "I will," then added a terse, "Thank you."

Her large eyes darted to mine, a bit wild within their restraint. "Don't mess it up. We can't do anything for the Eastern Network, or ourselves by extension, if the rebellion gains power soon. Despite all of Cristian's attempts to fix his Network, there's a shot we can prevent many deaths and much loss."

With that, she snapped her fingers and headed for her desk, her back to me as if I didn't exist. A strong gust of wind wrestled me out her door, slamming it shut in my wake.

* * *

A voice curled out from the dungeon cell like a snoring dragon.

"Is that fresh bread?"

With a clatter, I set the tray on the floor at my feet. "Coffee, too. There's a pot of cream, some sugar, fresh bread, whipped butter, cream of potato soup, and, if you're really chatty, there's a wedge of pie."

The top of an overturned bowl lifted enough to reveal glazed cherries, a flaky brown crust, and oozing syrup around

179

plump fruits. My stomach growled with the scent of fresh yeast.

Greyson emerged, eyes gleaming from the fresh torch I'd brought, and a spare after it. Faking a neutral attitude around him made my stomach curl. This was a man that happily tried to kill me and Scarlett two months ago. To stand before him with fresh food and a bargain at the tip of my tongue made me ill.

I set a hand on my hip, gestured into the cell with my other. "How was the apple?"

"Dry."

"Really?"

Every attempt to keep his attention on me failed. Micro glances whipped between myself and the food, occupying passing seconds until he stared at the tray. His desperation must be worse than I expected. The Greyson of days past showed nothing but restraint.

"Have you tried this soup before?" I asked. "Very delicious. Contains little flecks of clam, but not enough to overtake the potato. If you cook it too long, you lose the right texture. Fina has it just right. An Eastern Network specialty, I hear."

He blinked his attention onto me. Scathing dripped from his eyes. "What do you want, Bianca?"

With a flick of my fingers, I conjured the medallion. It glinted in the torchlight, hovering in the air. To my surprise, he smiled.

"You found it."

"You didn't hide it well."

With confounding innocence, he stated, "I didn't hide it."

Tucking it away, I straightened and casually said, "No, of course not. Ricardo Gallo hid it on your behalf."

His eyes darted to mine. "I never said that name to you."

I smiled.

Greyson blinked once before he stepped away from the bars to murmur, "Interesting."

"Want to talk about Ricardo?"

"No."

"No problem." Nudging aside the tray, I folded my legs beneath me and sat. My fingers plucked a dainty silver spoon from next to the bowl. "I'll enjoy my lunch." The bread elevated to my hand. I tore a piece of the warm crust off, butter slippery on the tips of my fingers. My teeth tore a bite off the end.

Crooning, I whispered, "Delicious."

His lips pinched.

With a chunk of the bread in my hand, I motioned toward him. "You had porridge today?"

He snarled. The fluffy aroma of bread filled the room, expanding into the iron-scented corners of his hovel. Coffee tumbled out of the pot and into a cup, followed by a thin stream of cream and a heaping spoonful of sugar. The spoon rotated, clockwise, as it stirred the hazelnut-colored amalgamation together.

Sipping, I moaned low.

"So yummy."

Greyson closed the space between him and the bars, face pressed into them. He gripped the iron tightly as I had another sip, meeting his gaze over the top of the mug. Feigning surprise, I whispered, "Did you want some?"

Deepest loathing replied. His silence spoke of imperious hatred. Coffee poured into the second cup, suffusing the room with bitter scents that twined into the bread, every bit as welcoming and homey as the yeasty warmth.

"You liked it black, didn't you?"

The cream and sugar hovered nearby.

He licked his lips.

"I'll add both," I said brightly. "Considering how long you've been here. The nourishment might do you some good. That is . . . *if* your lips happen to tell me a little bit about

Ricardo Gallo." With a spoonful of creamy soup halfway to my lips, I asked, "Did you have anything to say?"

The coffee elevated to a horizontal access slot in the bars, just above eye level, and a few handspans wide. Enough to allow a plate or drink to pass through. The mug hovered out of reach.

His eyes dilated. He struggled not to smell it, not to react, by staring harder than before. I rubbed a piece of bread between my thumb and forefinger as I stood. His rancid breath billowed between us when I closed the distance.

"Carcere was different this time," I said with less false cheer. "The last month provided plenty of opportunity and time for the magic to bleed free. It's little more than a building now, really. Good thing you didn't wait any longer to play your little game with Scarlett and me. You wouldn't have had so many assets working on your side."

His nostrils remained wide and livid. His arms trembled where they gripped the bars, knuckles white. I couldn't help but wonder what *would* push him to succumb to my demands. Greyson rarely had any compunction about getting what he wanted by whatever means necessary. His suppressed rage made less sense than ever.

The coffee cup settled onto the horizontal ledge. There, the magic would fail. I reached up, tapped it farther in.

"A free one."

He didn't reach for it, nor move. I spun, retreated to the tray, and had another sip of my own coffee. His eyes tracked my every move. If I didn't keep things moving forward, I'd lose the power. His refusal to eat or drink would sway everything into his court, and I couldn't afford to lose a single confrontation. He must know this.

I popped the bite of bread into my mouth and kept talking.

"With Carcere bleeding free, it was simple enough to return to the sight where the breakage of the magic occurred and find this."

The ledger hovered above my hands, a deception spell. Leda kept a tight hold on the original one. Greyson flicked a quick glance to it, back to me, and then the coffee hovering at my side. He didn't look at the tray, with its steamy bread and pie, but almost all of his concentration focused on it.

"Interesting ledger," I continued with a thoughtful hum. "Names listed as part of the rebellion. Whether they had promised loyalty or not. Proof that the Carcere explosion is directly related to the rebellion, no matter how you look at it. That's where you come in."

I lifted the handle of my mug and had another drink.

"Any thoughts?"

The bread elevated to his eye level.

Greyson tensed as if he braced for a blow. Hard as he tried not to see the bread, he couldn't tear his gaze away. Sensing a window, I conjured the final trick up my sleeve.

"Tell me how you escaped Carcere and you'll have the rest of this tray, as well as something else to occupy your mind."

Aurora's book landed in my outstretched hand. His upper lip twitched. Greyson studied the cover, the tray, and then me.

"Aren't you asking me the wrong question?" he rasped.

"Am I?"

"Don't you want to know about . . ."

"Ricardo Gallo?"

Pained, he nodded.

"Mmm . . . yes, but I have a feeling you'll only offer one answer."

"Correct."

I elevated my brow in silent expectation.

He whispered, "I can't tell you how it was done." His hand rose to his throat, insinuating a vow prevented him. "But I can ask you a question."

Remember this, I said to Leda. With Greyson, every word would be intentional.

She said, *Ready.*

"Please proceed."

"Given a choice, where would you have attended school in the Eastern Network?"

I stared.

"What?"

With patience, he repeated, "Given a choice, where would you have attended school in the Eastern Network?"

"Give me something worthwhile, Greyson."

He stared stony-faced. "You are prone to desiring the very best of things, and seeking knowledge from the deepest of troves. You, who covet all the grand things, all the desirables, all the luxuries. Where would you have attended school?"

Suspicion crawled over me as I repeated what he said to Leda through the communication magic. I regarded him while asking her, *Any idea what he could be getting at?*

Not yet, she said.

"That's hardly an answer," I shot back.

"It is more *answer* than you think. My food," he hissed, "if you don't mind?"

But I did mind, because his lackluster hint wasn't worth the wasted time. Still, he'd set my mind thinking on a track that I hadn't considered before, and I didn't want to darken my information source too soon.

Besides, I had trust to build. I'd need Greyson again, and both of us knew it. I commanded the tray into the air. The book, the bread, the coffee, the creamer, and the sugar—even my cup of coffee—filtered through the access slot. As soon as they crossed through the metal, they dropped. The magic wouldn't take them within.

Greyson was ready. He caught the tray and greedily retreated toward the corner, his gaunt shoulders scrunched protectively over it, as if afraid I'd take it away.

I called over my shoulder, "Merry part, Greyson. I'm sure you'll see me again soon."

Chapter Seventeen

After speaking with Greyson, I retreated to the one place that made sense.

Carcere.

The hollow shell hummed in the wind. A lonely sound. No answers became readily apparent, so I held a silent, invisible vigil for hours.

No answer about Ricardo Gallo appeared, but I hadn't expected it. Instead, my mind cleared. Something about the unfurled sky, wild winds, ragged sea, erased the tightness in my chest from the dungeons.

While sitting on the edge of a staircase, I sent a note to Caroline, at the Great Library of Burke. Then another to Priscilla, an update to Leda, one to Papa, and finally spelled my parchment and pencil back to the treehouse.

Caroline replied within minutes.

Find the Gallo family yourself. We have no sources.

Eyes rolling, I torched her refusal with a fire spell.

Researching the Gallo family in the Eastern Network would be a fraught affair. Triggering suspicion would only breed trouble, and I needed to stay quiet. If the Great Library of Burke had information, it would have been helpful, however unlikely.

I lay on the Volare, which hovered a few paces above the sand, with my hands propped behind my head. Hours passed while I pondered and sorted in the calm air, considering Greyson and riddles and the Gallo family and Eastern Network schools—called Academies—and whether he played me for a fool.

With the whispering sea in my ear, I waited.

A reply from Priscilla popped up in front of my eyes, so close it brushed my nose. Hastily, I sat up and flipped it open. Her neat handwriting filled the bottom of the page.

No, I can't think of any schools that take place in the Eastern Network woods, *as you put it. Why would you ask?*

Frowning, I skipped over a lengthy elaboration of different Academies that loosely mimicked the Central Network's structure around Network schools, and a too-long exposition on the state of their structure. My mind tangled into an unhelpful knot.

Jikes, but what did Greyson *mean* by his question?

Given a choice, where would you have attended school in the Eastern Network?

The forest, naturally.

Kicking a sand clod, I recalled his next words.

You are prone to desiring the very best of things, and seeking knowledge from the deepest of troves. You, who covet all the grand things, all the desirables, all the luxuries.

None of that was true.

Grand things. Desirables. Luxuries. I lived in a treehouse in the forest, ran barefoot, and ate bread, goat cheese, and bitter greens for most of my meals. The utter lack of truth in his statement made it stand out.

In fact, the deeper I considered his tone—ever-so-slightly stable and filled with loathing—the more my heart pounded.

Wait.

I missed it.

The obvious clue.

He said something so preposterous on purpose. The reference to the school, grand things, desirables, and luxury meant something about where to go next—not about me. To speak around a binding, perhaps?

Breathless, I flipped Priscilla's letter over, conjured my pencil, and scrawled a question across the back.

*If you wanted to attend a grand, desirable, luxurious
school in the Eastern Network, where would you go?*

It fluttered away with a flap. Chewing on my bottom lip, I paced across the tempestuous spit of land, ignoring the foamy sea and churning weather. Her reply came with uncanny speed.

*Oh, that's an easy one. I'd attend the Archives of Ancient
and Current Academies in Magnolia Castle. It's a combi-
nation of a museum, a library, and a college. I worked
with them often when I lived there.*

I reared back.

Magnolia Castle? Since when did Magnolia Castle house a college? Then again, there had been many facets of the grand palace I'd never considered.

Come to think of it, the Academy is your best starting point on historical genealogies as you search for more information on the Gallo family.

It's a quiet, lovely place. Magical, too. Most witches call it the Academy instead of its full name. They're protective, which is why you haven't heard of it until now, I'd wager.

"Protective? No kidding," I muttered.

Pompous, too. Oh, and don't be fooled by the entrance, which you can find at the end of the south wing. It's bigger than it appears.

The Academy holds the truest jewels of the Eastern Network—mostly heirlooms and literature and pedigrees. Some of the greater families store family jewels and other expensive things there, whether on display or tucked in the recesses.

Just be careful.

They really don't like strangers. If you're going to go there, which I would be foolish to assume not, then don't transform. Don't try to be an Eastern Network witch.

Approach as if you work for my school and need a genealogy.

They're pompous enough to enjoy the ego.

"Challenge accepted," I said as I tucked it in my pocket. I had an Academy to find.

* * *

The Archives of Ancient and Current Academies was a derelict-appearing doorway on the outside of Magnolia Castle. The limp facade led to a hallway that widened ever-so-slightly before attaching to Magnolia Castle proper. I'd hazard a guess that, at most, thirty witches might fit within.

Metallic letters gleamed from the dim light of day as I strode beyond an old gate and up to a wooden door lined with tiny seashells that spelled *The Academy*. The downpour didn't help the already lackluster appearance when I reached for the knob, my hair tied out of my face in a braid.

I twisted.

The door opened.

A bell rang when I pushed inside, drying myself with a spell that diffused the water from my clothes. When the door creaked shut behind me, I pulled up short out of sheer surprise.

Expansive marble floors, sleek statues, and whispering witches greeted me. A room thirty times larger than I expected awaited. The perfect meeting point of a library, a museum, and a fancy mansion. Leda might faint.

Before I could walk onto pristinely tiled marble floors, a witch bustled up to my side from behind a mahogany desk. He had a bristling mustache, a twitchy nose, and inquiring eyes.

As he opened his mouth to speak, I gave a wide smile and intercepted him. "*Allo*, signor," I spoke in the best Ilese I could manage, but didn't attempt to hide my accent. "I hope you're having a good day?"

"Ah . . . *allo*." He nodded once and followed my cues by responding in the common language. "How may I help you?"

Withdrawing a piece of parchment splashed with rain and smudged ink, I handed it over. He opened the ends, inspecting the forged document. I'd hastily cobbled together a teacher's note, using Priscilla's signature from her former letter.

"I'm a teacher Assistant, and I'm conducting research on Eastern Network family genealogies on behalf of our students.

We want to teach them of the great families from history and how they've navigated tempestuous times with ease."

He inspected me, the letter, and me again. Thankfully, the drying spell had also evaporated water spots. While he didn't immediately buy into my flattery, it bought me a few more minutes to attempt.

"We are not a library." He spoke in the common language, lightly accented. "We are the Academy. The heart of Magnolia Castle."

Sagely, I pressed a hand to my heart. "A distinction and truth that I hold sacred. It's not a library that I seek. Our students are studying the advancement of society and culture across different Networks and their most distinctive citizens. Descriptions of artifacts on the great Eastern Network families throughout history would be most helpful. You have these, don't you?"

His nose twitched. "Yes." His hands folded behind his back as he gazed over his shoulder. No one else stood with us in the room. "Yes, we have the most extensive collection available, but many of our pupils are in class, using the display rooms."

I had *so* many questions, but I withheld them to ask Priscilla later. Pupils? Extensive collections? Displays?

How big was this place?

"I can wait until your pupils are out of class."

A roll of his eyes made it clear that wasn't an option. With a twitch of his fingers, so similar to that of his nose, he bade me follow him. We strode past an elegant staircase lazily ribboning higher, higher, higher. From my cursory glance at the bottom, I counted at least five floors. Crushed crimson carpet covered each step.

So strange how much space hid here.

Almost like Carcere.

As we walked, I tried not to gawk at a display of jewels the size of my fist, hidden behind glass panes as thick as my palm. Hastily, I turned my attention to sensing the magic that surrounded it. As if a fire had exploded, my brain woke up. The sheer power of the protective incantations surrounding it shocked me.

Stumbling to the side, I caught myself as the man glanced back. I had a feeling my sheepish smile didn't fool him.

"Each family protects its own interests at the Academy," he said. "None of them suffer fools."

More carefully, I followed him past a display of previous Guardian uniforms, around hand-carved wooden jigsaw puzzles as large as a table, and strange pottery with painted designs.

"The greater families have displays on the floors above us," he said in time with the crisp staccato of his shoes. "They're located in rooms occupied by our students. You may view the displays of the lesser families. It should be sufficient for your classroom requirements."

And that encapsulated the Eastern Network in a nutshell. *Greater families* and *lesser families*. Sometimes, I thought I understood the marsh witch's urge to rebel against a disdain this thick.

He led me to a darkened room with subdued wood paneling, wide windows revealing the murky storm, and candles pressed against mirrored sconces. The moment we stepped across the threshold, the lights bounced awake, casting a cozy glow on the dreary day. With a cup of tea, Leda would have been set for the rest of the week.

"Touch nothing."

"What happens if I do?"

He repeated, "The families do not suffer fools." I watched him go, amused by the violence of his sincerity.

With my hands folded behind my back, I approached the closest cupboard. Two paces away and just out of reach, I stopped. A rustle of noise at the door caught my ear. Casting a sidelong glance, I caught my new friend glowering from around the doorway, poorly spying on my every move.

Acting as if I didn't notice, I leaned closer, peering at writing along the ledge. *The Talledora family*. Beneath it, an elaborate scrollwork of names sprawled to the left and right. Literal branches in an artistic family tree, each name brushed in a gold paint, with letters that formed the shape of a leaf.

Near the bottom, a new leaf unfurled near to a cluster of others.

Sofia.

"A new baby at this moment?" I cried, smiling. "How lovely."

For an Eastern Network *lesser family*, they didn't have as many descendants as others. A quick glance confirmed that several genealogies sprawled three times as wide as the Talledora family.

The shelves below the artistic display revealed baby bonnets, notebooks, favored quills, a recipe book, and a tattered painting of an old woman with a bright smile. She sat next to an old man with a scowl.

I slipped to the right, studying the next. *The Montes Family* stood next to *The Noferi Family* and *The Pistone Family*. Behind each crest hung a painted map, highlighting in vivid emerald a different section of the Eastern Network. Their ruling province, presumably.

Pausing, head tilted, I spun the other way, skimming over each golden family until I stopped at the one I sought.

The Gallo Family.

The familiar family crest was painted rather . . . differently. Instead of the symbolic cypress tree of the Eastern Network swamplands, the Gallo family pedigree resembled a wild marsh. Clumps of bushes formed little families, the grasses themselves a string of names. Embedded within the heart of each grassy bundle was a near-exact replica of the medallion I found in Carcere.

They had no items on display except a swath of dried grass

and a medallion propped against it. A lower, southeast portion of the Eastern Network map illuminated to a fervent emerald. The edge of swamps and into marshlands. They were the only family without a strange assortment of keepsakes.

Just their name.

Their crest.

Dried grass.

Standing there for a minute, I forced myself to focus on the gold painted words. An amalgamation of witch names that I couldn't hope to remember petaled out. Starting at the bottom, I skimmed upward. *Nicolette, Amaya, Danila.* All of them formed tiny grass blades at the bottom, branching from slightly larger above. As the husks ascended, they grew bigger. An indication of age, I presumed.

Resisting the urge to run my fingers along it, I studied the row of names three levels above the youngest.

There.

Ricardo.

His name, painted next to a Theodore, branched to the side with a woman's name given in rose gold. A marriage, I presumed. It appeared all spouses were rose gold instead of pure gold.

Ten different seeds emerged from their union. Children, presumably. Ten, like Leda's family. With wealth, was there as much chaos for expansive families? Each grass seed held a different name. The stems of witches most likely dead had a darker emerald hue, and not all ten had the characteristic lightness I assumed signified they were alive.

Jikes.

Much loss for the Gallo family.

I found the Gallo family display at the Academy in the Eastern Network, I said hastily to Leda. *I need to ask Priscilla something.*

You're in the Academy?

Yes.

How?

I walked up to the door.

No, she said impatiently, *how did you know about it?*

Priscilla.

Hmmm.

You knew?

Of course I knew, she retorted.

We can discuss why you never mentioned it later, all right? Any chance you've invited Priscilla into the magic in the last half an hour? There's no time for me to send her messages.

Believe it or not, she said testily, *I have a job that I do rather well and very consistently. So, no. I haven't brought Priscilla into the communication magic on the off-hand chance you might desire a chat with her in the middle of her day.*

Ignoring her dramatics, I asked as kindly as irritation would allow, *Can you please bring her in?*

If sighs could have traveled, hers would have.

Fine. Give me two minutes. But you're lucky I have leftover time at lunch!

To maintain the illusion of not caring about the Gallo family, I sidled farther to the left. Undoubtedly, my new Eastern Network friend continued to spy, though I hoped he left.

While waiting, I switched my attention to the protective spells on each display. Sensing magic in here was almost pointless unless I focused. The protective incantations were powerful and loud and similar. Each one had a different energy from the individual casters. Cast magic was often distinct to the witch who issued it. When different witches cast the same spell, a slight variance existed. Like a cup of coffee that smelled like vanilla instead of cream.

When Leda said, *Priscilla, Bianca has a question for you,* I returned to focus. With a lot less congeniality, she sniped, *Bianca, I would appreciate it if you keep in mind that some of us work and have other requirements in the middle of the day. I will not be skipping around Alkarra, making connections for you like this again.*

Thank you, Leda, I said with full sincerity. Meanwhile, I rolled my eyes so hard my head bobbed onto my shoulders.

Don't forget that we have a dinner in the Western Network tomorrow evening. Scarlett requested you join. If you do something stupid in the meantime, Scarlett will not be happy to replace you with a Protector, and the Council is always watching.

Thanks, Mama.

Oh, Priscilla said. *This is . . . so weird. Do you two also fight in the magic? That's not altogether surprising. Can you hear me, Bianca?*

A lack of resonance in her voice meant Leda had blocked out the conversation.

Thank Alkarra.

Yes, I said. *I hear you.*

Neat!

Did we interrupt anything?

Not at this moment.

You can use this magic to get a hold of me anytime you want. Especially if something happens and you need help.

Thank you.

I stopped in front of *The Valenti Family* and stared at what appeared to be a shrunken head, but might have only been an artistic rendition of a coconut. Head tilted, I continued our silent conversation by asking, *May I pose a quick question about the Academy?*

You're at the Academy?

Yes, looking at lesser family genealogies. Your idea to act as if I worked for a school was a good one.

Ask away.

The man who escorted me inside said the Academy was the heart of Magnolia Castle. What does that mean?

It's very loved by any who enter as students, teachers, or families who contain precious artifacts there. Though they try to protect it by not speaking much about it, it still has a fame all its own. The cultural center of the East, I suppose.

If you're wealthy, I thought.

To Priscilla, I asked, *What would happen if I touched one of the artifacts on display?*

I'm not sure, she said slowly. *Bianca . . .what are you thinking?*

With a languid drawl, I returned to the Gallo family crest and stared at the grasses. *Oh . . . I don't know.*

Bianca . . .

They cast their own protective spells over display items, correct?

Don't you dare try to touch any of the items! Rumor has it you'll be pulled into that individual family's prison. They all have one, you know. Of various sizes, of course. You should see—

Cilla, focus.

Don't do it! she said with more desperation. *Aren't you supposed to be careful and quiet?*

The temptation swelled inside me to say, *No one ever solved a problem by being meek, Priscilla,* but it would only make her more concerned. The words, *you'll be pulled into that individual family's prison,* spiraled through my head like a promise.

That might be exactly what I wanted.

I sought the Gallo family, after all . . .

Thank you, Cilla. I'll chat with you later.

Bianca—

With a thought, I closed her out. To Rognvald, I said, *I'm in the Eastern Network working on something. If it goes awry, Leda knows where I am. If you haven't heard from me in three hours, send Brody or Merrick to Leda and she'll explain.*

A heartbeat later, his gruff voice said, *Don't be stupid and don't waste my time in three hours.*

Understood, I said with a smile. After one last glance over my shoulder to guarantee I was alone, I reached my fingers out. They grazed the top of the medallion, which felt icy cold. A jerking sensation tugged my navel and the world spun.

I departed with a crack of sound.

Chapter Eighteen

I expected darkness, but water enveloped me.

The plunge sent me reeling. Several seconds of pure panic passed before I recovered and fought for footing. Sour bog water and a fetid taste raced into my mouth. I suppressed an instinctive gasp, arms flailing. After what felt like an eternity, I clawed my way to air.

My giant breath was followed by utter silence.

Flipping the hair out of my eyes, I batted them open to find a saturated swampland. Cypress trees extended twisting arms overhead, their trunks plunging into mossy water. Clumps of algae spread like islands. I gripped a tree, the furrowed bark rigid. When I tried to connect with it, the way I did with Letum Wood, no voices entered my head. A distant, sleepy awareness stirred, but it didn't speak. More song than sentience.

Deasylva? I asked.

No reply.

Rain thrummed on top of the water. Fat drops caused heavy *plunks* and streamed off branches. It dribbled on top of my head. Algae parted as I swam in a circle, attempting to see through the hazy gloom.

Why here? There was nothing awful about a swamp, except the smell. Certainly, nothing enclosed like the prisons Priscilla told me to expect.

I'm in a swamp, I said to Leda.

Congratulations.

No, I touched an artifact and I wasn't supposed to. It brought me to a swamp.

Screeching, she asked, *THAT was your question? You touched one of the artifacts in the Academy? Are you absolutely senseless, Bianca Monroe?*

Before I could reply, something stirred the water beneath and behind me. A terrible dread swirled in my gut as a low and sonorous growl filled the vacuum of silence.

Uh oh.

Leda, I spoke over her continuing reprimands, *what kind of dangerous animals live in the Eastern Network swamps?*

Terrible ones, she snapped. *And if you touched an artifact, probably deserved ones!*

Whirling around, I sucked in a sharp breath. Looming a full ten paces overhead was a gigantic and terrifying presence. Two teeth jutted out from leathery skin, a light green along a sinewy body that elevated from the water.

A *serpente.*

Flashing, yellow eyes preceded a hiss so sibilant it hurt my eardrums. I ducked at the last second, plunging into the bog just in time. Its heavy tail slapped the water where I once swam. The end of it grazed my arm as it swooped by in a narrow, under-water miss.

I began a transportation spell, but I didn't cast fast enough. The tail slithered around my body and tightened in an instant hold. The serpente—definitely too monstrous to transport—negated my escape attempt. I didn't have the power.

As the monstrous snake tightened around me, bubbles escaped my chest. My lungs burned. It pinned my left arm to the side when I attempted to flail. Ripping my right arm free at the last second, I flung the Volare off my back and into the water. A blur shot out of the case.

Viveet, commanded by a spell, detached from my thigh. She squeaked her way out of my nearly-bound legs and into the water. Her brilliant sapphire flames sped into my waiting hand. When a black tunnel began to form, the tightening snake's tail elevated me above the water. I surfaced, gasping.

A fresh deluge of rain thrummed onto the swamp. The giant beast hissed, a forked tongue flickering up and down. From what little I could see, the thickest part of its body was as wide as I was tall. Hair clogged my sight when I plunged Viveet into the tail. With a grunt, I embedded her to the hilt.

The snake screamed.

I held onto Viveet's handle as the tail loosened, flinging wide. Viveet slid free, like a hot knife through butter. Blood arced in a spray, dribbling to the water. The Volare caught me mid air, rolling me tight and whisking me out of reach of the flailing serpente's head. A ripping sound grazed the top of the Volare as the snake dragged its teeth across the magical tapestry. They didn't penetrate. Viveet smoked gently, pressed to my stomach and chest within the Volare's protective cocoon.

The Volare raced into the swamp, dodging the heady wrath of the serpente monster by its exquisite navigation. Once the ruckus quieted, I commanded the Volare to slow with a thought. It opened, edges uncurling.

Pushing to my elbows, I asked, "Are you all right?" and felt under the carpet.

No torn fibers.

How was that possible? Those giant, gleaming teeth could have ripped me in half at the lightest pressure.

Shaking the mystery off, I shoved the hair out of my eyes. Viveet lay on the carpet, smoldering, and then nothing. The return to her typical metal sword was a relief. If we were in immediate danger, she'd burn with sapphire flames.

For many minutes, we hovered in the same spot, listening to the pouring rain. I didn't understand my hesitation to leave, but obeyed the instinct that said something awaited. The Gallo family pulled me into that serpente nest. Surely, they wouldn't be far away. Was the snake their family pet? A different kind of heirloom?

The serpente didn't intend to kill me or it wouldn't have pulled me to air. Deliver me to the Gallo family, more likely. If the rumors Priscilla mentioned had roots in reality, as rumors often did, then the Gallo family might live somewhere near here. No one would have a guardian snake like that and not keep it close.

I stood as the Volare became rigid underfoot. Viveet in hand, but flames quenched, we slid between trees, moving sedately under the soaked cypress branches and curtains of moss. In the swampy forest protection, I breathed easier. Notes of Deasylva rang here. Hums, buried in roots and water, that sang a different melody. A primitive, ethereal place, with moss as bright as flowers, and weeping branches sinking into earth.

A flicker of light whipped my attention to the left.

The Volare stopped.

Elevating higher into the branches, we wound through a tree until we hovered near the edge. Shadows hid us from view. It would have been easier to crawl off the Volare and navigate bare foot, but the cypress trees might give my location away. In Letum Wood, the branches covered my tracks. I could run and not jostle a leaf. Leap and find a vine that hadn't been there before.

Here, I'd have no such support.

So I waited.

Below, glimmers of candlelight illuminated a gloomy house cloaked in fog. Cobwebs and dim boards reminded me of the dark paneling in the Academy's lesser families room. Dismal and unappealing and utterly coated in magic.

Was the pulsing power a concealing spell? Like the Academy, it probably lay behind deceptive exteriors meant to warn witches away. Based on their minimal and lackluster display alone, the Gallo family weren't like the others.

I lowered my hand and the Volare obeyed the silent command to drop several paces. Movement drew my gaze to two witches crossing a marshy field. They waded through the weeds and toward the house. If my sense of direction was correct, they strode away from the swamp. This higher vantage provided visibility over the swamplands, which cut a half circle around the house itself, like a giant scythe.

Had they seen me fighting the serpente?

Undoubtedly.

Throwing caution to the wind, I cast an ancient invisibility spell that Grandfather had given me from his extensive collection. With it, I'd been able to sneak into the Gatehouse, through the Great Library of Burke, and around Scarlett's office without detection.

The moment I cast it, a witch's head popped up.

He stared right at me.

Heart in my throat, I quickly cast a different spell. One of the men raised an arm, pointing to the branch where I hid. Retracting the Volare, I ducked. A powerful curse slammed into the tree behind me, splintering the closest branch. If I'd been standing there, I'd be halfway to the swamp again.

A hastily-drawn shield shattered under a rapid-fire curse powerful enough to send the Volare reeling backward. Clutching the rug, I removed my invisibility spell and banked around a tree. With a response like that, they detected active magic.

I wanted that spell.

Voices shouted, congregating lower. Three other witches

appeared from transportation spells, elevating above the marsh with levitation. A flash below made one of them visible.

Two.

Ten.

Jikes, how fast could they congregate?

Grabbing the edge of the Volare in one hand, I whipped around, closed myself in the tube, and transported away before their third attempt at a curse landed.

<h1 style="text-align:center">Chapter Nineteen</h1>

Leda patted the back of her hair, inspecting it in a long, oval mirror littered with tiny candles that illuminated the edges in a lovely way. Her eyes, brightened by the close light, shone in her reflection. Loops of her fine, snowy hair tucked into an elegant bun, simple as the emerald dress covering her torso. Her bare shoulders gave her a timeless look.

"Yet again, you're lucky to be alive."

"Was it luck?" I countered, irritated that she assigned everything to chance. "Or was there some level of skill involved?"

Nonplussed, she stated, "You tell me," in a tone that couldn't have cared less. Realizing I fought a losing battle, I shoved away from the wall and rubbed a hand over my eyes.

"Those witches were fast, Leda. Too fast. Suspiciously fast."

"Sounds like it."

"Not just fast but . . . ready. Trained. Almost like . . ."

"Guardians?"

"More like a militia."

Eyebrow high, she asked, "Did you see any interior details?"

"Not really."

"Just witches?"

"Besides the serpente, you mean?"

She glared.

Nodding, I cricked my neck to the side until it popped. "Yes, just witches. There wasn't much to see outside, really. They masked the house. Presumably, the Gallo family mansion."

"Could you transport to that spot again?"

"Yes."

"They're detecting spells, so that might not be wise."

"There's always the Academy."

She rolled her eyes. "Yes, there's always that. And the gargantuan snake whom, I'd like to add, you pulled to your side by splashing around. If you're going to swim with snakes, don't move."

"Thanks. I'll tuck that away for next time."

"For what it's worth, I think Greyson's approach is extraordinary, taken from a villainous and fiendish slant. He led you to the Academy, which eventually led you to the Gallo family house, which you sought."

"It makes me think Ricardo Gallo is behind Carcere and the rebellion. Why the militia? Why hide the family mansion? Why the serpente?"

"With what proof?"

"None," I mumbled. "Except his medallion in Carcere, which could have been from anybody."

Leda turned to face me. Instead of a moderately full skirt with a benign and somewhat vague print, her green gown highlighted her pale features. Leda's pay raise not only covered the currency she sent to support her siblings attending a Network school, but her own new wardrobe as well.

"You look very nice, Leda."

"Thank you."

"You are also supporting our mortal enemy by saying that Greyson is a wise villain."

She rolled her eyes. "Greyson is hardly *our* mortal enemy. Yours, perhaps. Certainly Camila's," she added. "If you consider this from his angle, he's proceeding exactly how I would expect. He won't give real information until you guarantee what he wants. The longer he strings you out, the more benefits he receives."

"Like delicious food?"

"And a bloody book," she muttered. "What else will you take him. Pillows?"

Thoughtful, I said, "Not a bad idea."

Leda ignored me.

A window at my left side overlooked the lower floors of the Western Network Arck Castle. I stared through the open windows into the heart of the desert. Custos, the capital city of the West, utterly lacked rain, so shield spells thrummed over windows and protected the interior from projectiles.

On my left, the subtle swish of a moving skirt and muttered curses came from beneath a door. Within the adjoining room, Scarlett prepared for an intimate Network-sanctioned dinner with the Western Network High Priestess, Lana, and both Ambassadors. Lana, who still had no High Priest and no plans to appoint one, invited Scarlett for a *friendly discussion that isn't focused on politics.*

I had my doubts. Though I liked Lana, she always had an angle. Regina, who had a long-standing and distant sort of friendship with the Western Network High Priestess, warned me about her years ago. *Lana is smart, almost a sister to me. Her motivation to win trumps all else in her life. Although she's social, there's always an angle.* I kept an eye on it.

"Greyson understands that I'm not going to give him perks without a real exchange," I countered, stepping away from the window.

Leda hummed. "Maybe."

"I believe him," I added. "And I believe there's a binding that prevents him from speaking about Ricardo Gallo, which explains why he spoke in such a coded way."

As lightly as before, she said, "Maybe," and I scowled. Couldn't she agree with anything I said?

Her gaze narrowed. "Are you wearing that?" Her openly judgmental tone gave little surprise. I suppressed the urge to study my simple linen dress that, unlike her own, breathed easily in the sultry heat.

"Yes."

Her prim lips pressed. "Of course you are," she muttered.

"Will you be providing security?"

"No."

"Outside, checking for problems?"

"No," she said as quickly. "Neither will you. The West Guards are in charge of security for this event. You're to stay inside with Scarlett, as we've already discussed."

"It's still bloody hot in here."

The door opened. Leda and I whirled around to face Scarlett, who emerged in a subdued, dusky red dress. It matched the rock Arck walls in a brilliant way, as if she meant to be one with the desert. A self conscious hand smoothed the front of the dress, which cascaded in ruffles past her waist.

"Well?" she asked.

"You're lovely, as always Scarlett," I said.

Her rueful glance was one shade shy of an eye roll. Nodding once, she said, "Thank you. Leda, are you ready?"

"I am."

Scarlett held up a hand. "No notes tonight. This is meant to be a . . . semi informal affair with Lana."

"I understand."

"Do I have to command you to have a good time?"

If she wanted you to have a good time, I said through the communication magic, *she would have soundproofed your room and given you a book to read.*

"No, Your Highness," Leda countered, sending me a murderous glare when Scarlett turned to study her already smooth hair in the mirror.

I winked.

The door creaked open, revealing a rather handsome but unexpected sight. Dressed in a crisp white shirt and a black vest, new pants, and shiny shoes, Baxter entered the room with his usual debonair style.

"Baxter," I said with surprise. "What are you doing here?"

He smiled at Scarlett and extended a bent arm. "I'm here to escort you to dinner with the rest of the guests, Your Highness. Lana has invited me to join the gathering. If you don't mind?"

Scarlett accepted his arm with a smile.

"Lead the way, Baxter. I'm grateful for your company."

* * *

An hour into the drollest and driest dinner conversation I had ever experienced, I resisted the urge to stab my eye out with a fork.

Leda, eyes alight with curiosity and enthrallment as she spoke directly to Lana and her male Assistant, had never been more in her element. She perched at the edge of her seat next to Scarlett, who wore a relaxed smile.

Despite my own disparagement of the dull proceedings, Scarlett was enjoying herself. That made the routine security worth it. Whatever the Sisterhood became in the future, boring trivialities were *not* on my priority list. Though I supposed I couldn't love every single minute of my work.

Or could I?

Did Papa suffer through hours like this?

The conundrum occupied too many minutes while I invisibly lapped the room a fifteenth time and waited for something interesting to happen. No *wonder* Guardians normally provided security patrols.

Another hour later, when a fluffy, coconut-based dessert settled in front of the participants, Baxter sidled up next to me. Though I was invisible so I didn't annoy them with my pacing, I had a feeling he'd been tracking me around the room. By smell, probably.

Demigods did everything better.

If the rebels in the Eastern Network were smart, they'd attempt to pull demigods onto their side. Of course, most witches continued to act as if the Battle for Letum Wood and short-lived war of the gods didn't happen. Unless one lived in the Southern Network, where demigods were more common, but still not *common*, most witches acted oblivious. At most, a demigod would be a more powerful fighter. With Gelas, god of ice, keeping a strict hold on all raw magic, the demigods couldn't magically aid the rebellion.

Baxter leaned against the wall, enjoying the cool breeze with a wine glass in his hand. He pressed his shoulder to the wall. His lips barely moved when he peered outside and asked, "Are you bored out of your mind?"

Irritated that I'd given myself away—I was the fool that stood in front of the cross breeze—I said, "Yes."

"Are you the one who upset the House of Gallo yesterday?"

I tensed.

He smiled.

"Define *upset*."

Though I'd kept an eye out, none of the newsbooks mentioned the Gallo family or a serpente or even the Academy. For all the warnings the male Academy instructor had given, relatively little came of my touching the artifact.

Well.

Giant serpente aside.

"Oh," Baxter sang, swirling his wine, "when one walks in the right circles, one hears things others might not expect. Subterranean things. Questions may have arisen about a witch sneaking through the Academy and onto a lesser family estate."

"How intriguing."

"Very. The question came from a female witch named Maria Donnatello. You might recognize her maiden surname: Gallo."

My blood prickled. Well, I'd certainly made enough of a scene to stir up suspicion. I had no fear they might have recognized me. The rain, distance, and darkness made it impossible for me to identify them, too, but any gentle uproar was informative.

"Maria approached you?"

"Yes."

"What did you say?"

"The truth. I hadn't heard anything. This pleased her."

Startled, I blinked. "Did she suspect demigod involvement?"

He made an affirmative noise in his throat.

Lana stumbled to her feet, half drunk. Giggling, she called, "Baxter! We're going into the other room. I've hired a comedian to tell us stories for the next hour, and I know you'll enjoy him. He's ribald, and I love him."

Baxter shoved away from the wall. "I am doing a little reconnaissance myself and will let you know."

"Thank you. I'll inform Camila."

"Wise."

While the congregants shuffled toward a doorway into an adjoining sitting room, Baxter joined them. I tailed at the back, counting the minutes to departure.

* * *

Yawning amidst early morning sunshine, I half-listened to a discussion between Rognvald and Brody and Merrick through the communication magic. They spoke to increasing rebel factions in marshes far south of Necce, where chaos multiplied.

As I slipped through Magnolia Castle to find Camila, I didn't trust the silence.

Burgeoning light illuminated the roaring sea, casting rippled shadows over the distant seascape. The sun rose in the far horizon, casting a shimmering rainbow. I turned from the churning white caps, grateful the days-long storm had finally passed. When I saw the sea, I thought of Prana.

Twenty minutes of calm observation assured me that I hadn't been followed, so I rapped on the High Priestess' personal chamber door with a very defined tap. Three quick raps with my knuckles, and then two taps with a finger. I repeated it once.

The door opened.

I slid inside.

Almost as soon as I entered, it closed behind me. Camila peered at me, eyes wide, until I allowed the transformative magic to bleed away. My transformed skin, frizzy hair, and bay-colored eyes bled into my usual gray gaze and wavy locks.

Camila sighed.

"It's good to see you."

She wore a fluffy white robe and slippers. When she sat, a relaxed breath rippled through her in a slow wave. I lowered on a seat across from her, enjoying the cool whisper of air from her open doors. A balcony overlooked the sea, which lay in a blanket of darkness. Buckets littered the floor at strange internals, half filled with water. Wet seams cracked above, spider webbing through the ceiling.

Seeing my gaze, Camila cast a spell. The cracks vanished. "Do you have an update?" she asked, tucking her robe more tightly around her waist.

"A rather interesting one."

With eagerness, she swept a hand in front of her. "Please, tell me all that you have to say."

My recitation of events at the Academy, Gallo house, and Baxter's information required only a few minutes. Camila took it in with little more than a blink and a stormy stare. Her fingers tapped on her pursed lips.

"Yes," she murmured, "there is a very discreet noise amongst the Gallo family, but nothing concerning."

"Have you been to Gallo house?"

"No."

"Do you know anyone who has?"

"No."

"Doesn't that seem odd?"

Her fingers dropped to her arms, drumming there instead. "When you say it that way, yes. It does seem odd. They live by Portafina."

I shrugged. "I'm not sure where that is in relation to where I went. Isn't sociality an important part of being one of the famed Eastern Network families?"

"Mmm, yes. For the greater families."

"Not the lesser?"

She clicked her tongue in thought. "Expectations are different. The Gallo family is quiet. They show up when obligation requires it. They do their work, they report their taxes, they marry their daughters to advantageous sons, and their sons to advantageous daughters, and they adore their marshes. There's not much else to say."

They adore their marshes.

It felt revealing.

"Do you think Ricardo Gallo is capable of facilitating this rebellion?"

She sighed. "Anymore? I don't know. Perhaps. More likely, it's one of his sons."

"Would you like me to keep looking?"

"Yes, please. If you don't mind?"

"I look forward to it."

More ruefully, she added, "You have done well, Miss Bianca. I am jealous that the Eastern Network doesn't also have a Sisterhood."

"Let's start with putting a High Priestess into power, first."

Her eyes sparkled when she laughed. "Yes, that is a wonderful starting point."

In her amusement, I saw Niko. He had been easy going and charming for most of our acquaintance. Things hadn't always been perfect, but he died with my respect.

"Before I leave, I have a question about Magnolia Castle," I said. "Do you know what year it was built? How old is it?"

Camila opened her mouth to speak, then paused when a distant, percussive thumping issued from down the hall. The rhythmic noise set my instincts on edge. I whirled around, invisibility incantation at the tip of my tongue, but stalled when she put a hand on my arm.

"Don't leave." She tightened the sash around her waist and murmured a calm, "This is fine. It's Cristian."

"Doing what?"

"Relieving stress. Make yourself invisible and follow me. This is something you should see." Quietly, she added, "As heartbreaking as it is."

Camila headed for the door again. My protective incantation dissolved as she pulled the door open. The magnifying sounds rippled down the corridor. Without the door as a barrier, the distinct sounds of shouting grew louder. Camila, unbothered by plunging toward a problem, moved like liquid. No fear claimed her eyes, only a steely and maternal determination that I recognized from Priscilla.

The face of a woman that understood no one else would clean up this mess.

I trailed close, hand on Viveet's hilt, understanding that whatever Camila wanted me to see, this was not my fight.

* * *

We entered an odd scene.

Two Guardians stood near a doorway, at attention. Their High Priest gripped a chair leg in one arm and half a broken vase in the other. I recognized Cristian first by his height, then his fierce scowl. His panting, erratic movements made it difficult to discern him otherwise. Breathing hard, he set the vase on a table, gripped the chair leg in both hands, and swung.

The vase shattered.

A spray of glass skittered across the black tile floor, interrupted by white tiles forming repetitive magnolia flowers that glowed crimson in the torchlight.

"Leave us," Camila commanded. The Guardians leaped to obey. As Camila approached, the broken glass shards swirled into a sparkling funnel and reformed into the original vase. With a grunt, Cristian swung again. It shattered. Reformed.

He did it again.

Again.

Again.

Camila closed the distance between them without fear. Despite his sweaty, heaving chest, his shirt buttons done apart at the top, and his eyes which flickered with wild rage, she didn't hesitate. She plucked the chair leg from his steadfast grip. It soared across the hallway, landed on an upturned chair, and reattached. The chair stood, slid across the floor, and returned to its previous position near a partially open door.

Cristian doubled over. "Mere . . . leave me . . . alone."

"No."

"Please."

"No."

She folded her arms across her chest and affected a stubborn stare. Her elevated dark brows sent a clear message.

She wasn't leaving.

I waited near the seam of two hallways, ten paces away. If Camila needed help, I could cross to her in three leaps.

"What's wrong, Cristian?" Concern filled her voice, beneath the firm tones of a mother who wasn't going to take abuse. To my greatest surprise, she spoke in the common language instead of Ilese.

Cristian turned away, jaw taut.

"The rebels have overtaken the Sartucci province, aided by Council Member Giuseppi."

She gasped. "No!"

His reply in the common language also surprised me. "The High Witch and populace are threatening to no longer recognize the Aldana family name on the throne, nor any laws I enforce. The Giuseppi province followed shortly after. Both are in open rebellion together."

She paused, soaking that horrible news in.

To Rognvald, I said, *You know about the rebellion in the Eastern Network Giuseppi and Sartucci provinces?*

A pause, then, *Now I do.*

It's ugly.

I'll inform Merrick and Brody. Thanks.

"This sets a precedent, Mere," he muttered, wiping the sweat off his forehead with an arm swipe. Blood trailed his skin, but he didn't notice. "If they can resist our Guardian attack, other provinces will do the same. Probably by morning. This could be the beginning of the end."

"It won't be."

"It could be."

"Every moment of every day *could* be the end, but it isn't. We have the ability to do something now, so we will. So what will you do?"

Her ability to give him the decision power when she must be itching to take over amazed me. Cristian's fingers trembled as he shoved a sweaty hand through his hair. One knuckle bled in a slash of crimson. He leaned on a side table.

"I don't know."

"Cristian, I will say it again: let go of the Council. They are the problem! If we had new representatives, we could more easily host discussions with the unhappy witches, determine ways to improve their lives and—"

He sliced a hand through the air.

"It's not that simple, Mere."

Camila set her hands on her hips. "You may be the Highest Witch, but you are still my son. I didn't raise you to cut off a woman while she is speaking!"

Cristian ran his tongue over his teeth. His upper lip twitched when he patiently lifted a hand in front of him.

"I apologize. Please proceed."

"At least get rid of Giuseppi and Nicoli! You know they want the Aldana dynasty to be over as much as you want it to continue. It's no surprise to me that his witches have rebelled so thoroughly first. He's a monster!"

"Do I?" he asked so quietly I might have imagined it. "Do I want our dynasty to continue, Mere?"

She reared back.

"What?"

He straightened, acting as if he hadn't said it. "To remove them from the Council is not the problem. Stoking the rebellion to greatest fervor after we did *is* the problem. We have three loyal Council Members and a low Guardian force. It's not a guarantee we can win."

Cristian said something in Ilese that I couldn't follow. The blur of his words was so great that several seconds passed before I heard his suspicion. Camila's reply, also in Ilese, held sorrow. Tears glazed her eyes

Priscilla? I asked.

Yes?

What does ventata mean in Ilese?
Frightened.
And paninica?
Paranoid. Where are you?
I'll explain later.

Priscilla fell quiet when I pressed my back to the wall and waited. Camila and Cristian continued a far more sedate discussion in the corridor. Was anyone else here? Protective incantations colored the air.

Understanding their words was wasted effort. Cristian spoke rapid-fire Ilese and Camila responded in kind. I had no hope of comprehending more than snatches.

Ten minutes later, Cristian was restored to his usual docile confidence. Camila rounded the corner, her expression serene as she smiled at the Guardians and returned to her room. I closed her door, locked it, sealed it with spells, and removed my incantation. Camila stared at the ocean, one hand on top of a chair.

"What do you do when there is no book written on how to guide witches?" she asked.

Her haunted tone sent a shiver through me. Was this the price of a mother's love? Camila had to watch him endure a harrowing responsibility and let him experience it. The terror of this situation struck me as incalculably sad.

How to reconcile a High Priest who wanted the best for his kingdom with a handful of others that made it impossible to execute?

"The situation is . . . " She shook her head, breathing hard. ". . . bleak."

At first, I repressed the urge to comfort her. Too bold of a move to touch the High Priestess. Befriending the Eastern Network High Priestess last time led to terrible ends. Yet, I couldn't help myself. I put a hand on her arm.

"You're not alone, Your Majesty."

My words held no promise. Hardly more than a statement

of fact that probably wouldn't provide comfort. Based on the welling in her eyes, it was enough.

"For the next several days, things here will be tentative. Cristian is going to mount an offense of some kind, and reach out to the other Council Members to stop this . . . death cascade. They must find ways to speak directly to all witches—including the marsh witches.

"In the meantime, please do what you can to find out more about the Gallo family without my interference, for things are more tentative than before. I will do the same. Wait for my word," she whispered, husky, but brave. "We shall be in touch. Thank you, Bianca."

She gave me a wan smile and a hand squeeze, and bade me leave with a nod to the door. Five minutes later, I stood on the outskirts of Necce. Wind flapped my skirt from where I stood on top of a building. It perched at the apex of a rising hill that allowed an expansive view of the horizon and Magnolia Castle. The flickering lights illuminated white walls, sprawling suites, and drawing beauty.

And yet . . .

Something was missing. The hallowed walls were lackluster. The energy . . . waning. I couldn't put my finger on it, beyond the dimness that came with closing summer days and cooler winter nights.

Leda's voice shook me out of my stupor. *Do I need to call for Merrick, or have you managed to survive?*

I made it out. I'm on my way to Letum Wood.

Shall I expect you?

Not tonight.

Then I'll see you tomorrow morning. As a reminder, Council Member Frederick expects you for lunch in two days. After a pause, she added, *Glad you're all right.*

Chapter Twenty

errick's burly arms clamped around my waist, securing me at the top of a disarming mountain scene. He brought me to the rocky heights of an incline where snow and barren rock fields and raw blue sky abounded. Winds tossed his hair with careless abandon, unraveling his braid. The shivering morning air cut through all my layers. I needed a coat.

"I don't have long," he said in warning. "Brody will be returning to the Central Network soon, and I need to head to the East. But I wanted to show you this first."

"What is this place?" I asked.

"Somewhere very special."

Merrick kept a hold of me, and I realized why. A pace away, a sheer cliff face plummeted into a distant ravine. I thought of Papa. The skinny trail where we stood wound to the edge of a mountaintop, spiraling higher through loose shale and smoky rock. The chilly air curled through my bones when I spun in his arms. "Where is this?"

He splayed his hand against my back. "The bowyer's cottage."

"Bowyer's cottage?"

"An old friend of my family. I wanted you to see it. Technically, it's my cottage now, according to a law we call *bequeathment*. The old bowyer bequeathed it to me before he died. I still have the paper with his signature."

"Oh?"

His smile widened. "Ours, I should say."

"Not officially."

"It is for me."

I smiled. "You have your wild, I have mine."

Merrick pressed a quick kiss to my lips in agreement. Turning, his hand sprinted down the inside of my arm and stopped at the palm, entangling our fingers.

"Come, little troublemaker. I want to show it to you."

His powerful legs led us toward craggy heights. With each step, a stout shack came into better view, half stone, half wooden boards. Windows sparkled in the errant sunshine, occasionally masked by trailing clouds. Winter already descended at these daunting heights. Its initial approach had only just begun in the Central Network.

"I haven't been here in awhile," Merrick admitted as the trail petered into pebbles. A rocky floor ballooned instead, thick with dried moss and scraggly undergrowth clinging to life.

"When did you last come?"

"A couple of years ago. My father brought me to first meet the bowyer as a young lad. I learned how to use a bow and arrow here. The bowyer taught me how to take care of them, keep the bow taut, make the arrows, that sort of thing. He corrected my breathing so I had better aim. You know." He gifted me with a wry smile. "Little kid impatience, and all that."

"You would come this far?"

"Definitely. Father really admired the bowyer. Looked up to him as a friend. He was almost like a father figure to him. When my father died, the bowyer came down the mountain to speak with me, which was unheard of. The bowyer lived up here all the time. Few ever saw him leave."

The cliff evened into an ascending plateau that led to the cottage. We cut across the windy slope and to the house. Rocks skittered away from my boots as I trod over them, past the loose dirt, and to the door. A strip of leather tied the entry shut. Animal hides covered windows. The place had the air of being abandoned. Merrick studied the ramshackle amalgam of stones and wooden boards while memories replayed in his eyes.

With a shake of his head, he pulled out of it.

"No one has lived here in years, and few witches stay this high on the mountain. He craved isolation," Merrick added as a thoughtful aside.

The idea of living at the top of the earth with unfettered stone and sky as the only companion made my blood race. Heady. Intoxicating. Also, lonely. Being so far from trees made my stomach queasy, though these stone bulwarks compelled me in a different way.

Still holding my hand, Merrick reached up with his other one to undo the leather cord. With a kick from his boot, the door gave way.

For being abandoned, the cottage had a tidy feel. A few cracked window panes whistled lightly after the wind slammed into them, and light spilled into the space. A spell untacked the animal hides and rolled them up, anchoring them. Flat light illuminated a square room.

A table stood in the middle with chairs stacked around it. Empty cupboards, nailed to the far wall, occupied the space between windows. Dusty books lay on their sides, falling on top of each other like wooden toys. Mice had eaten through a wicker broom propped against the wall, knocking it to the floor. Near the fireplace stood a bed with the rope underbelly exposed. No mattress.

Merrick released me and stopped in the middle of the room. "There's nothing here."

"Only memories."

I rubbed my hand along the grimy table and wandered to the stone fireplace. A cast iron tea kettle rusted on a long arm, and an abandoned fire poker propped against the stones. Merrick strode to the fallen books and thumbed through their well-loved, delicate pages.

"Books on arrows," he said. He transported one away. "They're old, but the information is sound."

Lost in thoughts about bowyers and lost lives and time, I didn't realize that a stretch of silence had filled the room. Merrick stood in the doorway, staring out. I came up behind him and pressed my cheek to his shoulder.

"This is definitely *not* our winter home."

Chuckling, he wrapped an arm around my shoulders and tucked me into his side.

"Why did you want to come here, Merrick?"

"I wanted to see what you thought of it."

"Are you sure you're not escaping handfasting plans?" I drawled with a teasing smile.

He didn't retort with the anticipated wry quip, but ran his hand along the sensitive skin inside my arm and grasped my wrist. His thumb and fingers circled it. He pressed a gentle kiss to my forehead, gripped my shoulders, and said, "I spoke to Mother yesterday, but they're still fast at work planning dinners. They want a date."

I sighed. "Yes. We should probably give them one. It's just . . . with things so unstable in the East, and both of us involved . . ."

"Agreed. Also, there are a lot of things that my sister and my mother want. It's a daunting task, looking at their list. Listen, B. I brought you here because I wanted to give this cottage to you instead of a cord of engagement. I want it to belong to both of us."

His forehead tilted to mine.

Ah.

This *wasn't* an idle visit.

"You want to live here," I whispered.

He didn't immediately contradict me. My statement rolled for several minutes before he nodded.

"I do."

My surprise was not great. I could immediately understand why he felt that way. The rustic, remote energy. The distance from the world. The sheer force of memories, tying him to his long-lost father and the bowyer. Potential oozed from it, especially if we had the chance to sink time into repairs.

The bowyer's house was Merrick's escape.

"Not to live permanently," he said, voicing my next thought. "But as a place to go that is ours. Not yours. Not mine. Ours. We both have to live in the Central Network for the Brotherhood, obviously. This would be our . . ."

"Escape."

He smiled, then grimaced. "Do you hate it?"

"I love it."

Surprise registered in his eyes. They softened into a hopeful smile that reminded me of a little boy.

"Really?"

"It reminds me of you, and I love it. Do you have to do something to officially make it yours? Besides the bequeathment, I mean."

He shrugged. "I doubt it. The bowyer has been forgotten. No one comes here anymore. The house is in good shape, but it needs work before it's winter ready. After we handfast, I can put our names on it in the Coven registry. We'd have physical claim instead of bequeathment . . ."

He trailed away.

I reached for his hand with a brilliant smile. "I'd rather this over a cord of engagement any day. How can I help make it ready for us? Put me to work! I have an appointment with Council Member Frederick soon, and I'd really rather not think about it."

* * *

A male witch with a ruffled cream shirt, a vest littered with white stains across the left breast pocket, and pants a thumbs-width too short sat across from me. He moved quick as a feline.

Council Member Frederick.

Two crocks of jam and three of butter followed him in a hovering trail, like dancing food. A coy smile stretched from ear to ear as he lowered to the chair, his plate of food and silverware rattling as he set them down.

"Miss Monroe."

"Council Member Frederick."

A heap of dinner rolls—five, to be exact—stood in a tower on his plate. Nothing more. Despite mouthwatering ham and baked potatoes, he gathered bread, jam, and butter that arranged itself in a fan around the upper edges. I stabbed a square of brown sugar cured ham and smiled.

"Thank you for this conversation, Council Member. I—"

He fluttered his hand. "Yes, yes. We'll get to that in a minute." Folding both of his arms on the tabletop, he leaned forward. The smell of yeast and sugared strawberries drifted closer. "Tell me: how good are you with invisibility spells?"

After a sip of cool water, I said, "I'm good. Why?"

"Which incantation do you use?"

"I'd rather not say."

"Muran magic?"

"That's one of them."

"Everyone knows Muran," he said crisply, an eyebrow arched

as if I'd offended him with my choice. "Everyone knows that invisibility spell. Don't you think that's a poor choice for the Head of the Sisters?"

"Sister*hood.*"

"Sure."

He stared hard, and I realized he expected me to defend myself or confess my other invisibility spells.

"Why do you ask, Council Member?" I held his intent gaze until he finally cracked.

His entire body loosened like jelly. "There's this neighbor that lives next door to my house."

Dread filled me from the bottom up.

Oh, no.

"And she is a *raving lunatic*, Miss Monroe." He held both hands to his eyes, covering them. "I can't get her to leave us alone. She's always throwing tomatoes over the fence or plucking up my wife's rose bushes, claiming they're spying on her. Have you ever lived near someone that constantly throws rotten tubers?"

"I haven't."

"I need someone to go to her house and figure out if she's stolen the key to our gate. She must have! We cannot figure out how she gets into the yard if not with a key."

What have you done to me? I asked Leda.

If laughter had a voice in this magic, she might have been cackling.

During my brief, disbelieving inattention, he'd rearranged his rolls into a strategic map previewing his yard and the problems within. I ran my tongue over my teeth when he used a spoon to projectile a bit of strawberry over one roll. As I considered the array, and drew in a slow, deep breath through my nose, I wondered if this was real.

Or a test.

"Let me clarify something, Council Member. You want me

to use an invisibility spell to sneak into your old neighbor's house and see if she has your gate key?"

He tossed both hands skyward.

"Yes! It's not so hard." He paused, head tilted and eyes tapered. "Why? Do you think this is beyond your ability? Just how good *are* you, Miss Monroe? Better than a scheming old neighbor?"

Ah. There sat the angle. While I couldn't be certain, this reeked of Council Member Frederick testing me. If I agreed, there would probably be some kind of ambush on the other side.

"Why don't you just spell the gate shut?"

"We've tried!" he cried. "She still gets around it. Every single spell we cast, she's countered. She knows, Miss Monroe." His voice lowered. "She *knows everything.*"

His reddened, bloodshot eyes altered my belief that this was a joke. I had no idea what to say to his rampant desperation.

"Forgive me, Council Member. This is not something within the purview of the Sisterhood."

He straightened so fast his chair skidded backward.

"What?"

"I will not help you break into your neighbor's house," I repeated carefully, modulating my inflection to remove what incredulousness I could. "Forgive me. I hope you can resolve it in other ways."

Council Member Frederick stared at me with a bold surprise that I couldn't hope to interpret. "Miss Monroe, I was not expecting you to refuse me."

"No?"

"The precarious position of the Sisterhood surely requires any work you can find. Does it not? Are you not seeking to prove yourself?"

"I'm not seeking to prove myself."

He reared away with another overly stunned reaction. His

palms slapped the table top. "You *are*, Miss Monroe. That is the purpose of this meeting."

"No, Council Member."

A moment of hesitation almost stole my gusto. Was he right? If this wasn't a chance to prove myself, what was it?

Before too much time had passed, I swallowed and said, "This meeting was to get to know you and your Covens. I'm not seeking to prove myself. I have proven myself time and again. Daily, I work with the Protectors. I have weathered Mabel, Almorran magic, the land of the gods, losing my magic, regaining it, fighting demigods and gods in Letum Wood, and coming out victorious. I have nothing left to prove, Council Member."

He spread his hands. "Then why?"

Smiling, I said, "I am a witch of great value. A witch that can show up, be what the High Priestess needs when the High Priestess needs it, and create safety for our Network. In order to do that, I'm asking the Council to formally acknowledge my value with a payment structure that ensures fair compensation for my work."

There.

Phew.

Words semi-political and maybe-not-that-bad came from this, and without Leda's coaching. The conversation reeked of something that almost made my nose wrinkle, but I kept my composure by threads.

His tense, gaping mouth calmed.

"Oh."

With a spell, I summoned a book that Leda gave me as a housewarming present. *How to Deal With Pests of the Witchy Variety*. Thanks to the forest, I no longer required it.

"This might help your situation with your neighbor. I sincerely hope it does."

I stood. Council Member Frederick lowered his hands onto his lap as he watched.

"You might be upset that I won't act as a personal squad for you, Council Member. If so, that's too bad. There's so much potential in the Sisterhood for good, and I know I'm the best witch to lead it. When it comes time for you to support or reject the Sisterhood, I hope you do so out of a fair sense of whether or not the Sisterhood can make Alkarra a better place."

Chapter Twenty-One

amila sent information about Ricardo Gallo to Priscilla last night, Leda said. *I was knitting with Priscilla at the time, so she passed it on to me. It's in Scarlett's office, if you want to stop by.*

Leda's announcement came as I slurped the last of my coffee the next morning. I set the mug into my wash bucket, pressed a kiss to Merrick's sleepy lips as he stumbled into his half-armor in preparation for more Eastern Network sleuthing.

I'll be right there.

Chatham Castle bustled with low energy as I navigated away from the main staircase and over to Scarlett's office. Assistants, Underassistants, and Council Members swept in and out of sight, occupying meeting rooms and hallway corners. When I arrived at Scarlett's office, Hiddleston perched behind a desk outside.

Seeing me, he nodded.

"Morning, Hiddleston."

"Her Highness is in a meeting elsewhere, but Leda is waiting for you inside."

He lifted one eyebrow in silent warning. Leda could be a

hard potion to swallow this early. I saluted and breezed by without stopping.

Leda muttered to herself from behind Scarlett's desk as she gathered piles of parchment, shuffled through scrolls, and simultaneously batted off incoming messages that fluttered around her head.

When it came to politics, every message tended to be marked URGENT. Leda's learned indifference toward presumed emergencies was impressive. *True emergencies rarely manifest in a letter,* she'd once said. *Witches in dire need always show up in person.*

"Merry meet, Leda."

Under her breath, she counted papers as she turned them this way and that, stacking them horizontally and vertically. By the time she finished, half of the mess on Scarlett's desk had vanished. Her hand twirled once over the top. The clutter righted itself and left a gleaming desk in its wake.

Leda set the stack of papers in the exact middle.

"Camila sent this."

She extracted a scroll from her pocket. I broke the emerald wax seal by sliding my finger under the page and unfurling it with a wrist flick. Within the rolled page lay another, smaller scroll. The yellowing paper curled into itself, only as long as my hand.

Leda continued to tidy the desk as I skimmed the page.

To my friend,

Our mutual acquaintance has not returned to his position since the breaking, which I know you are aware of. This I can confirm.

My caretaker has been my ears within this place. He says that the lower members of which we've spoken have not reported any suspicious activity. Nor has the place of education.

I paused. *Mutual acquaintance* would be Council Member Giuseppi, while *caretaker* likely meant her trustworthy Guardian, Ronaldo. The *lower members of which we've spoken* were the Gallo family, and the place of education the Academy.

How interesting.

Leda glanced at me before I continued on.

Considering your final question about my place of residence before departure, I have included a smaller scroll you might find interesting. This is all that remains, and had to be carefully extracted at my request and by my caretaker.

No signature accompanied it.

Stymied, I flipped open the thin parchment. My eyes paused on the very first line, which perched atop several others, all of them smaller, in a descending pattern that looked like an inverted triangle.

The True and Honest History of Magnolia Castle
as told by Allegra Rossi, who, at one
time, was a very trusted witch;
This is before her great
and tragic
downfall

Studying the back of the paper, which lay empty, I read it again. Leda, growing impatient, asked, "Well?"

I thrust them both at her. "Tell me what you think?"

Leda's lips bunched to one side after perusing. "I think it's cryptic and confusing to me, but probably makes sense to you.

The second paper? Looks like the ripped out front page to a history book."

"Yes," I murmured, running my fingers over it. Before Cristian had caught our attention smashing a vase into oblivion over and over again, I'd asked Camila about the year Magnolia Castle was built. I'd forgotten. Impressive that she remembered.

Leda picked up the stack of papers, propped them in the crook of her arm, and swayed toward the door. Over her shoulder, she called, "The Great Library of Burke might have a copy of that book, if you're looking. Since it originates in the Eastern Network and appears very old, though, it may not," and rushed into the hallway as a final dismissal.

"No." My eyes narrowed in study. "But I think someone else does."

* * *

Grandfather didn't own many books—not after clearing out his extensive collection—but the ones he owned meant something.

I had a hunch.

I loved hunches.

Reeves answered my persistent knock on the High Priest's apartment door. His astute stare appeared slightly less irritated as he regarded me, which was the closest approximation to a smile that I'd seen on Reeves.

"Miss Bianca."

"Reeves."

He pulled the door open, allowing me passage. To my delight, a wizened voice called out, "Is that my granddaughter?"

Grandfather stood by the table, a tea cup in his hand. He beamed, smiling with a gusto that didn't quite reach his eyes. I wrapped my arms around him in a warm embrace.

"How are you?" I asked.

He nodded. "Getting through, getting through. On my way to a meeting in ten minutes. How about you?"

I motioned to his bookshelf. "Do you mind if I look at your collection? I'm interested in a rather familiar title . . ."

"By all means."

He joined me as I stood before the bookcase, which loomed paces above my head. Though he'd dejunked and sorted his collection, plenty of tomes survived the culling and graced his shelves. They didn't clutter each cubby, like before. Reeves left them dusted, cared for, and neat, like everything else in this apartment. Papa and I hadn't made it easy on our esteemed butler.

"What title are you looking for, my dear?"

I passed him the paper from Camila. He studied it and brightened. "As luck would have it, I have that exact book."

"I thought you might."

"It was very popular in my early years. Many copies circulated, but then faded, as books do."

He reached for a book with a refurbished spine. Faded gold lettering, painted into the tough leather exterior, proclaimed the expected title. When I carefully cracked it open, the same front page was there in an exact mimicry.

"It's an old one." He tapped the first page. "Rare, too. I kept it because one finds so little information about Magnolia Castle anywhere else. In fact, if you were to attempt to study its history, you'd have a hard time."

"Why?"

He shrugged. "They don't want you to know?"

"Because there's something to hide?"

"Presumably."

"Have you ever been to the Academy in the Eastern Network?"

"Surprisingly, no." His tone elevated. "I've heard of it, but never ventured inside, nor had an invitation extended to me. As

Ambassador, I spent far more time speaking with the leadership."

I settled on the edge of his closest divan, suspicion guiding me into the book. He stood behind me and peered over my shoulder.

"What are you looking for?"

"Answers about Magnolia Castle's origins. Do you know when it was built?"

"Hundreds of years ago."

"Yes." I hummed with growing interest. "But how many? And by whom?"

Grandfather tilted his head to one side. "You know? I've not thought about it much. Same as Chatham Castle, I suppose. Someone—or many *someones*—built them. After this long, does it matter?"

An urging inside told me it did matter.

A lot.

The beginning of the book contained mostly boring drivel about the life of Allegra Rossi, mentioned in the title page, and her sordid past dealing with different magical systems. Most of them dark.

"Allegra Rossi." I trailed my fingers down the left page. "She's credited with building Magnolia Castle."

"The name is vaguely familiar."

Chapter one covered the strange fame Allegra created for herself around Magnolia Castle and her magical workings.

Chapter two discussed the Eastern Network at the time of the construction, which finally divested a year.

976.

"Could it really be seven hundred years old?" I asked. My finger tapped on the year. Grandfather sent a quick check to a nearby clock and pushed away from the divan.

"Possibly. Like Chatham Castle, spells would sustain it on a yearly basis, providing necessary repairs, particularly with witches actively living inside. It's not too surprising, really. Some historians date the Arck back much farther than that."

"Chatham is . . ."

"Older by a wide margin. But the history of Chatham is vague and sordid, with spurts of growth, some collapses, etc. It began well over sixteen hundred years ago, but not to the same size . . ."

He trailed away as Reeves cleared his throat, tapping on the face of a pocket watch. Grandfather nodded.

"Yes, thank you Reeves. My dear, I must go. Stay as long as you like, as always."

Peeling my gaze from the paper, I smiled up at him. "Thank you, Grandfather," and returned to my perusal. The door closed behind him as I sank in again. The book had a largely academic feel, meant for more than a casual reading of history, with cross-referenced books, annotated interviews, and a sundry of other items.

I hit something important on Chapter Six.

Not a date, but two lines.

Little was known about Allegra Rossi's past before she became friends with the current High Priest and began to instill in him ideas about a magical castle that could withstand time. There is some substantiated history that ties her into the house of Gallo, though this is imperfect. We have no documented evidence that the Gallo family ever claimed a relationship with her.

House of Gallo.

The book slammed shut. I tucked it under my arm and hustled past Reeves, who eyed the spot on the divan where I had mussed the pillows.

"Merry part, Reeves!" I called as I hurried past. "Thank you for the time!"

* * *

A full meal and five lengthy, boring books accompanied me to Greyson's cell, floating on spells. The Guardians allowed me to pass without a word.

The thought to invite Aurora slid in and out of my mind. She visited the Southern Network Ambassador at the moment, which would put her in a foul mood, further depressing my desire to see her.

I'd tell her later.

This had to be dealt with now.

Holding a torch ahead of each step, I entered the antechamber into Greyson's dank world with little preamble. Greyson barely had time to stand before I asked, "What do you know about Allegra Rossi?"

He smiled.

"Ah ha. Someone has been doing her research."

A feral, hungry gaze overcame him when his eyes alighted on the books. Nevermind the salty ham and potato soup, the pot of steaming tea, saucer of cream, and tower of sugar blocks. Buttered dinner rolls formed a pyramid near a brimming soup boat that had my stomach watering.

I shoved the first three books through the slot. He accepted them with a greedy sweep of his arms, immediately stepping out of reach.

"Talk," I demanded.

To my delight, he held up one of the books and began to speak.

"Allegra *Gallo* Rossi was a divisive woman."

"Gallo Rossi?"

"A Gallo by birth."

"Do you have proof?"

"Do I need it?"

Sealing my lips shut, I motioned for him to continue.

"Allegra was both powerful with magic and hungry for attention. Few witches knew that she originated from one of the original lesser families because the Gallos refused to own her after what she did."

He lowered the first book, lifted the second. "When she was in her early thirties, she befriended the unmarried High Priest—this is before the Law of Vittoria—and convinced him that the divided kingdoms required a symbol in order to unite. Why not make it a magical castle?"

Greyson tossed the second book onto the bed, holding the third aloft. "The High Priest had no reason to disparage the idea, so he put Allegra in charge of the construction of a powerful, magical castle. She is now credited as the main creator of Magnolia Castle." He paused, ready to throw the book on the bed, but stopped. "Whether that's a good thing or not is up to you."

The book landed on the others with a thud.

He went silent.

"I went to the Academy after your strange hint."

He brightened. "Oh, did you? And what did you think of the buffoons inside?"

"Nothing much. I touched the Gallo medallion in the lesser family room."

A delighted laugh, rangy and manic, rolled out of him. He pressed a hand to his stomach, allowing his mirth to roll free in a sound so unnerving, I cringed.

"Oh, Bianca. You do delight me. I presumed you would research and figure it out eventually, but to touch the medallion? Lovely. Not even my little riddle frightened you?"

"I figured it out."

Smiling with all his teeth, he murmured, "But did you?"

"The medallion took me to the Gallo family house in the marshes. They're an interesting family, aren't they? No artifacts to boast of except a medallion and a swatch of grass. Yet, when I arrived and fought off their serpente, witches swarmed me. They had a powerful spell that revealed any spell caster, too.

Whatever the Gallos are, or aren't, they're prepared. They're fighters."

Greyson yawned. "How interesting."

I shoved the last two books into the slot. Accepting them, he held one in each hand. "They have been the most underestimated and boring house in the history of the Eastern Network because they don't stir up trouble. By design. They don't say much. They do what they're supposed to, like good witches do, and thus stay out of trouble."

He grinned again, and I loathed his enjoyment of such power. As if this truly was a game, and I played into it at every turn. Knowing Greyson, it *was* a game. I just had to stay a few moves ahead.

"The only witches that play quietly are witches that want to hide something, if you ask me," he said in a contemplative tone. "But what are they hiding? A troubled legacy? Almost like they're . . . *atoning* . . . for something?"

"Magnolia Castle?"

"That is for history to yet reveal. Rumors abound, you know. I hear them the way one hears such things. But they are *costly*."

Both books joined the knot of others. He eyed the food, and then me. Although I expected this back-and-forth, it irked me to play into his hands. That Greyson should still have any power rankled.

I set the bowl of sugar blocks on the slot first. He plucked it free and carefully set it aside, in shadows near the wall, where I suspected he'd savor and nurse it for days.

"Despite this woman having lived hundreds of years ago, the family legacy of staying quiet but ready continues on today. You see, the Eastern Network isn't easy or quick to forgive. If any of them stirred up a problem, they'd be immediately silenced. Tainted blood runs in their veins. No High Priest can afford a resurrection of her terrible legacy."

Noting his unwillingness to say both Allegra's name, or the Gallo family name, I asked, "If she's credited with Magnolia Castle, what did she do that was so terrible?"

He flicked two fingers.

Teeth grinding, I set the creamer on the slot next.

Accepting it, he continued to speak with a jovial air, as if we attended high tea. "It's not that Magnolia Castle wasn't a great accomplishment, but it's *other* works that haunt. No good deed goes unpunished. There are terrible places where light cannot penetrate. There are deeds so foul one can never recover. Not without redemption. Some witches toy with dark magic as much as they master regular magic."

Any dark magic had undertones of Prana in it, in my estimation. The goddess of the sea enjoyed her black spaces a little too much.

So what had Allegra entangled herself in?

Greyson's rambling words were yet another clue, I felt marginally certain. *There are terrible places where light cannot penetrate. There are deeds so foul one can never recover.* Leda confirmed receipt of them when I repeated it to her.

Meanwhile, Greyson eyed the plate, as if ready to select his next option.

"What dark magic is Allegra known for?"

With a gesture to his throat, he said, "That is the question, isn't it?" His indication of a binding that prevented his speech became far more obvious. He couldn't speak about Allegra or the Gallo family, which explained his reason for sending me to the Academy with vague hints. That, or Greyson liked to toy with witches.

Both, probably.

"Did you work directly with the Gallo family?"

"Finally, the *right* question." Greyson leaned forward, fingers hooked around the bars. "Keep asking."

The readiness of their witches to fight, the existence of the serpente, and the likelihood that a lesser family like the Gallos might hold resentment and a grudge stirred my thoughts.

"You say the Gallos are trying to atone for something? That Allegra was a Gallo, though history has erased her name from them? Not culture, obviously."

He stared.

I continued, faster with each word.

"If what you say is true, then I think that Ricardo Gallo is tired of being blamed for Allegra Rossi. He's tired of playing *nice witch*. So he began a rebellion by exploding Carcere, releasing the worst criminals back into the Network, and laying low right after."

"Bad blood foments, and so does anger," he retorted hotly. "Unfortunately, Cristian is just a little too overwhelmed to save the Network. Seven Council Members against three?" He scoffed. "The Aldanas won't survive what's coming, Miss Monroe."

Seven, I thought.

How did Greyson know?

He hadn't answered directly to my conjecture about Ricardo Gallo, I couldn't help but notice. By design, no doubt. The Gallo family might have put a restrictive binding on Greyson when they released him. Maybe, they explained their whole plan in order to fit the criminals within it.

If true, Greyson might know . . . everything.

The tray floated into my hands, drawing the hunger from his eyes. I propped it on my shoulder, surprised by the heft. The electrifying scent of fresh yeast rolls and creamy soup thickened the air. He pulled in a deep breath, closed his eyes, and let his head tip back onto his shoulders. When he faced me again, his pupils dilated.

To speed the process and his motivation, I removed the lid from his soup boat.

"I'm curious," I sang, "how this rebellion happened. Curious enough to impart a little soup, if you're so inclined."

"The prisoners were recruited to the rebellion while in Carcere," he said quickly, licking his lips. "If they promised to help the rebellion, they were set free with the breaking of the magic. They had to swear to it."

"You can tell me about it?"

Irritated with my interruption, he said, "Yes, because any idiot could have figured *that* out. It's not protected information, Bianca. Why hide how extensively one is willing to go to achieve their goal?"

Ignoring his insult, I asked, "And you joined the rebellion?"

He scoffed. "Everyone joined. There may have been one or two almost-dead fools that didn't comprehend enough what the *lealta* meant, but anyone with half a brain agreed to join a murderous rebellion to overthrow the leadership who put them there. Yes, Miss Monroe. I can promise you, I joined."

Within his scathing response, he never said *Gallo* or *Ricardo* or any other detail. He remained vague, with terms *murderous rebellion* and *leadership*.

Inching the tray a little closer, I asked, "Who initiated the plan to help you escape Carcere?"

"A Guardian named Aurelio, but he answered to someone else."

"Who?"

Greyson stared.

"Fine." I shrugged that off, inching closer to confirmation that Ricardo Gallo had a key position. "How long had they been planning it?"

Snarling, he hissed, "Ever since I arrived, and that's suddenly all I remember. If you want more information, I need the nourishment of food and a long nap, Miss Monroe."

With a spell, I sent the tea cup onto his slot. Panic filled his eyes when I took a step back, the tray hovering behind me.

"You'll get the soup when you tell me how long they were planning it."

Gritting his teeth, he muttered, "I can't."

"Then tell me more about the Gallo family."

"I can't."

"Allegra?"

"No."

"Why not?" I asked innocently.

His throat bobbed. He shook his head, nostrils flared. Sweat broke out on his forehead, a sure indication that some sort of binding held him fast. Did I trust it?

Was he pretending?

Unlikely, though it seemed odd that he could talk about the traitorous Guard who engineered the breakout, but not Allegra Rossi. If I couldn't glean more information on Allegra from him, I'd have to search elsewhere. Somewhere. History hid her, I wagered. It wouldn't be easy.

Deciding that Greyson owed me one final answer, I said, "I decide when we're done with questions, Greyson, not you. If you want this tray, you will drudge up the energy to answer one more question to my satisfaction, or I will leave you with nothing but tea, cream, and sugar."

Greyson's lips pressed into a thin line.

"Are the rebels planning for a slow assault on Magnolia Castle in order to remove the Aldanas?"

"Why do you ask?"

"The castle is . . . I don't know. Different. *Something* seems different. There are cracks in the foundation and the ceiling," I added, thinking of the weakness Camila covered up with a spell during my last visit.

He lifted his chin. "It's over seven hundred years old."

"And maintained by magic," I snapped. "There shouldn't be cracks in the foundation or the ceiling. Is the rebellion planning to use Magnolia's weakening infrastructure to get rid of the Aldanas?"

With an uncomfortable grunt, and a grimace, he barely managed to nod once.

No lie appeared in his gaze.

He meant it.

I shoved the tray into the slot so quickly he scrambled to grab it before it fell. Soup sloshed over the edges.

"I hope you can stay useful with a binding in place that prevents you from telling me the most important information. You will live a very long time in this cell if you're not useful. The Council might suddenly think an execution is too good for you."

When I left with my torch, Greyson was busy slurping the spilled remnants from the bottom of the tray.

* * *

Aurora glowered at me.

I returned it.

"Why?" she demanded, tossing her hands toward the dungeons, which I had just exited. My arms loosened to my side with a heavy breath. If she hadn't interjected hurt into her tone, I might have been able to stand her questioning. As it stood, my conscience pricked too forcefully, and my irritation over walking away with incomplete information didn't help my bad mood.

"I'm sorry, Aurora. It was a spur-of-the-moment mental connection and I had to speak with Greyson right away." My fingers touched my temple to illustrate it. "It wasn't meant to angle you out."

"Yet you had time to go to the kitchen and find a tray, as well as the library to find books?"

"What do you want from me?"

The question rattled her. Aurora frowned, arms crossed over

her middle. Despite her creased forehead and heavy glower, she cut a vulnerable figure. Real annoyance, a step beyond exasperation, flickered in her eyes. Her meeting with the Southern Network may not have gone very well.

She regarded me with deeper curiosity before concluding, "Nothing. If I wanted something from you, the fault would be mine."

Her snippy comment circled my head. It had the markers of emotional depth that Grandfather sent my way constantly, but I rarely felt up to fulfilling. With a sigh, I set it aside in my mental space reserved for examining in the quiet, when I had the luxury of thinking.

"Look, it wasn't personal."

Her features rearranged into stone cold distrust. "We're done with this side of the conversation. Whatever you think," she muttered, "I am not your enemy, Bianca Monroe. What did you learn?"

"Nothing concrete. There is a witch named Allegra Rossi that I need to research more. Greyson did give me the name of a Guardian that helped to engineer his escape from Carcere, and linked the rebellion with the Gallo family."

She tilted her head. "Fascinating."

"I'm going to report it to Camila."

A moment's pause preceded her, "Keep me apprised of any further information." She held a formal card in her hand, shaking it from side to side. I caught a glimpse of golden writing against a darker backdrop. "This arrived from the Eastern Network today."

"What is it?"

"An invitation."

"To what?"

"A ball. Cristian is throwing a ball."

My eyes widened. "You're kidding?"

Wryly, she said, "I wish that I was."

"At Magnolia Castle?"

"Where else?"

"I just . . . I wondered."

Thus far, I hadn't shared my suspicions about Magnolia Castle with anyone except Scarlett, who had been indifferent to the idea, and Leda, who didn't summon any excitement over it, either. Until I could confirm my hunch about the castle, I didn't have proof. Arguably, no one would believe the confirmation of a prisoner. Aurora didn't strike me as the smartest witch to open up to.

"The ball is exclusive to political witches. Council Members, Ambassadors, etc. He's attempting to put on a good front, if you ask me, and make everything appear to be business as usual."

I accepted the proffered card and skimmed the benign invitation. After observing Cristian and Camila the other day, I couldn't agree with Aurora. Cristian had an angle.

But what?

Nothing shocking lay on the invitation, an elegantly wrought set of information about the ball. The words extended the offer to Scarlett, Grandfather, and any Council Members who desired to attend. Grandfather wouldn't go. The long transportation spells tired him, not to mention the socializing. I couldn't say that I wanted Scarlett to attend, either.

"It's not going to end well," I said.

Aurora sighed. "I agree. Anyway, I've given a copy to Scarlett. She has not yet decided whether she'll attend. Alina from the Southern Network plans to go for the first half hour, with the demigod Tipa, of course. Lana confirmed immediately, from what my sources say. I imagine she'll stay the entire time. Nadira has declined."

Considering that Nadira was once a rebellious Northern Network Council Member who usurped a rabid authority within the last several years, the rebuff made sense.

"Are you going?"

She scoffed. "No, thank you. The instability of the Eastern Network combined with a bunch of ornery Council Members? Not happening. I don't do balls. They're not a part of the diplomatic process. *That* happens in offices and meetings, not around swishing skirts and inebriated idiots."

"Isn't it your job?"

Nose in the air, she sniffed. "My job is to manage our relationship with other Networks, not flitter around a ballroom in a dangerous situation assessing what information I can find. That sounds like a job for the Brotherhood, so naturally, I came to you first."

For all her eccentricities and oddities, I couldn't say that I disagreed. Given the opportunity, I wouldn't choose to attend the Eastern Network ball, either. Unless it provided an unparalleled opportunity for information, as she mentioned.

Aurora shifted to the side, her skirt wavering. "Let me know what you find out, and I look forward to your report. Oh, and by the way? Regarding Greyson. Books and a tray of food will not satisfy him next time. Might I suggest having him put in a room with a window before your appointment? Just for an hour. Then remove him and speak with him before another hour has passed. If you need permission, I'll appeal to Scarlett with you. She can move him to a different room without Council approval, even if it is an upgrade, without much implication."

Aurora retreated up the narrow stone steps leading away from the little landing where she'd cornered me. I watched her go, thinking over her wise suggestion, and wondered if she wasn't better at this job than I'd given her credit for.

Chapter Twenty-Two

Jacqueline's bouncing energy, barely contained within my calm treehouse, rattled the dishwater. She flounced around my table, alternately exclaiming and muttering, as she sped through to do lists, firing off questions at rapid speed.

"What color do you want your dress?"

"Will your hair be up, or down?"

"Do you think Merrick will cut his hair?"

"He needs to cut his hair."

"Don't tell him I said he should cut his hair, or he'll grow it longer!"

Half-rolled scrolls, a rainbow of ink bottles, and several quills scattered the once-neat space. With every half muttered reply I managed to give, she marked something on one of many parchments.

"Everything is coming together *so* nicely!" she cried while idly perusing a scroll. "I pictured it being far more complicated. Drogo has one brother still alive, and he's confirmed that he'll come. That'll be neat. Never met him before, but really . . . this is more important than Drogo's second marriage to Mother."

Suppressing the urge to ask why Merrick's handfasting would be of greater importance than Drogo's, I had a sip of coffee to keep my tongue occupied. The effort wouldn't be worth the answers.

Jacqui skidded to a stop, drawing up with surprise.

"Oh no! I forgot to order new table cloths; we've got ten already. Do you think we'll need more than twenty? We can gather at least that many."

I choked.

"Twenty?"

"For the initial family dinner! Mother and I anticipate up to twenty tables filled. And we can't have half of them not-clothed."

"I . . . I don't . . ."

Clearly not requiring an answer, she returned to another sprawling list. The sheer force of her to-dos intimidated me into silence for the next ten minutes. My courage slowly came around when she muttered her annoyance at great aunt Matilda, whoever that was.

"Jacqueline?"

She lifted her gaze with a distracted, "Hmmm?" and the soft end of a quill stroking her chin.

"Is all of this *really* necessary?"

Jacqueline's delighted expression lowered. Her brows crashed together in a hurt look.

"Necessary?"

Scrambling to recover my mistake, I hastily said, "You're just working so hard! I don't want you to overwork."

Recovering quick as a finger snap, she laughed. "Oh, that! No, no. Are you jesting? This gives me life!" She breathed deep, eyes closed. "I adore all these plans and preparations. And, anyway, it's been far too long since we've seen our second cousins twice removed. We can't get them into town for anything less than a handfasting!"

Her chuckle had a nervous edge that inspired some fear. Second cousins twice removed? What did that mean, anyway?

Jacqui glanced around. "Where is my brother?"

"Working."

"Oh."

Amused because she'd been here for over an hour and hadn't noticed him missing, I asked, "Do you need him?"

"No, not at all."

Affecting as casual a stance as I could manage, I finished my coffee and asked, "Is there anything I can do to help?"

She paused, one hand halfway to a fourth to-do list titled *Family Dinner Without Cousins* across the top. Thus far, I hadn't offered to help beyond essentials, since Jacqui had it well in hand.

As carefully benign as me, she asked, "Do you mean it?"

Hiding a gulp, I nodded. The very last thing I wanted anything to do with was handfasting plans. Even my own. But Jacqui's tireless work and dedication to Merrick and myself wore me down. I couldn't, in good conscience, let her plan *everything*.

Even if she would.

Happily.

Jacqui motioned to the paperwork. "This is all theoretical. Because there's no—"

"Date."

"Can you set a date? That would help loads."

"That seems like something Merrick and I should do together, don't you think?"

"Yes." She set a hand on her hip and cocked it to the side. "But you aren't."

"We will!"

Jacqui eyed me with deepening distrust. "I've heard that before. We need to know. And soon. Aunt Matilda has health issues and we need to plan for her departure and duration! She refuses to transport because she almost lost a nose. She has to come over the mountain pass on a donkey, and if there's one thing you don't want, it's Matilda attending a handfasting before she's had enough recovery from the donkey."

With that in mind, I said, "I'll finalize a date with Merrick when he returns home tonight. Fair?"

"Fair."

"In the meantime, could you help with something else?"

"What is it?"

"A ballgown."

Infused with new life, she zipped upright with a gasp. "A ballgown?" she cried. "Why didn't you *say* so? Of course I'll help you with a ballgown!"

With a rustle of wind, the plans and papers vanished. Ribbons, string, bolts of fabric, buttons, a dizzying array of thin brown parchment, and packs of needles took their place. In the space of a minute, my treehouse looked like a dressmaker had attacked.

Well . . . if nothing else, I'd properly distracted her.

Jacqui beamed.

"Tell me everything!"

* * *

A letter from Papa arrived later that evening. I lay on my back, staring into leeching daylight with the forest singing into the halcyon quiet.

Utter quiet.

Jacqueline-free quiet.

How are you?

Lips twitching, I summoned a pencil and replied.

Good. How are you?

His response returned within a minute.

Better. I apologize for our last visit. I've been thinking about what you said, and you were right.

Any results? I asked.

Yes.

Staring at the single word, my head tilted to the side, I wondered whether Papa understood the cue to elaborate, or if he dodged it. Before I could decide which applied, the trees whispered.

You belong to us.
The joy returns.

Merrick appeared at the far end of the branch, striding closer. He often transported away from the house and took a lap around, mostly for a lazy perimeter check. As I sent the message to Papa away, Merrick settled at my side with an *oomph*.

"You dodged Jacqui," I announced, wrapping my arms around him. He smelled like seaspray and fish.

He tensed. "Is she here?"

Laughing, I said, "Not anymore," and threaded our fingers together. The reassurance of his presence ebbed the overheated anxiety in my chest. Jacqui, though she meant well, inspired all kinds of panic.

Merrick melted into my side, squeezing my palm.

"Tough day?" I asked.

"Yes."

For several minutes, we studied the canopy in silence until I couldn't bear it any longer.

"How is the Eastern Network?"

"A mess." He drove a hand through his hair and yawned. "But I made headway with Ronaldo, which feels like progress.

After watching him for a while, I decided to take a risk and speak with him directly. He's open to using Brotherhood intelligence and reports."

"Would Cristian?"

"I think he will now."

"Oh?"

"I gave Ronaldo a warning about an incoming rebel raid and he listened to us. Because of it, Magnolia avoided another attack. Cristian expressed his gratitude and interest. Brody is following up tonight."

A little knot unwound in my chest.

Progress.

"There are a lot of attacks on Magnolia Castle."

"I noticed."

Yawning, I stretched my arms over my head. "You're right. That is headway. I thought Ronaldo would be an ally if necessary. He's one of the only ones with his wits about him, at least for Camila's sake."

"On Brody's recommendation, Cristian is sending trusted Guardians into the marshes as emissaries. No armor, no weapons. They're marsh witches returning to their families and trying to broker . . . something."

"Like peace?"

He shrugged. "Whatever they can manage. It's like sending a sixteen-year-old kid into an Ambassadorial meeting, but they don't have a lot of choices. The marsh witches are rising and they must be stopped."

Random Guardians plunging into angry marshlands testified to the dire straights in the Eastern Network. I couldn't fathom a hapless young man returning to Letum Wood and attempting to convince old foresters that the Highest Witch had their best interests in hand. Witches at the intersection of poverty stricken wild places and progress didn't have the luxury of trust.

Camila hadn't responded to my updates on what Greyson reported, except to say, *I will conduct what research I can, thank you,* and left me wondering what she could discover.

"Let's hope the Guardians can do something to bridge peace," I said quietly. Merrick tightened his fingers around mine in a reassuring squeeze.

"Returning to my original point," I stated. "We need to pick a handfasting day." My nose wrinkled. "Jacqueline mentioned something about great aunt Matilda and a donkey?"

He swore under his breath.

"And a fourth dinner?"

Another curse.

Deciding his emotional state couldn't handle another exposition on the depths of handfasting planning Jacqui dove, I summarized with, "I promised her we'd decide on a date. She really *is* putting so much time and heart into it."

"Next week?"

"She'd die," I said immediately. "Absolutely fall over, dead. There's a tablecloth issue, you see."

He snorted. "Might be easier, though."

I nudged him with an elbow. Merrick fended it off. "I'm jesting," he said. "Jacqueline is so much . . . energy. She cares more about this handfasting than we do."

"Not true." I elbowed him again. "She cares more about the celebration and honor and tradition of it. *We* care more about the handfasting."

Merrick quirked his lips at the semantics, but he let it go. Our eyes met. "When do you want to handfast?"

"Ah . . ."

Silence stretched like drying animal hide. Neither of us wanted to peg down a date. Not because we didn't want it, but because of unknown variables far outside our control. Papa's idea to elope had new appeal every hour.

"What about a month from now?" he suggested. "That's

enough time for old aunt Matilda, but not yet the depths of winter, when food is more scarce. This allows us to take advantage of the final push around fall vegetables and wheat grinding, but before we have to slaughter sick goats."

A month.

One whole month for . . . not much to change. Another month of Jacqueline's energy escalating with everyday that passed.

"We *could* elope," I added.

He laughed. "Say the word and I'm ready."

My love for his family kept me from agreeing. The light in Jacqueline's eyes, as well as the warmth in Kalli's as they sorted through the items of inheritance, removed the temptation. Was it fair to take that opportunity from them? Not really. Especially when they did most of the planning, and we only had to show up.

"One month." I agreed with a punctuated nod. "We'll handfast in one month."

Chapter Twenty-Three

Flutes and violins warbled in the backdrop of Magnolia Castle three days later. Swooping dresses, crisp suit coats, and elaborate hair designs wrought by pomade littered the ballroom. The seductive smell of magnolia flowers, combined with a cool breeze off the sea, enticed me farther inside.

If we must attend a ball, the ambience could be worse.

Rognvald's gruff voice, occasionally interrupted by Leda's returning snipe, broke the symphonic flow as I followed Scarlett across a black-and-white tiled floor. We aimed for the middle, where Cristian stood with Camila. Scarlett, focused on her target, distributed her usual smile while I watched the periphery.

Thus far, no concerns.

There are no active expectations of an attack, Rognvald said. *Chatter in the Eastern Network hasn't yet spoken about any rebels targeting this ball. Partly because he announced it so late.*

And yet, Leda countered as smoothly, *we will act as such. Thank you. Do you have any Protectors on the ground?*

Brody outside. Chi within the castle, but away from the ball, and Merrick embedded within the ballroom.

Invisible or transformed?

Depends on the Protector.

Thank you. Bianca will be updating both primaries when she desires.

Merrick filtered through the crowd not far away, hidden behind Eastern Network influenced jet-black hair. Sleek and smooth, it hung to his shoulders in glossy locks. Umber eyes instead of lush green, and no hint of a beard on his square jaw or handsome face. He'd taken pains to adjust the nose, too. A clever trick. His skin, distinctly more brown, created hollows and contours beyond his usual tanned roughness.

Quite handsome, no matter where he hailed from.

Catching me in the act of ogling him, Merrick surveyed me with an equally appreciative perusal, then winked before disappearing behind a group of flounce-covered women. My stomach swooped with molten heat before I returned my whole attention to Scarlett.

Jikes.

He held my heart in his hands.

Jacqueline had concocted an extravagant dress with too many layers of silk, tulle, and skirts, leaving my shoulders open to the air and silk gloves up my arms. After thanking her profusely, I waited until she left to alter it with a few spells.

Tonight, I wore a tulle-free, single skirt variation that kept the silk, but altered the color to deepest sapphire. The tones blended nicely with my hair, and the simplistic style guaranteed I'd have no trouble defending Scarlett, should necessity require. The gloves remained at home. No transformation from me.

Scarlett wanted witches to see me.

How did you convince Rognvald to let you come into the ballroom? I asked Merrick through the communication magic, blithely aware that Leda and Rognvald could listen in. If they eavesdropped, which I doubted, they'd likely find his answer equally as curious.

Amusement laced his response. *It wasn't that hard. He owed me one. Besides, it was better for safety and mission observation.*

Mmmm, I replied, unconvinced. Whatever *he owed me one* meant, I wasn't sure I wanted to know. When Protectors banded together without intense Network-saving missions to distract them, they devolved into a group of capable, rowdy five-year-old boys.

Besides, this is good practice, he murmured, his voice loose as steam.

For what?

Dancing.

While dodging an incoming witch who didn't see me with Scarlett, I hedged a smile. *You need practice dancing, do you?*

Well, yes. But also for . . . His sense of hesitation told me exactly what he meant. The handfasting festivities. Far less confidently, he added, *It's part of the expectations.*

The expectations rang long after he said it, removing the flirty exchange entirely. Sometimes, I couldn't wait for the handfasting to end.

Scarlett paused to speak with an Eastern Network Council Member—presumably, one of three left that was welcomed into the castle. He grinned broadly, and I gladly ripped my concentration away from yet another handfasting expectation to assess this witch. A male. Not towering in height, but slender and small. An Assistant sniveled at his left elbow, mostly harmless. The Council Member had a gusty way of speaking and a too-fixed smile.

Leda, what does Council Member Colombo look like?

Medium height, broad facial features, with a prominent chin and whiskers, despite shaving.

Definitely Council Member Colombo.

He's a kind man, and open to logic and facts. Not only Cristian, but also Aldo, Cristian's Assistant, has been very impressed by his loyalty to justice and order.

Good to know. Don't you think something is weird about this ball? I asked.

Like the fact that Cristian is hosting it?

Yes.

Something stinks about it, she admitted.

Are you enjoying your night off? I asked. Scarlett had kindly deferred Leda's presence at this ball, as Hiddleston's family had a yearly dinner that he requested she attend.

Immensely. Now, I'm going to be with Hiddleston's family and will not respond. If you need something, you have a plethora of Protectors at your disposal. I imagine you'll be fine.

Got it, I replied, and let her go.

Scarlett, doing her best to find the two remaining Council Members as we navigated closer to Cristian, gracefully executed her job. At a questioning glance from me, she would nod, indicating we would continue, and proceed to the next one. Not all High Priestesses took care to meet with other Network Council Members, but Scarlett did. With all their current drama, it certainly helped get a better feel for their struggles.

Free flowing wine, elegant butlers, waiters with pristinely white cravats, and a general air of plenty still couldn't hide the stink of rebellion that tightened the air. Each noble witch had a glaze to their smile. Darting eyes. Uncouth fear.

While marsh witches died in the far reaches, and insurrectionists built up power through recruitment and promises of protection, it seemed that Cristian attempted to rally leaders under the guise of sheer, raw political prowess. But that couldn't be right. He wasn't turning a blind eye to his problems.

So what was his angle?

There are more witches here than I expected, Merrick said.

Agreed.

Chi, how is the castle?

Quiet, came his raspy reply.

Brody?

Also quiet outside.

Scarlett spun to the right, nodded to someone passing by, and kept a convincing smile pasted on her face. Thankfully, Scarlett kept us moving to avoid conversation. After a minimal introduction to it, she found she didn't enjoy using the communication magic, so I kept my queries to a minimum.

Are you well, Your Highness?

Yes.

Any particular plan?

I have one more Council Member to greet before speaking to Camila and Cristian, and then I'll return to the Central Network. Beyond well wishing, my presence here is a mere formality. We're not required to stay.

Thank Alkarra, I almost said.

Thank you, Your Highness, I replied instead, then updated Rognvald. The way the magic rippled ever-so-slightly indicated that the message went to Brody, Chi, Merrick, and Rognvald, as I intended.

Each Protector replied, *Understood.*

Witches gravitated toward a table filled with elaborate and lush foods. Scarlett skirted the edge of a table burdened by macarons, puffed pastries dusted with sugar, and other delicious treats. Amidst the swirls of skirts and slippers, old men with refined goatees, taut necks, and tense bodies abounded.

While Scarlett hailed the final Council Member—a man named Alfonso that greeted her with a kiss on both cheeks and a mostly toothless smile—I studied the room. The structure made me nervous. It wasn't until I glimpsed some of the windows on the far side that I understood why.

Except for the carriage-sized entrance door at our backs, all the other exits went directly outside. Fresh air and space meant little control over entry points, exits, and witches.

How many East Guards are outside? I asked Brody.

Ten.

Stationed where?

Various entry points.

How many around the interior ballroom?

Four.

As Scarlett withdrew from her conversation and re-steeled herself to find the elusive Cristian and Camila, a *tink-tink-tink* of a utensil tapping glass swelled over the cacophony. Propelled by a spell, undoubtedly. The room settled. All eyes swiveled to the wall near the wide entrance.

Cristian stood on an elevated platform, handsome in a freshly-pressed gray suit. His hair waved in shiny black perfection, like freshly-washed raven feathers. Camila stood to his left with a pinched smile that appeared to require great effort. Resplendent in an emerald dress, with layers of blue silk sprouting chiffon and tulle, she commanded attention by her presence. Peacock feather eyes decorated the bottom of her bell skirt, bedecked with the great burden of material that the Eastern Network women tended to wear.

Cristian's voice rang out in Ilese.

"Welcome, my friends, to our celebration of life!"

Did you hear that? I asked Merrick. *I think we should call our handfasting a celebration of life.*

Too sappy.

You're right. Jacqueline wouldn't approve.

It's not about Jacqueline, he parried with amusement, *but pride. Believe it or not, I have some. The Protectors would never let me live it down.*

As the smattering of applause calmed, Cristian continued.

"Tonight, we gather to celebrate the Eastern Network and *all* her witches." His careful emphasis created a shuffling stir amongst the patrons. "We are celebrating a willingness to be peaceful. To align, meet, and agree. It is time to put down swords and come together."

My confidence faltered. Did he say *align, meet, and agree* or had I translated that incorrectly? With whom? Or what? Blinking, I glanced at Scarlett. She schooled her expression so carefully neutral that it confirmed her own surprise. This was a ball, not a political reformation.

Or was it?

"These are difficult days. Together, we can weather them. We can hear all sides. We can create peace. There is still much light amidst the dark."

Hear all sides.

Create peace.

Surely, I translated correctly. He spoke with assurance.

This sounds more like an indirect romantic plea to the rebellion, I said to Scarlett. *Is he trying to say something?*

Her lips thinned. *It certainly seems like it.*

Would you do this?

I don't know.

To Merrick, I said, *I don't see anyone protecting Camila. Do you?*

It's too hard to be certain with this many witches together. Magic systems are too thick to delineate unless I'm much closer. There must be East Guards protecting Cristian. If she's near him, she'll be fine.

We didn't share that confidence.

Any chance you have an interest in leaving now, Scarlett?

Her gaze fluttered to me. I met her questioning stare with the most serious expression I could manage.

Are you concerned? she asked.

Yes, Your Highness.

Cristian, glass elevated, continued a similar diatribe. She hesitated, seemed to understand the elevating strain in the room, and said, *We're agreed. I suppose no one will notice us leaving, and I did catch Cristian's eyes at one point. Our social agreement has finished.*

I plan to stay, Your Highness. I can give your regards to Camila.

She hesitated, but looked to the High Priestess across the room. Understanding what I didn't say, she nodded.

It's for the best. Be careful, Bianca.

While Cristian continued his extrapolation, Scarlett quietly transported away. No one stirred, seeming not to miss her. At the same moment, I went invisible. Any observant witch would presume we left together.

Scarlett has returned to Chatham Castle, I said to the Protectors.

Rognvald replied, *Confirmed. She transported to the Gatehouse. Speaking with her now.*

Swift as I could, I stepped out of the gown. Thanks to my simplification, removal was as easy as a few buttons, which a spell took care of. The silk whispered to the floor, leaving me in my binder and slip. The creamy linen capped my shoulders and dropped to my knees. Fine in a pinch, and far less restrictive. Unconventional, but then, no one knew me, anyway.

Besides, I didn't plan to get caught.

Spelling the dress back to the Central Network, I edged along the periphery, where fewer witches left plenty of room to navigate. Particularly without a bothersome dress. I paused near a wall where a cluster of sconces marched a sedate rhythm. Cristian and Camila stood at the north edge of the ballroom, I on the west.

The room held its breath when servants stopped moving and congregated near the edge, their rapt attention focused on Cristian.

"The Eastern Network has weathered many hard times . . ."

I'm going to make my way toward Camila.

Camila? Merrick asked.

No one is visibly protecting her.

Merrick, your mission, Rognvald said with a growl, *is not to protect the Eastern Network High Priestess. You are there to watch for signs of an insurrection and return with pertinent intelligence. That's it.*

Understood, Merrick said immediately.

I gave no such acquiescence. Rognvald asked for none.

Cristian gained more fervor as he spoke, but something tempered his voice. Fear, I wagered, though his expression hid it well.

"We must pull together!" Cristian declared. "We must become one body. A united front."

United front? I quipped to Leda, forgetting she closed her mind off to communications already. Though tempted to say the same to Merrick, I withheld. This wasn't a moment for confusing chatter, but I missed the chance to make sense of it with Leda.

Restlessness stirred in the crowd as I edged around the corner and along the north wall, creeping closer to Camila. Magically, I detected nothing in my way. No hidden East Guards, anyway. Ronaldo stood behind Cristian, near Camila but not quite in position to protect her. Unencumbered, I hurried the rest of the way to Camila's side.

I'm behind Camila on the north wall, by the entrance. I'll stay here.

I'm watching the back doors, Brody said.

A gradual lessening slowed Cristians words. "The Eastern Network shall return to her former grace," he promised with a voice that should have thundered, but rolled instead. "The Aldana dynasty will lead us to peace."

With a nod to the orchestra, Cristian commanded the festivities to life. A pause several seconds long tripled through the room before witches appeared to unlock. Movement flowed when the violins ballooned, easing into a merry tune.

Cristian stepped off the platform and turned to his

Assistant, Aldo. "Any sign of them?" he asked. HIs low words are almost incomprehensible.

"No, Your Majesty."

Irritation scored Cristian's features. "Not a single one?"

"No visible or known rebels present, Your Majesty." Aldo's head snapped to the side in silent question, and Ronaldo confirmed with a nod.

"If the rebels don't come as we requested," Cristian's voice dropped into a hiss, "this whole event is wasted. All of the currency, the time. The risk."

The risk.

Had Cristian staged an attack? He spouted talks of peace but planned to destroy? The feeling of being flipped upside down overcame me, and I floundered in a moment of confusion, unable to decide if he was brilliant or a bloody fool.

Aldo drew me from my spiraling thoughts. "I understand, Your Majesty. We can try to communicate again with the rebel leaders."

Cristian buttoned his coat, head high. "Send another missive. Whatever happens, we need to speak to them before the Mizzuni province falls. Do you hear me? Tonight. Mere, enjoy your ball."

Aldo and Cristian peeled away without giving Camila a chance to reply. Ronaldo hesitated, clearly torn between loyalties. Did he follow the High Priest or stay with the High Priestess? I stepped up to his side, careful to brush his arm as I whispered, "I will watch Her Majesty."

Ronaldo stiffened. "Can I trust you?"

"She does."

Camila, hearing my voice, whipped round. Her assessing stare slid past my invisible form. Under her breath, she said, "It's well, Ronaldo. Go. Bianca will take care of me."

With great hesitation, Ronaldo left.

* * *

"You're here?" Camila breathed. Her glittering smile beamed at a passing witch. Camila waved, blew a kiss, but angled her body toward me.

"Of course."

"I confess, Miss Monroe. I didn't expect you to be *this* willing and present."

Amused, I asked, "Would you like me to leave?"

"No! Goodness," she cried under her breath, "please don't go. Thank you for being here. I am overwhelmed with gratitude for your support. Have you observed anything that should give us alarm?"

Before I could reassure her that all appeared well, Chi and Brody spoke at the same time.

Witches approaching.

Rebels outside.

"Your Majesty, please come with me."

Camila didn't protest as I gently grabbed her arm and tugged her away from a swirl of oncoming witches.

Robed men, Brody continued, *approaching from the north. They're wearing black cloaks and robes. I count seven. Eight. Ten.*

More on the south, Chi confirmed. *They're moving towards the interior in one group.*

Merrick asked, *Armed?*

Very armed, Chi continued in his bland, whispery way. *Fifteen approach from the south, converging near the Academy. Others are fanning out. They have scimitars, axes, and swords. More weapons than I've seen the East Guard carry. They're organized.*

Same on the north, Brody interjected.

As I led Camila out of the ballroom and into the hallway, increasing sounds of hilarity flowed from within. For extra precaution, I cast my invisibility spell farther, to cloak Camila. In situations like this, with large groups of witches in a closed space, invisibility could be more dangerous than it was worth.

Tonight, I'd hedge my bet.

Camilla offered no resistance, but walked more carefully.

"What are the odds the rebels would attack?" I asked Camila.

"Very high."

"Did Cristian mean what he said?"

"About peace?"

"Yes."

"Of course he wants peace."

"Did he ask the rebels to come tonight?"

"Yes."

"Why?"

"To speak with them."

We slipped down a side staircase. I had no idea where it went, but it didn't matter. Away from the ballroom was all I focused on.

"He wanted to invite them to the ball as a sign that he sees them all as equals. He wants a chance to discuss the rebellion, and their desires, without the Council Members to influence them. He's speaking to the marsh witches, not the Council Members. It's an opportunity to get ahead of Giuseppi's rampage amongst our witches."

Smart, but fraught.

"Where does this staircase go?" I asked.

"To the East Wing."

"Perfect."

"Bianca, what's wrong?"

"Rebels approach."

She sucked in a sharp breath. "From where?"

"North and south."

Camila swirled to a stop, groping blindly for my arms. I accepted her hands. She squeezed tight. "You must find him!"

"Cristian?"

"Yes, tell him. There's an opportunity to stave off an attack."

"Or create one," I snapped. "He could also be luring them in, right? He pretended to want peace, but he really plans to shred them as they arrive."

"No!" she cried. "He truly wants to come to a resolution with the witches who are suffering the most. He did it in front of all the Eastern Network society to send a message to Council Members and rebels alike: he cares about marsh witches."

After a hasty glance to ensure we were alone, I removed the invisibility spell. If possible, her terror deepened when she saw me, morphing into astonishment.

"Miss Monroe. Is that . . . are you wearing . . . a slip?"

Waving that aside, I insisted, "Tell me where to find Cristian."

"In his office, most likely. Attempting to contact the rebel leadership. If he can find them. That's all I know. He doesn't tell me everything!"

The distinct sense that I'd buried myself too far into this conundrum rose like tide waters, but I refused to give into it.

Putting an arm around her shoulders, I said, "Hold tight," and issued a transportation spell. Magic swept us with pressure and discomfort and darkness into another place, then deposited us ten paces away from the same room where Ronaldo hid her after the previous breach of Magnolia Castle.

"Stay in here," I whispered. "I'll find Cristian and tell him."

"It might be too late!"

"It might not. I'll return as soon as I can. Stay here. Ronaldo or I will return for you. Do you promise?"

Pale, she nodded. "Yes, Miss Bianca. I will remain here. Thank you, and please be safe."

While Camila hurried inside the room and cast spells to secure it, I updated the Brotherhood. *The High Priestess is secured. Cristian has retreated to his office. Camila revealed that*

Cristian is trying to bring rebel leaders to the castle to discuss peace without the Council Members. The Council Members might be conflating the marsh witches true desires.

That's . . . smart, Rognvald said.

Let's hope, I countered.

The rebels coming from the south don't appear interested in diplomacy, Chi muttered.

Merrick repeated similarly for the north edge, while Brody said, *I'm attempting to secure the ballroom, but there are too many witches.*

The ocean might discourage the rebels from gathering or attacking from that side, Chi said.

Unlikely, but I admired his optimism. Seconds after I left Camila's side, invisibility spell in place, I stood in the hallway across from Cristian's office. Ronaldo occupied the open doorway. Over his uniformed shoulder, I could see Cristian pacing near a voluminous desk, where Aldo sat. Four quills scribbled on floating parchments.

I sidled up next to Ronaldo, brushing his sleeve again. "Her Majesty is safe in the same room as before."

His lips barely moved when he said, "Thank you."

Keeping a wary eye on Cristian, who paced so fast he might run into a wall, I said, "Rebels approach from the north and south in two separate groups. Last count was twenty-five, but might be more, both armed heavily. One group is congregating near the Academy. Hidden Protectors are attempting to delay them."

Ronaldo's entire body squeezed. "This is confirmed?"

"Yes."

Clearing his throat, Ronaldo called, "Your Majesty, the rebels have arrived."

Aldo's head snapped up.

Breathless, Cristian asked, "Which ones?"

"Unclear. They approach from the north and the south. They're heavily armed."

After another dazed moment, Cristian shook out of his stupor, crossed the room in four strides, and commanded, "We cannot bring armed rebels into the castle under any circumstances, so we will go to them. Ronaldo, accompany me with your East Guards."

Chapter Twenty-Four

Five rebels awaited Cristian. The rest hid in shadows.

They lounged at the Academy entrance wearing flowing robes over wide shoulders. Caustic glares were their only greeting. Searching for signs of the Gallo family crest amongst them was futile. Except for their faces, I observed no details and recognized no one. Certainly not Ricardo.

A man of middle height, with no outstanding characteristics, stood in the center. The presumed leader. He had the classic bold features and tawny skin of the East, with a beard hiding a strong jaw and glittering eyes. Malice hardened them. He tilted his head with an arrogance that bordered on amusement, but tension tightened his lips.

Cristian strode with impressive confidence toward the imposing group. Ronaldo's three most trusted Guardians accompanied him. They fanned out, with Ronaldo at Cristian's immediate side. Shield spells preceded them as a group, and each one individually. Wisely, Ronaldo had altered the spells, which made it less likely to overpower in one magical pulse.

I'm flanking Cristian on the left, Chi said.

On the right, said Merrick.

I'm inside Magnolia Castle, Brody replied. *Shall I aid an evacuation of witches?*

It would be wise, Rognvald said. *Remain unseen. Make it look like the witches decided it themselves. I repeat: our presence shall remain undetected.*

Understood.

Cristian spoke as soon as he stopped fifteen paces from the rebel group. "Thank you for meeting with me. I presume you are Luca?"

The standing witch smiled like a chary cat. "I am Luca, yes."

"It's a pleasure to meet you. Finally," Cristian added, as if he couldn't help himself. The formal exchange was easy to translate.

Luca tilted his chin, regarding Cristian through slotted eyes. "We came to Magnolia for our purposes, Mr. Aldana. Not to speak with you. The rebellion is beyond the point of diplomacy."

"Other marsh witches have assured me that diplomacy is never off the table."

Luca scoffed.

Cristian folded his hands in front of him. For a flash, he looked like Niko. The stern inquisition, ridged grooves in his forehead. For the first time since I'd known him, he cut an imposing figure.

Any chance we can bring Ronaldo into the magic? Chi asked.

I said, *If Rognvald wants to come and do it.*

Not a good time, Rognvald muttered.

Be ready to act, Merrick countered. *There's more happening than we thought. I recognize Luca. He's a leader of one of the bigger splinter groups that are forming within the rebellion, and not likely one that Cristian wanted to speak with. They all have different ideas, different focuses.*

"What brought you to Magnolia Castle in dark robes, at night, during a ball?" Cristian asked.

Luca sniffed. "That is our business."

"The moment you step foot on castle grounds, it is *my* business," Cristian said firmly. I silently cheered. "Where is your leader?"

"Where he belongs."

Despite the volatile situation, Cristian maintained a hard tone. "Does Gisueppi know you're here?"

Immediately incensed, Luca growled. "I'm not a child!" A knife appeared in his hands. With a spell as quick as his reaction, I knocked it out of his grip and sent it skittering across the ground. It landed at Ronaldo's feet. Ronaldo pressed his foot on it until the metal shattered into hundreds of pieces, assisted by a burst of magic.

Luca glanced down, eyes wide. Cristian ignored his shock and leaned into his advantage, as if he'd expected this reaction.

"I'll take that as a no. Information has come to my ears, Luca. Information that states you are not in charge of your rebellious group, no matter how much you try to convince witches otherwise. That you have lost control of your own rebels."

Luca shouted, "This group is mine!"

Cristian countered with a cool, "Perhaps tonight's hoped-for rebellion against my castle is yours, but most marsh witches do not align with *you*. That is what we hear. If you desire violence, you will lose."

A low laugh ballooned from Luca. His frenetic movements jarred the top of his robe loose. The hood slipped to his shoulders, revealing flowing black hair and wide ears, the only definable trait on him.

"Ronaldo," Cristian called. "Imprison them."

Cheeks red and eyes apoplectic, Luca issued a string of words I couldn't understand. He reached to a rounded pocket on his left side. A yelp followed as he jerked his hand free. Chi or Merrick or Ronaldo sent a spell to prevent him from grabbing a weapon, probably.

"Stop it!" he shouted. Rage clouded his features. "We will topple the dynasties. In the chaos, we create order."

Ronaldo leaped.

Luca screamed, "*Incendio!*" as he toppled to the ground.

An explosion tore across the night, slamming into my back. Ducking my head into my knees, I rolled away from a shockwave of heat and pressure. Two East Guards and Cristian vanished. Luca, another rebel, and Ronaldo also disappeared.

As I regained my feet, Merrick stated, *I have Luca,* at the same time Chi said, *I have a rebel.*

Ronaldo rushed into sight again, dazed.

East Guards swarmed an inferno raging over the Academy, shouting spells. Magical flames swept over the building in a sheet, but didn't press into the structure. A protective spell held the flames at bay until, with a powerful surge, an East Guard summoned water from the nearby ocean and spread it over the flames. Smoke hissed, belching slate plumes.

Coughing, I stumbled toward Ronaldo. "We have them," I said, wrenching him off the ground. "We have Luca and another one."

"Thank you," he said, gaining his feet.

The three remaining rebels already departed. In the distance, ball guests called to each other. Some screamed, others ran. Lines of them poured out of the castle, transporting and racing toward Necce in all their finery.

Brody, do you need help? I asked.

No, all clear.

Retreat to the Gatehouse, Brody, Rognvald said. *Sisterhood, if you would be so kind, we would like to find Cristian and Ronaldo. We have his rebels and are willing to wait for him to question them.*

Already spoke to Ronaldo, I said. *I'll locate Cristian and return.*

Chapter Twenty-Five

Frost nipped my nose when Scarlett, Leda, and I met Aurora, at her request, in a distant, walled off garden on Chatham Castle grounds the next morning. Exhaustion weakened every footfall in the half-frozen grass.

Clad in an ashen dress with full skirts and shiny leather boots, Aurora watched us approach with the solemnity of a prisoner awaiting execution. Scarlett, glimpsing her from afar, asked, "Why are we meeting out here?"

Leda controlled her tone when she said, "Privacy, apparently."

Scarlett lifted an eyebrow. "There's none in her turret?"

"Considering the request, I wager not."

"It's Aurora," I said with far less decorum. "Nothing she does makes sense. Paranoia is her natural state."

Fading flowers welcomed us into the garden that most witches referred to as *The Storm*, but the gardeners dubbed, *Roaring Waterfall and Other Growing Things*. Creeping plants coated a stone wall with designs that mimicked a blowing wind. Brilliant orange flowers combined with darkest green, as if a gale blew along the wall and scattered them to distant reaches. When touched, the flowers snapped shut and trembled.

Turbulent fountains, aggressive birds that nested within certain conditions, and a general sharp feel to the architecture made *Roaring Waterfall and Other Growing Things* an odd place. Namely, one bench with spikes protruding out the top.

Whoever designed it had a rough day.

Considering the ambiance, it made perfect sense for Aurora to find safety here.

"Your Highness," Aurora called as a hedge slid closed behind us. "Thank you for humoring my odd request to meet in the gardens. I also appreciate your offer to update me on the events from last night. The entire castle is abuzz."

The hedge sealed us in, preventing others from finding the entrance. Not far from where Aurora stood, a fountain bubbled and slurped with frenzy. No one would hear us over that monstrosity.

"You have my attention, Aurora."

"While it may seem strange to discuss these things with you right here, you may not be surprised at my call for caution. Rebels clearly infuse the East to greater numbers than even *they* knew. I think all of us owe it to them to be cautious. Also," she added, head canted, "my turret is . . . in dishabille. Winter approaches, and a walk around the garden would be a refreshing start to the day before it's too cold to do so."

Her turret in dishabille is the understatement of this lifetime, I said to Leda. She tucked her lips to avoid a smile.

Aurora motioned with a sweep of her hand. "If you're willing, Your Highness." Bemused, Scarlett complied. Odd request or not, it *was* a crisp morning to stroll around a garden, and I never turned down an opportunity to work outside.

Leda and I fell in behind them as Scarlett recounted the hours and hours of debriefing that occupied most of my night. The Brotherhood and I spared Scarlett and Leda the worst of it

—we didn't wake them until four in the morning. Since she hadn't taken part of it, Aurora remained fresh-faced and rosy. Scarlett, Leda, and myself struggled to contain our yawns.

Why is Aurora the Ambassador if she doesn't attend any of the pertinent events? Leda asked in a growl. *We didn't wake up at four in the morning to make her life easier.*

Someone else wasn't at the ball last night, I quipped.

Leda cut me a murderous glare.

Scarlett has better work boundaries than most, I added. *Speaking of, how was Hiddleston's family?*

Fine.

Busy?

Perpetually.

Not unlike yours.

Correct.

Her chin remained high, gaze straight ahead. A subtle defiance. She wouldn't give me more details because I'd upset her with my jab. Time had a way of wearing her down, particularly about Hiddleston. Relationships so thoroughly confounded her, she'd have to speak about it with me, Cilla, or Michelle eventually.

Cristian will arrive to interrogate the rebels in a few hours, Leda said. *Ten minutes before he arrives, Rognvald has agreed to force feed Veritas to Luca and the other one, Gustav. Tysen will do it. Apparently, as the newest Protector, he needs practice.*

Or no one else wants to, I countered.

I assumed that.

I didn't suppress a grimace. Forcing another witch to drink Veritas, a very unpleasant truth potion, sounded horrendous. Necessary, though. Unwinding the events of last night with Cristian, Ronaldo, the Brotherhood, Scarlett, and eventually Leda, made it clear that the Eastern Network had more than one rebel group. The rebellion had splintered. Many witches claimed to align with Giuseppi, others with Mizzuni. Still more with *other* Council Members whose names I couldn't remember.

Unwinding the truth from fiction had been impossible. A complicated tapestry moved over there, which necessitated whatever insight Luca might divulge.

What a delightful day, I said.

After that, she continued as if I hadn't spoken, *Scarlett plans to meet with Cristian alone to form a plan for the Eastern Network rebellion. After the help that our Protectors provided, and the obvious issues that the Eastern Network faces, Cristian has formally requested and accepted Scarlett's offer.*

Leda cast me a sidelong glance. Ahead of us, Scarlett spoke with her hands, making idle motions while Aurora, listening attentively, didn't take her gaze from Scarlett's face. The two of them cut a powerful duo together. A study of contrasts. One steady, one wild. One light, the other dark. One subtle, one bold.

For the first time, I could see why Scarlett chose her.

Scarlett angled her and Aurora's trajectory around another rabid fountain decorated with a sculpture of a ship cracking in half and sliding below stormy waves. Bodies spilled out in half-mangled torrents.

Macabre, this garden.

This is where you have to let go, Bianca, Leda said primly.

Of what?

The illusion that you have anything to do with this. Yes, you agreed to assist Camila. You have assisted her greatly. Yes, Cristian is asking for more help, but not from the Sisterhood. The Brotherhood is a better fit for him. Our focus is Scarlett. Unless Scarlett returns to the Eastern Network, it's not your business.

To punctuate the opinion, she met my stare.

I swallowed.

I started this to keep Priscilla safe.

You've done that. Or started her on the path to being safer. Now it's out of the Sisterhood's hands . . . unless that changes.

What about the Gallo family?

Cristian thinks it highly unlikely Ricardo Gallo has anything to do with it, she said smoothly. *There's no chatter around that family. Scarlett asked this morning, while you caught a quick nap.*

I drew up.

What?

Nodding, she continued. *If Ricardo did break Carcere, there's still no definitive link that puts him in the rebellion, or even related to it.*

The ledger!

As I said it, I understood it didn't count.

The ledger could have belonged to a Guardian or a worker or anyone else, she countered. *The assumption that it belonged to Ricardo Gallo is a long jump. While the ledger creates an implication that a rebel leader had their hand in breaking Carcere, it points no fingers to Ricardo Gallo. And,* she added somewhat delicately, *is a potential waste of time.*

With a sigh, Leda tucked her hands into her coat pocket. The furry interior, a soft white rabbit's fur, highlighted her differently-colored eyes. Strange, when her voice spoke in my head but her lips didn't move.

Cristian trusts the Protectors and is asking for help, she said. *They're receiving inside information on the rebellion this morning, and with it should have a chance at turning the tides. Ricardo Gallo is a distraction.*

Every instinct in me rebelled, but what could I say? All my proof lay on the words of a convicted criminal.

Greyson.

Leda folded her hands behind her back, falling into the ponderous, pursed lip stare that bespoke heavy thinking.

On that note, she continued in a musing tone, *I've considered a way we can angle this work with the Eastern Network for our good. Scarlett plans to debrief the Council now that she's promised more help. The Council will know by the end of the week that you were . . . extensively . . . involved.*

My mind spun with counter arguments, but all turned to ash in the face of logic and the raw fact that Cristian didn't ask for my help. Camila did. Camila, the all-but-defunct High Priestess who had as much political power as a child.

Jikes.

This situation stunk.

Instead of your involvement working against us, Leda continued, oblivious to my mental flailing, *I think we can make it work for us. We highlight how you stepped in, removed yourself, and focused on Scarlett afterward. Not to mention the trust that another High Priestess placed in you, as well as your seamless work with Rognvald. In a way, this builds a steady picture of involvement.*

Distracted, I said, *Hmmm.*

Consider it a . . . strategic angling . . . of less-than-ideal circumstances, she countered haughtily. *It's not easy finessing the reputation of someone as impetuous as you, Bianca. You give me very little to work with.*

Mollified by my silence, her shoulders drifted low again. *I long ago accepted the futility of boxing you into anything unless absolutely necessary or immediate. But to that end, the time has come for you to meet with another Council Member.*

A niggling frustration drew my thoughts to Camila. Several instances of not caring for her had arisen. Last night, in particular. Ronaldo, forced to go with the High Priest and use the few East Guards they could trust, would have abandoned Camila.

To whom?

Bianca?

Sorry. I shook my head. *Lost in thought. What do you need?*

Council Member Alice, over the Letum Wood Covens, wants to meet with you next.

Aurora's shocked gasp caused Leda and I to pause. Scarlett,

speaking more rapidly, continued to walk. Aurora kept up, her full lips gaping open.

"And then the Protectors and the Sisterhood converged on the scene to provide hidden support . . ."

While Scarlett's story trailed into greater details, I asked Leda, *Why Alice?*

The connection between both of you should be quite strong. She grew up a forester, and has been in position since your father took power and then left. Though she's historically quite neutral, she has a tendency toward aligning with the Highest Witch. Scarlett knew her from her time as a teacher, too. As I said before, she added, *I'm doing everything I can to avoid Georgette until the very last minute.*

I understand. Thank you.

Leda closed the conversation, and we trailed in silence.

I kicked aside a dirt clod, lost in thought again. A bird bounced onto the walled-off garden and hopped inside, prancing along the top edge of sweeping vines. Scarlett stopped in the middle of the garden as the story wound to a close.

Maybe Aurora had the right idea bringing us out here. The autumn chill kept me awake and my mind engaged. If we sat by a cozy fire, I would have fallen asleep. My eyelids felt like I'd rubbed sand inside them. Merrick, Brody, and Chi still hadn't left their debriefing. Rognvald required deeper examinations and reports than Scarlett or Cristian asked.

Sometimes, I didn't envy the Brotherhood.

Aurora's astonishment cleared. Her gaze flowed up and down Scarlett's profile, to Leda, and then myself. Her perusal lingered on me for a beat longer than the other two.

"Thank you for your summary, Your Highness. You look exhausted. Since I am well rested and up to date, might I suggest that I step in and oversee the next several hours of events? That will free you up to rest, or finish other duties. As Ambassador," Aurora added with a confident smile, "it is my duty."

Scarlett suppressed a yawn as she considered the idea. A quick flutter of her eyes to Leda likely meant they exchanged options through the communication magic before she said, "Thank you, Aurora. That initiative and offer would be most appreciated. I trust you to represent us well and that you understand our place in these . . . hostilities."

Something like relief flickered through Aurora's dark eyes. "I will strive to live up to your standards, High Priestess." She turned her focus to me. "Now, if Miss Monroe will stay behind, I have a request to make."

* * *

Aurora didn't wait for Scarlett and Leda to leave the garden before she rounded on me. Her hands clasped behind her back, lips pressed. Strands of silver dusted her close-cropped black curls.

"Bianca, I would appreciate your help."

"With?"

"Greyson."

My lips parted. I'd expected *many* things from her, but not that.

"Greyson?"

"Before Cristian arrives, I believe it would be advantageous to have more information from him."

"Did Scarlett approve?"

"Does she have to?"

"Well . . . no."

"She voiced her trust, did she not?"

"Yes," I drawled.

"These rebel splinter groups are not, I think, the same as the rebels that overtook Carcere and broke it. As such, Greyson may have more information that we can offer the High Priest before he arrives. I feel they're looking at this too narrowly, and the problem may be bigger. Unless we can prove it, however, Cristian will be too focused to see it. Scarlett didn't even mention the Gallo family when she reported suspicious names."

My jaw dropped.

Hadn't I just thought the same?

She quirked an eyebrow. "Are you catching flies, Miss Monroe?"

"No." I snapped my mouth shut. "I just . . . I didn't expect anyone to agree with me. That's all."

"You agree?"

"Yes."

"Leda doesn't?"

I shook my head. Perhaps Aurora's penchant for sleep over dramatics had an advantage. She often surprised me.

"I hadn't considered that you might see it also," I admitted. "I'm sorry."

"That's why you're not the Ambassador," she retorted. "It would be helpful to this process if we knew what splinter group Greyson originated with, if one at all. To offer that information to Cristian before the official interrogation would be wise."

"What advantage do you chase?" I asked. "The Central Network already has good standing with the East, and we can likely extract information on splinter groups from Luca when he has Veritas."

Her icy tone didn't cut all that deep, considering Aurora rarely approved of anything I said. "An Ambassador never takes risks that one can mitigate."

"Well . . . *never* is a big word . . ."

"As Head of the Sisterhood, I expected you to understand. There will be angles upon angles to this situation and Veritas only lasts so long. If we can anticipate angles, that allows us a deeper and more effective interrogation."

Realizing I had it wrong, I nodded. "You're right. I didn't see that."

"Try upgrading Greyson to a different room for the interrogation, and make it clear the information he gives will decide whether he stays. He needs to divulge more than he has ever divulged. You and I? We need proof that it's the Gallo family. Irrefutable proof that doesn't rely on Greyson's testimony."

Diabolical, but wise. Grandfather would have approached from an entirely different angle, if at all. Which made Aurora even more intriguing.

"I know what to do, Ambassador, but it will take at least a day to get results on the information that you want. Maybe two days. There's a binding in place, you see."

"Well . . . do the best you can. If we can't get it now, we'll still need it later."

She turned to go, then stopped. Calling over her shoulder, she said, "Oh, and have the kitchen send light ipsum with you."

"Light ipsum?"

"He favored it as a Council Member. Do it," she commanded, expression twisting with irritation. "You'll get better results."

Aurora vanished without another word. Sighing in the midst of a garden tempest, I trudged to the corner. Decidedly, Greyson was the last witch I wanted to talk to.

No.

Strike that.

Georgette was the last witch I wanted to talk to. With a groan, I forced my feet to move across the dying grass.

Sometimes, the Sisterhood wasn't all that *fun* either.

* * *

Greyson's upgraded cell remained in the dungeons, but offered a rectangular slit to the outside. The air vent stood a handspan wide, the length of my arm, with a grate-lined, magic-protected visibility to the outside which provided a little light. Fresh air streamed weakly in, though not much. I couldn't fathom where it peered out on.

While nothing to brag about, it was still far better than his previous situation buried in the earth and stone. A positive step toward his desire to be house-bound outside. Basic accouterments didn't change, either. One moldy mattress, a bucket for refuse, and rats for company. He must have hidden the five books, because I couldn't fathom he would have surrendered them.

"Well," I said brightly. "You smell a little less rank down here. Oh, look! There's a hint of sunshine coming in as well. Look at you! Moving up in the world."

Greyson pouted from the cell, his spine nearly touching the far wall. A mug of light ipsum floated at my side, the glass edges frosted despite the warm castle air. He eyed it, then me.

I waited.

So did he.

A full twenty seconds passed while we stared. I realized I assumed he'd be as willing to speak as before. If not more, considering he held an upgraded situation in his hands.

"Do you like it?" I asked.

He said nothing.

"No?" I reared back. "How interesting. Because you can stay here, where you have some fresh air and certainly a little more light, if you're willing to answer some questions."

Greyson swallowed hard.

"What questions?"

"Things happened in the East last night."

"Things are always happening there," he said with lazy disregard. "Why should I care about anything that happened last night?"

"The rebellion has splintered into several different groups. It's now beyond logical control. The Protectors are helping the

Eastern leaders now. They plan to attack the splinter groups, I believe."

Surprise registered in his eyes. He turned to his mattress, lifted a dank corner, and withdrew a book. Perusing it, he said, "I couldn't care less. Did you have a question?"

"Who broke you out of Carcere?"

His nose twitched. "You know that I can't say."

Smiling, I lifted the mug of ipsum as if to give a toast and had a sip. The malty flavor slid down my throat, cool and yeasty. He glowered. Twirling my finger in a circle, I said, "If you want to stay in this cell, you'll say."

"I. can't."

Leaning closer, I said, "Bindings can be broken, Greyson. You know that as well as I do."

"You want me to break a magical binding," he hissed, "to tell you information about an Eastern Network rebellion?"

"No." I set the ipsum down and stepped closer. "I want you to break the binding to give me the insider information that proves Ricardo Gallo is the head of this rebellion."

So I can keep Camila and Tomasso and Priscilla safe, I added silently.

"Give it to you?" he said. "No one else wants that information? How very expected. The Eastern Network has never appreciated the underdog, you see."

"Do you miss your previous cell?"

"Breaking a binding is not worth it."

I shrugged. "That's your call, not mine."

"You can get the information elsewhere."

"From who?"

His lips pressed, as if under sudden and great strain. I waited, brow lifted in expectation. He grunted, sweat beading on his brow.

"All I'm asking for is names. Confirmation that proves the true origin point for the upheaval."

The ipsum elevated, froth still high at the top. Greyson glanced around the cell. His hands clenched at his side as he slyly cut his gaze to mine. "To break a binding might be more than my weakened body can take. I better have a full meal first. Or, to that end, several."

Scoffing, I spelled the ipsum away.

"Break the binding and tell me everything you know about the witches that freed you from Carcere, Greyson. If you haven't done so by the time I return, you're back to the old cell where I will advise the Council to let you rot instead of kill you."

The reverberating door slam escorted me out. To the Guardian outside his cell, I said, "I'll be back tomorrow. Keep an eye on him, and alert me quietly of any changes."

<h1 style="text-align:center">Chapter Twenty-Six</h1>

That evening, I slipped into the Gatehouse. Frozen rain pelted the windows, invisible under the shadow of night. The storm cast a dreary pall on an already difficult evening.

Two Protectors—Tysen and Caffrey—stood near the shared fireplace in the middle of the room, next to Rognvald. The bass rumble of male voices issued from the right, where the Head of Guardian's door was closed. Talmund must be inside with his Captains.

"Stay a minute," Rognvald called to me. "I'm finishing with these two and need to speak with you."

Tysen sent me a smile, but returned his attention to Rognvald with all the sincerity and interest of a new recruit. Their assignment finalized two minutes later, and they dispersed. Rognvald lowered into a chair that magically expanded to accommodate his broad shoulders. He motioned me into another one.

"Rough day?" I asked.

"Where were you during the interrogation?"

"Busy."

"Where?"

"With Greyson."

"Huh. Has Scarlett updated you?"

"No. She's been in meetings at the castle all day."

He smoothed a hand over his face. "Nothing shocking came of the interrogation. Luca revealed at least fifteen different splinter groups, and more constantly forming. The seven Council Members made it worse for the rebellion, certainly. Their attempts to assert power just created yet more chaos."

"Any central figure identified?"

"No."

Insecurity nudged me with Leda's voice. *Of course no central figure is identified,* it said. *Because Greyson is sending you on a wild goose chase and you're wasting your time, not to mention the Sisterhood's opportunity.*

"Protectors have been sent to the Eastern Network. Assuming all goes well, the different splinter groups will be leaderless by tomorrow."

"You think it'll work?"

"How do you stop a rebellion?" he countered.

"Destroy their leaders."

"Or you increase their chaos until they can't handle it." With a sobriety that perfectly matched the low evening energy, he said, "Chaos kills even the ugliest motivation."

Setting aside my insecurities, I studied Rognvald. Seeing his exhausted state, I found the courage to ask a question that had been burning for weeks.

"Is it worth it?"

He peered at me through two fingers.

"What?"

I waved a hand around the Gatehouse. "This. The sacrifices. The work. Do you ever regret becoming a Protector?"

His eyes narrowed. "Have you ever asked your father that question?"

"I have."

"What did he say?"

I offered a slow smile. "That's his business, not yours." More gently, I added, "If you don't want to tell me, I understand. I can see how the answer might be . . . closely held. I'm just curious what years of this work ends in."

Rognvald scoffed. "I have nothing to hide. It's worth it. For the most part," he added. "Some weeks are harder than others."

"Why is it worth it?"

"Because of this week."

"This week?"

"Things happened. We were ready. We received intelligence, supplied it to leadership, and they made decisions to improve witches' lives. *That* is worth it."

The fire crackled as I pondered his answer. How many years had Rognvald fought without an affirmative response? How dark were the nights when they didn't manage to discover the secrets and keep witches safe?

What if I *hadn't* stopped Greyson?

"Can you accept a career that will be similar?" he inquired.

"I don't know."

Rognvald paused, head tilted. After five seconds, he straightened up. An incoming message from a Protector, probably. He'd already moved on from our brief discussion, which was a relief.

"Initial attacks on the splinter group leaders start in four hours. Protectors are moving into place as we speak."

"My protector, too?"

"Yours, too." He tilted an eyebrow. "You don't talk to him through the magic, do you?"

"No."

"Good."

Merrick and I hadn't spoken since our last internal conversation at the Eastern Network ball. With this moving in the background, I anticipated it would be days before we spoke in person again.

"I'll include you in the updates, if you want," Rognvald offered.

"Yes, thank you."

Exhaustion pushed me out of the chair and away from the cozy fire. More sitting and I'd fall asleep in the Gatehouse. I paused halfway out the door. "Thanks, Rognvald. I know that was a personal question to ask."

Rognvald said, "You're welcome," and I opened the door. Stinging raindrops shattered against my shoulders as I entered the storm. I paused halfway outside to glance over my shoulder. Rognvald's chin rested in his palm. He slumped to the side, yawning. As exhausted as I felt, he must be worse, and another almost full night of raids to track.

"Do you know if Cristian has any plans to search for a single leader?"

"He didn't mention any."

"Are all Protectors assigned to the rebellion?"

"All of them except me and Tysen."

"Tysen?" I reared back. "What did he do wrong?"

"Nothing." He hefted his beefy shoulders in a shrug. "He's the youngest. The older guys wanted the opportunity, so they received it." Another wide yawn split his lips. "Sometimes, it sucks to be the new guy."

Chapter Twenty-Seven

T he sound of clashing wooden swords met me at Papa's house in Letum Wood. Two figures—one tall, the other medium height and spry—circled each other in his yard. Ava and Papa had returned to practicing.

A good sign.

"Elbow up," he called. Then an approving, "That's it."

Ava smirked and advanced. She was forever sloppy with her footwork, just like I had been at her age. Focusing on the basics was particularly difficult for her. Like any teenager, she wanted to stop the boring stuff and get into the meat of sword fighting, but she wasn't ready.

Having an Inheritance curse lurking over my shoulder had shoved me out of teenage angst and right into must-save-myself territory.

Amused, I folded my arms over my chest and leaned my shoulder against the house. Ava growled when Papa tapped her on the shoulder with his sword, swerving out of her reach with his perfect footwork. He laughed, displaying a vivid smile I hadn't seen in months.

"Nice try, Ava. If you're going to ignore your footwork, you either have to be faster, or more deliberate. Since you're already fast enough, you know what you need to do."

Panting, she lowered the sword.

"I hate footwork."

"I know."

"It's boring."

He leaned the tip of his sword into the dirt. "But you still have to do it. And no," he said quickly, tapping her on the shin with his foot for emphasis, "you can't ask Baxter to use god magic to bequeath the skills, like you did with the common language."

Ava scowled as she shoved curls out of her eyes. Priscilla convinced her to grow her hair longer, instead of chopped short. Often, she put it into rows. Hiddleston, who had locks halfway to his elbow, nearly had her convinced to try them. A year before she graduated from the Network school, she planned to try them in order to prepare for her year at sea.

"I wouldn't have asked Baxter," she muttered, sweat trickling down her neck as her breath caught up. They cut a picturesque scene that made my throat tighten. Is this what Mama saw when Papa and I worked together? No wonder Mama laughed from the sidelines while Papa taught me with the same long suffering and patience. Like cutting a piece of cloth out of the past and waving it.

I cleared my throat.

"Mind if I join?"

They turned to me at the same moment. Smiles broke out. Ava reached me with a barreling hug first. I caught her, laughing, as Papa set his wooden sword aside.

"He's mean," she whispered in my ear.

I laughed harder.

"But I'll be mean back," she said with determination. When I pulled away, she had a stubborn glint in her smile. "I'll get him. One day."

"If you perfect your footwork."

Rolling her eyes, she released me. At Papa's unstated insistence, Ava gathered up his sword and hers, coiled a rope out of the dirt, wound it together, and bound them tight. The tidying was critical to the routine. A necessary addition to teach thoroughness and follow through.

I saw the lesson now.

So clearly.

Papa glanced overhead. As always, no direct sun was visible from this low in the canopy, but after enough time in the forest, a general idea of time passage became apparent.

"Great timing." He propped his foot on a stump and leaned his forearm on his bent knee. "Ava has to return to school for dinner."

She neatly set the wooden swords and rope inside of a box on his porch before closing it and securing the clasp. Just like my *outside box* as a young girl. How strange, living history from the other side.

Ava paused in front of Papa and inclined her head. "Thank you for the lesson, Mr. Black. I appreciate your time and patience. When should I return?"

His lips twitched. Yet another eternal facet of his sword work routines. Gratitude and scheduling, no doubt sprinkled with a touch of etiquette as required by Miss Priscilla.

"Tomorrow, same time."

Ava's eyes illuminated. "Tomorrow! See you then."

Before I could ask how she planned to return, vines wrapped her ankles. She disappeared into a spell cast by Letum Wood itself. Ava, a mortal, had no ability to use goddess magic, nor could she have access to god magic. The forest stepped in often. Deasylva, it seemed, was fond of Ava.

Papa nudged me in the shoulder. "What are you doing here?"

"Came to check on Cat."

"Oh?"

A purring sound came from overhead. Cat lounged on a tree limb, tail swishing lazily back and forth. She licked her paws, narrowly regarding me through judgmental eyes.

"Cat is thriving. Doing better than me, in fact." His head craned up to study her. "I've never seen a cat so wholly dedicated to pest removal."

"The ideal feline."

"So I hear."

"What about you?" I asked, arms spread. "I didn't think you'd be here. Looks like you've been home for a day or two."

Scoffing, he crossed his arms over his chest and headed toward the open door. I followed him inside, where the windows spilled fresh air and shadows congregated in the far corners.

"I got bored in the desert."

"Too much survival?"

He grimaced. "And dust."

"You mean you want to *use* the home you so painstakingly and lovingly built?" I gasped dramatically. "What a shock!"

"Har har," he said flatly. "But also that, yes. Seemed like a waste of my time not to do more here. Also, I missed the forest."

"Did you?"

"Didn't realize how much until I left it. Letum Wood kind of gets into the skin."

I sat at the table across from him. A tea kettle swung toward the fire, which blazed with sudden life. A tray filled with sugar and tea floated closer. Two cups separated, hovering until they nimbly settled in front of us.

"How are you *really* doing Papa?" I asked. "We parted after a tough conversation."

"Better."

"Really?"

He nodded. "It's like Marten says—sometimes, you just gotta shake the past out. I'm sorry, B, if my absence was hard for you, or if I missed anything because of it. I wasn't trying to abandon you."

"Papa, stop. It's fine. You're allowed to flail."

"Thanks."

He spun the tea mug around on the table, teeth tapping together in thought. His eyes had cleared since last time. The oppressive weight he tried to hide didn't exist in the same recesses. Had he truly let go of his demons?

"Well, fine or not," he eventually said, "I am sorry. I've returned home to . . . think through a few things. For one, I need to figure out what's next in my life. I can't vagabond forever, though it did feel good."

A subtle glance around confirmed nothing of Regina visible. Papa kept his home neat, even in the midst of construction, but little signs of life existed. Not even the heel of her favorite bread loaf or short sword.

"Regina?"

He shook his head. "I'm not sure. I might have really mucked this up."

"How?"

"Too little," he whispered, "too late."

He must have spoken with her—or tried to. My heart ached at the thought. It didn't sound like Regina, but then, Regina hadn't been herself last time I spoke with her. Seeing the reality of my parental figures flopping their way through decisions was disheartening. Didn't this get any easier?

By my observation, not at all.

"I haven't given up on her," he said, "and I'm doing what I can to make amends. It'll just take time. She's going through a lot also, and she's transitioning out of the Masters. I haven't been there to support her, which was my fault. Both of us are a mess."

I laughed to keep from crying, and he looked the same.

When the forced hilarity settled, he asked, "So? Merrick and you."

"Merrick and me," I repeated. "We set a date."

"Oh?"

"About a month away. Third month of fall, third week, third day." I shot a quick smile. "Easy anniversary."

Barking a laugh, he promised, "I'll be there."

"Bring Regina, if you can. I'd love to have her."

"I hope she comes. Who else are you inviting?"

"Not sure." I flashed a quick smile. "I haven't tackled that yet. Probably my friends, you, Grandfather."

"Castle staff?"

"Ugh." I moaned. "Let's not get into this right now. I have no idea who to invite and the thought makes me sick to my stomach."

He brought the boiling tea kettle closer with a chortle that, had it appeared as more of a laugh, might have instigated a battle.

"No shield yet, either," I said, just to change the conversation.

"No?"

"Can't find the right one."

A low silence followed.

"Why are you here, B?" he asked gently. The lilt in his questioning tone set me back. I'd expected him to know I hadn't come here just for Cat, but it happened quicker than I anticipated.

Exhaling, I said, "I'm not sure."

"Why you're here?"

"What I'm doing."

Papa tilted his head back, hooting with laughter. "Here I thought I was the only one! If you want answers, you might have come to the exact wrong witch."

Chuckling with him, I reached for a tea sachet, grateful to have something to do with my hands.

"No, it's not like that. I . . . I'm confused. I might be focusing on the wrong thing and setting the Sisterhood up to fail. My path is against conventional wisdom, and nothing stacks up to support my gut."

He leaned back, hands resting on the table. Two fingers twitched in an encouraging gesture. With a sigh, I unloaded the situation with the East, Camila, the unfinished nature of the work, the narrowness of working for Scarlett. By the time I wound to an end, daylight ebbed. The tea had gone cold, and Papa's concentrated stare hadn't wavered. Candles illuminated around us with flickering light.

"In the end," I finished, "I don't want to run a Sisterhood that can't take missions I'm able to do. That scope is too narrow. But Leda is right. I can't save everyone." I trailed away, thinking of what Leda said in the gardens about letting go. "How do I . . . how do I let go?"

Papa's brow lifted as I finally stopped speaking, my voice hoarse. I swallowed cold tea, grateful to take a break, while he puffed his cheeks and blew out a breath. The relief was an unleashed burden.

"It's a tough situation, B. Most of your missions will be. There's no single answer here, either. They're all intricate, dependent on multiple factors. You have to get rid of the idea that a single path exists. It's just not true."

As flat as he had been earlier, I said, "Well, that's frustrating."

Papa chuckled soundlessly, shaking his head. "No, not like that. Sometimes, it's easy to walk away from a mission. Sometimes it isn't. Letting go is less about unresolved tasks and more about what's up here."

He tapped his temple with the tip of his finger.

My gaze softened.

"You have to rearrange how you look at each mission. You're viewing your work with Camila through the lens of fixing the Eastern Network. Leda is correct—that's not your job. But you don't really believe it yet."

Searching within myself, I realized how correctly he spoke. "I guess . . . you're right. But that doesn't change my thoughts on Ricardo Gallo."

He held up a finger. "Ah, but *finishing* isn't the same as letting go."

"True."

"When you run the Sisterhood, you have to look at each day, sometimes each hour, sometimes each *minute*, through the lens of *what good can I do here today?* Instead of *what problems can I fix?* Saving isn't always fixing. Sometimes, saving is walking away and letting *them* save themselves."

"But what if it's not enough?" My voice sounded small in the descending night. "Camila can't stop the rebellion. Neither can I. Cristian—or anyone else for that matter—won't consider my worries about Ricardo. Everything feels futile."

Papa's affectionate smile cut right through me. "It's not about achieving, B. It's about *being*. You will never do enough. There's always more. More missions, more people in pain, more struggles to resolve. But if you can *be* the witch you want to be— a witch that changes the world for someone else in some small way—then it's enough. It's always enough."

Tears collected in my eyes. "That's how you did it?"

"Eventually, yes. Except, you're much wiser than me and are asking for advice. I didn't do that. This realization took years for me to understand. You let go of expectation," he reasserted with a sage wisdom that made me think of Grandfather, "and you stay with yourself in *this* moment. Did you save the Eastern Network? No. Did you aid Camila?"

"Yes."

"Greatly," he added. "You aided her *greatly*. You fought for her alone. You empowered her when no one else did. Those small acts could change the entire course of the Eastern Network. Now, frame your question around who you want to be. Do you want to be a witch that leaves unresolved questions behind that no one else is asking?"

"Absolutely not."

He grinned. "There you go. There's still work to do. What if it's a false lead?" He shrugged. "Doesn't matter. You showed up in the most important way possible, and you negated a potential threat. It's a win."

"But the Council?"

"What of them?"

Bobbing for an answer, I could find none.

"I guess . . . I don't know."

"Do you need the approval of the Council to be Bianca?"

"No."

"Exactly."

The aimless map I wandered illuminated with greater clarity. What had once been cast in the shadow of doubt and insecurity now had texture.

I understood.

"I did good," I breathed. "I didn't fail her."

"Did you give up on her?"

"No. At least . . . not when she needed me."

"Would you help her if she asked again?"

"In a heartbeat."

"Then there's no failure. You're being a witch that is helping someone who needs it *when* they need it. You're being, not doing. There's a difference."

"Expectation," I repeated.

He nodded through a sigh. "Expectation." With a snap of two fingers, he added, "By the way? I should take a dose of my own advice. Thank you for coming to me. Apparently, we both needed to hear what I had to say."

The chair scuttled as I shifted it across the floor to sit next to him. Leaning against his side, Papa draped an arm around the back of my chair. I tilted my head to his shoulder, content to stare at the crackling fire and let his thoughts sink in.

He ruffled my hair.

"I love you, B."

"I love you too, Papa."

* * *

A letter flapped in front of me as I ascended the main staircase of Chatham Castle and turned down the Royal Hall, heading for Scarlett's office. Unknown handwriting filled a scroll that I read as I walked.

The prisoner is ill.

No signature. I didn't subdue my smile. Greyson being ill meant he was trying—perhaps succeeding—to break the binding.

What perfect timing.

I tucked it into my pocket for later. Amusement brightened Leda's expression when I stalked into Scarlett's office. Hiddleston sat at Scarlett's desk, using the pad of his thumb to speed through an assortment of parchments.

"Fifty-seven," he declared.

"Excellent," Leda said. "We can send those on their way and be ready to close for lunch."

Scarlett bustled into the room. "I'm proud of you, Bianca," she declared.

"Really?" I whirled. "For what?"

Huffing, she tugged at the bottom of her bodice, sent me her typical assessing stare that spoke more to teacher than to High

Priestess, and said, "I just had a conversation with Council Member Frederick."

I gulped.

"He relayed the conversation in full. Mostly to inform me," she gave a delighted smile, "of the *questionable choice of witches you work with.*"

Leda frowned.

"It's a powerful thing when a woman begins to understand her worth," Scarlett continued. "You stood up to him admirably, though I'm sure he didn't relay the full story. His picture painted enough words I can read between the lines. Fortunately, you understand your value early in your career. Could have been helpful even earlier," she muttered, "but this is acceptable."

Leda, torn between irritation and relief, appeared in a bind. After several twisted expressions, she said, *Just be careful with this newfound confidence, or our strategically sculpted deck of cards will ignite in the flames of your arrogance.*

I shot her a smile.

She seethed.

Scarlett gathered several scrolls as she headed for the doorway. "I'll be meeting with Aurora in the Council Hall, Leda. I need a break from the office, and it should only take an hour."

"Thank you, Your Highness."

After Scarlett left, Leda faced me. "Regardless of what Council Member Frederick thinks of you, Council Member Henry has been singing your praises to anyone who will listen. According to him, you took him on a grand adventure and introduced him to several toadstools."

"With that support, witches will flock to approve the Sisterhood."

Leda paused behind Scarlett's desk, surveyed the very careful arrangement of items on top, tweaked an inkwell, and gave a nod of satisfaction. Perfection abounded, from the angled lines of her notepad to the purple-tipped quill resting on the side, without a smudge of ink to blur the parchment blot pad below it.

"Let's not get ahead of ourselves," she said lightly. "One Council Member does not give a Council majority. If we want salaries for this work, we need a majority of them to vote for the budget. Also, the budget has to come from somewhere. Who do you think will sacrifice it?"

"Covens?" I guessed.

She clicked her tongue. "Yes, that's it. A minimal amount per year across all Covens, but still. It adds up. They're old ladies clutching their pearls."

Cast in that light, we had a snowball chance in Hatha of surviving, even if the currency for our salaries wasn't all that grand in the scheme of all that the Network required to run.

Precedent, and all that.

Change, too.

The Council Members fought more than Leda and myself. They fought the unknown. The frightening. Change. Currency. Not unlike Papa, they gave the impression of flailing and not knowing everything. In the wake of my discussion with Papa, my former stress about the Council's approval ebbed.

How could they know any better than the rest of us?

Weren't we all flailing together?

The Council Members in the Eastern Network floated through my mind. Had their closed-mindedness started small, then expanded? When an intricate problem such as dissatisfaction grew to be a Network-wide blanket solution, problems resulted. I imagined that most Council Members attempted to build guardrails and prevent the worst.

"Regardless," Leda said in her prim way, drawing me back to the office, "things went so well with Council Member Henry that Alice reports she's very excited to meet with you. In that vein, I think it'll be wisest for you to scatter in some women next."

"Why?"

"A hunch."

I attempted to hide a yawn. I'd stayed up far too late last night waiting for Merrick to return. He hadn't. The bed had been empty in the morning, and my stomach with it.

She studied me. "There have been no updates from the Brotherhood. Scarlett asked Rognvald not to provide them through the night, but to give her a summary after she notifies him she's ready. He hasn't requested a time to stop in, and Scarlett's schedule isn't very forgiving today."

"I wondered why it was so quiet. Rognvald promised me updates, too. I haven't heard any."

But I hadn't had the courage to ask. Not with Merrick tangled into the mission. It might look too much like an obsessed partner, and not a professional desire to not miss out.

"Last I heard, things were progressing in their attempts to remove rebel leadership, but slower than planned," Leda said. "The Protectors went in a little hot, if you ask me, and too big for their britches."

"The first two splinter groups were the initial targets, right?"

She nodded. "I take it Merrick didn't return?"

I shook my head.

"You would have heard if he was hurt, so that's a small consolation."

"True."

A towering figure appeared in the doorframe. Hiddleston. Seeing us in the middle of Scarlett's office, he paused. Leda glanced up and her expression softened into a smile I'd never seen her give before.

"Good morning," she said.

He smiled back. A soft gift of a thing. Not wide and brimming with energy, as he often gave. A reserved one, just for Leda. It faded as quickly as it appeared.

"There have been updates from the Brotherhood," Hiddleston said. "Tysen came by just now, asked if you'd heard. When I said that we hadn't, he filled me in on the last things Rognvald relayed and asked him to report."

"What are they?" I asked.

Hiddleston swiveled to face me. "The Protectors are all fine. Only two of the splinter group leaders were findable by those they planned to scout. Some of them were more organized than Luca led us to believe."

"The Veritas failed?" Leda asked.

Hiddleston shrugged.

I shook my head. "No, not that. The biggest tool they have is chaos, and the chaos itself probably made it so Luca didn't have the best information. That, or he was Veritas tolerant, which would make it easier to soften the truth into something less . . . pure."

"That's Tysen's assumption," he said.

"What now?" Leda asked.

At her question, Hiddleston lifted a hand, holding a *Chatham Chatterer* scroll, half unrolled. The top headline said everything we needed to know.

Chaos in the East

"The Eastern Network Council has issued demands prior to extermination," he said.

My eyes blew wide open.

"What?"

"From what Brody and Merrick have said, the rebellion has come to a tipping point. They gathered intelligence while scouting splinter group heads. Both Merrick and Brody are having a hard time finding their previous contacts. Everyone has scattered, many to aid the individual rebellions. Some splinter groups have killed suspected Aldana allies, and Necce emptied out."

Blood turned to slush in my veins at the thought. "It must be pure mayhem over there."

"Beyond that. Looting, crimes, devastation. Homes burned down. It's wild."

Hiddleston flipped the scroll so that it closed, then floated it to Leda. She accepted, but didn't take her gaze off of him.

"What does it mean, Hiddleston?"

"Cristian has lost control," he said. "Utterly. He and his very few trusted staff have secured themselves in Magnolia Castle. They locked it down with spells and withdrew the East Guards to keep the Guardian force safe. As long as Magnolia Castle holds, they can weather whatever happens. But not forever. At some point . . ."

He trailed away.

A lump formed in my throat when I thought of Camila. She'd be safe with her son, surely. He wouldn't have forgotten her under this sort of duress, but did she *know*? Undoubtedly, she had no chance to send me a message and request help. The thought of Ronaldo being present with her comforted me.

"With all this going on in the meantime, what are the Protectors planning?" I asked.

He shook his head. "No idea." Before he finished speaking, my words to Rognvald were already in progress.

Just heard the updates from Tysen. I conjured my *Chatterer* scroll and glimpsed the ink columns. *What is the plan? Do you need help?*

The individual Protectors have it under control for now, as much as they can, he immediately replied. Despite his fatigue from the day before, he clearly hadn't gotten any sleep. Despair threatened. How could I fix this?

No, wait.

I couldn't fix this.

Not for the East. Nor Camila. Nor Merrick. Nor could I fix this for Rognvald. That wasn't my job.

It's not about achieving, B, Papa had said. *It's about being.*

Drawing in a deep breath, I set aside expectations and asked, *How can I help you, Rognvald? You must be exhausted and Scarlett has no plans to leave the castle today.*

I'm going to sleep for two hours. Tysen will be in the Gatehouse, monitoring chatter on the communication magic. If any of the on-site Protectors tell him to wake me, he will. They have their orders. Stay available, he added. *We might need you.*

Understood, I said.

Thank you for offering.

Leda and Hiddleston stood together near the windows. Hiddleston gripped her tiny hand in his expansive one. Leda set aside the paperwork to hold his hands and murmur quietly. When I turned to face them again, she didn't pull away.

"I didn't listen to whatever conversation you just dropped into," she said, "but I presume it was with Rognvald. What did he say?"

While I tied my hair into a braid out of my face, I updated her on the breezy conversation. Relief showed in her eyes.

"I'm glad he's getting sleep."

Reaching down to remove my shoes, I said, "Me too."

Leda eyed me with growing resignation. "I don't think I need to ask, but I'm going to anyway. Are you heading to the Eastern Network?"

Spelling my shoes back to the house, and whipping my braid off my shoulder, I faced her again. "Yes. I'm going to find Camila and check on her. Let Scarlett know what I'm doing. Don't let her leave the castle without me."

Chapter Twenty-Eight

L ife deserted Magnolia Castle.

No visible Guardians patrolled the exterior, but magical signatures roved at every entrance and below clusters of windows. They rotated on a short schedule that must have a timer. I heard no verbal exchanges.

An impatient ocean slammed against the sandbar behind the castle, occluding the air with thick humidity and layers of frosting-like clouds. A cool breeze whispered by, trailing the hair off my shoulders in cutting staccatos.

Far more unsettling was the inaudible blanket over Necce. The bustling city had fallen into a calm that I couldn't equate. The *Chatterer* updated their article to say that most splinter groups circled Necce and spread outward, toward other cities.

The faint, humming sheen of magic meant someone had cast a powerful spell—or several someones—to trigger a warning or prevent someone from transporting into the building. I'd have to find another way inside.

Easiest path first.

I summoned a small slip of paper, a pencil, and scrawled a quick note.

Outside. I want to check on you. Where should I come in?

Camila replied within thirty seconds.

Around the back, by the sea. Stand below my windows. I'll send a friend.

Instead of transporting to the exact spot, I kept my invisibility spell in place and worked my way around the edges of Magnolia Castle barefoot, keeping an eye on the exterior. It wasn't my imagination. The building itself seemed to be weeping. The stone turned gray instead of white. The spiderweb crack that I had seen briefly before stuck out more obviously now.

The chance that Magnolia Castle had always been in this state of disrepair and the Eastern Network hid it with magic was possible, though unlikely.

Something caused this.

Ten minutes passed before I arrived at the place Camila indicated, which wasn't hard to find. Several Guardians stood nearby, but they must have been forewarned, because they made no move to stop me. As soon as I stopped walking, a familiar face appeared.

Baxter.

He pressed a finger to his lips, vanished into thin air. A hand wrapped my arm, and we immediately stood in the High Priestess' personal chamber. God magic washed through me in a light tingle. It worked differently—so differently. Moving from one place to another with god magic took little more than a thought before arrival. Transportation pressed, prodded, until it finally worked. The ease of god magic always vexed me.

Camila shuffled across the room, fuzzy slippers in place, when Baxter revealed us. Relief smoothed her features as Camila clasped me into her arms and cried, "Thank you!"

Over the top of her petite head, I sent Baxter a questioning glance. He pressed his lips together, shaking his head once. Whatever had happened in Magnolia Castle since the official revolt of the Council Members, it must have been nothing good.

Camila pulled away. "What do you know?" she pleaded.

"Not much."

"I just returned to the East," Baxter said, "so I also don't know much of what's happening within or without the Council. I was in the Southern Network until a few minutes ago. As soon as I heard . . ."

He trailed away in a sublime reminder that Baxter didn't live here, either. As demigod representative across the Networks, he traveled from place to place.

"Are you welcome here?"

"Yes. I promised Cristian I will ensure no demigod involvement in the rebellion, and that's all he cares about."

"Which isn't surprising."

"Fair, yes."

"Does Gelas know about the Eastern Network rebellion?"

"If he does, he doesn't care. The gods have other things on their minds."

Also unsurprising.

Sensing Baxter's compounding frustration, I turned the topic of our conversation. "Most of what you'll read in the *Chatterer* is what I know, Camila. The Protectors haven't shared many updates through the night, but I know two splinter leaders have been subdued. It wasn't easy, apparently."

She paled. "That's it?"

Reluctantly, I nodded.

"But I thought—"

"They planned to have them all taken care of by now? It must have gone awry. From what I hear, the chaos is too much to easily battle. The leaders are disappearing, killed, hidden, or lying about their identities and pretending to not be the leader."

Camila pressed a shaking hand to her forehead, returning her attention to the newsscroll. Baxter asked, "Any Protectors harmed?"

"Not yet."

"I've been trying to eavesdrop on conversations when I can," Camila said, "but Cristian moves from room to room. He's upset. Ronaldo and Aldo are doing the best they can to obtain trustworthy information. It's hard."

Camila reached for my hand, clutching it. "I'm safe in Magnolia Castle. As long as our spells hold, and they will, we can weather out the rebellion while Cristian and the Protectors attempt to speak to the splinter group leaders and stem the violence."

"What can I do?"

She squeezed my hand, then loosened her white-knuckled grip. Haunted, she shook her head. "Nothing." Camila sank to her divan, propped her chin on her hands. "There's nothing we can do right now."

Glancing at Baxter, I tossed my ace. "What about Ricardo Gallo, Your Majesty? Who is looking for him?"

Camila blinked. "Ricardo Gallo? Oh." She drew up. "Yes. I forgot. They are so quiet. You were looking into him, no?"

I nodded.

Puzzled, she said, "You still think they have responsibility?"

"I do."

"I hear you. We need to check everything. How can I help?"

The extension of her trust settled a tight knot in my throat. Few strong reasons existed to chase my hunch.

"My plan hinges on Greyson breaking a magical binding and providing confirmation. I'll let you know what I plan from there, but we require a prisoner willing to endure unspeakable agony in order to tell us the truth about Ricardo Gallo."

Camila patted my arm in a gesture that reminded me of Grandfather and stared into my eyes.

"Do what you must. I will call you if I need help. For now, we wait. We let Cristian and the Protectors work. You can transport onto my balcony anytime. Only you. Bring no one else, it won't work. I will set the magic very specifically. Let's hope you don't have to use it."

Chapter Twenty-Nine

Greyson groaned on the prison floor, thrashing. Sweat soaked his pitiful clothing, saturating it to a rank yellow. His skeletal figure was ghostly white and shuddering.

Broken bindings took a physical toll as punishment for going against the agreement. Days could often pass of a fever-like agony, filled with hallucinations. Depending on the type of binding wrought—magical, blood, verbal, written, or a sundry of rare others—the consequences could also be devastating. Non-recoverable, or death.

Awful.

"Been like that for hours," Jack the Guardian said with a shrug. "Isn't responding to questions or food, even. You know it's rough when he doesn't respond to food."

"That," I said quietly, "is what you get when you make a binding with a demon. Well, he's certainly in the middle of it, isn't he?" Patting Jack's shoulder, I said, "Let me know when he calms, please? Should be soon."

* * *

While ascending the spiral stairs away from the prison, I quickly decided my plans. With Greyson breaking his binding, things in the East reliant on Protectors and Cristian, and Scarlett not requiring me for the next several days, I had time to complete my research on Magnolia Castle.

Unfortunately, a far worse enemy awaited. I skidded to a fast stop right before slamming into a pile of blonde curls with natural dark streaks, coiffed ringlets, a defined set of bright lips, and a cold smile.

Council Member Georgette purred, "Merry meet, Bianca."

Help! I said to Leda. *Georgette has cornered me on the landing to the dungeon.*

"It's a pleasure to see you, Council Member."

Georgette's amusement appeared real enough when she chuckled. "I'm sure you think that's true. The opportunity to run into you is rather welcome. Would you mind stepping into a different room? I've been meaning to speak with you."

She paused, brow arched high. A hint of challenge underlined her tone. "If you're not busy with the Sisterhood and its many . . . opportunities?"

A jab, definitely.

Shock prevented me from fully feeling my disdain. With equal steadiness, I replied, "I can make space for a chat."

Georgette bustled ahead of me. We slid away from the staircase and toward a lesser-trafficked portion of the castle.

We left and are heading to a different room.

I have no idea what she wants with you, Leda said. *But it probably isn't going to be good. Brace yourself.*

Oh, it wasn't difficult to guess what Georgette wanted to speak about. Whether or not I wanted to hear it was a different question.

Where are you headed? she asked.

Looks like the storage rooms.

Georgette led us into a room that branched off the main

hallway, used by former Highest Witches as a storage area. The empty shelves and lack of beating heart testified to a recent cleansing. A few errant parchments stacked on one shelf, gathering new dust.

Georgette spun in the middle of the room, facing me with the same calculation that I'd come to expect. A broach pinned at her neck glistened in an errant strand of sun from the grimy windows. She folded her hands in front her, her petite, pale fingers a veritable testament to living indoors.

We couldn't have been more different.

She released a tight smile. "Word has it that you're speaking to individual Council Members about the Sisterhood."

"I am."

"Why?"

"Is there a reason not to speak with them?"

"Not necessarily."

"Do you have concerns around me speaking about the Sisterhood?"

"None at all." Georgette swept her hands in front of her. "I was simply inquiring whether there were other motives."

"Aside from understanding what Council Members may not understand about the mission of the Sisterhood you mean?"

A cat-like smile gleamed in her eyes.

"Yes."

"Or the fact that the Council has to approve the currency to pay the Sisterhood?"

Her smile turned brittle.

Calling out the point she tried to sidle around shifted the conversation ever-so-gently into my purview. I kept my expression neutral, though I wanted to chuckle. Victory never lasted long when it came to Georgette. She had intelligence and quick thinking down to an art.

"That was my assumption," she said. "Are there other reasons?"

"Multiple."

"Are you willing to share them?"

"Of course." I attempted to channel my inner Leda. "The Sisterhood is trying to have an open discourse with the Council so we can be of greater service to Scarlett, and others."

Too late, I realized my mistake.

"Others?"

"Well—"

"Is that your plan?" she asked, quick as lightning. "To serve others outside the High Priestess? Because I understood that your *mission statement* focused on Scarlett."

My throat locked.

I couldn't say a definitive statement either way.

"The Council will vote on whether or not the Sisterhood should receive currency compensation for your work with Scarlett. If you plan to widen your scope of work—"

"I didn't say that."

Her smile turned feral. "But you did."

Irritated, I fell back to Leda's original talking points. "We thought it would be advantageous for the Sisterhood to be understood."

"We?"

Jikes.

Another slip.

Does she know about you? I asked Leda.

Only that I helped to arrange these appointments.

A gleam came into Georgette's eyes. "There are others in the Sisterhood? Now that is news."

Was it?

Wasn't it clear to everyone? Apparently not.

"It must be Leda," she concluded with easy grace. "Who else would you trust? Before now, I wasn't aware that the Assistant to the High Priestess also worked in the Sisterhood."

My heart raced as I decided to play it calm and easy. "I thought it was common knowledge."

"Well, Miss Monroe," Georgette said with a soft smile, and all the ballast I earned slid into her delighted victory, "that's just a testament to how all of us have inherent bias we can't detect. You see, it's not common knowledge. I have immediate concerns."

It took all my power to keep my tone under control when I asked, "Please, do share?" and attempted to maintain a steady inflection.

"The High Priestess is a very busy witch that requires all the attention her Assistant can give. If Leda is working on something for the Sisterhood instead of our esteemed leader, it could present a security threat."

Don't react, Leda said. *Don't react. Acknowledge.*

She must be listening from outside the room, and goddess bless her for it.

"I hear you," I said.

Nothing more.

Georgette fumbled for half a breath before she continued. "Not to mention a potential conflict of interest. You, Scarlett, and Leda have intersecting backgrounds. Certainly, more intertwined than most leaders and their subordinates. Many of us have concerns that you and Leda received preferential treatment because of your history at the school together."

Act interested, Leda said hastily. *Make no other statements.*

A strangled noise issued from my throat. When Georgette waited for a reply, I finally said, "Interesting."

Good, Leda said. *Nothing else. Let the silence be uncomfortable. It will force her to feel it and keep talking. She'll mess up somehow. Time to take the power back. We want her to reveal her own motivations, which you can force her to do through indifference.*

My heart pounded under the speed of this unexpected interrogation. No wonder Leda strove to save Georgette's meeting until the very end. Every ounce of venom in Georgette's stare dropped the temperature in this quaint room a breath above frozen.

Distrust, then a glimmer of scrutiny, appeared in Georgette's gelid stare.

"Miss Monroe, I think it's no secret that you and I have never seen eye-to-eye. Scarlett is well aware that I do not agree with you interacting with Greyson without supervision, nor do I feel the need for a Sisterhood is obvious."

Acknowledge, Leda said.

"Y-yes," I stammered, though it didn't make sense. Mildly befuddled by the odd statement, Georgette continued.

"That being said, I am not in charge of the Sisterhood, you, or the Network."

A pity, I imagined her silently adding.

"You are, obviously, free to express any intentions to the Council Members that you wish, but I feel it's fair to let you know that I am tracking all of your conversations. If promises are made, those promises will require fulfillment."

She means if we promise to do something, like keep the Council Members safe or fulfill something for them personally, Leda hastily said. *Doesn't apply to our current motivations, unless you guarantee something stupid.*

"By your own admission today," Georgette continued, a hand lifted toward me, "you are seeking to be useful to the Council?"

No! Leda almost shouted. *Fast no!*

"I didn't say that," I said.

"But you said, only a few minutes ago, that you sought feedback from the Council on how the Sisterhood could be useful to *others*, did you not?"

Her innocent-but-straightforward response, without even a head cock to soften it, cut to my innermost fears. The ones that pulsed brightly at night. The ones that whispered I didn't know *what* I wanted. That my instability would be the downfall of the Sisterhood and my own dreams.

Could one recover from broken dreams?

Papa's courage saved me.

That, I thought, *is not who I am.*

"On the contrary, Council Member," I managed to say without tripping over my frothy rage, "I said that we sought a discourse with the Council so they understood how we may be helpful to Scarlett."

"And others."

"Through Scarlett. I've made no admission to helping others."

Georgette set her jaw, eyes narrowed.

Say that the Sisterhood is seeking feedback to discover risks in the Network that we may not have considered, Leda said.

"We seek feedback from the Council to discover risks that we may not have considered."

Georgette's attention flicked to the doorway and back to me. She made a sound with her mouth, elevating her chin.

She knew about Leda.

Of course.

"I see," she drawled with elongating hilarity. "What is the Sisterhood's mission, Miss Monroe? Surely, you know it already."

My heart slammed. She warned me that whatever I stated, it would lock me in. She told me, in no unequivocal terms, that she planned to hold me responsible for everything I said. If I was corralled into serving only Scarlett, I'd have to stay there or risk losing legitimacy in front of the Council.

To ensure the wellbeing of the High Priestess and protect her from enemies foreign and internal, Leda hissed.

I couldn't say it.

And *that* is what Georgette knew.

The curl of her lips told me she understood exactly how to corner me. Knew that I'd silence when confronted with the bold question of what the Sisterhood was doing, because though we'd defined a path, I knew it wasn't the right one.

There had to be space for something in between. A Sisterhood that served Scarlett and those who needed our work and abilities. We had to live in the shades of gray, not purely black and white. Black and white didn't work. The words issued from me almost before I knew them myself.

"Our mission is to create safety."

"For whom?" she countered.

"Whoever asks it of us."

Georgette's toying smile unleashed, and the full weight of it gave way. She leaned a little closer, looking like a cat that finally caught the mouse.

"Like Camila, the Eastern Network High Priestess?"

Having no defense, I said nothing. Chances that my involvement had remained quiet amongst the Council were almost null. I'd spent too much time in and out of Greyson's cell, reporting with the Protectors, and involved with Scarlett to hide it. For all I knew, Aurora and Georgette had been speaking about my work with Camila, though I doubted the Ambassador cared for Georgette all that much.

Thankfully, neither did Leda. Her shock must have been too grand for words.

Georgette set her shoulders.

"*That* is my problem, Miss Monroe. Why should the Central Network have to pay for you to frolic in the Eastern Network when the Brotherhood is already involved, established, and trusted? According to the reports I read and heard, you weren't involved in the interrogation of the prisoner. Which means that the Brotherhood was able to complete the mission to their satisfaction and without your involvement. We pay the Protectors. We don't require another entity."

She trapped me. I couldn't rebut her. Nor could I say that the Brotherhood hadn't thought to go into the recesses of Magnolia, hadn't whisked away the High Priestess. She could only counter with, *how will we ever know? You removed their opportunity.* Or some other such drivel.

"You've made your position very clear, Council Member."

"Good," Georgette replied, and managed to mean it. "Please, Miss Monroe, don't take this personally. As a witch, I'm sure you're lovely. But your history, your family's history, and the current state of the Network is . . ." She paused, drummed her fingers on top of her other hand, and finished with a loathsome, ". . . not a great mix."

"My history?" I sputtered.

She tutted, giving me a piteous look. "Rognvald, yet another witch who I fear has allowed you this position out of favoritism, seems not to mind that our former Head of Protectors and High Priest was a reckless witch whose daughter has an equally reckless reputation. I have not forgotten, Miss Monroe."

Just don't speak, Leda said weakly.

Flashes of Alaysia, Tontes, the land of the gods, the drumming thunder, the fire in my throat, replayed through my head.

Reckless witch.

Indeed.

Licking my lips, I said, "I'm sure you haven't forgotten."

"I seek to protect the Central Network from unnecessary bloating and favoritism amongst ranks. Please, continue your work speaking with Council Members, but understand that I shall be speaking my own ideas into their other ear. If Scarlett wants a Sisterhood so badly, she can pay for it out of her own currency."

She swept out of the room, taking all the air with her. I stood there, tensed, staring at the dust motes dancing in the stirring air. The retreat of her footsteps blurred into the gentle chaos of the passage.

Georgette's cutting tone carried a promise that I wouldn't soon forget.

A sigh entered the room and closed the door. I turned around to find Leda standing there, eyes wide as saucers. She looked so much like the reticent, constantly irritated teenager that I first met years ago in a Network school that I struggled to stay present.

What was real?

"When you know it's poison," Leda whispered. She didn't finish the thought.

I nodded.

"I get it."

"Don't let her in your head, Bianca. I meant it when I said she's poisonous. She does this. She assesses weakness, then uses them to her advantage and goes for the kill. The best way to beat her is to keep going. Ignore her."

"She's a real problem."

"It depends on what we ask of the Council."

I asked the question that haunted me. "Without currency from the Council to compensate us for our time, to legitimize the operation, does the Sisterhood exist? I'm living off Letum Wood and access to Chatham Castle's dining room because of Grandfather, but he won't always be here. I'll need currency at some point."

Leda rubbed her lips together and swallowed. "It exists simply because you say it exists, but . . . it wouldn't receive the same chance to survive. If Scarlett paid you from her salary, that would put pressure and strain on Scarlett's relationship with the Council, her political reputation. Without the Council acknowledging the Sisterhood, it may as well not exist."

"Is Georgette that vindictive?"

"As much as I disagree with her methods and attitude, I don't think it's vindictiveness." Leda spoke with concern more than rage. "I think she believes she's doing the right thing by leashing that which she doesn't control. She's efficient and functional and productive as a Council Member because she asks questions no one else asks. For good or ill."

"Thanks." I struggled to meet her haunted gaze. "I appreciate you coming."

Her expression schooled into something more neutral. Hurt, even. My words to Georgette hung between us.

Our mission is to create safety.

Without another word, Leda spun and walked away.

* * *

Jacqueline bunched her fists up, pressed them to her chin, and squealed.

"It's *perfect*!"

Across the table, Kalli chuckled. A polishing cloth, several pieces of ornate silver, and a box lined in velvet scattered her area. She rubbed each tarnished silver piece with tender care and infinite patience.

Jacqueline flittered around the table singing, "Three weeks! Your handfasting is three weeks awaaaaaay."

She tweaked, moved, altered, shifted, and changed the layout of plates, cups, and spoons with wild abandon and no logical pattern. She'd rotated different settings for the past twenty minutes.

Merrick, sleeping after a very late mission, deftly avoided this preparatory meeting to finalize decorations and menu items before the introductory family dinner. Twenty immediate family members—the definition of *immediate* was vastly different in the Northern Network than the Central Network—were invited.

Though I desperately attempted to drudge up the power to care, the ability evaded me. My agitated parting with Leda, terrible details from the insurrections in the East, the escalating issue of Camila and Cristian locked in Magnolia Castle, and the Protectors' difficulty finding splinter group leaders distracted me. Per Guardian reports, Greyson lost consciousness sometime around midnight. He lived, but hadn't awoken.

It set me on edge.

Not to mention Priscilla and Tomasso's safety. Per Scarlett's order, two Central Guards protected the school grounds day and night. Jorge, the gardener, slept in the dining room and kept an ear on the school at night. Priscilla transported several bags of extra clothes and baby toys to my tree house, just in case. Most of all, the trees kept a constant vigil on her behalf. Thick shrubs formed tube-like structures around the school, keeping students in and other witches out.

But that could change in a heartbeat. The rebels had already proven their ability to transport in, wreak havoc, and depart.

For now, the violence remained in the Eastern Network. Unlikely that the rebels would have much concern over Tomasso unless the tide decisively turned toward Cristian or the rebels. Tomasso was in the most danger when the rebels gained power, or when Cristian died.

So far, no one was winning. Certainly not me. My overnight attempts to learn more about Magnolia, find a way into Gallo house, or drudge up information on the Gallo family, came to naught.

"Bianca?"

Startled out of my spiraling thoughts, I straightened.

"Sorry, what?"

Jacqueline bounced over with a pomp of her overfull skirts. Hands spread, she inquired, "Well? What do you think? I'm done. For now," she tacked on, eyeing a particularly troublesome gravy boat.

A glittering array of empty plates, cups, saucers, utensils, serving dishes, candlestick holders, and other dishes I couldn't fathom a use for awaited. They washed the table in gleaming perfection. One place setting lacked a full set of forks and spoons and knives, and Kalli placed the utensils she finished near that one.

"It's beautiful, Jacqui."

"I know," she said solemnly. "This one is made to impress. Some of the others are more formal, but at the introductory dinner, we're making a statement. We need to set expectations about the rest of the gatherings."

She swept a hand over the table. The pit in my stomach fell hard. Across the way, Kalli set down a spoon, rag in her hands, and watched me closely. Jacqueline side-stepped around the table, straightening a few chairs.

She cast Kalli a long glance. "Mother? Does it gain your approval?"

"It's beautiful."

Satisfied, Jacqueline clapped. "Then let's put it away! We eat in a week."

I almost choked on my tongue.

"A week?"

Puzzled, she glanced over her shoulder. "Yes, a week! Bianca, the dinners begin weeks before the big day! You do remember?"

"Yes. Of course."

"Ideally, we would have had the introductory dinner *months* ago when he gave you the cord of engagement . . ."

Her eyes dropped to my wrist, which would remain perpetually empty. She smiled with a hint of bemusement, as if she couldn't fathom *why* we didn't care as much as she did.

"Thank you, Jacqui. It's beautiful."

Beaming, she snapped two fingers. All the plates sidled together, slipping into a box within less than a minute. Once finished, it jangled as a spell levitated it off the ground, whisking it into the attic. A pile of fabric replaced it, flying into her arms.

"I need to run to the castle," she said around a bundle of

tulle that I prayed had nothing to do with my handfasting. "Have a few alterations there! Merry part!"

Jacqueline departed, and her absence rang in a hollow, empty way. I sank to the bench across from Kalli, who set aside the final utensil and scrutinized me.

"This is a lot."

I smiled and forced a forgiving nod. "It's a *little* overwhelming."

Laughing, Kalli said, "It's a lot overwhelming. The Northern Network has always held very fondly to handfasting traditions, but I didn't realize just how much we relied on them until I saw them through your eyes. This is our first child's handfasting," she said with a touch of wistfulness. "I suppose I hadn't had reason to think much of it before."

She reached across the table, set her warm hand on top of mine. "It's appropriate for you to say no at any time, B. You don't have to do this."

"Jacqui would be so sad."

Wryly, Kalli said, "Jacqui has suffered far worse episodes of sadness. She's doing more than taking advantage of a joyous situation. She's . . . "

"Finding purpose?"

"Finding *happiness*. She believes it's not in her immediate situation, so she's finding it wherever she can. Unfortunately, you were in her direct path for the perfect excuse to look at everyone and everything else except herself."

"I never thought of it that way."

Kalli squeezed. "Our traditions are important to us, and sharing them with you is part of a gift we give when you join our family. But not *all* of them have to be done right away. We can cut down on the dinners. We can sort through the items of inheritance at a different time. It's *your* handfasting; you decide."

"With everything developing in the East, there's no guarantee Merrick will be around in three weeks. If Cristian asks for the Protectors to help more often, and if Rognvald lets them . . ."

I trailed away.

Kalli's concern tightened the skin around her eyes. "Is that likely?"

I shrugged. "I don't know. Technically, this rebellion has nothing to do with the Central Network."

"Do you side with Cristian?"

The question haunted me many nights. Who did I support? The situation in the East had more texture than simplicity. Marsh witches. Greater and lesser families. Carcere. Magnolia Castle. The crossing threads built disarray, nothing that made sense.

"I don't know if there can be sides. Only confusion. I don't think anyone is entirely to blame, either. Whether it's the Aldanas, the Council Members, the splinter group leaders, or the rebels . . ."

With an apologetic smile, I returned her friendly squeeze. "If Merrick is here, we'll be handfasted. If he's not, we'll make the best of it."

Kalli nodded. "Spoken like a sensible woman. You let me deal with Jacqui. She'll survive. I promise."

Before I could counter that questionable point, a voice floated into my head. Brody. Probably an accident that he included me, since he had no reason to speak with me, and the resonance indicated he spoke to many witches.

One of the splinter groups, led by Council Member Giuseppi, has surrounded Magnolia Castle.

I frowned.

"Bianca?"

Holding up a hand, I indicated a pause. Brody's breathless voice continued, panting even in his thoughts, though the magic didn't allow the physical voice to transmit through. Panic had a way of communicating, regardless.

Brody continued, *I can't get a good view on the Necce side, but I can hear them. I'm estimating hundreds.*

Hold, Rognvald said. *I'm joining you. Merrick?*

Already there.

Chi?

On my way.

Their voices faded as quickly as they came. When they ebbed, Leda spoke to me. *I don't know what's going on. I'd tell you if I had more information than what we just heard.*

Thanks.

My jaw tightened, and I tapped my teeth together. Council Member Giuseppi made his final move. My thoughts streamed to Camila, then the bigger issue of who pulled the strings of this rebellion puppet. Even chaos had a coordinator. For my part, I didn't credit Giuseppi.

My bets landed on Ricardo.

Glancing at Kalli, I opened my mouth to explain, but she laughed and shook her head.

"Go. Go save who you must, Bianca. While you're there, please tell my son to be wise? I haven't polished all this silver for nothing."

<h1 style="text-align:center">Chapter Thirty</h1>

Urgency swept me to Camila's balcony at Magnolia Castle. I landed invisibly, amazed that transportation had worked as she promised despite the layers of magical power protecting the castle.

Magnolia Castle had seen better days. Witches swarmed it with torches and aggressive screams. Fires burned in piles along the grounds—they'd dashed to pieces several decorative gazebos. Smoke columns rose from the magnolia trees that surrounded the perimeter. Had they tried to torch the historic trees, enchanted to survive anything? My throat thickened at the thought.

Until that moment, it hadn't seemed real.

On the southern edge, protective magic kept the Academy safe despite the onslaught. Witches surrounded it, too.

All felt ragged.

With my knuckle, I rapped on Camila's window. The door slid open. Before I entered, I called within. "It's me, Bianca Monroe. Camila gave me permission to land on her balcony."

"Prove it."

"Uh . . ." I cast about for any small detail. "I have an honorary nephew named Tom whom I love."

A second later, the glass door gave way. I slipped inside, surprised to find Camila alone. She waved the door closed with a spell. Double lights zipped around the edge as both of us sent spells to seal it. Mine from listening ears, hers from intruders. Although the porch was already protected with magic, who could blame her careful approach?

She gripped my wrist. Her fingers were ice cold, and terror thinned her desperate whisper. "Cristian thinks they will try to overpower Magnolia Castle tonight. All the splinter groups are working together. Protectors have identified previously singular groups merging."

"Give me a second, Camila?"

Wide eyed, she nodded. I turned my gaze to the far wall, fixing it on an elaborate painting of a former High Priestess. Vittoria, if I remembered correctly. She had an elegant profile, kind eyes, and hair glossy as onyx in the portrait. Poverty abounded behind her, but wealth regaled her full dress and glittering, subtle necklace. I turned my attention to my thoughts.

I'm inside Magnolia Castle with the Eastern Network High Priestess, I said to the Brotherhood at large. All of them would be listening in at this point. Leda was automatically looped in, as well as Scarlett. *Camila reports that they believe that the rebels plan to work together to overthrow Magnolia Castle tonight.*

It fits what we're observing on the ground and what Cristian has shared with us, Rognvald replied, and my blood cooled a few degrees. The current government wouldn't survive if the rebels managed to crack the castle and slaughter Cristian and Camila.

Your Highness, I said so that only Scarlett and Leda could hear, *can we grant Cristian and Camila safety in the Central Network?*

A long pause followed. My heart thudded in the meantime.

The implications are grave depending on how this goes, Scarlett said. *If the rebels win, they may take it as an occasion to have issues with the Central Network.*

They're not going to be all that organized at first, Your Highness

So we think, she said with a demure tone that surprised me. *Nadira would prove otherwise.*

I almost cursed at the reminder. The Northern Network weathered a similar-but-different situation with shocking grace and ripples, instead of explosive issues.

Scarlett accepting Cristian and Camila would incite the Council, Leda added.

If I never heard *the Council* again, it would be too soon.

Scarlett asked, *Based on your observations of the situation in which you stand, how would you advise me to act, Sisterhood? My decisions are my own. I seek your perspective.*

My breath hung on a ledge. I released Camila to peer out her window. Gathering bodies continued to amass, torches flickering in a wide circle. They hurled curse after curse, spell after spell, hoping to wear the magic down. Over time, they would.

With a shake of my head, I considered all the splinter groups converging together to break down the castle.

This wasn't chaos.

This was *planned.*

My instincts had been spot on.

It's my belief that Camila should be protected, as her only crime is being part of the Aldana family, and her reputation is sterling amongst her witches. The rebellion will see her as a key pawn to destroy, but I don't think they'll be prepared. Cristian will be their focus. We can quietly take Camila to Priscilla's, gather Tomasso and Priscilla, and send them somewhere safe.

Where do you recommend? Leda asked.

My father's house.

The moment the suggestion left my brain, it felt right. Papa needed purpose. Papa needed someone to save except himself, and where would they be more secure? Not only would my trees look after them, but Papa.

I agree with this plan, Scarlett said succinctly. *Present it to Camila. Do you believe we should extend the same to Cristian?*

I do. I don't think he'd take it.

I agree.

What about the Council, High Priestess?

You let me deal with them.

Yes, Your Highness.

Leda's voice interjected into a sudden silence. *I will bring Priscilla and Tomasso to your father's house. We'll expect you and Camila there soon, Bianca.*

Update Leda and I as soon as you have news, Scarlett concluded. *I am closely tracking these events as they unfold.*

Camila, studying my every move, haunted me like a shadow. I shoved away from the window to spare her the agony of all those amassed against their reign. Unbidden, Georgette floated through my mind. If there was one course of action that Georgette would hate, and happily rally the Council against support of, this was it.

I didn't care.

To reassure Camila, I reached for her hand, gripped it. "One more minute. I have a plan."

She clutched my offered fingers, closed her eyes, and drained a slow breath. Relief played vividly across her features.

To the Brotherhood, I said, *I'm going to take the High Priestess to the Central Network, just to be safe.* I switched to Rognvald alone. *I have an idea of how to quell this. Perhaps not stop the rebellion itself, but squash the attempted coup tonight. How busy are you?*

His instant reply didn't surprise me.

Extremely.

Do you have any Protectors to spare?

Only Tysen. He was the youngest, and I wanted someone at the castle in case.

If Talmund puts extra protection on Chatham Castle, can the Sisterhood borrow Tysen's expertise?

The beginnings of a plan cobbled together in my mind. A plan that I hadn't been able to figure out yet, but now I would. While I waited with a pounding heart for Rognvald to reply, I considered the long-term ramifications of what this could mean for the Sisterhood.

Failure.

Death.

Rejection by the Council.

Georgette would have a celebration if it went awry.

What surprised me most was how little I cared. Let the Council mutter and talk and gossip about the Sisterhood, our purpose, or our value. Papa was right. They didn't matter. Not really. *This* mattered.

This moment.

I wanted to be the witch who saved, not the witch who feared.

Finally, Rognvald hastily snapped, *I don't care. We're swamped. Do what you can. If you see a way to stop it, do it.*

I turned to Camila.

"Your Highness, do you trust me?"

* * *

Camila, to my shock, didn't protest.

Whether her faith in the Sisterhood was complete, her fear of death that potent, or she simply understood the corner in which she stood, Camila humbly and gratefully accepted the offer of sanctuary. After a few incantations packed her bag, and I spelled them to Papa's house, we departed.

A warm fire blazed through open windows when Camila

and I arrived in Letum Wood. The moment I landed, the trees hummed in my ears.

She returns.

You belong to us.

In response, my heart whispered, *Protect this house and these witches? They are very important to me.* The forest rose in instant agreement. Subtle movements began. Saplings shifting. Roots pulling. Undergrowth expanding. Camila didn't notice the world alter before her eyes, but I felt it all the way in my watery veins.

To Deasylva, I said, *Thank you.*

A streak of sapphire light raced through the ground to my feet in acknowledgment.

The long transportation with another witch drained parts of my magical reserve, awakening an instinct to conserve my powers. But a memory of that night in Carcere, standing against Greyson, certain I would meet my demise in a battle of magic, reminded me that I didn't have to fear.

Because of Deasylva, I had power.

Loads of it.

At the moment of need, I always had enough. As Papa had said.

Always enough.

Before I could rap on Papa's door, it swung open. Delighted to see me, his brow raised high, he opened his mouth in greeting, but stopped. I had an arm around Camilla, hidden in a cloak and a hood. She stood at my side, demure but proud. The hood obscured her features. Papa's mouth snapped shut.

"Care to lend a hand for a desperate noble?" I asked.

He blinked. "Noble?"

"Her Majesty Camila Aldana seeks sanctuary. The forest has already agreed."

Papa's eyes snapped to the undergrowth. A slow smile grew. He recognized the subtle rearranging. His eyes sparkled as he grinned and opened the door. Just beyond him, I spied Camila's bag waiting in the middle of the room.

"I had a feeling you were up to something when a random bag of women's clothing arrived."

"The Eastern Network is falling apart. Camila needs somewhere safe. Priscilla and Tomasso, too. Leda is on her way with them shortly."

"It would be my delight to host all of them. This house is too quiet, and someone needs to put Cat in her place. She thinks she owns the attic. Regina spoils her."

Regina's name, spoken so casually, gave a thrill of hope that caught me by surprise. Had he fixed things? Or was Regina like me—concerned about the cat that, for all intents and purposes, ruled this house?

Now wasn't the time to ask, but I burned to know.

Camila elevated her hand, pulling aside her hood to peer at him.

"Derek Black?"

Papa bowed. He extended a friendly hand, his smile wide. "Your Majesty, it's very good to see you again. It's been too long, and we had little time together in previous years. Welcome to Letum Wood. My home is yours."

* * *

While Leda settled Priscilla, Camila, and Tomasso at Papa's house, I departed for Chatham Castle. The prickling discomfort around Priscilla and Tomasso's safety ebbed, freeing mental space I would need. They'd be fine.

More than fine.

They'd be *safe*.

Tysen sat alone in front of the massive fireplace in the Chatham Castle dining hall. It wasn't the first time I'd found him there, pondering the mysteries of Protector life in front of the flames. He cut a dreary figure, alone in the darkness, brooding with a scowl the size of Alkarra.

My footsteps echoed as I crossed the stone floor and sat at his side. His spine pressed against the table edge, legs stretched out and crossed at the ankles. Glowing firelight illuminated his face.

I mimicked his pose, arms folded over my chest. My thoughts flickered to Merrick. Which splinter group leader was he in charge of? The most dangerous, probably. Between him and Brody, they would have first pick. Honor amongst the Protectors let those involved in a long-term mission choose first advantage. Merrick would have chosen the most difficult in order to shield his Brothers.

Not only for his Protector reputation, but sheer power of personality.

That was Merrick.

My soulmate.

"Tysen," I said, low.

He responded in kind. "Bianca."

"How are you?"

"Fine."

"You don't seem fine."

His curt reply was no surprise. "I'm *fine*."

"Something on your mind?"

"No."

I hid an eye roll. If Tysen was distracted by something else, he'd be a terrible mission companion. Glancing at an ornate wrought-iron clock over the fire, I promised two silent minutes dedicated to digging to the bottom of it. This wasn't the time for therapy . . . yet, it was. I needed a clear-headed mission partner.

We had a rebel to locate.

"Last chance—want to talk about it?" I asked.

With an amused spread of his hands, he cried, "I just said nothing was wrong!"

"Yes, but I can tell you're lying and I need your help. I won't have you distracted."

Tysen hung his head in defeat. "You're right, I am lying. And no, I don't want to talk about it."

"It's a girl?"

"Yes."

"Broken up?"

Jaw clenched, he muttered, "Yes. But it's for the best. She didn't like how much I was gone."

With a whistle, I said, "It's not easy."

"I keep forgetting you grew up with a father as a Protector. It's so rare."

I shrugged. "It's also definitive."

"Well, this got ugly." He blew out a hard breath.

"I'm sorry, Tysen."

"It's my own fault. I should never have fallen for her. Chi is right. Protectors shouldn't be handfasted." He sucked in a sharp breath, sent an insecure and sidelong glance in my direction. "Sorry." He winced. "Well . . . I mean . . . that is . . ."

Laughing, I said, "It's fine. You can have your own opinion."

"It's different with you and Merrick. You're . . . stable and strong. You understand this life and you aren't resentful about it, from what I can see. Merrick is good at what he does, *and* he's a Master. I'm still new. There's a lot to learn and figure out, and a lot of ways for me to mess it up. I'm a better Protector than boyfriend."

"Maybe. Or maybe you're just trying to make it through the first years of a really tough position."

The tension drained from him.

"Let her go." I nudged him with an elbow. "She wasn't the one for you."

He flicked the tip of his finger against my wrist, tossing the hair out of his eyes. "I don't see a cord of engagement yet."

"You won't, either."

"No handfasting?"

"We are. In a month. Or wait. Maybe less? Three weeks."

His brow shot up. "Really?"

"Yes."

"What about—" he motioned to my empty wrist again.

"Merrick isn't wearing one, and I'm not either."

"Why?"

"Neither of us want to wear them on missions. Besides, he gifted me a house. That's way better."

"And the surprises keep coming," he said softly.

"Listen, are you over it yet? I have something I need you to help me with in the Eastern Network."

He straightened with interest, then slumped. Tysen cast me a sidelong glance and returned his focus to the fire. "I messed up."

"When?"

"During the interrogation."

"How?"

He ran his tongue over his front teeth. "No idea. But clearly I did because I wasn't invited and all the Protectors are in the East tonight." He spread his fingers in that direction. "I'm stuck at Chatham Castle. It's worse than babysitting duty."

A chuckle rolled out of me. "No, *Merrick* had babysitting duty. When he was still a recruit, he had to tail me everywhere and keep me from killing myself."

"I've heard it wasn't easy."

His dry tone delighted me. I laughed at the memories of Merrick's almost constant irritation. No wonder he had me splitting wood and running trails for hours. I needed the outlet.

Shifting my focus to the matter at hand, I said, "Well, Rognvald didn't say anything about you being an abject failure when I asked if you could help the Sisterhood. He told me to go for it."

Tysen's eyes shot to mine.

"What?"

"I spoke with Rognvald half an hour ago. He said you didn't

get on the mission because of seniority. There were only so many slots and the older Protectors wanted them. You didn't know?"

He grumbled a defensive, "No."

"Why didn't you ask?"

"I'm still the newest recruit. Things get weird if you look petulant or frustrated. If I asked, I would have seemed . . ."

"Too eager?"

"Yes."

He remained pensive as he stared at the dying coals. When we recruited other women to the Sisterhood, I made a mental note to train against *this* reaction. The culture of the Brotherhood acted against it. Undoubtedly, one day, the Sisterhood would face the same issues.

Good thing we had Leda.

With a pep in my voice, I slapped his knee and stood. "Come on, mopey. I'm doing my own expedition into the Eastern Network, and need your help."

Suspicious, he pressed his hands to the bottom of his seat, as if about to stand, but not quite ready.

"What is your plan?"

"We're going after Ricardo Gallo."

"Ricardo Gallo?"

"Yep. No one else thinks he's worth chasing, but it's clear there's a mastermind coordinating the attack on Magnolia Castle. While all the others are focused on the splinter groups amassing, we have an open spot to break into the Gallo family mansion. I still have no idea how," I added.

Tysen stood.

"I'm in."

I held up a hand and curled it, beckoning him to follow as I spun toward the exit.

"Come with me. We have a kitchen to raid and a prisoner to visit before we go. Let's hope said prisoner has been hard at work breaking a binding, or my plan is doomed."

Chapter Thirty-One

Greyson sprawled on the floor of his cell, a stinky, sweaty mess. Vomit splattered the floor next to him. He'd stripped off his clothes, set them aside in what appeared to be a fevered frenzy, and lay in his undergarments. Heat brightened his cheeks to a dangerously red hue.

Greyson had descended to an all-time low.

"Been like this for a few hours," Jack whispered at my right shoulder. "Thought he was going to die. Sent for an Apothecary, just in case. They left a few tinctures, but he hasn't been able to take them. He's moaning, at least. Breathing."

"Thanks, Jack."

He nodded once and left, nose wrinkled at the horrific smell. The small patch of window didn't stir the air much, if at all. Unwashed body, human refuse, and vomit combined to a cesspool of smells. I set an incantation that would sweep air out the small hole. It wouldn't remove the stench, but it would help.

"What's wrong?" Tysen asked, appearing unaffected. Working with the Factios thugs in underground Chatham City, he'd probably smelled worse.

"I told him to break a magical binding if he wanted to stay in

340

this new cell. Apparently, he decided to try. If we're lucky, he's suffered enough to speak."

"Didn't kill him." Tysen whistled. "Impressive."

"Yet."

A tray burdened with broth, fresh croissants, a crock of butter, and cooked carrots steamed to a glazed perfection settled on the slot. The suppressive magic of Greyson's cell prevented me from magically lowering it all the way in. The coffee piped a hot, aromatic smell that helped to cover the rest.

With another spell, I sent a message to the housekeeper, requesting a hot bucket of soapy water and towels, as well as someone to clean the cell.

I crouched. "Greyson?"

Shivering, he lifted his eyes to mine. His upper lip snarled. Dirt caked his skin and neck, smearing flecks of vomit and spittle. Despite the fact that he attempted to murder me and had machinations to murder Scarlett, not to mention take over the Central Network, I couldn't help pity him.

Was there a worse bottom than this?

I nodded toward the tray on the slot. "Food is here. Easy stuff for a sick stomach, as well as an extra pint of light ipsum for when you're feeling recovered. I've heard it's your favorite. I've also sent for housekeeping to clean the cell, and a bucket of sudsy water for you to wash."

The blankness of his expression made me wonder if he comprehended what I said. At the words *sudsy water*, he showed a modicum of life.

"Talk to me," I said.

Greyson licked dry lips. His voice was a mere croak. "Ricardo." He braced himself. Able to speak it, he continued. "Ricardo Gallo set me free from Carcere with the help of his youngest son, Nelo. Nelo is an East Guard, but he posed under a different surname. The surname of a distant cousin, I believe. Nelo earned his station at Carcere through trickery. While there, he infiltrated the interior. Provided maps to his father. Learned the layout, the secrets, and the history. He brought Ricardo inside, and Ricardo promised us escape."

"Ricardo was the caretaker of Carcere, I thought?"

"The island, not the interior. He didn't interact with prisoners."

"Oh."

His voice was a painful rasp. "Nelo and Ricardo said they would destroy the turret and avenge the Gallo family name and change the Network."

"Why?"

"To clear the Gallo family name."

"From what?"

"The curse of Allegra Rossi," he spat, panting. Greyson tilted his head with a moan. A shudder raced through him. Extra agony, no doubt, for the act of betraying his promised secrets. I failed to feel sorry for him.

Greyson lowered his head to the ground, exhausted. "Ricardo has many children. The girls have been sick, ill, dying. He's lost . . . two. Three?" Delirious, he shook his head and winced. "Because of Allegra's terrible legacy with Carcere, their position in society is abysmal, and he's tired of it. The marsh witches that the Gallo family serves are unhappy and blaming the curse of Allegra Rossi. They threatened revolt. He decided it sounded like a good idea."

My mind stirred, thinking of Allegra Gallo Rossi and Carcere. Of Ricardo Gallo and rebellion.

Something *else* linked them. I couldn't quite touch it yet.

"Think!" Greyson barked, hoarse. "Think, you mindless ingrate. What's happening to Magnolia Castle? What happened to Carcere? Why would Ricardo Gallo instigate a rebellion by destroying the magic of a worthless tower on the sea?"

Greyson gripped his stomach, cheeks contorted in a

perpetual grimace. At this rate, he wouldn't be conscious long enough for us to hear the confession.

"What is the . . . number one . . . rule of magic systems?"

"Balance."

"Balance," he breathed.

My mind raced. Carcere's magic was broken, offsetting the Eastern Network rebellion in full. And why *then*? Why hadn't Ricardo acted before that? Because Carcere's explosion was the key moment to create a rebellion and bring down the Aldana family.

Because of magical balance.

That meant there had to be a sister magick. Another place similar to Carcere, but completely opposite. A building of impressive size, with a magical counterpart that hid great . . . what? What opposed a prison?

Freedom.

"Magnolia Castle," I whispered.

"Yes!" Greyson howled. "Yes, Magnolia Castle, you spineless drivel! Magnolia Castle is linked to Carcere through its origin with Allegra. They are sister magicks. The equivalent and opposite. For every good magic, there is an equal and opposite darkness. Carcere is the darkness. Magnolia Castle is the light. Specifically, the Academy. It's why Allegra was such a hated figure. She established Carcere first, so that Magnolia might be its opposite. The darkness of her soul to create Carcere . . . cursed her family . . ."

Terrible understanding washed through me, cold as death. It breathed down my neck, alighting a swirl of understanding.

"The good gods," I whispered.

Sister magicks.

Where Carcere hoarded darkness and evilness and suppression, the Academy inspired openness and wisdom and light. Carcere was closed, locked down. The Academy was open, prolific. One secreted away, the other kept in a spotlight. One hated, the other revered. In all things they were opposites.

One was broken.

"The other will fall," I stated. "Magnolia Castle *is* falling apart. Something *is* wrong with it! I was right."

"Carcere is dying, and so will Magnolia Castle. I don't know how long," Greyson added weakly. "It's Ricardo's plan. Weaken the symbol, bring down the Network."

Another agonized groan. Greyson curled into himself. I gripped Tysen's arm. No puzzlement showed in his expression, only growing clarity. Thank the goddess he appeared to track the developments.

"Breaking Carcere made a statement," I said quickly, understanding it all. "Not only to break Allegra Rossi's curse, but to eventually weaken Magnolia Castle. He's been ramping up his attacks on Magnolia to speed the process."

"Yes."

Greyson groaned.

"Which means that Ricardo *has* been behind this." I slammed my palm on my knee. "I knew it! What about the splinter groups?"

With drooping energy, Greyson whispered, "His plan from the beginning. He hid behind them." His head shook back and forth. Each word sounded lower than the last. "He made me swear to sow chaos and discord for the Central Network and never speak his name, or Allegra's."

Which explained his cryptic clues.

"Sow chaos and discord?"

He glared at me with new energy. "My *game* was more than just sweet revenge, Miss Monroe. It fulfilled a promise."

Understanding shuttered into place.

Oh.

"In exchange for your freedom, you vowed to create chaos in

the Central Network in order to help the Eastern Network fall to rebel hands?"

"The goal," he rasped, "was for me to so thoroughly distract Central Network leadership that they couldn't provide Protector support."

He curled onto his other side with a shriek of agony.

There it was.

The heart of his secrets. The closeted skeletons. The bitter reality. Greyson sought more than my demise. More than revenge.

He sought chaos.

Jikes.

"Killing Scarlett would certainly do that," I hissed.

He coughed. I reared away from his foul-smelling breath curling across the prison floor. His eyes fluttered closed.

"I failed," he breathed.

"Spectacularly."

"If the Central Network doesn't kill me, the Gallo family will." He rocked on his sides, hands clutching his abdomen. "Nothing matters anymore. Nothing."

"No wonder you want a cozy little house in the middle of Letum Wood," I muttered.

He panted, his cheeks brighter than ever. I'd never observed the process of a broken magical binding, and never wanted to again.

"Give me something else, Greyson," I demanded. "I'll give you the food and you can keep this upgraded cell in exchange for admitting Ricardo set this into motion, but I need more if you want the bath and a cleaner to come in here."

He forced his weak eyes open.

"Ricardo has . . . one weak spot. He won't be fighting. He's hiding until the last moment. Hiding behind . . . Council Members. Letting them take the brunt to protect . . . him. His weak spot."

"What is his weak spot?"

Every fluttery breath seemed less powerful. He spoke in a whisper. "His daughters."

Greyson passed out.

* * *

Air as thick as water awaited Tysen and me.

I breathed deeply of the marshy smells: soil, greenery turned to air, and humidity so heavy that it weighed like a cloak. The vapor assaulted me with each swirling breath, clearing the lingering malodor of Greyson's cell. The disgusting filth exited my mind when I closed my eyes.

Centered myself.

The vibrant souls of the marshland and swamp trees weren't the same as Letum Wood. Cypress trees had an entirely different personality. Where Letum Wood crackled with hostility in places, and brightened with delight in others, the cypress had steadiness down to an art form. They dozed, never inquiring, but watchful. I felt their presence, but didn't interact with it. Still, they calmed me. Or, rather, Deasylva's presence in their stalwart companionship calmed me.

Tysen surveyed with a traveling, wary gaze as I stabilized my thoughts. Attempting to sort through all Greyson said, and the implications of his treachery, would occupy me for days. In this moment, I needed to comprehend the basics and move on. Which, in itself, took skill enough. The details spiraled into delicate, interwoven braids.

Ricardo.

Allegra's curse.

Rebellion.

The goal was clear: we capture Ricardo and take him to Cristian. Come what may. The successful completion of said mission gave us a chance at restoring peace in the Eastern Network, and safety for Tomasso.

"How well do you know Ilese?" I whispered.

Tysen pivoted to the left. He crouched, ready to spring. "I can make my way through the Network without making a fool of myself."

"Me too. Hopefully, that's enough. Don't use magic unless you must, and look out for serpentes."

"No magic?"

"They had the land around the house cloaked last time, and I triggered the spell when I used magic. I'm not sure how far out the cloaking extends, so I transported us as far away as I could."

He nodded to the Volare case on my back. "Can we ride your rug?"

"No. Just in case it uses too much magic. We'll have to climb the trees and go limb to limb to close in. Go slow. We don't want them seeing our movement in the branches."

Tysen agreed with a nod.

Thanks to a lack of moonlight on rippling water, invisibility wasn't needed. Blackness filled every corner as I stepped off land and set a firm foothold onto the closest trunk. The rough edges scratched my fingertips as I clambered higher. Deftly, Tysen followed. Rognvald couldn't have managed the same finesse.

Working across the midstory required time and focus. As we hopped and scurried from branch to branch, lapping waves raced around tree trunks. Did the serpente glide around underwater? It must. Something tracked us.

The Central Network experienced thick humidity in the summer months, when the air became oppressive and difficult to breathe, but nothing like this. This slurping water world dominated by lichen lent an entirely different energy, making it difficult to breathe. Swamp noises occluded other sounds. The entire operation felt like groping in the dark, monsters underfoot.

As we progressed closer to the mansion, the Brotherhood

updated rarely and briefly from Magnolia Castle. Their short spurts set my heart racing.

Attempt near the east wing.

Supporting the south.

More gathered at the Academy.

Ronaldo holding from within. Not looking good outside.

Cracks in the stairs.

What few updates I garnered made it sound like the Protectors surrounded Magnolia Castle's exterior and attempted to hold the protective magic steady against an onslaught of spells. They could only last so long. Not only would their own magical reserves deplete with time, but the spells themselves.

The rebels had sheer numbers on their side.

We closed in on an area of swamp that I recognized—the spot where the medallion in the Academy had brought me, near the serpente's underwater lair. Emerald water, littered with floating lily pads and a skim of loose algae, swirled. Thick tree trunks, vines, plush foliage carpeted us. Water lapped at everything.

It would have been breathtaking if it wasn't so ready to kill us.

Land appeared as we leaped from one cypress tree to another. The branch where I settled to study my next move bowed beneath my weight, leaves pirouetting in circles that would draw any eye. I held my breath, crouching.

No one shouted.

No witches appeared.

Emboldened, yet suspicious, I crept toward the end of the long arm. Land appeared ahead, swelling to the grassy bank. The old mansion from before perched on top. Miserable and lonely, not a single sign of life stirred within. Only blazing magic, hot and pulsing, when I turned my senses to it.

The structure reminded me of a miniature Chatham Castle, with turret-like structures and gabled windows. Steep eaves framed cracked windows hiding shadows instead of life, and no beckoning lights. Double wooden doors peaked sharply at the top like an inverted, chiseled diamond. Spires jutted from behind, almost innumerable. A family house fallen into disrepair.

Tysen peered ahead. "I know that house."

"How?"

"Merrick and I have been here before. It's a small marsh outside of Portafina, one of the main hubs for marshes. The village is part of the southeastern portion of the Eastern Network."

"The marshlands."

"Yes."

Vague memories stirred my mind from my lunch with Council Member Henry, when Merrick and Tysen chased potential rebels. The map that displayed the Gallo family crest at the Academy resurrected. Yes, Portafina is where the map indicated the Gallo family lived.

The Eastern Network conjured gems like Magnolia Castle or Necce when spoken about. The artistic city of Livorno, too, where art and humanities converged. But *this* was the real beating heart of the Eastern Network.

"Portafina and the outlying marshes cover much of the lower peninsulas," Tysen continued. "I came with Merrick when I was helping him gather information. We staked this out, but never saw witches. Is this the Gallo family house?"

"Yes. We need to go inside."

"That's the mission?"

"Yes. Ricardo should be there."

"Why would he be here and not Magnolia Castle?" he asked. "If he's coordinating this rebellion, it makes more sense he'd be there."

I shook my head. According to the Academy, Ricardo had ten children, and Greyson mentioned that Ricardo's daughters had fallen ill. Some died. They were his *weakness*. Instinct told me he'd be here.

"He's hiding out until the end, per Greyson's report," I said. Tysen, unconvinced, frowned.

"Take it as a hunch," I added. "I think he's here."

Tysen grunted. "Fine. What's your plan to get inside?"

I scoured the facade, seeking clues. Wasn't that the biggest question? I'd puzzled over it for several days. Attic rooms led to windows with steep eaves. Moisture dripped off the shingled roof, raining in intermittent bursts through the humid night. Fog crept past, alternately obscuring it.

"I don't have a plan," I admitted.

Tysen hid his exasperation behind a neutral, yet somehow loaded with emotion, facade. "You didn't plan this far?"

"Not yet. Have any ideas?"

After a minute perusing this edge of the exterior, and divining no further clues, Tysen pointed. "See the far right wall, on the ground?"

A porch wrapped the bottom floor, elevated nearly a story off the grass. Staircases on either side elevated the main entrance above the marsh. Creepers wound through a latticed cover, hiding what lay within.

"Yes."

"See the lattice?"

I nodded.

"I bet there's something under the porch."

I lifted an eyebrow. "Yes, a house foundation."

"Or a cellar entrance?"

"That's a big hope."

"The attic would be a better target." He squinted. "On the left, there's a gable that looks as if a window pane might be cracked. You could use a spell to remove it without having to break it and cause a sound."

"Assuming this is the true exterior."

He shrugged. "True. They have at least five detectable, protective magicks surrounding it. How are you going to close in on the attic? And when you do," he quickly added, "the protective spells will evaporate, revealing something we can't predict. The house might look totally different. Might be full of witches with arrows drawn, aiming right for your heart. For all we know, it's a tent encampment with a thousand ready rebels."

"Which means it's futile to plan and we press forward on a moment-to-moment basis," I sang.

He threw his hands in the air. "We can't go in without a plan!"

"Listen, Protector. You're with the Sisterhood. Over here, we strategize on the go."

A sucking sound drew my attention to the swamp thirty paces below. Slithering scales peaked out of the water and vanished without a sound.

Inspiration struck.

Based on my previous experience in the swamp, the serpente was little more than a guard dog for the Gallo family. *It* would be allowed through the magic. To test my assembling plan, I sent a spell that stirred the bushes nearest the house. They swayed and I ducked.

Nothing happened.

No one surged forward, detecting my magical use. A second test resulted in further quiet. If Ricardo sent all his witches to the front lines of the rebellion, we might have a chance of making this happen.

A wild chance.

A fool's prayer.

But something.

I readjusted my weight and braced myself. "Hold on tight, Tysen. I have a plan."

* * *

Tysen's silent litany of curse words followed me when I transported onto the bank of the grassy knoll leading to Gallo house. Croaking bullfrogs made it easy to ignore him, though I couldn't block him out entirely. Funny how the Brotherhood shared so many characteristics, yet applied them so variantly.

Around a giant tree trunk, land stretched out of the water like rising fingers. Sucking mud grabbed my ankles as I climbed free of the damp earth and onto higher ground. It smelled rotten and sweet, a strange mixture that clung to my nostrils.

The overwhelming magic blasted from the house as I slunk through the dark with swift, measured steps. Who maintained these emanating spells? Exhausting, even for a short time. I resisted the urge to hold Viveet in my hands. She'd draw more attention. The serpente would remember the taste of her metal.

Ten steps out of the swamp, I paused. The thickest magical loci pulsed from just ahead, almost like an invisible shield. No visible line existed, but the shell of a protective spell might. One more step and I'd cross it. Probably die, too. An incantation of this power often led to morbid consequences.

Unless.

I held my breath, counting.

No sign, Tysen muttered. I sidled to the right, carefully following the edge of the shell. No splashing serpente or predatory hissing noises erupted behind me, but the swamp quieted into brackish waters and vague starlight.

Are you ready? I asked.

Yes.

I removed my invisibility spell.

If the serpente lived according to legends, magic drew its attention, but it also relied on visual clues. If my sudden appearance on its home ground wouldn't be distracting enough, I conjured blighters that glowed with bright colors along my spine, hidden from prying eyes. The serpente would see them.

Go, I commanded Tysen.

A glimmer of subtle magic drew my attention to the left. Tysen transported invisibly, landing closer to the other side of the house, nearest the cypress trees I escaped. I vanished at the same moment to keep the attention on me.

No entrances, he said. *I detect no break in the magic.*

Keep searching.

The slither of shifting grasses and a gentle *plop* of water sent my heart racing. Breath thready, I angled for the exact opposite side of the mansion to cover more ground. The barrier power made the hairs on my arms rise. Never did it waver.

No entrances here, either, I said.

Confirmed sighting of the serpente, Tysen said. *Ten paces behind you.*

Ten.

Not close enough yet. A hiss turned my blood cold. It took all my willpower not to run or scream or throw myself into a transportation spell. Tysen's voice vibrated with tension when he said, *Five paces away.*

To guarantee as much power as possible, I extinguished the blighters. The serpente didn't need them to find me anymore.

Is my position correct?

Yes, if you don't move.

I froze, posed toward the creepy house. *The serpente is following?*

As desired.

A rumbling growl issued from somewhere behind me. I scooted another breath closer to the protective shell, until I couldn't even breathe without touching it. The magic had a resonance. A hum that wasn't unpleasant.

Three paces, he whispered. *Waaaait for it . . . now!*

I ducked.

The serpente's head soared over the top of me, piercing the protective shell as it lunged. Spread jaws snapped shut, but captured nothing. A ripple broke the shell, splitting the magic apart like separating drapes.

I glimpsed the serpente's underbelly before I raced ahead, shooting through the magical gap it created. Tysen transported so close behind me he trod on my feet.

Surprise drew the serpente up short. The snake recoiled as it sensed our movement from below, withdrawing from the barrier as it thrashed, head roving from side to side, seeking us. Tysen barely had time to lunge within, drawing his feet into the shell, before the serpente retracted all the way. The magic closed behind us.

"We did it!

"Yes," I muttered, "but why did it leave so quickly?"

An entirely different mansion glittered in front of us. Instead of age and cobwebs, a brilliant house with a glimmering facade, shining windows, and blue-gabled turrets sprawled far and wide, twice as expansive as the illusion. Light shone from within, betraying bodies that paced back and forth.

A roar interrupted our study.

The serpente thrust back through the magical barrier, lunging as it screamed. Air raced over me as it wriggled closer. The edge of its mouth skimmed my spine as I rolled out of the way. With a grunt, I shoved down the hill, jostling sideways. Its teeth sank into the ground near my head, then my shoulders, then my torso.

The serpente yanked its fangs out of the mushy soil while Tysen shouted, tossing spells. Its thick coat deflected them. I gained speed, but so did the snake. A dizzying spell right in the nose sent the serpente swirling in circles, buying me a second to stop and gather my feet.

Got it! he called.

Tysen grabbed my shirt and hauled me up. We raced up the knoll while the serpente whirled and hissed, attempting to follow. A blinding curse stopped it. Two witches appeared in front of me so unexpectedly I nearly screamed. I skidded to a stop and put my weight on my right foot, ready to pivot to the side and dodge a beefy hand. A second witch stopped me, then another.

They surrounded us.

Tysen slammed his back into mine and we circled, caught in the middle of a wall of livid marsh witches holding daunting bows. Arrows notched, aimed straight for our hearts.

Told you, Tysen muttered.

One of the witches shouted, startling me. Before I could make sense of his guttural words, he advanced to shove a boot into my chest. I barely had time to brace for impact before I tripped over Tysen. We collided with something hard and shimmery.

Not a witch.

A spell.

I jolted into a paralysis curse, my eyes squeezed shut as I braced myself to hit the ground. Unable to move, I toppled. Hands pinned me to damp soil. Attempts to overwhelm the curse with magic of my own were futile. Shock shoved me out of the short window of time I had to overpower the paralysis.

A muffled grunt told me Tysen suffered the same.

At first, only the serpente's retreating scales could be heard. Boots, a curious mouth noise, and then I sensed someone leaning far over me.

"Well, well," drawled a familiar voice. "What a delight to see you again, Miss Monroe. Take her inside," Ricardo commanded. "We have some talking to do."

The moment he spoke, silence fell.

Only the bullfrogs sang.

Chapter Thirty-Two

After taking the Volare and Viveet, Ricardo and his witches abandoned us in a damp place.

I lay on a ground that smelled like moss and cast spell after spell. Whatever paralyzing incantation they used, I'd never encountered it before. Different Networks emphasized variant spells more commonly, which made it all the more important that I venture into the world and learn.

But this one?

No idea.

Frustration oozed through me with every passing minute.

Can you hear me? Tysen asked.

Yes.

Can you overpower the spell?

I've been trying. You?

Frustrated, he growled, *No. I've never seen this spell.*

Me, either. Are your eyes open?

Yes. They hurt. I can't blink. It's awful.

Mine are closed. What can you see?

Black.

Did you notice anything inside? They brought us to a base-ment, right?

Yes. There were a lot of women and all of them appeared shocked. They carried us through the house, down stairs, and into these makeshift holding cells, from what I can see.

Suppressive magic?

Maybe? We're talking, aren't we?

Yes, but there could still be something in place. Priscilla says it's common in the East for the lesser and greater families to have their own prison cells.

Weird.

Any other observations?

Two males carried you, two carried me. An older male witch, presumably Ricardo, appeared to be in charge. That's all I've been able to observe. Both of us are facing the wall, in two different cells.

After taking a moment to absorb his report and appreciate how little opportunity we had to do anything, I asked, *How long do you think this spell will last?*

No idea. It's not showing signs of fading. Stop wasting your energy.

Though his advice made sense, I didn't like it. Our limited options funneled to one point: asking for help. The Protectors were already occupied beyond aid, but the communication magic still worked.

Leda?

She didn't reply within ten seconds, so I sent a second query.

Leda? Are you there?

My sense of confidence evanesced into panic when a third and fourth attempt went unanswered.

Do you hear anything from the Brotherhood? I asked.

No. You?

No. Leda isn't responding either. Why can we hear each other, but no one else?

We're close in proximity. Maybe that changes it.

Whether a suppressive magic that selective existed, I didn't know. The communication magic might also have limits we weren't aware of, but I doubted it. The Brotherhood had used it for generations without reporting a weakness like this. Either way, the landscape bleakened considerably.

While we lay in a hovel, the Eastern Network fell apart.

I hated it.

My only consolation existed in knowing that Papa had Camila, Priscilla, and Tomasso. That meant something.

Minutes passed. I strained to hear anything. Footsteps, voices, movement that might indicate life, but it was futile.

We lay in the dark.

Doing nothing.

Unable to plan, respond, or prepare, my mind spiraled to dark places. To Georgette. To Greyson writhing on the ground, potentially dead from his own binding. Maybe I should have offered to help Council Member Frederick after all. The Sisterhood's future could lie in petty thievery and Council Member service.

The thought made me want to vomit.

When the despair threatened to overwhelm me, and I considered apologizing for roping Tysen into this, a clanking sound echoed through the dungeon.

Someone's coming, Tysen said. *I see a light.*

Footsteps clunked down stairs. One set. I could make out a flare of light from behind closed lids. The paralysis evaporated. I jerked upright.

Ricardo Gallo sat on a chair, peering at me with a curious expression. Amusement elevated the corner of his lips. A basement made of dripping, moss-covered stones surrounded him. The two cells in which we lay were square. My curled up body filled most of the miniscule space, and the metal bars vibrated with a chill, despite the heat outside.

To my right, Tysen gently rubbed his closed eyes. I tucked my legs beneath me. Ricardo met my level stare with his own.

Are you all right? I asked Tysen.

Fine.

Can you do magic?

I'll check.

You try, I'll distract.

"Merry meet, Miss Monroe." Ricardo smiled, eyes alight. "What a pleasure to see you here today."

"Merry meet."

Before Greyson and I met in Carcere to play his game, I had met Ricardo. Alone on La Torra island, he cut a mournful figure. He was a time-wizened witch with soulful eyes, but a burning interior. The intensity I noticed in him on La Torra island when we first met was more blatant today. Heightened by the rebellion, no doubt.

"If you wanted to meet with me, you could have written," he quipped in the common language. His command of the words hinted at a deeper intricacy beneath the surface. Less broken than when we first met.

"You're a busy witch, Ricardo, and I do hate imposing."

Laughing, Ricardo patted his knee with one hand. "I have a feeling we could have been friends in different circumstances. Please, what can I do for you? Sneaking onto my property is impressive. No one has used my darling Decora to enter. Quite clever."

He tapped the side of his nose with a wink, a sign of approval in the Eastern Network. Decora meant *darling* in the language of the ancients.

"Decora is a pet of yours?"

"Family servant, I would say. She's been around longer than I have."

Any luck? I asked.

Not yet.

"How many generations?" I asked.

"Ten."

My eyes widened. "So long?"

He shrugged and said, "Serpente," as if that explained a colossal snake hundreds of years old.

Horrifying.

No magic, Tysen reported.

While Ricardo turned his attention to Tysen, I attempted to contact Leda again. She gave no response.

"And you?" Ricardo inquired.

"I'm a friend of Bianca's."

Ricardo's eyes gleamed. "Protectors never want to claim their title. You're all the same, you know that?"

Tysen's deadpan expression revealed nothing. Rognvald would have been proud. Ricardo swung back to face me.

There's a chance the spell around these cells could be worn down, I hastily said, *at least enough to get a message out. We need to contact Leda and tell her to send help. Keep doing it over and over.*

Understood.

Ricardo leaned his forearms onto his bent knees. "Since you are here, I am forced to believe that someone—our High Priest, perhaps—has asked for your help finding me. But this does not follow."

He shook his head softly, speaking with the cadence of a witch who already knew what he sought.

"Cristian would not ask for your help, nor would he think of me as a threat." With a coy grin, he lifted both clasped hands. "But Camila would send you."

Whatever Ricardo thought of my presence, I couldn't tell for certain. He believed I came to Gallo house on orders from Camila, but that didn't reveal perceived motivation. Had Greyson even entered his thoughts? Greyson promised to distract the Central Network, and failed. I doubted Ricardo thought of him again.

The one advantage I held.

"On the contrary," I said breezily. "You're not someone that Camila has concerns for. Which was frustrating for me, naturally. I have been suspicious since I first heard about you."

A gleam of interest entered that cold smile.

"Oh?"

"Camila didn't send me, Ricardo."

"Then whom?"

To defer answering and buy more time, I said, "Camila believes you're harmless. Well, mostly. The word she used was *quiet*. She thinks that the rebellion is firmly in Council Member Giuseppi's hand. But that's just what you wanted them to think, isn't it?"

He shrugged lightly, as if to say, *what can you do?* "They believe what they want, the Aldanas."

"They also believe that the splinter groups are out of control, and chaos rules."

At this, Ricardo laughed. A thin, wheezy sound that rattled my bones. I couldn't wait for him to stop.

"I'll say it again," he cried. "They believe what they want, the Aldanas."

Keep trying, I said to Tysen.

I am. No luck.

Before Ricardo could speak again, I casually said, "At least, I can tell you one thing that I know for certain: Camila isn't aware that you are the one who broke Carcere. Though, I would hazard a guess she won't be very surprised when I tell her that I've confirmed my hunch. The curse of Allegra Rossi, and all that."

Ricardo went very still. I held his disquieted study, aware that I'd completely flipped the tables. If luck had a benevolent hand, she'd nudge Tysen's magical use along.

Rather delicately, Ricardo asked, "If not on behalf of Camila, why are you here, Miss Monroe?"

"Why do you think?"

With hands uplifted, and in a mild tone, he said, "I don't know anymore."

"The rebellion could harm witches that I love and have promised to protect. I'm here for them."

"Do I know these witches?"

"I couldn't say."

"We could guarantee their safety."

"You wouldn't."

His slitted gaze grew ballast. He hummed in his throat, slipped a quick glance to Tysen, and me again. Tysen sat with his knees propped, elbows pressed onto them, hands gripping his hair. The picture of a sorrowful, captured Protector.

Clever witch.

Ricardo ignored him.

"I want to know, Miss Monroe. Why are you here?"

"Free us and I'll tell you."

"We both have impossible desires."

I stood, lifted my hand. "Shall we vow it? I'll give you the information you seek, you grant us freedom."

Ricardo shook his head. Frustration, perhaps despair, clouded his features.

"No," he said. "It is not necessary. Tonight, Cristian will die. Camila, too. When I wrest final control from the Aldana's and kill all of them, then we will also destroy all of Magnolia Castle and Carcere together. Then," he whispered with brimming despair, "then will the curse of Allegra Rossi, the Gallo family tie to that horrible island, finally break. We shall not be *quiet* or *lesser* anymore."

After a pause, Ricardo shook his head. "In destroying Carcere, Allegra Rossi will finally die. In destroying Magnolia

Castle, the oppressive system of the Eastern Network government will also die. You see? The path ahead is bright."

"You're slaughtering other witches, too! Think of the marsh witches that have died in the insurrection. There are better ways."

He shrugged. "Revolution requires blood. I tire of lesser and greater families, Miss Monroe. I tire of the Aldana's and their instability." He had an oddly sorrowful look about him when he promised, "The Eastern Network will be mine."

He stood, shuffled to the stairs. My heart leaped in my throat. I engaged all my control not to shout after him.

Tysen glanced up, bleary-eyed. *I'm making progress, I think. Let him go and we'll get through to Leda together.*

A bad feeling ballooned in my gut. No, we couldn't let Ricardo leave. Ricardo didn't need to know why we came. The rebellion would proceed otherwise, and killing us would be far simpler than an interrogation. A decisive win, too. A blow against the Central Network, that they caught and killed a Protector and the leader of the Sisterhood.

"I went inside Carcere," I called.

Ricardo paused.

"Inside Carcere, I confronted a man named Greyson. A former prisoner, but you already know that."

Ricardo pivoted, expression blank. My words hung in the air.

"Go on," he whispered.

"Greyson told me things."

Ricardo chortled. "I'm sure he did."

"After he survived the breaking of his vow."

Another wave of stillness washed through Ricardo. When I said the words, understanding of our precarious position swept me. What did it matter? Ricardo's rebellion would proceed as planned with us in this dungeon. He didn't need to fear me, locked in the basement. The Eastern Network leadership had ignored him, allowing Ricardo to pull together disparate factions and overthrow Magnolia Castle.

None of what I knew mattered.

Unless . . .

"How odd," he murmured.

"Greyson told me how to defeat you. He told me your weakness."

Interest piqued his tone. "Did he? Please, share."

"Not without reassurance."

"Of what?"

"You'll release us out of this basement and back to the Central Network. You won't bar our path home."

Ricardo considered, head tilted. His eyelashes fluttered until, at the top of the stairs, the creak issued again. A door swung open, spilling torchlight down the steps.

"It's begun," a deep voice said.

Ricardo spun. He might hide behind simple marsh clothing, but a witch of power and culture lurked beneath. There was no interest or forgiveness in his voice when he said, "Merry part, Miss Monroe. You're clever. It's too bad we'll have to kill you. But first, there are other deaths to attend to."

My choked disbelief escorted him out.

Chapter Thirty-Three

Tysen tilted his head against the damp wall and squeezed his eyes shut. Exhaustion permeated his features. He must have tried in a constant refrain to get Leda's attention. Thus far, she'd given no response.

What now? he asked.

I swallowed the rising dread. *We have to tell someone what Greyson said about Ricardo's weakness.*

His daughters?

Yes.

What will that do?

It's something. If Cristian can kill Ricardo, he has a chance at cutting off the insurrection, getting rid of the rebellious Council Members, and starting over again.

You think that's the right path?

His question stalled me.

I don't know.

Quietly, he said, *Me, either. I've seen the marsh witches, the hovels, the desperation. Cristian should never have let such poverty grow so rampant.*

It wasn't Cristian's legacy.

Sure. It was his brother. Tysen met my uncertain stare. *Niko turned a terrible Council over to his brother, and the Council Members also failed the witches. No matter how you look at it, the Aldanas have failed.*

To that truth, I had no rebuttal.

Thankfully, Tysen learned the invaluable skill of utter calm in a threatening situation. If he experienced vexation, he didn't state it. He pushed to his feet and paced, managing two strides before he had to spin.

After a few attempts, he stopped.

Whatever incantation they're using to prevent our magic must be on the outer bars. I ran my fingers along the bars separating our cells. *Not these inner ones.*

Which explains why we can talk.

Exactly.

A tidbit that offered explanation, but not help. "We need to find Cristian and extract him from Magnolia Castle," I muttered. "Second, we tell him about Ricardo. If Ricardo does take over, the witches won't be any better for it. He's planning to rule amidst absolute mayhem and murder."

A voice came from the darkness.

"I'd like to help with that."

I gasped.

Tysen blinked.

Papa appeared, jogging out of the staircase shadows and next to my cell. He carried a ring of keys in one hand, his fingers clasping them to keep them from singing. Overhead, bedlam unfurled. Stomping boots and startled cries raced across the creaking wooden floors.

Shock tied my voice.

"We have a handful of seconds before they come to check on you," he said smoothly, as if he sprang me free from dungeons all the time. With a winning smile, he shoved a key into the lock on my door and twisted. "Fifteen seconds, I think?"

A percussive *boom.*

"Well," he clarified brightly, "maybe thirty."

"Papa!"

"Leda heard all eight hundred of your messages. As soon as you stopped responding, she told me where you'd gone. Regina was home; she stayed with the others. I followed you here, but had to find a way past the snake. They like owls, by the way." He twisted the lock and flung the door open with a flick of his wrist. "Remind me to get a serpente."

"Sure. Next week, at the market."

"Well, you never know. I snuck into the house and levitated to the ceiling when Ricardo came down here, then waited. Once you clear these cells, you should be able to transport to the Central Network."

I rushed free, threw my arms around his neck, and whispered, "Thank you." When I stepped away, Papa unlocked Tysen's door. He nodded upward.

"Go."

"No," I said.

Three seconds passed before he registered my response. "Forgive me, what?"

"They have Viveet and the Volare. I'm not leaving."

He rolled his eyes. "Summon them while Ricardo and his men are distracted."

"I'm going after Ricardo."

He jabbed a thumb into his breastbone. "*I* am going after Ricardo." He pointed with his index finger outside. "You are going home."

"No. The Sisterhood is staying here. We need to take Ricardo to Cristian and warn them that Magnolia Castle is doomed."

His eyes clouded.

"Sisterhood?"

"That's me, thank you very much. Good to meet you. If you're going to stay and help, I'd welcome it. But only if you're willing to work *with* the Sisterhood, who is in command of this mission."

The storm in his gaze intensified. "The good gods," he whispered, "you really are the Sisterhood. I guess I haven't seen you on a mission before. This is . . . odd. But . . . neat, too. I'm not sure if I like this, but I'm also wildly proud of you. Strange."

"Now is not the time, Papa!"

He hesitated, clearly uncomfortable, but the turmoil cleared more quickly than I expected. "Fine, *Sisterhood*," he intoned carefully. "I'm here to support your mission."

"Good. You're welcome to stay. Oh, and thanks for the help."

Amused, he braced his legs, arms folded over his chest. "What is the target, and why?"

"Ricardo is the instigator of the entire Eastern Network rebellion, and he's our target. He's pulling the puppet strings, so to speak. Commanding the Council Members to rebel, and creating a smoke screen to hide himself. I want him alive. Paralyzed is acceptable. Dead is less than ideal. We're taking him to Cristian regardless."

"Understood."

"Ricardo broke the magic of Carcere, thus crippling Magnolia Castle as well." At his look of confusion, I waved both hands. "I'll explain those details later. If we can deliver Ricardo to Cristian, we stand a chance of stopping the insurrection before it destroys Magnolia Castle and murders the entire Aldana family."

Another nod.

"Continue."

All of my hard work attempting to understand the Brotherhood, the Council, and how things worked in an adult world culminated in this moment. Not only was I running a mission, but I was *recovering* a mission. Thanks to strategic partnerships, I pierced enemy boundaries, received help out of a pinch, proved out a tyrant others overlooked, and could prevent further rebellion with the truth.

This mattered.

So did the Sisterhood.

In all her glorious versatility.

"If we capture Ricardo alive," I continued with greater confidence, "Cristian can build a new structure and Council based on justice. We can put an end to all of this. The rotten Council, the uprisings. All of it. The Eastern Network will have a chance."

A distant *boom* split the air. Papa chuckled. "Whoops. Forgot about that one. Probably buys us another minute before they descend."

"What *are* those?" I cried.

"Not important."

"Spells?"

"Or a little powder from the West," he sang innocently. "Perhaps I found it in a market outside Custos . . . " He snapped two fingers. "See! You can find lots of things in markets."

Tysen laughed. "Sweet idea, High Priest. I mean . . . er . . . "

Papa clapped him on the shoulder.

"Derek, is fine."

The slack-jawed expression on Tysen's face made it clear he'd never be able to address Papa as Derek, but he could deal with it later.

"I understand the target and motivation," Papa said, "but what's the plan?"

I chewed on the inside of my cheek, thinking fast. "Did you see anything noteworthy about the interior of the house when you snuck down here?"

"Open floor plan, few side walls. Maybe five witches are visible, with three males and two women. More noises upstairs."

"Any ideas?"

A *bang-bang-bang* preceded strange silence. Papa and Tysen glanced above while feet raced overhead. Girlish cries followed, and then tears. The female noises spurred another idea. "Ricardo's greatest weakness is his daughters. He's lost several of them lately."

Papa's voice elevated with interest.

"Oh?"

"I have it on fairly trustworthy authority."

"Now that," Papa said, "changes things."

"Yes," I drawled. "I have an idea, and it involves all three of us. Do you have any more of that explosive stuff you found in the West?"

"A bit."

"Perfect. Tysen, you're the most important part. Papa, you're going to stay with me. Here's what we're going to do."

* * *

Papa and I stood at the top of the staircase, a thin line of light illuminating the bottom. The frenzy of boots and racing feet had calmed. Only occasional shuffles of sounds, opening and closing cupboards, pouring drinks, and whistling tea kettles followed.

Papa cut me a roguish smile.

Leda let me back into the communication magic.

Returning his grin, I said, *Welcome. How's it feel?*

He shook out his shoulders. *It feels* really *good. Like coming home.*

Leda?

You're back! she instantly cried. *Derek made it?*

Yes. Thanks for sending help.

Are you all right?

Fine. We're about to rush Ricardo.

Oh.

Tysen is going to send you an update in a minute. Whenever Rognvald is free, can you communicate Tysen's update to him? We won't have time.

Yes, but they're busy and not very responsive. We haven't heard much, nor spoken much. Only brief updates here and there. The rebels managed to breach one side of Magnolia, but the East Guards and our Protectors stopped an invasion. With renewed spells, Cristian's forces are stopping other attempts. The Academy will be overrun soon, though. The rebels are focused there.

My heart cracked at the thought. While I didn't love the pompous attitude of so many witches in the Eastern Network, they didn't deserve a total annihilation of their culture and history, either.

Thanks for the update.

Shaking my head as I returned to the moment, Papa asked, *It's weird, isn't it? The communication magic. You're there, but you're not.*

I'm still not used to it.

You probably never will be. Ready to go?

Ready, Tysen said.

Ready, I confirmed.

Though tempted to blast the prison door wide open and emerge in a dazzle of fireworks and glory, I carefully lifted the handle and let it creep forward. No witches became immediately apparent, nor could I hear signs.

It whispered wide enough to allow Tysen passage. He slipped by, his smell sliding through and vanishing into the house.

Clear, he said.

Papa and I followed suit. I closed the door as quietly as possible.

Ricardo's house opened in a sprawling square without walls to break up the wide space. Columns and structures built around bookshelves or staircases provided support beams, but it was largely an unbroken area. The far right corner, walled off, issued the sound of crashing pans. A kitchen, most likely.

The north wall, which led to the serpente and the grassy knoll I had inexpertly infiltrated, crackled with a giant hearth tall enough for me to do a cartwheel inside. Flames danced despite the steamy air.

Going right, I said, following Papa's suggested path.

Left.

Outside, Tysen chimed.

We scattered as quickly as we'd left the staircase.

Tysen reported in next, as expected. *I've updated Rognvald. There are two witches on the porch, keeping an eye on the front door. The rest are out in the swamp, near the serpente. They're shouting at each other.*

Ricardo?

Not with them.

Tysen, who crawled out an already open window Papa had observed, would stalk the perimeter in the shadows, keeping an eye on comings and goings. I peeled to the right, gliding beyond plush divans, elaborate paintings, and an entire section of plants. There was no destination. I pursued the slight scent of plumeria and an errant giggle upstairs. One of Ricardo's daughters, I presumed.

The floor is empty down here. I hurried up a carpet-covered staircase. *No sign of Ricardo from my vantage on the right. I'll check the bedrooms on the next floor.*

No one on the left, Papa said. *I'll join you in a minute. I found an interesting closet.*

A closet?

Never know, he sang.

This was a side of Papa I wanted to meet again and again. Was he this pleasant for all missions?

At the top of the stairs, I turned right, then skidded to a halt.

A hallway greeted me. Ten doors total, five on each side, most of them thrown open. The plumeria that I chased faded into antiseptic and medicinal scents. Dark ipsum, often used to dull pain, thickened the air.

I advanced more slowly, recalling Greyson's warning about Ricardo's daughter. *The girls have been sick, ill, dying. He's lost . . . two. Three?* Based on information in the Academy, Ricardo had ten children. Five female and five male. This truth hovered in my brain, making it thick and swampy, when I crept up on the first door.

A witch coughed.

I paused outside, peering in. A fluffy white bed sat against the far wall, underneath a closed window. It overlooked the far marshes, which stretched into oblivion before the last gasp of swamp .

A young woman lay amidst thin blankets, sweaty hair parted to either side of a thin face. Her raspy breath staggered as she drew it in, then released a desperate gasp. Whatever sickness plagued her, it made her skin pale, her arms bony. Her eyes sank into a too-thin, skeletal head. My livid heart softened.

What a terrible sight.

The trill of a too-happy voice issued from the room across the hallway. I drew back just in time. A flounce of wild black hair and a billowing skirt rushed into the room with a laugh. In Ilese, the young woman said, "I'm back, Antoinetta. Did the potion help?"

A painful rasp and weak shake of the head answered. The woman's bright countenance drooped for a moment, recovering quickly.

"Well, we'll try again in an hour!"

Found two women, I said. *One is very sick.*

Heading upstairs now, Papa replied. *Cleared the bottom floor, plus the kitchen. No sign of Ricardo down here.*

Four men returning from the swamp, Tysen said.

Are you ready for them? I asked.

I am.

Caution slowed Papa's response. *Go easy on it. Use the exact amount I told you.*

I stole down the hall, hurrying past two other rooms with no one inside. The last one on the left stopped me. When I peered within, my breath arrested.

Ricardo sat on the edge of a bed, gripping the hand of a young girl who couldn't be older than eight. Her chest bucked up and down in the same horrific, inefficient breathing as the first young woman I observed. A woman sat on her other side, crying into a handkerchief. The girl, a shade away from ghostly white, kept her eyes closed.

A pall hung over the room.

Imminent death.

But first, Ricardo had said, *there are other deaths to attend to.*

My heart hurt. At the time, I thought he meant the Aldanas. He meant his daughters.

I found Ricardo, I said quietly. *Second floor, final door on the left.*

Moments later, Papa brushed against me. Questions of why we weren't detected, why no one checked for invaders, dissolved. The answer lay before us: Ricardo's young daughter dwindled on her deathbed while his rebellion played out at the castle.

Weakness, indeed.

Neither Papa nor I made a move. We cast no curse, no paralyzing spell. For too long we stood there, watching the cycle of her breaths slow. Ricardo's expression slackened. His cheeks fell. Brows crashed.

Her inefficient rasps became rattles. Agonal gasps.

I can't, Papa, I said.

I know.

I can't take him to Cristian at this moment. I can't do it.

He set a hand on my invisible shoulder, somehow knowing right where I stood. *There is a right time for everything.*

What do you mean?

You'll see. Trust.

Finally, the young girl's limp hand sank into Ricardo's. The anticipated next breath didn't come. Like a winnowing candle, a change overcame the room. The woman on the other side of the bed doubled forward and shrieked into the pillow.

"Maria!"

Tears dribbled down Ricardo's cheek. "Maria," he whispered in softest Ilese. "Oh, *ma bellissima. Ma bellissima.*"

Now, Tysen, I commanded.

Tysen said, *Powder deployed.*

Another *boom*, this grander than all the others combined, broke the world outside. The window rattled. Porcelain shifted on top of the dressers, tinkling hanging crystals off expensive lamps.

Ricardo lifted his head, blinking through an emotional daze. From a distant room, a woman screamed. Shouting men raced under the window, returning to the marsh.

Successful, Tysen said.

Thank you.

Ricardo shot to his feet, watery eyes aflame with passion and vengeance. He cried as he stood there, wiping his eyes with the back of his wrist.

"Cristian!" he bellowed, wrestling a sob. "Cristian, this is because of you! I will have my revenge."

There is a right time for everything, Papa had said. He trusted this moment would lead to the correct next moment.

So would I.

Heart in my throat, I tucked away my emotions. Fought the rising grief I felt on behalf of this weeping father, and I leaped into action.

Literally.

Springing into the room, I toppled Ricardo from behind, curled my arms around his weakened form, and transported both of us away.

* * *

The transportation spell ended on a familiar balcony. The moment the spell dissipated, Ricardo turned to a wildcat. An elbow to my nose and a screech in my ear almost knocked me senseless. With blood streaming down my face, I managed to clamp a hand on his arm and issue a paralyzing spell.

It didn't work.

A flailing backhand smacked my cheek. I stomped his foot, swiped a leg, and followed him to the ground with my knee. Blood dribbled onto his shirt as I put pressure on his ribs. Viveet and the Volare appeared at my magical summons.

Yanking Viveet free, I pressed her tip into Ricardo's neck. "Stop."

Ricardo's expression contorted into one of pure hatred, and I couldn't fault him. My stomach knotted at the thought of what I'd just ripped him from. The understanding that thousands of witches would continue to die if he didn't call a halt to this madness kept me going.

"Not a word."

With Viveet in reach of his neck, I stood. The double blow to the head left me a little woozy, but I overcame it. Blood slipped to my upper lip. I ignored it while searching around his wrists, then his ankles. A glimmer confirmed he wore a charm bracelet that repelled hexes and curses. No wonder the paralyzing incantation didn't work. I sliced it free with Viveet and shoved it into a pocket.

"You'll live to regret this," he shouted, then choked on a painful exclamation of, "My Maria!"

Bile rose in my throat as I sent the paralyzing incantation a second time. It worked. Without the protective bracelet, he became limp. He fought it, attempting to overcome with another spell. I countered, not letting him. For several minutes, we battled silently.

Eventually, he lost power.

Ricardo succumbed.

I didn't envy him, trapped in the spell, unable to think about anything except his lost daughter, his crumbling revenge. With a heavy heart, I levitated him off the floor and into Camila's quarters.

I transported outside the main doors, Tysen said. *I'm in contact with Rognvald and am answering his orders now.*

Understood, I said.

I'm here with you, B, Papa said, though I couldn't physically detect him.

How?

Followed you.

There's magic preventing transportation onto Camila's balcony. She created it to only allow myself.

Not anymore.

His grim reply made me shudder. Magnolia Castle must have truly unraveled, then. I kept my focus on Ricardo, layering several spells, to be certain. The question of whether I could have subdued him if I hadn't found him in such an emotionally weak moment tugged at my mind. I sent it away.

Scout around, will you? I asked Papa. *I have him under control.*

You have a bloody nose again.

That's enough from you, I muttered.

He laughed.

We've returned to Magnolia, I told Leda, including Papa and Tysen. *We have Ricardo. What's happening?*

Total breach on all four sides, she reported. *The rebels are within the structure. Reports say it's crumbling, so be careful. Chi says the Academy is a total loss.*

That escalated quickly, I muttered.

Understood, Papa and Tysen said together.

I fought not to roll my eyes.

Protectors.

Find Rognvald, Leda continued. *He's with Cristian in the interior. They're hoping to see you.*

Chapter Thirty-Four

Blood, chaos, and crumbling masonry ruled Magnolia Castle.

Shouts, screams of the dying, and thudding feet came from everywhere. Papa prowled ahead of Ricardo's floating form, invisible, his sword leading the way.

We slinked along, alternating between being visible and invisible depending on the situations we encountered. For the most part, the fighting seemed relegated to the first floor. The East Guards held the upper floors by bold tenacity.

For now.

Where are you? I asked Merrick.

At the front doors. It's a bloodbath.

Papa and I sped up. We rounded a corner, almost colliding with a group of five witches. Blood marred their cheeks. Their wild eyes cast around, maniacal and shocked. These weren't East Guards. They weren't trained Guardians, but marsh witches, inspired to rebellion and ready to lose their lives.

One of them locked eyes on us. Though invisible, he likely sensed our spells. His desperation was almost palpable. Perhaps that's why Papa slowed and said, "Keep moving," in Ilese instead

379

of fighting. There was room for mercy and compassion, even in the most horrifying circumstances.

The men stalled, their ragged shirts hanging loose, pants wrinkled on the floor over their shoes. To forestall more problems, I removed the invisibility spell from myself and Ricardo's paralyzed form. One witch glanced down, saw Ricardo hovering above the floor. His cheeks slackened, eyes widened. He whispered, "*El capo?*"

Leader in Ilese.

The front marsh witch swung. Papa caught his sword with his own, using momentum to swing it down. The slice of metal on metal sang as I recast the invisibility spell on myself and Ricardo.

On your way, then, Papa said to me.

He enjoyed this a little too much.

Have fun with your frolick. I'll deliver this tyrant and return home before dinner.

With another push of magic, I levitated Ricardo and myself over their heads and down the hallway, leaving Papa to deal with them.

Like that, I found Cristian's office.

Ronaldo stood outside, hands crossed in front of him, a mixture of loathing and fear and frustration rotating across his face. I couldn't fathom an internal combustion of this size in the Central Network and how much it would sting. I hadn't expected so many emotions in the course of one mission.

He registered my magic before I fully descended, so I removed the invisibility spell. He elevated his sword, knees braced, but paused when his eyes fell onto Ricardo's paralyzed form. A repetition of the paralysis spell strengthened the magic a third time, just in case.

Mouth agape, Ronaldo whispered, "Ricardo?"

"He's the source of the rebellion," I said. "Everything. He admitted it to me and Tysen at Gallo house. The splinter leaders are taking orders from him, and so is Council Member Giuseppi."

"Is he—"

"He's alive. Please, we have to tell Cristian. Right now! If the splinter groups see that we have their ultimate leader, there's a chance you can cut this off before it grows out of control."

Ronaldo scrambled to open the door. Inside, Cristian stood at the window, hand to his mouth, staring without. He cut a bleak profile against the dark sky, brightened with torches and bursts of fire. Magnolia shook, prescient ripples that spoke to impending doom. He didn't know yet.

Did he?

Did they know about Carcere and the link with Magnolia Castle? That her time as the jewel of the East was limited, perhaps to days? Maybe hours?

Rognvald stepped into sight. "The gods," he muttered. "Tysen said you did it, but I wasn't sure . . ."

I canted an irritated eyebrow. "You didn't believe him?"

"I did, but . . ."

He shook his head. Rognvald's usual attempts at humor, his occasional jovial glint, had utterly disappeared into his role as the Head of Protectors.

Cristian spun.

His eyes widened.

"What is this?"

The door slammed shut behind Ronaldo.

"We don't have long, Your Majesty," I said. "Ricardo Gallo is the instigator, the leader, and the ultimate end to Magnolia Castle. If you want to save the Aldana dynasty and the Eastern Network, you need to act right now."

* * *

After my hasty explanation, Baxter, Rognvald, Cristian, and Ronaldo fell into instant discussion. Ricardo had attempted to overwhelm my incantation, but I layered it too heavily.

While Cristian finalized his next steps, I wondered if this is what it would always feel like. The Sisterhood. Stretches of empty hours, training for an unknown state, and then a burst of excitement that culminated in emotions like sorrow, terror, and despair.

There were no true heroes.

No accolades.

No sense of having created safety and saved lives for certainty. Questions abounded. Terrible emotions. Looming monsters that, at a later time, I'd have to battle and re-battle. The monsters that many tucked away, and I could see why.

The memory of Ricardo weeping over his young daughter moments before I snatched him to his probable and violent death would forever haunt me.

Justice or not, I'd never forget.

Helping in the East Wing, Papa said to the Brotherhood at large. Rognvald's eyes snapped to mine.

"Derek?" he mouthed.

I smiled.

So did he.

Welcome back, Rognvald drawled. *About time you stopped traveling the world to do something that matters. Now get to work. They don't need you in the east wing. Merrick needs you in the foyer, by the main doors.*

Understood, Papa replied, giddy.

I won't have you taking over, thinking you know everything, old man.

Oh, no. Never.

The moment of levity made my lips twitch, steeling me for what lay ahead. Cristian, more grim faced with each moment that passed, nodded as he conferred with Ronaldo. Three other witches entered. Council Members, I thought. Loyalists.

The only ones left.

The five of them whispered in a circle, nodded to Cristian, and spun on their heels.

"The plan is ready. Miss Monroe," Cristian said, "please follow us. For your own safety, and the request of your High Priestess, I would suggest you remain invisible and stay on guard."

* * *

While the others split separate ways to fulfill Cristians commands, Rognvald and I accompanied Cristian down the main staircase in the heart of Magnolia Castle, hidden behind invisibility spells. We passed cracked window panes, columns turned to rubble, and paintings askew.

Fallen East Guards, abandoned in dark pools of blood, lay off to the side. Fissures raced through walls, and dust and debris skittered around the floors in piles. Dust clogged each breath, which I took through my nose, and slowly.

Oh, Magnolia.

Once a jewel.

Soon to be ruins. My heart would sever like these storied walls.

The ignoble symphony of the rebellion sprawled at the bottom of the staircase, and my guilt at pulling Ricardo from his family assuaged. For all the torment he experienced, he created unfathomably more. I sent the emotions away, tucking them into a far corner of my mind until I had space to soothe.

The staircase led to a view of the foyer. Cristian stood at the top, peering out on a teeming mass of the desperate. Dead rebels' bodies occluded the doorway. Their compatriots climbed over the piles, throwing themselves into the awaiting East Guards and invisible Protectors. The East Guard force had been lean to begin with, but it was stark in comparison to the rebel ranks pressing in from outside.

Scarlett, can we send Guardians? I asked.

Rognvald hasn't requested it.

What if I can guarantee they won't fight? They'll stand behind Cristian, just to pose a force.

This throws our support firmly onto him as leader, and that wouldn't be wise.

Haven't the Protectors already done that? I cried.

Not in the same way. The Brotherhood operates by a different standard and expectation, and have remained largely invisible. They've stayed off the radar thus far, from the newsbooks and scrolls.

Cristian's bellow broke through Magnolia Castle, expanding on a spell. "Insurrectionists, I have your leader!"

The bloodbath paused. Slowly, at first. He had to expound with magic, shouting it three times, before silence fell. With a spell, I elevated Ricardo into the air. The silence absorbed the sobs, the pleas, the grunts.

All paused.

Ricardo hovered in position, rotating in a circle. Tied, limp, pale, as grim as death. His features hung in saggy, pathetic lines off lumpy bones. For all they knew, he was dead. Gasps rang out. Whispers swelled. In the aftermath, littered with dying groans and crashing shelves in the far distance, I thought we glimpsed their first chance at peace.

"House of Gallo!" Cristian boomed. "Sons of Ricardo, your father is mine. Advance from your rebels and step onto the stairs."

Horror tripled through the room as understanding dawned. Murmuring broke from the crowd.

Desperate to find Merrick, I scanned everything I could see, but it was pointless. In the end, I sensed his magic near the middle of the foyer, not far from the stairs. A circle of bodies and destruction lay around him.

The awfulness of this . . .

He couldn't see me because I made sure to remain invisible, but surely he'd detect my magic in the same way. He had to sense me. I felt him like a thousand burning suns.

"This," Cristian shouted, "is what you can expect with a rebellion against the House of Aldana. Come forward, you cowards. Now!"

Three men shuffled out of the crowd, hatred contorting their faces. The similarities to Ricardo were undeniable, particularly around the eyes, the firm chin. They amassed at the bottom of the stairs. My already churning stomach took on greater weight, but I forced myself to see it through.

That's when the truth lay manifest. The rebels didn't have it in them anymore, either. The hordes of witches once colluding on the veranda dispersed. Whether to home, to invisibility, or different parts of the castle wasn't clear.

"Look at me!" Cristian demanded.

Sullenly, Ricardo's three sons refused.

"You brought this upon yourself," Cristian said with a fiery wrath. "I would have *worked* with you. I would have *helped* you, but you spoke to Council Members instead of me and stoked an insurrection for which you'll pay with your lives. Where is Giuseppi?"

Movement near the front doors caught my eye. A rebel notched an arrow. I sent a spell, yanking it out of his hands.

He glowered.

Another stirring rebel was subdued by invisible means, allowing Cristian to continue speaking. Ensuring Ricardo remained airborne, I crept down the stairs, watching carefully for other interlopers that may want to kill Cristian. A powerful protective incantation radiated in an aura around him that should repel most weapons, at least long enough for him to get away, but I wouldn't take chances.

"Giuseppi!" Cristian shouted.

At the doorway, rebels broke apart. They peeled to the side as a familiar figure strode through them, stumbling over fallen witches, discarded swords. His face twisted into a sneer. Burly men who might have once been former East Guards stalked behind him. The hatred on Cristian's face confirmed that this must be Council Member Giuseppi.

Giuseppi's narrow gaze flickered to Ricardo, then Cristian. Amidst the swirls of darkness and hatred radiating from his snarling expression, I thought I detected surprise.

"Your Majesty," Giuseppi crooned through a sneer.

"Why?" Cristian asked.

Giuseppi hesitated. "Because it was time for better."

Not a noise broke the silence. Every eye riveted on them. Cristian standing tall and proud above. Giuseppi, his aged head tipped back, glowering from below, destruction petaling around him in death and chaos. A painting brought to life.

To my surprise, Cristian said, "You're right, Council Member. It is time for better. Our witches have already endured enough death at your hands."

Giuseppi gasped.

Then moaned.

Crimson bloomed across his chest as a sword shoved through, a bloody tip protruding. Ronaldo appeared from behind Giuseppi as the Council Member dropped to a knee. Blood bubbled out of his lips as he toppled, sliding off Ronaldo's sword.

Now fully visible, Ronald swung, bloody sword pointed to the witches that tailed Giuseppi. "Who's next?" he bellowed.

One former East Guard dropped his sword and held up both hands. Another, sneering, dropped his surly glare. A third vanished into a transportation spell. At the same moment, swords sliced into Ricardo's three sons from unseen hands. One from the back, one from the side, another from the front.

The middle one dropped to his knees, and the youngest rolled to the side. The tallest lifted his glittering stare to Cristian before his eyes rolled back. He fell, teeth stained crimson, in the final slaughter of rebel leadership.

I expected rage to broil from the remaining witches as they prepared to unleash an onslaught on the High Priest, but no such response came. Their exhausted state prevented them. With their leaders bleeding on the floor, and Cristian commanding so powerfully above, all the energy left the room. The air shifted to one of expectant surprise.

Cristian leaned his hands on the sidewall. A spell carried his whisper over the room. "Let us be done fighting. Together, we will create a better dynasty for ourselves and those who come after us. Please."

His calm plea rippled through the room.

Weapons dropped.

Swords clattered.

The rebellion stopped.

Chapter Thirty-Five

The Eastern Network insurrection lost all heart. The rebel force disintegrated into retreat and panic. Some sprinted away, others transported. East Guards focused on recovering the wounded instead of chasing the rebels. The Western Network and Central Network sent apothecaries and supplies.

Cristian, the three remaining Council Members, and the East Guards retreated minutes before the Academy and all of Magnolia Castle collapsed.

The aftermath moved steadily without the jewel of the Eastern Network. Loyal East Guards cleaned up the old castle site, clearing around the surviving magnolia trees. Scholars and volunteers retrieved what artifacts could be saved from the Academy rubble—and hadn't already been surreptitiously removed during the siege on Magnolia Castle. Cristian executed the rebellious Council Members that survived, along with Ricardo and all his remaining family.

The hard work of repairs had already begun. Cristian focused on finding new, upstanding witches to represent the provinces and boroughs, while Camila returned to Necce to assist her son in reparations with marsh witches and others.

A week after the rebellious conclusion, Papa, Grandfather, Merrick, and I sat on Grandfather's balcony overlooking Chatham Castle grounds and Letum Wood. A crisp breeze brushed our cheeks, and autumn sunshine warmed our skin. Merrick kept a tight hold on my hand while he closed his eyes and soaked up the delicious quiet.

Grandfather finished his update on the Eastern Network by saying, "All in all, the cards have fallen in very interesting ways. As Voice of the Council, Georgette scheduled a meeting with Scarlett and myself to discuss what happened in the East. Scarlett has agreed. We'll meet in a few days. You are, of course, invited to eavesdrop and remain unknown, my dear."

I laughed and opened my eyes. "That is one meeting I look forward to dropping in on."

"Might join you," Merrick purred.

Grandfather turned to Papa. "What about you? Are you ready to rejoin Alkarra?"

Papa chuckled.

"Yes, I am."

"What about Regina?" I asked, eyebrows raised high. So far, she remained elusive, but signs of her existed at Papa's again.

Another smile. "Just fine. We've . . . worked things out. As you'll see very soon. A few changes are coming to my place."

A story lurked behind that smile. A story I couldn't *wait* to hear.

"And we shall have a handfasting soon," Grandfather said with a quick clap of his palms. "I, for one, am rather excited to see what comes of it."

Merrick hid a grimace.

My lips twitched.

Oh, it guaranteed to be interesting, all right.

"The first family dinner is coming up next week," Merrick said. He straightened, running a hand through his sandy hair. "I sent you a flow chart, Derek, in case you needed help keeping track."

Papa grumbled under his breath, but shot me a wink.

"The wonderful thing about this life," Grandfather said with a sage eye on Papa, too, "is the unknown. We're always looking into the dark place, and then trusting ourselves. The path will lead. It's not always clear until it's behind you."

My nose wrinkled. "That is not what I thought being an adult would be. I expected it to be far more straightforward and less . . . messy."

"Expectations," Papa said with a droll smile.

Grandfather's quick laughter pealed through the air like bells. "Yes, messy and uncertain and changing and wonderful. That is everything this life is, and was meant to be."

* * *

The chaos of Michelle's house was a lovely thing. A little wild, a little shrill. With three kids careening in and out of the wide open door, and Michelle bustling from place to place with the steady ease of a pregnant woman, there was a sense of *home* in the ruckus.

Priscilla, who stood at Michelle's side at the table, kneading dough, looked up when I rapped on the outside of the house. Fresh autumn air drifted around us, stirring my hair. Michelle's subdued smile, and Priscilla's wide one, welcomed me without words.

Sanna, Isadora, and Tomasso scuttled around my ankles, attempting to pull me into the pretend bog in which they floundered desperately. Growling like a bog monster, I waded into the kitchen with them on my legs, scared them out of the house with happy shrieks, and then plunked onto a chair near Priscilla with a breathless laugh.

"That's me," I declared, "the bog monster. Merrick would wholeheartedly agree."

"You," Priscilla said with a fake sharpness, "are going to get them all stirred up before nap time."

"It's my plan."

"How are you Bianca?" Michelle asked, knuckles deep in an elastic ball of dough. Flour skirted her table, powdering the tip of her nose. Her light hum ceased. Michelle sang her culinary spells. She swore that the music helped the food cook more evenly, which is why most of her meals tasted like a masterpiece. Soon enough, she'd be running the whole kitchen at Miss Priscilla's School for Girls.

"Handfasting plans are settling."

"You're only a few days away, right?"

Smiling, I said, "Right."

"Are you nervous?"

"Not at all."

Peering toward their tables with a hungry stomach, I asked, "What are you making?"

Ten bowls scattered the sideboard, and yeast thickened the air. Spoons sloshed around another wide bowl as yeast granules dumped within it from a small crock that usually held butter. Shortly after the yeast dissipated, the stirring spoon stopped and the bowl settled on the table.

"Bread for the school." Michelle deftly flipped the loaf on which she worked, tucked the ends in, and slung it into a butter-greased baking tin. "Celia asked me to take over the weekly bread making and breakfasts."

"Oh."

A shadow of sadness passed over Priscilla's expression. Celia, a most beloved figure, would be missed whenever she fully retired, though *full* retirement appeared less and less likely.

According to Priscilla, Celia planned to stay in the school until she couldn't, which made the arrangement of Michelle helping from home ideal. After so many decades serving young girls, Celia had nowhere to go. She'd stay at the school, her only home, until she passed. It was the beginning of her inevitable end. She grew more frail with each passing month.

Michelle, who loved the work but remained at home with her kids, found ways to take part of the burden off of Celia. The payment eased pressure on Nicholas as he worked odd forester jobs to make currency. Occasionally, he helped the forest dragons, but they didn't require much attention these days.

Priscilla's voice jarred me out of my reverie. Blinking, I lifted my head when her incurious voice queried, "Bianca?"

"Sorry, lost in thought."

"Are you really all right?" Michelle inquired.

No, I wasn't. But how to explain? *I captured a man moments after his daughter died, and led him to his death.* Ricardo's actions were his own. I didn't blame myself for his death.

But the trauma of it I would never forget. Nor the bloody battle. The desperate politicians. Though I'd fought in the Battle of Chatham Castle and the Battle for Letum Wood, my position in this uprising had been very . . . different.

Voluntary, in a way.

It exposed the shades of working in and for a Sisterhood that chose to face these challenges again and again. The weight of it bore down on me in the weeks following. The depressing depths that witches were willing to go for a little power, a little peace, a little stability.

All of it, preventable.

All of it, dependent on the desires of witches.

Swallowing the truth, I said, "I'm all right, but still working through what happened in the East." A flash of guilt appeared in Priscilla's eyes, but I squashed it with a glare. Her lips twitched in a little smile. "With or without you," I said, "I would have been there."

Nodding once, she accepted it.

This topic exhausted me, so I stood up with a bright smile. "Just popping in to say hi. Merrick is with his family, preparing for our next dinner. I promised him I wouldn't leave him alone with them for too long, considering it involves his extended family."

Priscilla laughed at my loose grin, which seemed to set her at ease. It was easy, fooling my friends. A quick smile, a skim-through of the difficulties that offered no real depth, and we were on our way to comfortable origins.

Only Michelle showed a flicker of concern and hesitancy, but she accepted my departing wave with a small smile and turned her attention back to her song.

* * *

I didn't go to the North.

Not immediately.

My steps sped me through Chatham Castle, hidden under a spell. *Chatterer* journalists, random witches, even a few Guardians would have attempted to speak with me otherwise. Word of my presence at Magnolia Castle had spread, though no one confirmed the rumors that I provided Ricardo's body.

They found out.

Somehow.

I didn't like the attention. It created a hemmed in feeling. Heightened expectations, like they all wanted a piece of me now that I'd done something important. The Protectors waved it off, but the reporters left them alone.

"Get mean," Rognvald advised. "It's the only way they respond."

No journalist had crossed far enough to inspire that level of wrath.

Yet.

Jack manned Greyson's cell again. With a smile and a nod, he allowed me to pass. The Volare bounced along my back, with Viveet on my hip. I didn't try to hide her today.

A patch of sunlight fell into Greyson's latest cell. Two windows on opposite sides brought an autumn breeze and the smell of decaying leaves. I paused after the door closed and stood there, hands folded, staring at him.

Greyson sat on the edge of his mattress, legs bent. He stared at me through thin, haggard eyes. The torture of breaking his binding had taken more life out of him than I expected. He hadn't recovered. A bath, a new cell, and some sleep kept him from the brink of death, only to die tomorrow. With the Eastern Network no longer requiring him, Scarlett sped his execution up.

Finality brought me to his doorway.

Greyson's fingers rubbed along the inside seam of his pants as he studied me, jaw tight. Hatred and resignation boiled from the same depths. When I met his stare, he glanced away.

"Tomorrow," I said.

He rolled his eyes.

"I hear your last dinner request is bread with fig flecks and fresh butter. An interesting choice."

"Very Central Networkian," he rasped.

"Is that why?"

"No," he said softly, and didn't explain himself. I didn't ask. Greyson motioned to his cell. "I understand this is your doing. The cell with fresh air and light."

"While I feel no debt to you, I requested Scarlett give you this cell for your final day of life."

"Why?"

I answered, "I don't know," because I was too tired to drum

up my own reasoning. Truly, I had no idea. Everything made me tired these days, and facing Greyson felt like a culmination point.

The end of a chapter.

Every peak had a down side. A plummet downhill, that, when one considered it, was the hardest part of the battle. Climbing up, you had inertia, energy. The will to fight and conquer. The way down?

Too much inertia combined with the trauma of the climb.

Clearing my throat, I said, "Thank you for providing the information about Ricardo. Whether it makes any sense to impart gratitude after you tried to murder me for a game, and an agreement," I added as a side note, "I don't know. I guess it doesn't matter. Thank you, anyway."

His eyes glittered as he regarded me.

"For what it's worth, Miss Monroe, I hope you stick it to all of them."

He stood up, turned his back, and dismissed me. I gratefully spun to leave. After this moment, I would never see Greyson again.

I felt no sorrow.

* * *

Sunshine and banter greeted me in the Northern Network, banishing the dark dredges in which I swam.

Ten seconds after I arrived, taking in a carefully-sculpted chaos, I felt a hand on my right arm. I spun to find Merrick smiling, sunshine tangled in his beard, highlighting the strands to a near-red. He wrapped me in his arms, holding tight.

Eyes closed, I sighed against him.

Respite.

The *only* respite.

Despite the eternal love of my friends, Greyson's certain

death sentence in the morning—alone, with only Guardians to escort him to the lands and lives beyond—and the Eastern Network working to repair, the only safety that truly existed was here.

With Merrick.

Our hearts thudded together for the space of several seconds. I drew in all the strength he offered, sucking it deep, locking it tight, letting it swirl. Merrick kept the darkness at bay. He brushed the hair out of my eyes with his rough hand.

"You all right, B?"

Smiling, I said, "Fine."

His thumb touched the crease of my eye. "You have shadows in your eyes. Are you sure?"

Nodding, I said, "I'm just . . . thinking."

"Greyson?"

Another nod. He stretched his fingertips into my hair, hand cradling my face, as he pressed our foreheads together. The scent of apples filled my nose with a sweet smell.

"I'm here," he said. "You're here. We're safe."

The same refrain he repeated at night, when nightmares startled me awake. I curled my fingers around his hair, letting the silky strands race through them.

"Can we go home after this?"

"Of course."

"No, to the mountain home."

Eyes alight, he said, "Yes, of course!" Suspicion narrowed his tone. "Are you sure? You haven't wanted to leave the forest since we returned from Magnolia Castle."

How I loved that he didn't halt his sentence, or try to restructure what happened. Other witches had been on eggshells about it, but not him.

"I'm sure."

"We can start working on it, if you like."

"I would!"

Like Papa, I needed work.

Creation.

Channel this darkness . . . somewhere else.

Wrestling those demons back, I summoned up a sincere smile. I squeezed him once more around the waist, pecked a kiss on his lips, and said, "Take me to great aunt Matilda! I've been waiting for weeks to finally meet her."

About the Author

Katie Cross is ALL ABOUT writing epic magic and wild places. Creating new fantasy worlds is her jam.

When she's not hiking or chasing her two littles through the Montana mountains, you can find her curled up reading a book or arguing with her husband over the best kind of sushi.

Visit her at www.katiecrossbooks.com for free short stories, extra savings on all her books (and some you can't buy on the retailers), and so much more.